Delta Blue Squadron

America's First Space Fleet

David Spriggs and Debbie Barnum

Delta Blue Squadron

ISBN 978-0-9815660-0-9

Will You Be Prepared?

Prepare to embark on a journey into the adventures of your mind and imagination, while, simultaneously discovering important and often even dangerous issues facing the United States of America today. Delta Blue Squadron will take you on a journey in America's race to space that will ultimately determine the fate of the country we call home...The United States of America.

Delta Blue Squadron contains significantly more FACT than FICTION. Facts that uncover government corruption and scandal in the United States, the many vulnerabilities in security that the United States is facing and that has left our country susceptible to frontal attacks by other nations, and, finally, Delta Blue Squadron takes you along on their race to space in an attempt to save America from these foreign attacks. The United States must conquer and develop our outer space before any other country; otherwise, America will risk losing the super-power status it currently holds to other nations. This race is reality, not fiction.

Will America be prepared...or is it already too late?

GET READY...Everything Changes in this Race.

Forward

Many, who read this book, if not most, will look at it as just another science fiction story. In my opinion, I have included more fact than fiction, and when you finish reading the book ... well, you can be the judge.

I will be seventy-three years old soon, and I have seen much advancement in technology. The changes have been so rapid that when a new item is invented, it's almost obsolete before it's been completed.

As a child in the 1930s and 1940s, I remember reading books about a character known as Flash Gordon, a space traveler. In those books, there were rockets going to the moon and beyond, and jet planes that could fly faster than the speed of sound. What did the older folks think of those stories back then? They scoffed at the ideas, saying they were impossible, that the moon was too far away, or an airplane couldn't fly without a propeller—no way!

We were still in the days of horses and buggies when, in 1903, Orville and Wilbur Wright made the first controlled, sustained flight of an airplane from a small village on the outer banks of North Carolina. After that, nothing seemed impossible.

Now, my friends, look how far we've come in the 100-plus years since then. Rockets and jet engines were developed just a mere thirty-nine years later, and now I hear that the Air Force is preparing to test its Mach 10 speedster, an unmanned Falcon, hypersonic test vehicle. I hear it will pave the way for jets that can fly faster than a bat out of hell on its way to dropping bombs and spying on everyone.

People ask, "Why do we spend so much money going to the moon and into space?" They don't realize all of the things that are derived from our advancement into space. Some might never have been thought of had they not been needed for space flight. Some products that come to mind are the simple microwave, solid circuit electronics, and of course, the microchip. People take for granted such things that drastically improve their lives. Was it not for the technology developed for space, I would venture to say that at least ninety percent, if not more, of the items we have today wouldn't even exist .

Years ago, man put his first footprints on the moon and returned to Mother Earth. Again, let's look at where we are today. We have developed what is now considered a fleet of antiquated shuttles, in which I believe, were built primarily to transport materials into space to build the International Space Station. Again, it is my belief that the space station was built as a stepping stone into deep space travel, but it is years behind schedule and as of this date, February 09, 2007, NASA has reported a base will be established on the moon within the next ten years.

Let's try to be as realistic as possible. Anyone who is familiar with the capsule that took our men to the moon would know it was barely large enough for the men, let alone any materials that needed to be transported. That is where I believe the space shuttle came into the picture. In order to transport the materials and equipment needed to maintain even a small base, it would take a ship at least the size of the space shuttle.

Most of us have heard about the Phoenix Lights and Area 51. I'm sure you can ask anyone in Phoenix, Arizona, and he or she will know about the lights. As far as Area 51 goes, I don't believe it has anything to do with captured aliens or any UFO. What I do believe is that our newest fleets of space ships are being built there, and are being tested in the dark Nevada and Arizona skies.

The ten years I served in the United States Air Force was a valuable tool for understanding the military's terminology, its speech, and its way of thinking.

With that in mind, you be the judge of what could be fiction and what could be truth.

Should this book be published, there will be a follow-up after considerably more research.

Thank you

Preface

The International Space Station is years behind in its completion for too many reasons, the main one being the antiquated fleet of space shuttles. After the loss of two shuttles and their crews, all of the other ships were grounded for many months. NASA scrambled to solve the problems that caused the losses. It was not helping that sabotage was suspected, which in turn caused long delays in projects that were crucial to the entire program.

In addition, certain countries did not want to see the space station completed — namely Russia and China — which were trying to prevent America from controlling outer space. U.S. Vice President Cynthia Alexander came to the realization that her Democratic party was trying to dismantle the U.S. military. When she spoke to the president about this matter, he told her not to be concerned with it. When she insisted that it was her concern, the president looked her square in the eyes and ordered her to stay out of it. She knew that would never happen. She could not, and would not, stay out of anything. She had to find a way to stop what her party was doing.

According to the CIA, both Russia and China were working hard to build their own space programs, yet the U.S. kept cutting the funding for NASA. When the president forced the sale of top secret technology to the Chinese, Vice President Alexander became infuriated and almost resigned. She changed her mind quickly though, for she knew if she resigned, she would lose access to key information. She decided she had to know everything if she was to fight her own party from within. She had no idea who to trust, but she knew she needed help.

That was when she thought of Thelma Ritter Estes, a life-long friend, schoolmate, and person she knew she could trust. She needed to talk to Thelma and see if her husband could be trusted as well. It would certainly help to have him on her side, as he had recently been promoted to a one-star general in the United States Air Force.

When she arrived in Houston, her escort was waiting for her on the tarmac. The black limo shimmered in the sun, and it looked as though pools of water were dancing on the asphalt. As she walked to the limo, the pools of water seemed to move farther away with each step. In the back seat, she could feel the cool air from the car wrap around her. She knew there was no turning back now.

At Thelma's, she was greeted with girlish laughter and hugs that brought the old days flooding back. After catching up, Thelma looked long and hard at her friend and got to the point, "Tell me what's on your mind."

Cynthia told Thelma the details of her problem, and then asked if her husband could be trusted not to give her away.

Thelma said everyone in the military hated the commander in chief for what he was doing. They hated that the president, as well as the party, were selling out their country.

General Estes met with Vice President Alexander and an alliance was formed. They were both concerned, not only for the Armed Forces, but also in the direction the race for space was heading. General Estes was a U.S. Air Force technical representative with NASA and was associated with Colonel Dennis Denehey, who was working on a new shuttle — one that could do the same duty as the original but was a true space ship. The slimmed down budget Denehey had to work with was no help, but he managed to do his job, and do it well.

Vice President Alexander put her plan into action and within a short period had diverted a few billion dollars to set up a secret facility where the first prototype of the newest shuttle could be launched from the drawing board and into a production stage.

She set up a secret meeting with the two top Republicans in the House and Senate, revealing everything and informing them she planned to resign and leave her party. They agreed to assist her with more funding if she would consider running for president in the next election on the Republican ticket. She agreed and was elected president by a landslide. With Cynthia Alexander as president, the rebuilding of the U.S. armed forces began in earnest, as did the race for space, under the genius of one Colonel Dennis Denehey.

This is the story of those involved in the project — Delta Blue Squadron, America's First Space Fleet.

Table of Contents

The Team ~ Space Program 1

Conspiracy ~ Revelations...14

Sabotage ~ Beginning Romance...33

Family Reunion 75

The Facility...86

Your Ship My Lady ~ Discovery 94

Test Flight ~ Internal Espionage 115

Proposal ~ Just Rewards...162

Air Battle 191

Preparations for Space Flight 221

Into Space ~ Deception...242

Space Station Protected ~ U.N. Speech............................260

Space Station Attacked 285

Abduction 297

The Rescue Plan 318

Rescue Attempt 339

Final Journey ~ Discovery...391

The Arrival 420

The Presidential Denial 475

Triple Marriage ~ Honeymoon Journey 496

General Robert Estes was sitting in his office at Wright-Patterson Air Force Base when his intercom sounded.

"Yes, Anna," he mumbled into the system.

"Lieutenant Denehey, sir."

He sat there a moment staring at the black phone, took a deep breath, and answered it.

"Dennis, what the hell happened? I can't believe they busted you to the bottom."

"Yes sir," Denehey replied. "They did give me a tough choice though, either a general discharge or take the reduction in rank."

"Damn it, Dennis!" exclaimed the general, as he leaned back into his chair. "Why did you have to hit the S.O.B.?"

"The same reason you would have, sir. No one questions my integrity, honesty, or loyalty to my country — and no one curses me on the floor of Congress either."

General Estes wiped a few beads of sweat from his forehead and took another deep breath. He knew that Dennis was right, but to strike a U.S. senator for whatever reason was still a no-no.

"There's something I need to know. Can you still work on the program?"

"There was no mention of my being relieved of my duties, sir. With or without me, the program must continue."

"Good, because I don't think we could move ahead as quickly without you. There is one more question. Do you believe you can still function after this bull crap?"

"That's no problem, sir. It's a huge disappointment to me, but I'm fine. I won't let you down."

"OK, Dennis, I'm sending a plane to bring you here. I have some new pilots to meet with in the morning. Their scores on the simulator, such as it is, look very good. The plane will be at Andrews in about two hours."

##

Dennis was sitting in the op's lounge at Andrews Air Force Base, dozing, when the intercom system broke the silence.

"Lieutenant Denehey. Lieutenant Denehey. Report to spot six, a plane is waiting for you," said the drowsy voice of someone who sounded like she could use another cup of coffee.

There was only one plane on the parking ramp and he was met on the steps by the flight engineer, who offered to stow his bags.

The lieutenant was surprised to see four other passengers on board. He felt their stares as he passed by their seats to find a spot where he could have some privacy. He was in no mood for any conversation after all he'd been through in the past few weeks. The court-martial was still fresh in his mind.

Dennis had married a U.S. senator's daughter — first mistake. Senator Tolbert, from the start, did not particularly like the idea of his daughter marrying a military man.

Dennis was among several called before a special hearing to testify concerning not closing certain strategic bases. He disagreed with the senator's stance on the subject, and said so before the board.

Senator Tolbert was furious. He made the mistake of walking up to Dennis, putting his finger an inch from Dennis' nose, while more or less accusing him of being a coward.

He had quietly told the senator to abide by the rules of protocol, get his finger out of his face, and be very careful of his accusations. Tolbert persisted and made the big mistake of repeating his previous action, and that's when Dennis knocked him out cold.

Then there was the court-martial. He almost accepted the general discharge, but then strongly considered the great need the United States had for the ship he had designed, and accepted the demotion instead.

Then came the divorce papers from his wife and now the call from General Estes.

He had been so wrapped up in his thoughts of the previous few weeks, Dennis didn't even realize the plane had taken off until he heard the familiar crackle from the intercom and the pilot announcing it was OK to move about. Dennis opened his laptop and brought up the plans for his ship. He would get lost in time when he studied the ship. It was his passion and an escape from past troubles.

"Interesting looking ship. A little farfetched though, don't you think?"

Dennis immediately closed his laptop and looked into the intense green eyes of a tall woman wearing the uniform of the U.S. Air Force. His eyes traveled down to the wings that were pinned to her blouse and then to the silver leaf of a lieutenant colonel.

She smiled and offered her hand, "Colonel Diane O'Hara."

Her perfect teeth gleamed through the sexiest lips Dennis had seen in a long time. He took the offered hand and introduced himself. A slight, cocky grin appeared. "Farfetched? Maybe it is, Colonel."

"Are you by any chance writing a science fiction book?"

Smiling in earnest now, he answered, "No, ma'am, I'm not a writer; just speculating."

"Looked pretty detailed for just speculating, Lieutenant."

"Sorry, Colonel, but at present I can't discuss my speculating with you."

"I see," she said with a hint of disappointment. "Well, Lieutenant, perhaps another time."

She turned sharply and went back to her seat. His eyes could not stay off of her. He felt as though his heart would beat out of his chest. He had never felt anything like this before, not even with his now ex-wife. Feelings stirred deep inside him and he wondered; *is this what love at first sight feels like? Or maybe it's lust at first sight. I don't believe in love at first sight...so it can't be that.*

Dennis closed his eyes. His mind wandered back to his marriage. He had really wanted it to work but it seemed doomed from the beginning. She was a daddy's girl and Daddy did not like

Dennis. He dozed off; when he opened his eyes again they had already landed.

Diane was standing, looking back at him.

"Are you coming with us, or are you sleeping all day?"

He grabbed his laptop and headed to the front of the plane.

The small waiting room seemed stuffy. No one was talking, which made it even worse. Everyone had other things on their minds, like what was in store for them here.

General Estes' secretary came in.

"Dennis, follow me, please. General Estes wants to see you. Sorry about the problems."

Dennis noticed the questioning looks on the faces of the others as he fell in behind Anna.

Forty-five minutes later, he and the general came out to the waiting room. The general fumbled with some files until he found the one he was looking for. He glanced at the name on the top of the file.

"Colonel Deana Kutchmark?"

Deana stood and saluted him

"That would be me, sir."

He returned the salute and shook her hand. "Welcome, Colonel Kutchmark."

"Thank you, sir."

The routine repeated with Lieutenant Colonel Diane O'Hara, Colonel James Matovich and Colonel Edward Mitchell. General Estes then handed all the files to Dennis.

"If you all would take a seat at the table, we can get started," Estes said, and the four recruits made themselves comfortable while Dennis sat across the room at a smaller table, alone, to study their files.

General Estes studied the faces of the recruits.

"Ladies and gentlemen, I'm not quite sure what conclusions you've reached concerning our simulator. We're sorry for the poor design of it, but due to budget crunches at that time, which are changing now in our favor, we did the best we could. Considering what you had to work with and what your records reflect, you have again excelled. That's why you're here now."

He glanced toward Dennis and then back to the four sitting at the table.

"I want you all to be aware of the job ahead and what your job will be. Since the clarity of our program was not fully revealed to you when you volunteered, you will have a chance to reconsider. You can walk away from the program and go back to your previous positions, but understand one thing, what I reveal to you is, and must remain, top secret."

The general paused and looked intently at each of the recruits.

"The new positions intended are not just as pilots but also as astronauts — astronauts in a much different sense than the present shuttle astronauts. America is going into space, and back to the moon."

General Estes smiled at the puzzled looks on each of their faces.

"Now before I go further, you can ask your questions and voice any doubts you may have, or even withdraw."

"You certainly have caught my interest, sir," Deana said. "I have many questions but my first two are, why back to the moon, sir, more rock samples? Furthermore, will our transportation be similar to the Apollo Lander?"

General Estes replied, "Back to the moon to install a manned base."

"Sorry to interrupt, sir," Colonel Matovich edged in before the general could respond to the last part of Deana's question. "We have had enormous problems just supplying the space station. How can we be sure we can sufficiently supply a base on the moon, and lastly, what is the value of a base on the moon?"

"To answer Colonel Kutchmark's last question, your transportation will not in any way resemble the Apollo. The new ship will be two and a half times larger than the present shuttle and capable of moving almost four times the tonnage of the shuttle."

General Estes walked over to the water fountain and took down a small cup. He offered the others a cup and they all declined. After taking a long, cold drink and tossing the cup into the tiny trash can beside the fountain, he continued.

"Why a base station on the moon? Several reasons, really, but the main reason is for national security. The United States has a new anti-missile weapon; a laser cannon. It's so powerful it can track any missile from the minute it's launched. It can track it, and if deems it is going in the wrong direction, it can blow that missile out of the sky within five to eight seconds."

"Excuse me, sir," Diane interrupted. "According to the Outer Space Treaty and Resolution; no country can put weapons into space. So, is it the intent of the United States to break that treaty?"

General Estes shook his head. "Russia and China have already broken that treaty, and we have solid proof of it. You already know that Russia is mad as hell since they got booted from the space station when they broke the ISS Code of Conduct rules three times. Now, before I reveal anything else, is there any of you who wish to withdraw and return to your previous duties?"

The four looked at each other and Diane quickly spoke up, "I certainly don't, sir."

The other three followed suit.

"Very well then, we have another flight to make." The general called out to his secretary.

"Anna? Has the luggage been transferred to my plane?"

"It's all on board your 747, sir."

"Is all the equipment and files on board the C-130?"

"Yes sir, once we wind everything down here, and you're on your way east, we should be airborne within the hour heading west."

"Thank you, Anna. Take care of yourself and my Thelma. Safe trip."

Anna smiled. "We will be fine, sir; see you at home base."

The general turned back to the recruits. "Ladies and gentlemen, Anna will take you to a van. I'll be right behind you and we'll be on our way."

Everyone filed out behind Anna except Colonel Mitchell, who followed the general back into his office.

"Excuse me, General, for being so curious, but what is with this Lieutenant Denehey? You have to almost twist his arm to get him to speak and his clipped answers are to the point, and then he clams up."

The general picked up the files from the desk and turned to face the colonel.

"Colonel Mitchell, that's not something I'm privy to speak of at this time." He paused at the door and offered an ushering gesture. "After you."

##

Diane and Deana were very comfortable. The seats in the plane were as good as any easy chair in one's living room. They were facing each other but gazing out the window as the huge plane lumbered toward a runway. The sun was setting behind them and the huge plane turned slowly to the south, onto the runway, and into the prevailing wind. The two women could see the top quarter of a huge fireball slowly dropping down behind the western horizon. Many streaks of white clouds, high above the earth, were turning a brilliant light pink, with the still-azure sky as a background.

Speaking softly and to no one in particular, Diane said, "God has his paint brush working on pure beauty."

"You're right," Deana answered. "I can never get enough of his art work."

The huge engines whined softly as the nose of the aircraft lifted gently into the air. The big bird was up and climbing for the heavens.

Dennis, once again, was sitting off by himself studying the files of the four new recruits.

An Air Force stewardess came down the stairwell and proceeded to the intercom to make an announcement.

"Lieutenant Denehey, the general would like to see you above. For all others, the general will hold a conference on the upper deck and all wishing to attend are welcome."

The recruits were on their way before she finished, loaded with questions. Dennis smiled at their enthusiasm as he, too, climbed the stairs.

Once they were seated, the general announced, "OK, I know this is turning into a very long day. I just want you to know that I'm not going to make you starve ... yet."

The recruits laughed and the tension seemed to ease somewhat.

"Dinner will be served in an hour, but in the meantime give the stewardess your orders for drinks. Alcohol is permissible at this time. Now, let's get down to business."

Diane jumped in immediately. "Sir, if the new ship is so big, what size booster rockets could possibly put that much weight into orbit? The booster rockets for the shuttle are what? Twenty percent marginal?"

"I guess I'll have to let Lieutenant Denehey answer that, Colonel."

Dennis put the files aside.

"We don't use booster rockets, Colonel, and we don't launch from a pad like the shuttle. We take off from a runway like a conventional aircraft."

Surprise registered on their faces as they stared at him, trying to comprehend what was just revealed.

Ed Mitchell cleared his throat. "Are you telling us, Lieutenant, that you genuinely believe you can take a ship that's two and a half times the size of the Space Shuttle, get it airborne from a runway, carry enough fuel to reach escape velocity and get into orbit? Is that a paper formula?"

Diane chimed in unbelievingly, "How so?"

The cocky grin appeared once more on Dennis' face.

"I've flown it seven times to the space station and back to base, ma'am."

All four of the recruits looked at Dennis anew.

Colonel Kutchmark leaned forward, folded her arms on the table and stared disbelievingly at Dennis. "You're telling us that you've test flown such a ship? How much fuel, of the ship's total capacity, did you use?"

Dennis smiled at her two quick questions. "Yes ma'am, the prototype has been on the runway for a year. She has quite a few hours on her, and I worked out the bugs long before I took her into space. I made seven trips at different times, for trial runs, and used less than twenty percent of the fuel to get into orbit."

"You flew a craft that size by yourself?" Colonel Matovich asked.

"More or less, yes, sir. I had my engineer, Sergeant Tensley, on board each time, but the computers did most of the work."

Diane was mesmerized by what she was hearing. "How many orbits around the earth did you have to make to get enough speed to slingshot the ship into orbit?"

"None. I avoid the jet streams and go to 35,000 feet, kick in the after burners and go vertical to get into quick orbit."

Ed Mitchell stood up with a look of disbelief on his face. "Lieutenant, I believe that what you're telling us is almost impossible. To reach for almost 25,000 miles per hour in a vertical flight, in a ship that size, just can't see it, sir!"

"OK, let's hold up," General Estes intervened. "What Lieutenant Denehey has told you is fact. He has worked years to not only design the ship, but ninety-nine percent of the computer system and the electronics are his baby." The general looked directly at Ed

Mitchell. "Without the new fuel — one hundred percent his — and the engines, which he almost totally designed, we could not have powered this ship to perform as it does. I personally guarantee that whatever he tells you is fact, not fiction."

A new respect for Dennis was formed at that moment.

In Moscow, Russian President Dimitri Kozolov was meeting with his defense minister, Vladimir Bienski, and several other high officials.

"Our radar outposts in Cuba and Mexico are giving reports of activity somewhere in the Nevada/Utah area," said Vladimir. "They can't pinpoint the exact area because of the distance. We have also learned that the Americans have developed a new aircraft that moves at speeds in excess of 25,000 miles per hour."

The president's eyebrows rose as he tried to imagine this, and the other men around the table looked at each other with questioning glances.

"The radar operators also reported that from the time they switched from narrow screen to wide screen, the aircraft would literally disappear."

"Disappear?" asked Dimitri. "Disappear to where?"

Vladimir read each of the solemn gazes of the men sitting around the table. His hands trembled slightly from his nervousness.

"We aren't sure, sir. The next thing that appears on the radar is the craft, in orbit, but what's so strange is that its configuration is different. The first has a set of delta wings while the one in orbit has no wings."

Dimitri thought for a moment, and then replied, "That difference is easily explainable. Delta wing planes can retract their wings, but that is not my main concern. If you are even half correct about the velocity, then we are half a century behind the U.S., and that we can't allow."

He stood up slowly and walked to the window. He stared into the thick blanket of fog that seemed to smother the land. After a few minutes, he quickly turned back to face the defense minister.

"I need proof. I can't believe any aircraft can fly at the speed you are telling me. Here's what I want."

Dimitri sat back down and scribbled some notes.

"I want a radar watch station put in the area where their new craft is first picked up on radar. If that craft is really what you say it is, it needs to be destroyed. We can't dismiss the possibility that it could be a new type of unmanned missile."

"That is a possibility," Vladimir said, "something similar to their interplanetary probes."

"Regardless, we need to know one way or the other. Can we get a radar site in that area, undetected?"

"I believe so, sir; we have a study of that area of the United States. They do much of their testing in the deserts and there are many abandoned airfields, and even missile silos, all over those deserts."

"Get on it as quickly as possible and keep me informed, Mr. Minister."

"Yes Mr. President, but one question, sir. If we do determine it's an aircraft, I'm wondering; how can we get close enough to destroy it? Once we make our presence known, the Americans will take it as a declaration of war. Are we ready to face that possibility?"

"Hmm," Dimitri murmured, as he leaned back in his chair. "No. We are in no way prepared for any war. As a matter of fact, if we got into a shooting war with the U.S. right now, we would be on the losing end. Then China would attack us like the mad dogs they are."

He leaned further back in his chair, rubbing his eyes and speaking to no one in particular.

"No, no confrontation with America."

Then, as if a brilliant idea hit him, he leaned forward.

"What are the chances of our people escaping if we used ground-to-air missiles?"

Vladimir replied solemnly, "I would say slim to none, sir. Even though there are thousands of miles of nothing but desert, it is surrounded by military installations. They would swarm the area within minutes with aircraft, helicopters and soldiers. With heat-seeking infrared technology ... well, I have no doubt our people would be found, sir."

"Suicide?"

"Mr. President, our people are totally demoralized. We have cut military spending so drastically that some are not getting paid for months as it is now. I doubt we would find one who would even consider a suicide mission."

"Arrest their families and kill them if there is a refusal!" Dimitri's face turned red as he slammed his fist down on the table.

Beads of sweat began showing on Vladimir's forehead as he tried to talk some sense into the president.

"That would be the final straw, Mr. President. Our military would revolt against us; they are almost at that point now."

"OK, OK ..." The president threw up his arms in a gesture he was laying that idea to rest. "Just get some viable ideas soon, and I do mean very soon. If it is as you say, that prototype must be destroyed."

He took his notepad from his pocket, and again began to scribble notes in it. "You may go, Mr. Minister," he said without looking up.

Just as Vladimir got to the door, the president shouted.

"Wait!"

Vladimir turned, with a questioning look on his face.

"Seven years ago, when I was head of KGB, there was a very workable plan to get our MiGs into America undetected. You will find those plans at KGB headquarters. How many countries are we selling our MiGs to?"

"At least ten or eleven that I can think of, sir."

"Very good, get seven or eight of our very best pilots, and find those plans. I want unmarked MiGs, and also get me the topographical maps of the area where this new craft is located."

A reassured, devilish grin came over the president's face. "We're going to put our MiGs into the U.S."

"Yes sir, right away!"

Vladimir turned back toward the door, and as he opened it, he remembered something else and turned back to face the president once more.

"Oh, Mr. President, Mr. Castro finally approved the mission into Florida."

The 747 taxied to the hangar at the Cape where the shuttles were housed, mounted on huge crawlers that transported them to the launch pad.

It was 11:30 p.m. and had been an extremely long day for everyone. When the plane stopped, General Estes stood and turned to face everyone.

"OK, people, listen up. I know it's been a long day. There are vehicles waiting to take you and your bags to a hotel just off the base. You can eat, drink or whatever. Just remember that they will pick you up at 1030 hours sharp. We will go to the base for a few hours, and then we're off for home base, so get some rest."

"And where is home base?" Colonel Matovich asked.

Smiling, the general answered, "You will see when we get there Colonel."

Diane was drying off and getting ready for bed. The thoughts of what she had learned today still flooded her mind. She had slept the last hour and a half on the flight and knew sleep was not going to come back soon. She slipped on some clothes, brushed her hair, and headed to the lounge.

The soft music began to relax her as soon as she walked in. Gazing around the room, she noticed about half a dozen people and was surprised to see one of them was Dennis, sitting in a booth, alone.

"Hi, care for some company?"

"Please, sit." He gestured to the empty seat across from him. "What's wrong? Couldn't you sleep either?"

"No, I couldn't. It's been such an exciting day; my mind just won't shut down. I thought a couple of drinks might relax me. You?"

"Yes, much the same, but more so trying to get the nightmare of the past few weeks out of my head."

"Problems with the ship?"

"Oh, no, Colonel, I'm very happy with that."

"Do you suppose we could drop the rank business for tonight? Diane would be just fine, Dennis."

"Suits me fine, Diane, so what would you like to drink?"

Diane ordered rum and Coke and Dennis ordered a refill for his half-empty beer glass.

"So, you're really excited about the program?" Dennis asked.

"Excited is the only word I can find that comes close to what I feel. I can't seem to find the right words to express myself. It's like something I would read in a sci-fi book, or see in a movie. I find it hard to realize that I'm to be part of a historical happening."

Diane sipped her drink and then sat up straighter in the booth. "C'mon Dennis, tell me, just how fast does this ship go?"

"To be truthful Diane, I don't really know. I've never exceeded sixty percent thrust, and that was for escape velocity. One day I'll push her a little more."

"Dennis, believe me, I don't doubt you. I just can't comprehend a ship as massive as you described reaching 25,000 miles per hour in vertical flight."

"I was amazed myself. When I designed the ship and modified the engines for the new fuel, I couldn't believe I could ever go into vertical flight without stalling out. I always thought we would have to work into orbit, like the shuttle."

Diane studied Dennis and decided to ask a question that had been nagging at her mind.

"Dennis, I'm, let's say, an average woman. We are animals that thrive on sticking our noses where they don't belong, and I'm sure you've heard the cliché that curiosity killed the cat. Well, I'm curious, and not ready to die, but I have to ask, how long have you been in the Air Force?"

Knowing what might be on her mind, Dennis replied, "Twelve years."

"OK, wait a minute, twelve years in the service, you design a historical craft probably fifty years before it's time, and you're just a second lieutenant? Something doesn't add up here."

Dennis leaned back against the cold vinyl of the booth and took a long drink of his beer. That crooked grin of his appeared once more. He thought it would take a little longer for someone to put two and two together.

"Guilty as charged. I went through a court-martial and was demoted from full bird to second lieutenant."

Diane's look of surprise could not be masked. "What the hell did you do to deserve that, threaten the president?"

"Not quite. I lost my temper and punched my ex-father-in-law, who happens to be a U.S. senator."

Diane leaned forward and dropped her voice even lower. "Oh my Lord, that was you? I read about that, and from what I read you had every right to do it."

"Unfortunately the court-martial board didn't see it that way."

"Oh, I'm so sorry. Don't they realize how valuable you are to this country?"

"They know nothing of the project, only a very select few do. Not even the vice president knows about it."

"I see, so you took the hit in silence. The way I heard it, you could have taken a general discharge under honorable conditions. If you'd done that, you could have taken your ship, and knowledge, to any aircraft firm. Hell, you could be a billionaire." Diane sat back and looked at him like he was nuts.

"What good are riches, if you don't have freedom?" Dennis leaned forward, looking straight into Diane's eyes, and said in a steady voice, "Diane, this program is vital to our national security. Should the Russians, Chinese, or anyone else find a way to control outer space, America would not exist very long. I promise you that."

##

It was 10:30 a.m. when the five were delivered to the large shuttle hangar. General Estes was waiting for them. The ground crew took their bags, and once again, loaded them on the 747. The general handed each a security badge.

"We'll cut this short, people. I'll explain a part of our plan here. Please take mental notes of the tiniest of flaws, anything you see, or feel could go wrong, and of anything you think may help us. Once on board the plane we'll have a conference to discuss this. Right now, Dennis and I feel it's a fly-by-night plan, but workable."

Two large Marines checked their security badges as they entered.

At the first sight of the shuttles, mounted piggy back on the huge booster rockets, Deana was in awe.

In a soft, yet audible voice, she said, "Lord, I knew they were huge, but never dreamed they were this big."

"There are two brand new inventions on board two of them, and they are the first part of our mission, prior to our trip to the moon," stated the general. "I'll explain their purpose on the plane. Meanwhile, follow me."

They walked around a dividing wall, and to everyone's surprise there were three supersonic Concordes.

"I thought those were retired," said Ed Mitchell.

"They were," Dennis replied, "but the French had no place to store them where they wouldn't deteriorate. We have permission to use them, and then we'll cocoon them and put them out to pasture in our desert graveyard. Now, here is a brief look at our plan."

Deana was still in awe and felt like a kid at Disney World for the first time, wondering how the next part could be more exciting than the previous.

Lieutenant Denehey continued. "First of all, we are being overly cautious. We are aware of being watched 24/7, but don't believe anyone will try to interfere with our mission, so this is a just-in-case scenario. On board one of the shuttles is a new, smaller version, of our laser cannon. Its prime purpose is to protect the space station. There are countries that don't want to see it finished, and if they could, they would destroy it. In the other shuttle is a shielding device. It will protect the station from junk in orbit, meteor showers, or missiles. We also know that once the shuttles are in orbit, chasing the station, our enemies' radar will see them, but the only time the shuttles will be vulnerable is when they are docked with the station."

He looked out over the faces of the new recruits and knew that he most definitely had their full attention

"We chose the Concorde because of its size. It's not the fastest plane but it is fast enough to keep up with the shuttle and create a shadow to confuse radar operators as to what they are actually seeing. The Concorde will create that image until the shuttles are out of range from the huge radar site the Russians have in Cuba. When the booster rockets separate from the shuttles, the Concorde will have done its job. I repeat, we are being overly cautious, just in case, somehow, the enemy finds out we have the laser cannon and the shielding device. China and Russia do have missiles that could reach the space station. When the shuttles are recognized, we hope that in their confusion, and while they are scrambling to contact higher commands, we will have enough time to get the shield installed."

"OK, these are just the highlights of our plan, people," the general interrupted. "Let's get back to the plane now. There will be a conference while we're in the air so we can address your concerns and questions."

##

Diane and Deana took their places across from each other and fastened their seatbelts.

Diane leaned back and closed her eyes as the 747 smoothly taxied toward the runway. She was trying to sort out all of the information she had accumulated in the past twenty-four hours.

Deana softly asked, "Are you asleep, Diane?"

Without moving from her comfortable position, Diane opened her eyes and smiled. "No, I'm not asleep. You know, I can normally sort things out and get everything in proper order with my eyes closed, but not this time."

"Same here, the last twenty-four hours seem surreal, so much information in such a short time. So tell me, Diane, any second thoughts about this mission?"

"Are you asking if I might consider changing my mind and backing out?"

"More or less."

"Oh, no way, I'm more excited now than when I first applied. I want to be a part of making history. To be quite honest with you, I've been thinking more about the path I walked for the past seven years to get here."

Deana shifted in her seat. "Mine was pretty intense. Years seem more like weeks and I've been in for almost nine years now. So enlighten me, just how did you get here?"

"Well, I would have to start back about fourteen years ago when my dream was to become a doctor, if you can believe that. I was full steam ahead until I met Ed. He was also a med student. We had a few dates, and one weekend he asked me if I wanted to go to the Blue Ridge Mountains, where his folks had a lodge. His family was there for the week on vacation."

"Wow that sounds like fun."

"I thought so, too. I believed we were going to drive, but the only driving was to a small airport not far from campus. He had an old Luscombe Silvaire and I assumed it was a new plane; it was so sleek and clean. That was my first time to fly and I fell in love with it. He taught me how to fly and in a short time I had my license. Then, one afternoon, we got into a no-fly zone and the next thing I knew, we had three F-16s surrounding us."

"Oh, boy!" Deana said, laughing. "I bet that wasn't much fun."

"Actually, it was. They told us to follow them and land. De-ana, I watched those beautiful birds as we followed them and I can't describe what I felt. They inspected us for contraband and whatever else they were looking for, and then escorted us out of the no-fly zone. When I watched them peel off and leave, I said to Ed, that's for me. I went the next day and enlisted! He thought I was crazy for throwing away three years of med school. I don't regret it at all. This is what I was meant to do and I love it!"

The intercom sounded and a sultry voice filled their ears, "Ladies and gentlemen, General Estes requests your presence in his conference room upstairs. Thank you."

When everyone had taken seats in the conference room, the general began, "OK, let's get back to business. First thing I defi-nitely need to discuss is Lieutenant Denehey. He is the squadron commander and your flight instructor. He will set all the schedules and he can qualify you, or flunk you out of the program. He will represent me in all aspects concerning the ships and the program. I am the base commander and will command the squadron until our mission is completed and beyond. Any comments on those sub-jects?"

They all shook their heads.

"About the briefing at the Cape, let's go in order around the table. Lieutenant Denehey, any comments?"

"None for now, sir."

"Very well, Colonel Kutchmark, you have the floor," the general said as he sat down.

"Where do I start, sir? I have so many questions."

The general stood up again. "Let me interrupt for one minute. We have a six hour flight ahead of us and if it takes that, Colonel Kutchmark, that's fine. There is one thing I need to mention, that I insist on. As of today, we are a team and a family. No questions are bad questions. We will feed on each other's knowledge and skills and we must all work together to accomplish our mission. You may continue, Colonel."

"Thank you, sir. You mentioned a shielding device for the space station. It sounds like something from the "Star Trek" TV series. Some years back, I read where a college was experimenting with the theory but it seemed that most believed it was a pipe dream. Will it actually deflect a rocket missile or meteor?"

"Missiles, yes. A meteor, say the size of a huge boulder and weighing approximately five tons, yes. The dome shape of the field itself helps a lot. They dropped a five-ton weight on a straight impact and it was deflected, but we don't know how much it will actually take before it starts to weaken the shield."

The general took a sip of his water and continued. "There will be a shield for the base on the moon. If our time schedule holds for the trip, the extra laser cannon and search radar won't be ready. The search radar is to scan for meteors and anything incoming, while the laser cannon will start picking away at it. Our scientists estimate that if we can fire at an object that is 239,000 miles away, a laser should pretty well destroy a meteor the size of a football field at 10,000 miles. Meanwhile, the existing cannon will be utilized, if needed, until the next one arrives. A smaller device is being worked on for the ships. Another question, Colonel Kutchmark?"

"Yes sir, you mentioned ships, plural; how many will we have, sir?"

"Dennis, that's your area."

"Colonel, when all is said and done, we will have twelve. I'm going to use number one to train with. Numbers two and three should be on the test stands now, or will be shortly. We have spread the contracts out to aircraft companies all around the world — primarily in the U.S., England and Australia. No one knows what it is they are building. It's the same with the electronics and hydraulics. When a fuselage section, or other part, is ready for us, they deliver it to a depot, and the pieces are secretly delivered to our base. Our own engineers assemble the units. I have been out of pocket for a few weeks and Sergeant Tensley has been in command of the assembly, and trust me, when I say no one, not even myself, knows every detail of our ships as well as he does, you can take it to the bank."

"OK, thank you Dennis," said General Estes, "and what is your next question, Colonel?"

"Why don't we use our ships to do the station mission?"

"We have to keep these ships as secret as possible. I'm sure the enemy knows we are experimenting with something, and if they had any idea of the ship's capabilities and the size of our fleet, well, I would venture to say that World War III would happen. The Chinese spy satellite started making passes over our area, and I strongly believe they are searching for our facility. We also think we have a leak somewhere and are searching for that; so, it's in our best interest to not use the ships when we don't have to. Unfortunately, it's going to affect your training. There will be no further flights into space until the actual mission. One thing in your favor is the computer system we have. There are two backup systems behind the main one. Colonel O'Hara, questions?"

"If I understood correctly, Lieutenant Denehey, you said you used less than twenty percent fuel to get into orbit from 35,000 feet, going vertical. When you are at orbit altitude, can you maintain that velocity indefinitely? Since you are then basically in a vacuum and pulling away from Earth's gravitational pull, then I could cut off the engines and coast to the moon?"

"Just like the Apollo missions. Since we're not sure how much pull the earth has on a ship, and at what point the pull is actually negative, I'm not sure. We will find out on the first trip. Since the Moon Lander actually traveled much slower than we intend to, I'm not positive on anything. My intent is to maintain a velocity of 17,500 miles per hour, which is the same velocity it takes to maintain an orbit around the earth when it is 124 miles above the surface. We will initially slow to approximately 8,000 miles per hour below escape velocity. Even with all the calculations from NASA, there are still some small unknowns, so we're going to be cautious at first. When we do get the shields for the ships, we can gradually increase the velocity. There are things in space like meteor showers, and we want plenty of time to make course corrections if radar picks them up. We will be in a new learning stage of space flight with this ship."

"What will constitute a full crew?"

"It will consist of a first and second seat, flight engineer, radar operator, and combination weapons and communications person."

"Are the ships themselves armed, and if so, with what?"

"A small version of the laser cannon along with forward and aft space torpedoes."

Diane looked puzzled. "Do we need that much armament, sir?"

Dennis picked up the pitcher from the table and poured more water.

"All I can say is, it's better to be ready." He held his glass forward as if he were toasting someone. "Don't you think?"

Diane smiled. "Yes sir, it is. So, we're looking at a little over a fourteen-hour trip. What about fuel and runways?"

"As far as the fuel goes, after we escape and shut down the engines, we should have at least seventy-seven to seventy-eight percent of fuel remaining. Since the moon has only one-sixth the gravitational pull of earth, we should not use more than five percent fuel for landing, unless the landing spot we have chosen is too rough, then the first ship down — mine — will search out a landing spot and direct the others in. All in-flight corrections will be with compressed air thrusters, even to slow down as we approach the moon. Regarding the runways, these ships have VTOL capabilities."

The phone beside the general buzzed. He picked it up and listened for a minute.

"Are you sure, Captain? Four course corrections and it's still there?"

A worried look appeared on the general's face.

"All right, Captain, call out the fighters. Where is the nearest place we can land?"

He paused, nodding his head in agreement. "Yes, that's fine, take us down. We can't do a damn thing about the satellite but I want that plane on the ground. Check their flight plan with the FAA and they had damn sure better have filed one."

He placed the phone down and scratched his forehead.

"Problems, General?"

"Yes, Dennis, the second time this month. I was followed a couple of weeks ago from Houston to Wright-Patterson, and now today we picked up a tail from Florida. The pilot has made four course changes and they have done the same, plus the Russian satellite is watching us again." He stood up and started gathering his files. "There are only three who know where I am – the president, the FAA, and base. There's nothing we can do about the satellite but the fighters are going to bring down the Lear jet. I want to see who is tailing us, so we are landing at an old Air Force base in Denison, Texas. We still man the main hangar there."

The intercom buzzed: "Fifteen minutes until final approach, General Estes."

"OK, people, back to your seats, and Dennis, I'll see you on the ground."

The 747 taxied to the open hangar doors and shut down its four engines.

As everyone disembarked, the sound of jet engines roared overhead. Three fighters flanked a small Lear jet; one fighter off each wing and one following close behind. As they all turned in the distance, on final approach, the two at the wing tips of the Lear jet followed it down—each fighter jet flying just a few feet off the ground. The third fighter touched down at almost the same time as the Lear jet. The two wingmen throttled up, gained altitude, circled, and then came in for a landing.

A young lieutenant came out of the hangar and approached the general.

"Lieutenant, would you please escort these four into the old briefing room?" General Estes asked. "Dennis, I need you to stay here."

The pilot of the 747 joined them, and was informing the general of information he had received.

"The FAA can find no flight plan for the numbers on the wings of that plane, sir."

"Call the local FBI," the general ordered.

The Lear jet taxied to within twenty yards of them. It was a couple of minutes before the door opened, and the first two out of the jet were women, followed by a large, burly man. The two women headed toward General Estes and Lieutenant Denehey, while the man stayed beside the plane. The lead woman looked very agitated, and her anger was clear in her voice.

"Are you in charge here?" she blurted out toward Estes.

"Yes, I am General Estes, your identification, please."

"What right do you have to force us to land here?"

"Excuse me, miss, I am in charge here, not you. ID, and who is the pilot here?"

"I don't have to show you one damn thing; I'm a civilian, not military."

The general faced the returning pilot of the 747.

"Did you get the FBI?"

"Yes, sir, the agent said it would take about fifteen minutes to get here."

"The FBI?" the woman asked. "Why are you calling them?"

"You have broken federal law by flying without a registered flight plan, refusing to identify yourself, following a United States military aircraft, do you need more reasons?"

The other woman stepped forward.

"Sir, I'm the pilot, what is it you need?"

"Your pilot license and a copy of the flight plan you are supposed to file. I want the ID of this woman, and that man also. Are you carrying anything illegal?"

"Sir, my license is in my briefcase, on the plane. May I talk to you in private, please?"

The other woman turned to the pilot and whispered in an angry tone, "Shut up, we are paying you!"

The pilot stepped toward the general and screamed at the woman, "You liar!"

She spun around to face the general.

"Sir, they hijacked me and my plane! That man has a gun!"

The other woman turned, as if to signal the giant man standing by the plane. Seeing the man pull a weapon, Dennis grabbed the woman, dragging her back, an arm around her neck. He positioned her between himself and the man with the gun, using her as a shield, and wishing he was armed himself.

He shouted.

"General! Get the pilot into the hangar."

The big man eased toward Dennis. General Estes grabbed the pilot's arm and ran through the hangar doors. The man shot at them, but the bullet ricocheted off the steel door, just as they ducked inside.

Dennis knew that he did not have a prayer. The woman was just a temporary shield and the man could easily outflank him.

Dennis kept backing away, toward the hangar, dragging the woman with him.

Just as the man made a quick move to his right, trying to get a shot at Dennis' side, the shattering noise of machine gun fire broke the silence. Chunks of concrete flew everywhere. Dennis felt the searing pain when splinters of concrete hit his arms and face; he fell backward, pulling the woman down on top of him.

Then, there was silence.

Dennis tried to move the woman. He felt something, a fluid, running over his fingers, which were still wrapped around the woman. Her dead weight was suddenly pulled from him, and he rolled away as fast as he could, thinking the man with the gun had lifted her.

"Easy, Lieutenant, it's all right, the gunman is dead."

Dennis looked up and saw two uniformed men, one offering his hand to help Dennis off the ground. They were two of the fighter pilots who helped bring down the Lear jet.

Dennis looked around and saw the body of the huge man, lying on the concrete. His body looked twisted. He was face down, yet the rest of him was in an almost fetal position.

Dennis' thinking was hazy. He shook his head, as if trying to chase a fog from his brain. He heard one of the fighter pilots apologizing, but it was not registering yet. It was the pilot who stayed on the tail end of the Lear jet. He had seen the man with the gun and waited, until the huge man had made a move to flank Dennis, then he fired a short burst from his M-61A1.

The 20 mm bullets tore the man apart, but the burst had also hit the walkway, showering Dennis and the woman with chunks of concrete, one of which killed the woman when it penetrated her forehead.

Dennis felt the blood trickle into his eye. Someone was softly wiping his forehead with paper towels and shouting.

"Someone get some water!"

"How serious is it?" asked the general.

Dennis recognized Diane's voice as she replied.

"The forehead has superficial scratches, not deep. There is blood on his left side, but I can't tell if it's his or the woman's. She took most of the fragments."

"Do we need an ambulance?"

"I don't think so, sir. Right now, I'm trying to stop the bleeding from his forehead."

The adrenaline rush had eased, and Dennis calmly said, "I'm fine, just take me to a bathroom where I can wash my face."

Diane led him inside, where he leaned over the sink and splashed water on his face.

She found a first aid station and soon was bathing his forehead with an antiseptic. She applied some antibacterial ointment and wrapped his head with.

"OK, now, off with that shirt, Lieutenant."

"I'm fine, Colonel. I don't think I'm hurt."

"Off with the shirt, Lieutenant … now!"

"Yes ma'am, Colonel," Dennis said with a slight grin, as he stood up and removed his shirt. He felt a stinging sensation as Diane removed a small splinter of concrete from his left side. She cleaned it up, put a gauze pad on the small wound, and taped it on. When he looked up, he saw several concerned faces in the doorway.

"I'm fine, just fine, and thanks, Colonel. Nice job."

Diane, leaning over to pick up the first aid kit, whispered in Dennis' ear.

"Nice chest, Lieutenant."

Dennis smiled, and walked out into the hangar. He saw General Estes and the three fighter pilots in one group, and some man in a civilian suit talking to the pilot of the Lear jet.

Another man Dennis did not recognize, in an Air Force uniform, walked up to Dennis and handed him a plaid shirt. Dennis smiled and thanked him. He slipped the shirt on as he walked to the general.

"You OK, Dennis?" asked the general.

"Yes, sir. I was just wondering which of these pilots I need to be thanking."

A young captain stepped forward.

"I am so sorry, sir. It was all I could think of to do."

"Oh no, Captain, no apologies are necessary. You saved my life, sir! It was just a matter of a few steps and he would have had me, woman or no woman. Thank you so much."

Dennis reached out and shook the captain's hand.

The FBI agent walked over to the general.

"General Estes, the man and woman have Canadian passports. I took their fingerprints and will run them when I get back to the office. If I had to guess, I would say the woman is Russian, and the man Cuban. I'll know more after I run their prints. The office has cleared Jennifer, the pilot. She has a very clean record in all respects, but if you want, I can hold her for seventy-two hours. There is nothing I can charge her with since she was obviously hijacked."

"No, there is no need to hold her," replied the general.

Jennifer stood.

"Does that mean I can go home?"

"Yes, young lady," the general replied. "You have been traumatized quite a bit today. Are you sure you feel up to flying home alone right now?"

"Oh, yes sir, I'm fine, thanks to all of you. Lieutenant, what you did was the bravest thing I have ever seen. Thank you!"

As the FBI agent prepared to leave, General Estes gave him a card with instructions to pass on further information.

"That is a White House phone number," the agent observed. "Who should I report to?"

"That is the president's phone, Agent Thomas; report to no one but her."

The general headed for the conference room and his team followed.

"Captain, what's the latest report on the satellite?"

"It is believed to be Russian, Sir, and since the collapse of the Soviet Union, we all know they only have one spy satellite over the United States, and it uses the film pods, so they won't even have images for at least a week. That is unless they have something we don't know about up there now."

"I can't afford to take any chances."

The general sat down and leaned back in the chair at the end of the table.

"I can pull the 747 into the hangar, General, all but the tail," said the captain.

"I doubt they have heat-seeking capabilities," Dennis replied, "but they could have some kind of infrared camera, if they have upgraded without us knowing it. With it being night, they may be able to see the plane, but I don't believe they can see us."

"Captain, do your people man this 'empty' base twenty-four hours a day?"

"Sir, looks are very deceiving. See that far wall over there that looks like offices? There's a stealth fighter behind it, and the pilots are in the old ops building that's connected to this hangar. Most closed bases now maintain a portion of it."

"Hmm, when did this all start?"

"Right after our new president was sworn in. She's a commander in chief truly worthy of the office, General."

The general leaned forward and wiped an imaginary spot of something from the table.

"Captain, you are indeed correct. Is there a good hotel where we can spend the night?"

"I would recommend the fairly new La Quinta Inn, sir. They have a good restaurant, nice lounge, and comfortable rooms. And they have vans that will pick you up, and deliver you back here in the morning."

"Good, we need ten rooms."

The general stood up and got everyone's attention.

"Listen up, folks; we'll be staying the night in a local hotel. There will be a van here to pick us up shortly, so in the meantime, get the bags you'll need from the plane."

##

There was a knock on Dennis' door. When he opened it, Diane was standing there with a bag in her hand.

"Hello, Lieutenant, the doctor has come to ply her trade."

Laughing, Dennis asked, "What are you talking about? I'm fine."

Dennis had forgotten his shirt was off, until Diane put her hand on his bare chest and pushed him back into the room, and closed the door.

"I'm the doctor, and I'll be the judge if you are fine or not. At the least, three years of med school taught me what infections can do. Now sit down in that chair, and let me get that awful head bandage off."

"Let me at least put on a shirt."

"Why? I'm going to check that side wound, too."

He obediently took the seat, and she began working on the bandage.

"If you had three years of med school, how did you end up here?"

Diane began to retell the story she told Deana earlier. After she had all the bandages off, and had checked each cut, she reached for her bag and dumped the contents out on the desk.

"Did you go shopping, doctor?"

"There's a pharmacy across the street. We can't afford for our instructor to be out of commission, ya know."

Diane picked up a container and handed it to Dennis.

"Here, this is antibacterial soap. Go take a shower, use this, and don't rub anything over the wounds. Use the palm of your hand, and just lightly smooth it over them. Rinse with warm water and pat them dry, I don't think we'll have to go back with the head bandage."

Dennis did as he was ordered, and Diane put clean bandages on his wounds, leaving off the head wrap. Dennis thanked her, and asked her to join him for dinner, which she gladly accepted.

Diane giggled.

"Is something funny?"

"I'm sorry, Dennis, but yes, it is funny!"

"What is?"

"I may not be the doctor I thought I was. Those band-aids I put on you, reminds me of the patch work on the fabric of a patched up Piper Cub."

"That bad, huh? Oh well, I hated that bandage around my head. I only kept it on because you put it there."

"Oh, you mean as a souvenir?"

"Something like that."

##

The phone was ringing. Dennis rolled over and finally found it.

Oh Lord, 3:40 in the morning?

He picked up the phone.

"Hello?"

He paused for a moment, listening.

"General Estes, yes sir, I'm half awake. Is there a problem, sir?"

Dennis sat up on the edge of his bed.

"You'll be here in a minute? Yes, sir, let me slip on some pants and I'll open the door."

He hung up the phone and a soft voice asked, "Problems?"

Diane rose up on an elbow.

"Oh hell, the general's coming here, something's up. I'll close the bedroom door and fill you in after he's gone."

"Umm, ok," Diane said sleepily.

She lay back down, pulling the covers over her head.

Dennis opened the door on the first knock, and the general rushed in, handing Dennis a cup of black coffee and sipping on his own.

"There's a problem at the Cape, eight commando-type men made a try at the shuttles. Damn, Dennis, they're getting serious. The Marines killed one, and captured the other seven. There is a definite leak somewhere. When they try to attack on American soil, and in crucial places, someone is talking to someone. Dennis, I hate to ask, but do you feel up to a trip to the Cape?"

"Yes, sir," Dennis replied, "but why me?"

"According to your records, you went through the Marine interrogation training sessions. We have some live prisoners here, and I would like to see what you might be able to find out. We have to stop this information leak, or this whole project is in jeopardy, particularly if it gets to some of our liberal politicians. Hell, they would love to impeach her."

"Yes, sir, I'll go. What about transport, sir?"

"The captain at the hangar is trying to line up a Lear jet for you at the field."

The general took another drink of his coffee.

"If you had a choice of one of our group to go with you, who would it be?"

"Excuse me, sir, why someone else?"

"The old cliché, two heads are better than one."

Dennis thought it over for a moment.

"For something like this, I would have to pick Colonel O'Hara. Three years of med school before she enlisted, her overall performance is superior to everyone else, even mine."

"Is that so?" the general mused. "OK, find her room number and give her a call. She didn't sign on for this kind of duty Dennis, so ask her if she will go. I've got to get back to my room and wait for the captain to call about the transportation. I'll call you when I find out."

Dennis locked the door and hurried back to the bedroom. He opened the door to find Diane sitting on the edge of the bed, putting on her shoes.

"Sorry, I was eavesdropping at the door; yes, I'll go. You men are getting too sharp for us women."

"How's that?

Dennis leaned against the door, thinking: *she is so beautiful ... this is crazy, we just met ... I can't be in love.*

"Apparently you men are learning our secrets. Asking, not ordering, even in the military. Is that good or bad?"

She stopped what she was doing and walked over to where Dennis stood.

"An example, Lieutenant. Had you ordered me to sleep with you, I would have told you off, and so, on that, you did well; it was great as a matter of fact. When I had to ask you if I could sleep with you ... well, that was bad. So, think that over and maybe we can discuss it on the way to the Cape."

##

The van pulled up to the hangar doors and Dennis got out, taking his and Diane's bags. A Lear jet was sitting nearby, the soft hum of its idling engines like music in the quiet, early morning hours.

A lieutenant came running from the jet.

"Morning, Lieutenant," he said to Dennis.

Seeing Diane's lieutenant colonel insignia, he stopped and saluted.

"The pilots are waiting sir, ready when you are."

They walked over to the plane and the lieutenant called out, "Hey Cathy, your passengers are here."

A tall, pretty woman appeared in the doorway.

"Welcome aboard."

Dennis stepped aside, allowing Diane to go up the steps first. He followed, carrying the bags.

As Dennis appeared inside, the pilot said, "Whoa, cowboy! Someone pepper you with a shotgun, or what?"

"Long story, ma'am."

"Let me have your bags, I'll stow them, grab any seat ya want."

The pilot took their bags.

"Hey, I see those wings, are ya both pilots?"

"Yes, we are," replied Diane.

"Wow, may I ask what birds you fly?"

"The lieutenant here is a shuttle pilot, amongst other things; I'm a fighter pilot."

"Wow, double-wow, would it bother you if I came back to talk to you guys, after we're airborne of course? I'm thinking of enlisting, but only if they allow me a chance to fly."

"Sure," Diane answered, "come on back."

"Great!" Oh, I'm Cathy, your pilot for the trip. There is fresh-brewed coffee, after we are up. Milk and other goodies are in the galley fridge. Make yourselves at home and we'll see you in a bit."

She turned to leave. While walking away, she looked back over her shoulder and with a big grin, said, "Oh, and please buckle up!"

She was no sooner gone, than the twin jet engines came alive. Dennis and Diane found their seats. The hangar disappeared as the jet moved down the taxiway.

"That young woman is a rarity these days, great attitude!" Diane said.

"It really is good to see women flying, just like that woman who had to face those hijackers."

"Are you telling me you don't resent us women competing with you men?" Diane asked, with a slight smirk on her face.

"Not at all. I believe women, in most cases, have faster and better reaction times. I guess you can say I'm sort of old-fashioned in my thinking though, it may be a male ego thing, but I don't want to see a woman hurt, wounded, or killed. That woman who literally died in my arms, no matter her motive, is going to eat at me for a long, long, time."

"You're just an old softy, Lieutenant. It's not ego, it's called caring, and personally, I appreciate a man who thinks as you do."

Dennis felt a slight "thump, thump" in his feet. He glanced out the window and saw the streetlights quickly falling away, as the quiet ship moved high into the pre-dawn sky.

"That was a smooth take off," he remarked. "These are great little planes."

He felt the main landing gear being retracted and locked into place, and looked up to see the seatbelt sign go off.

"I'm going for a cup of that black coffee, want some?"

Diane unbuckled her seatbelt and stood up.

"I'll get it. I'm going to the ladies room first."

Confident, that's what that woman is, he thought to himself as she walked down the aisle – *confident, beautiful and a personality to match – quite a woman.*

When Diane returned with two cups of coffee, Cathy followed, with a cup for herself.

"Mind if I sit for a bit with you two?"

"Not at all, but who's flying the plane?" Diane asked, in a joking manner.

"It's on autopilot, but my co-pilot is monitoring it. We never leave the cockpit unattended."

"So, you're thinking of enlisting? Oh, forgive my manners, I'm Diane O'Hara, and this pock-marked gentleman is Dennis Denehey."

"Denehey, Denehey," Cathy thought out loud. "I heard that name somewhere. Oh my God! The hero? I heard all about you when I landed. That's where you got shot gunned. Yes, sir, everyone on the base knows about you, sir." Cathy's excitement showed in her eyes.

Laughing, Dennis declared, "What they apparently don't know is how I was trying to save my hide also."

"Everyone is fully aware of what happened, Lieutenant. Is he always this modest, Diane?"

Diane laughed. She was really beginning to like this girl.

"You know," Diane remarked, "the pay in the military isn't quite as good as what you're making now."

"Oh, yes, I know that, but thanks for telling me. I've been flying since I was thirteen, got my pilot's license at fourteen. I was flying second seat on commercials when I was twenty. I'm doing this to keep my hours up, until I make up my mind just what I'm going to do. Shoot, I'm qualified for first seat on 747s, 727s and others. It's not only a family tradition; I guess you can say it's in our blood."

Cathy's face gleamed with pride as she continued.

"My great-grandfather was considered a pioneer in aviation—my grandfather, father, and even my grandmother, flew in the wars. I have three brothers, two of them still flying in the military, one a Marine pilot, the other Air Force."

"What did your grandmother fly, Cathy?"

"Oh Lord, lets see…C-47s, B-25s, B-17s ... well, let me put it this way, she flew lots of them. She ferried planes from the factory, to England and Scotland, during World War II."

"What is your last name?"

"Mitchell, Catherine Mitchell."

"So, you must be the great-granddaughter of Billy Mitchell. They named the Mitchell bombers after him, am I correct?

"Yes Sir," she said proudly. "William Mitchell, 1879 to 1936. Then you've heard of him?"

"There isn't a pilot worth his salt who hasn't heard of him," stated Dennis.

"You say you have a brother who is a Marine pilot?" asked Diane.

"Yes I do, a helluva man he is."

"Wouldn't happen to be Edward Mitchell, would it?"

Cathy's eyes opened wide. "Yes, yes, it's Ed. Do you know him?"

"Sure do, he's back in that town we just left."

"You mean Denison?"

"Actually, we were all housed at the La Quinta Inn in Sherman last night."

"Oh Lordy, what's he doing there?"

"They're waiting for a plane ride to our new base," said Dennis.

"Where? What new base?"

"Well…that's something we can't tell you, honey," Diane said sympathetically.

"Oh well, he'll contact us as soon as he can," Cathy said, with a small pout on her face.

"Yes, he will. I take it that Ed's your oldest brother?"

"He is now. My oldest brother was killed in Operation Desert Storm, and my youngest was killed in Pakistan. My mom is dying, maybe a couple of months left. Losing two sons has taken a heavy toll on her. She made me and Mattie promise to not join up while she was still alive; otherwise, we would have already enlisted."

"How many flight hours do you have?"

"I'm not sure of the exact hours, but I have a little over 1400 hours commercial — 747, 727 and others. Two hundred hours in helicopters from when I flew people, equipment and supplies to offshore rigs, and a little over two hundred hours with this job … somewhere between 2500 and 3000, I reckon."

"Any FAA violations?"

Laughing, Cathy answered, "None on record, but yes, I had one write-up. When I was sixteen, I took my finals and got my instrument and multi-engines rating. Now mind you, our house was in the middle of eleven hundred acres of farmland, the nearest house was over three miles away. Well, I was in a mood to celebrate, so I buzzed our house, three times, in a twin Cessna. Someone got my ship's number and turned me in. The FAA inspector thought it was a stupid complaint, but I did break regulations by buzzing a residence. I was grounded for one day, and they made me answer the phones and file reports in his office. The complaint was expunged."

"Oh, that's good," Diane said.

Dennis scribbled some phone numbers on his pad, tore it out, and handed it to Cathy.

"When you are ready to enlist, call this number, and tell him that I told you to call, and why. He is a very influential man, right up to the president. I'm sure he'll help you over the hurdles; you certainly impress me. Between the general and myself, I think we can give you a jump start."

"Gee, thanks, Dennis," Cathy said, adding in a shy, almost girlish voice, "I don't want to take advantage of your very wonderful offer, but I guess it never hurts to ask, do you think y'all might help my sister too, my younger sister?"

Dennis and Diane both had to laugh at the way she asked.

"What does she do?" asked Diane.

"She's my co-pilot."

"Oh my, this is just too much of a coincidence, Dennis. May I come forward and meet her, Cathy?"

Cathy introduced them to the pretty young girl in the co-pilot's seat. When told that Diane was a fighter pilot, Dennis an astronaut, and how they both knew Ed, Mattie's eyes opened wide and were bright as stars.

"Oh my," Mattie whispered. "That's my dream."

"What's that?" Diane asked.

"Fighters, then the stars, oh yeahhh!" exclaimed Mattie.

"You mean space flight?" asked Dennis.

"Yes Sir, you bet! It's going to happen, I just know it is, and I want to be there when it does!"

Mattie was so excited just thinking about it. Dennis and Diane smiled at each other; feeling refreshed at the wonder of the young girl's ambitions.

"It's going to happen, sooner than you think," said Diane.

Cathy and Mattie looked at her, waiting for an explanation. A more serious look came to Mattie's face as she straightened the earphones on her head.

"Incoming message."

Mattie expertly adjusted the radio frequency and began writing on the pad attached to her right thigh.

As Mattie signed off and moved the earphones back to their lopsided position, Cathy asked, "What's up, Sis?"

"Just a minute, I have to change our computer heading."

They watched as Mattie's fingers flew across a tiny keyboard, punched in numbers, and then pushed a red button. The immediate response was a slight bank of the plane, as they watched the compass readjust to a new, southeasterly setting.

Once satisfied, Mattie said, "I guess our passengers' mission is pretty important. We're cleared to land at the Cape, and we'll be escorted through the no-fly zone. If we get there before the escort, we're to circle at 24,000 feet 'til they arrive. We are to stay there until their business is completed and then take them to ... I don't know where, yet. We will be notified after their business is concluded, and we're supposed to be ready to roll."

Mattie tore off the piece of paper and handed it to Dennis.

"Cath, honey, would you take Lieutenant Denehey to the private phone? He is to call this number, immediately."

When Dennis got off the phone, he went back to his seat. Diane was already buckled in.

"What's wrong?"

"We only have two of the so-called commandos left. Apparently, they had some kind of suicide capsules implanted in them. They assumed that the two remaining could not get to theirs because of the way they were shackled. They sedated them both, and they don't believe we'll be able to talk to them for at least twenty-four to thirty-two hours. They located the capsules in the two that are alive, and are removing them as we speak."

The intercom came on, and they heard Cathy's voice, "Approximately fifteen minutes to no fly zone."

"So, we wait I guess," said Diane.

"Yep, we wait. They're making arrangements for all of us at a hotel. We'll stay there until the doctor gives us an all-clear to interview the prisoners."

"Well, the suns up, Dennis, maybe a stroll on the beach?"

"Could be possible, but I doubt it. This whole area is secured by beach patrols, cameras, and who knows what else. That's how they got these people. They have detectors of every kind on these beaches, as well as underwater."

"Oh well, there goes our stroll on the beach," said Diane, with her bottom lip curved into a cute little pout.

"I would guess, Diane, that most hotels and motels have swimming pools."

Dennis was trying hard not to laugh at how cute Diane was looking at that very moment.

"Oh sure, knowing the government, we'll be in some flea bag hotel, but that's OK, I didn't come prepared for swimming anyway."

"Maybe they allow skinny dipping," said Dennis, as he grinned from ear to ear.

Red faced, Diane came back at him, "You wish! I'm sure you would love that!"

"Only if no one else gets to see that beautiful body," Dennis said, sincerely.

Diane felt a little quiver in her stomach. She was not quite sure what to make of all this. Was Dennis just a smooth talker, or did he really mean what he said? She sure wanted to find out.

"I'll take that as a compliment."

Then touching his arm with innocent intention, she asked, "Do you really think so?"

Softly, Dennis replied, "So there are no misunderstandings here, I never say things I don't mean, and I'm really much more interested in the person that occupies that beautiful body, the rest is merely a bonus."

Diane's quiver in her stomach had turned into a full blown flip-flop now, but she made herself get back behind her safe wall before she answered.

"I think that's the best line I have ever heard, Dennis."

"Perhaps. To me, a line is an untruth, just to attract women, and my words are truth. The physical makeup does not matter; it's the heart, the soul, and the personality that reflects the real beauty, or ugliness, of a person."

Diane realized he was serious … very serious.

"Thank you for that confirmation, Dennis. I didn't mean it as such, but your affirmation makes it all the more lovely."

Diane returned to the position behind her safe wall, and said jokingly, "So, is that a preliminary proposal?"

Cathy's voice came over the intercom.

"Got escort on radar, approximately fifty miles out, coming fast."

"Lord, already 7:30. Where did the time go?"

"My theory is that it went to good conversation, and to meeting two very interesting young ladies. Ed's two sisters, who would have thought it? Those Mitchells are everywhere. Damned interesting family history in aviation they have. The last thing the general said he was going to do was to see if our pilots could be cleared to land at the Cape."

"Escorts here," said Cathy's voice over the intercom, "you two might want to buckle up, we're going to follow them down to 10,000."

Dennis and Diane buckled their seatbelts. They glanced out the window and were quiet. Diane could not remember when she had felt so alive.

The sound of hydraulics, as the landing gear went down, and the announcement from Cathy that they were two minutes from final, brought them back to reality.

The landing was so smooth that Dennis wasn't sure when they were actually on the ground. Even the reversing of the thrust, used to help brake the plane, was smooth.

"That was sweet! Someday I'm going to learn to do that."

"Do what, Dennis?

"Land an airplane that softly."

A guide truck met them at the taxiway, and soon they were parked at the huge hangar once more.

"Well, this is sure familiar," Diane said.

After Cathy and Mattie had completed their post flight check list, they met with Diane and Dennis.

"We're going to be staying overnight," Dennis told them.

"Oh Lord, another night in a flea bag motel," Mattie said acidly.

Dennis and Diane looked at each other and laughed, remembering their previous conversation about the same thing.

An Air Force sergeant was waiting, with a van, as they deplaned.

"Mattie, you take the left side and I'll take the right," said Cathy.

The sergeant stepped forward, "No ma'am, our crew will post flight and refuel your ship."

Cathy looked at him with eyebrows raised, "Sorry, Sergeant, I post and preflight my aircraft. You can do it again, after I'm done."

She turned and headed around the plane with the sergeant following her.

"Yes ma'am, do you want us to refuel?"

"Yes, thank you, you can do that."

"Yes ma'am. Also understand that your plane has to go in the hangar until you're ready to leave. No ships are left outside."

"Thank you, Sergeant. I'm not trying to be rude or difficult, it's just my policy."

"Oh, don't worry about that ma'am, I understand. Do you have flags and gear pins?"

"They're in the pouch, left side of door. Thank you."

Dennis, observing Cathy as she carried on, said to Diane, "Those girls are professionals."

"They certainly are."

"I wouldn't mind having a dozen just like them," Dennis said, not realizing what it sounded like.

Diane laughed.

"What? You saying you want your own harem, Dennis?"

"Ha! Not hardly," Dennis said, in a slightly sarcastic voice.

"I must have been the one at fault," he continued, "for you not remembering what I said on the plane, during our meeting with the general."

Diane gave him a puzzled look.

"Well, I hope it was my fault that you were daydreaming about me when I told everyone that we would have a total of twelve ships. Remember?"

Diane answered, totally feeling the fool, "Oh…my…gosh! You are so right, that's why you want twelve just like them! Ok, you got me on that one, and you are right about one thing."

"What's that?"

"It is your fault!"

While waiting in the van for Cathy and Mattie, Dennis seemed to be a million miles away in his thoughts.

"A penny for your thoughts."

"Oh, I was just thinking about the ships. Most of them are close to readiness for test flight, and once we prove their value, I'm hoping we'll get more."

"Sounds like we're building a separate Air Force."

"Space Force," Dennis replied. "The only way our country can survive is to stay superior in air and space. Eventually, we know China and Russia are going to get into space; we just can't allow them to control it."

"I agree with that, but what about arms in space?"

"There will be no stopping it. We know the Russians already have an armed spy satellite up there, and the Chinese probably do too. All we can do is try to stay ahead of them in technology. The last eight years with a liberal president has put us way behind. At least now we have a president that realizes the importance of our military and strong technology."

When Mattie and Cathy finished, they met the others at the van and headed to the hotel. The van turned into the drive leading up to the Hilton. Diane reached over and slapped Dennis on the arm.

"You knew about this, didn't you? I wondered why you had such a smirk on your face when I said we would be staying at some flea bag motel!"

"It's where we always stayed when I was here," Dennis said, laughing.

Diane slapped at his arm again, and Dennis laughed even louder.

"Say, are you two boyfriend and girlfriend, or married or something?" Mattie asked. "You sure act like it!"

The van stopped and Diane was out of it like a lightening bolt, still blushing from Mattie's remark, but loving it at the same time.

Dennis was still laughing as he helped Cathy and Mattie out of the van. The bellhop was getting their bags from the back.

"Well, Mattie, she did ask me if what I had said was a preliminary proposal!"

"So? Are you going to propose? I think the two of you are a cute couple."

Diane just stood there, looking dumbfounded and blushing more than she had ever done in her life.

"Aww, go on Diane, marry him! You ain't gonna find one much prettier than he is," Mattie taunted.

Diane wrinkled her face and put up her fist, pretending like she was going to punch them all, then turned and headed into the hotel.

Dennis, still laughing, called out after her, "Well, you did say that!"

As they walked into the lobby, Dennis asked, "Cathy? Do you and Mattie want separate rooms or one together?"

"Together, we can't afford separate rooms in this hotel."

"No worries, ladies, you aren't paying for this; it's on the government."

"Still together please, we get along good together."

Mattie could not resist.

"Are you two gonna have separate rooms?"

Dennis smiled and Diane got a little choked up.

"Separate!" Diane finally got the word out. "Separate rooms, Mattie."

"Aw, shucks," Dennis said, as he put his arm around Diane's shoulder. "I had such high hopes!"

"Dream on Lieutenant, dream on," Diane said.

They all laughed, and Dennis walked over to the desk to get their rooms. He came back with three cards and handed one to Mattie and Cathy.

"Ok ladies, you can order breakfast in your room or dine in the restaurant."

"Let's all eat together," said Mattie. "I'm having way to much fun watching you two make eyes at each other."

"Mattie, behave now, will ya?" Cathy scolded.

"Honey, Dennis and I only met a couple of days ago."

Mattie giggled and patted Diane on her arm. She put her lips to Diane's ear, acting as though she were going to whisper, but instead blurted out, "I understand, lust at first sight!"

This time, Cathy grabbed Mattie's arm and started pulling her toward the elevator.

"Ooooh, Mattie, what am I going to do with you?"

##

After a day of relaxing and catching up on sleep, the four planned to meet for dinner. Dennis and the two girls were seated at a table for four and he was amazed at how knowledgeable they where when it came to technology.

All of a sudden, Mattie gasped, "Oh, my word! Is that who I think it is? She's drop-dead gorgeous!"

Dennis and Cathy turned to see who Mattie was talking about, and Dennis's jaw fell to the floor.

Her wavy, deep auburn hair, flowing gently over her shoulders and down her back, glimmered, like fresh fallen dew, under the light of the chandeliers. Wisps of hair framed her face, bringing out her soft red lips, green cat eyes, and a smile as bright as sunshine. A shimmering gold necklace lay against her olive skin, dangling just above a cleavage that would make a man want to find out what was under her silky, emerald green blouse.

Dennis's eyes traveled further down, to the form-fitting black skirt that ended just above her knees. It revealed a shapely pair of legs, and a pair of open toed heels that made a slight clicking sound, as she walked confidently toward the group waiting for her.

In the dining room, many sets of eyes followed her.

"It is her!" Cathy whispered in amazement.

"My Lord, Diane, you are gorgeous! I'm astounded!" exclaimed Mattie. "I tell ya what, if Dennis doesn't marry you, I'm going to consider a sex change."

Everyone laughed at Mattie's comment and Dennis rose to seat Diane.

He could not keep his eyes off her. The girls laughed and talked, and Dennis seemed to stutter every time he tried to say anything. When the waiter came to take the orders, Dennis excused himself.

"You go ahead and order ladies. I forgot that I had some important phone calls to make, so please excuse me."

He left quickly, thinking, *this can't be happening, this does not happen in real life.*

He got to his room, removed his shirt and kicked off his shoes, all the way across the room. He grabbed a beer from the small refrigerator. In a daze, he flopped down on the couch. He stared at the blank screen on the television, trying to get his thoughts in order. When that did not work, he got another beer, then another, until he had guzzled down six of them. "I am hooked on this woman, and I just met her," he said to the empty room.

There was a knock at the door. Dennis opened it to Diane.

"Hi, you didn't come back."

"I know," he said, as he turned and stumbled back to the couch, leaving her standing there. "Come in if you want."

Diane walked in, closing the door behind her.

"Make your calls?"

"Yes. I mean, no."

"Well, which is it?

"No," he replied. "I didn't have any calls to make."

"Hmm, sorry, did I rattle your cage?"

He looked up at her, a wry smile on his face. "You didn't rattle my cage, Diane, you destroyed it."

"Does that mean you'll make love to me tonight?"

He looked up into her beautiful, sexy green eyes … searching them … though not sure what it was he sought. He stood, took her hand, and led her to the bedroom.

##

His eyes fluttered open, and it took a few moments for him to realize where he was. He had slept in so many strange beds the past few weeks; it was hard to keep up with where he was sometimes.

He looked next to him, where someone would be if she had slept with him, and found it empty.

"A dream," he said out loud.

He knew it was too wonderful to be real. He lay back on the pillow and closed his eyes again, thinking how real it had seemed. Then a noise startled him and he quickly sat upright.

There stood Diane, two cups of coffee in hand, smiling that gorgeous smile.

"Hello, sleepyhead, finally wake up?"

He sat up against the headboard, rubbing his eyes as if he were trying to make sure that what he was seeing was real.

She handed him a cup of coffee.

"What time is it?" Dennis asked.

"Almost eight; sleep well?"

"Oh, yes — oh, hell yes — like a baby. You?

"What little I got, but no complaints here," she said with a devilish grin.

She sat down on the edge of the bed.

"I went to my room to get my hairbrush. Cathy called wanting to know if I had talked to you, and if you were OK. I told her I would have breakfast with them and see if you felt like joining us."

"I'm starving; seems I worked up an appetite somehow. Gotta shower first, though."

"That's fine, I told her about nine. I'm going to my room and take a quick shower and change."

Dennis reached out, taking Diane's arm and pulling her down to him, almost spilling her coffee on him

"I'll give you a shower," he whispered into her ear.

Diane smiled and sat up.

"Oh, no. There's no time for that, mister. Once we start, we would not only miss breakfast but lunch too. Cathy would have the Army searching for us."

Diane kissed him gently on the forehead, and got up to leave. She turned back and smiled at him.

"See you downstairs."

##

Cathy and Mattie were already seated when Diane and Dennis came down. They were enjoying their coffee, when Mattie piped up.

"Did the two of you get a good night's sleep together?"

"Not much sleep, but," Diane started before she realized the trap Mattie had sprung.

Dennis had just taken a drink of coffee when Mattie asked the question. He grabbed a napkin to keep it from spewing from his mouth. He coughed, sputtered, and then died laughing at Mattie's prowess. Mattie was getting good at catching Diane off guard.

"Ha! I gotcha, Diane!"

"No fair, Mattie, you set a trap is what you did!" said Diane.

"Oh, yes I did. What a wonderful confession it was too, don't ya think?"

"Maybe so, but just remember one thing young lady: payback can be hell!"

Diane winked at Dennis.

"OK, enough now," Dennis replied. "I confessed to nothing!"

Mattie leaned over and grinned really big at Dennis.

"Yeah, but she did … woohooo … what a romance!"

A waiter appeared.

"Lieutenant Denehey, there's a phone call for you, sir, over by the door," he said, pointing.

"We have an hour," Dennis said when he returned. "A van will pick us up."

Dennis signed for the meal and they walked up to their rooms. Diane stopped at his door.

"So, they finally woke up?"

"Yup, but there may be a problem. They think he's speaking Russian. He also attacked a nurse and a doctor, before three Marines could get him down and shackled. They have him hung in the interrogation room."

"Hung?"

"Apparently, they have hooks in the ceiling and floor, and they hook his hands and feet to those, with chains."

"So, what's the problem, then?"

"No interpreter. All they ever caught were Cubans, so they never had a need for a Russian interpreter."

"Well, I would bet that if he was with Cubans, he speaks their language, bet he's playing dumb."

Dennis and Diane were met by a Marine at the Cape, and escorted to the captain of Marine Security.

"We knew a sub was in the Atlantic, but it was just outside our jurisdiction," the captain explained. They planned on coming ashore there, so when they deployed their raft we waited. When they pulled the rafts to shore, we intercepted, preventing them from going back into the water. One woman put up a fight, and was killed. Why the others waited so long to kill themselves is not known. The diesel sub let them out and then high-tailed it back to Cuban waters."

The captain led them into an observation room, where through a large, one-way window, they could view the prisoner. The prisoner was spread eagle, vertically, wrists bound to the ceiling with cold steel chains attached to hooks, while his ankles were bound to the floor.

"They tried to give him water and food, but he spit it on them and refused to drink or eat," explained the Captain. "He will spit on you if you get close enough."

"Any tags in their clothing, or any ID on them?" asked Diane.

"No ma'am," the Captain replied. "I'm betting that man there is Russian. All the others were Cubans, and the woman killed on the beach was a Cuban-American who was wanted by the FBI and the CIA."

"I'm going in," said Dennis.

"Stay at least three feet away from him Lieutenant; that's about his spit range."

After forty-five minutes, Dennis came out, wiping spit from his shoulder.

"I guess we're going to have to get an interpreter."

"Mind if I give it a shot?" Diane asked.

"His range is more than three feet," Dennis told her.

She turned to a Marine sergeant and in a blink of an eye had removed the large knife that was attached to his right thigh.

"Ma'am, please return my knife to its scabbard, immediately!"

"Sergeant," she stated, "see this silver leaf on my collar? Don't give me any crap. This knife is U.S. government property."

"Ma'am!" he said, frustrated, "the Geneva Convention!"

"Go study the Geneva Convention, Sergeant; it doesn't apply to this trash. He has no ID and no uniform to show what country he represents. I don't intend to hurt him, much, but he doesn't know that. Now, you can stay or go!"

She turned and went into the room.

Diane took a seat at a table in the room, facing the prisoner. She placed the knife on the table for him to see. For a minute or two, she just stared at him, and then he laughed and spit at her.

She began to speak to him … in fluent Russian.

At first, the prisoner looked surprised. Then he laughed and tried to gather more spit into his mouth.

Diane picked up the knife from the table, twirled it around expertly, in her hand, and said very calmly in English, "You spit at me one more time and you'll lose an inch of your cock."

The prisoner's eyes squinted. He stared long and hard at her, then at the knife she kept toying with, and spoke again in his native tongue.

Diane answered in English. "Kill you? No, I won't do that. The last prisoner wanted that, too. I started with his cock … a thin slice here."

She made a slashing motion with the knife.

"A thin slice there."

Another slashing motion.

"Just enough to bring blood and pain. Have you ever poured alcohol on an open wound?"

It was quite apparent to Dennis that this man understood English very well, as he had little beads of sweat on his forehead, and his Adam's apple was moving up and down often, as she talked to him.

He finally spoke again, in his language, and Diane threw her head back and laughed. She stood up, walked over to him, and pointed the knife at his face.

"This is your Geneva Convention. Show me a uniform, ID, papers — where are they? Your mother sent us a bastard; she must have been a whore!" Diane screamed at him.

That made the prisoner mad, and he started yanking on the chains, his face red with fury.

Diane calmly sat back down, waiting until he was weary from yanking on the chains.

"Are you done now? It must be true. Only a person guilty of having a whore for a mother would get so upset."

The prisoner, very quietly, but with animal fury in his tone, and in perfect English, said, "My mother is no whore, and somehow, I'll find a way to get you. I'll take that knife and slit you from your cunt to your throat!"

"Well, well. You do speak English. Wonderful!"

Diane stood again, "I really don't want to waste much more time with you, as I have much better things to do, so here's what will happen. I will ask you some questions and you will answer them."

"I don't think so. Fuck you!"

She walked over to a metal cabinet that displayed a red cross on it. She opened the cabinet, took out a first aid kit and placed it on the table. From the kit, she removed a bottle of alcohol and sat in on the table, along with some gauze pads and a pair of latex gloves.

After placing everything side by side, she pushed the big knife into the lineup. It was a wicked looking gut knife.

The prisoner's Adam's apple, once more, began to quiver slightly. Beads of sweat began to run down the side of his face.

"Fuck you, bitch, you don't scare me," he said, but not very convincingly.

Very calmly, she said, "I'm going to give you five minutes to think it over, while I get my tape recorder. If I don't hear the answers I want, I'm going to find out if you have enough cock to satisfy me. When I am finished, I'm quite sure you won't."

She turned, and calmly strolled out of the room.

"Is your tape recorder ready, Dennis?"

"Yes, but do you think he's really going to answer your questions?"

"I don't know. We'll wait and see. I'm thirsty."

She pulled a Styrofoam cup from the dispenser and filled it with cold water. She guzzled it down, refilled it, and stared in the window at the prisoner. He was staring down at the table with her tools on it, licking his lips every now and then, beads of sweat still trickling down the sides of his face.

"He is nervous. You aren't really going to do what you told him, are you?" Dennis asked.

"No, but he doesn't know that. Believe it or not, three years in med school did teach me a thing or two. I'm going to take the recorder in, but I want you to come in and ask the questions when he decides to answer them."

"Sure, no problem."

She sat the recorder on the table, alongside her tools. Standing in front of the prisoner, she put the cup of water to her lips, taking small sips as she stared into his eyes. She turned back to the table and put the cup down, picked up the gloves and pulled them on.

"You sure you don't want me to ask you some questions and you give me some answers? We could both get out of here and still have time for a few drinks?"

He shook his head.

"Fuck you!"

She took the cap off the alcohol and poured some over the knife blade, looking him in the eyes.

"We wouldn't want you to get an infection from a dirty blade now, would we?"

She walked up to the prisoner, found the zipper to his suit and pulled it all the way down to his crotch.

"Stop!" the prisoner demanded. "You are not allowed to do this!"

She looked around the room.

"I don't see anyone here to stop me."

She picked up the knife, reached into his suit, and grasped the band of his baggy shorts. With the knife, she slit them all the way down.

In a squeaky voice, he again said, "This is not allowed — the Geneva Convention!"

"As I said before, it doesn't apply to thugs and terrorists. You stupid people had every intention of killing a lot of my good friends here, so screw you." She pulled out his penis.

"Oh my!" she exclaimed, and then died laughing. "You don't have enough there to satisfy a flea! Hell, you're almost a woman, anyway."

She laid the cold metal against it, and Dennis could see the man shiver. With the knife, she twisted his penis sideways, and set the edge lightly against the skin. She let the weight of the blade rest on it, then, she pulled it back about a quarter of an inch. A thin line of blood appeared.

"Noooo, noooo," the man screamed. "You did it! You cut me, you bitch!"

"Oh, honey, not to worry!" Diane exclaimed. "It's just a scratch, very little blood, but hey, if I just cut the tip off this little pink head now," she said, moving the knife in that direction, "then the blood will gush!"

"No, oh my God, don't! Ask your questions! I will answer; just don't cut!"

Dennis entered the room.

For the next thirty-five minutes, questions were asked, and if the prisoner even hesitated for a moment, Diane would move the knife forward. That threat was all it took.

In the security captain's office, Diane pushed the knife back into the sergeant's scabbard.

"Thank you, Sergeant. I even sanitized it for you."

"Does the prisoner need a doctor?" asked the captain.

"Maybe a Band-Aid."

Mattie and Cathy were sitting under the wing of their plane, out of the hot sun, watching a crawler inch its way toward the launch pad. The huge booster rockets glowing white, in the sun.

Cathy saw Dennis and Diane, and stood up. She offered Mattie her hand, and helped her from the ground.

"Do we go now?" Cathy asked.

Yes, we do; we're all done here."

"Ok, Dennis, everything is stowed. I wonder where we're headed."

"Let's get airborne and set a heading for Nevada. Use that for your flight plan and I'll call the general. You can clear it with FAA and then we can change if needed."

The engines idled as Cathy talked to the tower. She was getting an altitude, and asking if an escort would be taking them out of the no-fly zone.

"Negative on the escort," said a voice from the tower, "cruise altitude 24,000 feet, cleared to roll, and runway number two cleared for take off."

Once airborne, Dennis called General Estes for a destination, and was told Las Vegas. The general told him that his new Lear jet had been delivered, and would pick them up at Vegas Municipal. Dennis filled him in on the details of the interrogation and hung up. He then went forward and told Cathy their destination.

Dennis returned to his seat.

"The general was very happy with the information you got from the Russian, and the president is sending Castro a nasty message. She's going to tell him that any more attempts like this one, and she'll consider it an act of war; the United States will level his cities. That woman is hell-bound on stopping aggression against us."

"Yes, she is, but let's face it; there are always countries whose leaders want to rule the world. Russia and China are jealous of us in every respect, and personally, I believe we are being attacked by the most dangerous people we have ever faced, the fanatical Muslims."

"I'm in total agreement with you. We're going to have to literally destroy the fanatical governments."

Dennis leaned closer.

"Meanwhile, one question, dear lady. Would you have really whacked off that prisoner's penis?"

"Oh, Dennis, hell no! I might have sliced it up a bit more, and had to apply a few more Band-Aids, but that's it!"

"Well, remind me to never make you mad. By the way, I have two surprises. General Estes said we could spend the weekend in Vegas, and fly back to base Sunday afternoon. Today is Thursday, so that will give us three nights and two days for some rest and relaxation. The general said we all need some R&R."

"Sounds interesting, but I've been so anxious to see home base and get settled in. I want most of all to see the ships."

"Actually, I've already accepted the R&R for all of us, but we can go to the base now, if you prefer."

"No, that's fine, but you did say two surprises, what's the other one?"

"The general is letting Ed pick us up in the Lear jet, so he can spend some time with his sisters."

"Great. Did you tell them yet?"

"No, I thought it might be a nice surprise."

"Will the R&R be BYOM?"

"BYOM?"

"Bring your own money, silly."

Dennis smiled.

"No, it's not. Our gracious president is providing everything except gambling money. The Crystal Palace Hilton, rooms, food, and all drinks are coming out of her pocket."

"What about Cathy and Mattie'?"

"All five of us, she wouldn't have left anyone out."

"Wow, one helluva generous president."

##

Diane and Dennis were standing beside another plane, about twenty feet from where Cathy and Mattie were beginning their post flight inspection.

Dennis softly whispered to Diane.

"That Lear sitting by the edge of the area there," he pointed off to the right of them. "I'll bet it's the general's new jet."

"Well, it's certainly a new one, but there are no military markings on it," Diane whispered back.

"Right, so no one can identify it, which hopefully means they won't be following it."

"Here comes a short limo; wonder if that's our ride," Diane said, jokingly.

Cathy and Mattie looked over at the vehicle as it pulled in front of their plane.

The rear door opened and a man appeared, back first, out of the limo. When he turned, it was easy to identify the uniform of a Marine.

Cathy was putting the landing gear pin in place when the Marine turned toward her. She looked at the man, dropped the gear pin, and bolted across the pavement.

"Oh, my God, Mattie! It's Ed!"

Mattie started jumping with joy, and ran over to where Ed and Cathy were hugging, laughing and crying.

The reunion was so touching; even Dennis had tears in his eyes.

At the hotel, Diane had not even changed yet when Mattie and Cathy, brimming with excitement, were at her door.

"Have you ever seen the likes of this place, Diane? These aren't rooms, they're palaces!" Mattie exclaimed.

"I know honey; I was just about to explore my bathroom. Come on in here."

"It's so big! The biggest shower I've ever seen, closets, a Jacuzzi as big as a small pool. I thought the rooms at the Hilton in Florida were nice, but this … wow…"

Cathy interrupted Mattie's ramblings.

"Diane, we came to ask a favor. Sometime in the morning, would you go shopping with us? You have such good taste in clothes and things. We only brought a couple of changes of our flight uniforms for this little journey."

"Yes, please," Mattie begged, "and our hair? Lord, girl, your hair is gorgeous. Can you help us with ours?"

Diane smiled, showing her pleasure. "Yes, of course I will. We'll make a party of it!"

"Knock, knock," a voice said. "You shouldn't leave your door open; anyone could walk right in."

"Come on in, Dennis. The girls and I were just making some plans for tomorrow morning."

"I couldn't help but overhear. I believe I'll stay out of this one."

"Awwww, come on Dennis, go with us," Mattie said, as she plopped down on the huge couch.

"Not on your life, Mattie, but, Diane, you have a phone call coming in a few minutes. You might want to put it on speaker phone."

"Who would be calling me?"

"It's a surprise."

"Is it private? Why the speaker phone?"

"You can take it either way you want, it's up to you."

"Dennis? What are you up to now?"

"Your phone is ringing, dear, better answer it."

Still staring at Dennis, she walked to the desk and pushed the button for the speaker phone.

"Colonel Diane O'Hara here."

"Diane, Cynthia Alexander here."

"Cynthia? Cynthia Alexander?"

Her quizzical look changed to one of surprise when it dawned on her.

"Oh, my Lord, Madam President! I'm so sorry, it didn't register immediately. How are you?"

"I'm fine dear. Look, I like the title, but since this is a private call, what do you say we just forget protocol for now, Cynthia will do just fine."

"Yes, Madam Pres ... I mean, Cynthia. And what do I owe for this privilege?"

Laughing, Cynthia said, "I owe you, Diane. You are one gutsy woman. I watched the video of your meeting with the prisoner at the Cape earlier. And I just watched it again!"

"Video? I had no idea it was on video. I ... I ..."

"Not to worry, Diane. I would dare anyone to question your logic, technique, or your interpretation of the Geneva accord. I'm proud of how you handled it. We suspected what you learned, and thanks to you, we now have viable proof."

Diane sat on the edge of the big bed, still looking as though she was in shock, but listening intently as the president continued.

"Mr. Castro should have gotten his notice today. Monday, the Russian president and I will talk. In no uncertain terms, I'll let him know that he's on notice to keep his people off American soil. You know Diane; I could sure use a gutsy woman here in D.C. Would you care to come and work with me?"

"Oh, that's a wonderful compliment, but I love what I'm doing here, and hopefully, I'm needed here more."

"I'm sure you are, dear. I've seen your record and it shows you are well above average, actually they show you are excellent. By the way, the videos will all be destroyed."

"That, Cynthia, I dearly appreciate."

"Good girl. Say, if you ever change your mind about D.C., just call me personally, OK?"

"Yes, yes I will, Cynthia, and thank you!"

"Have a good time in Vegas dear; we'll talk again. Goodnight."

"Goodnight, Cynthia."

Diane jumped straight up. She ran over and plopped down in a big easy chair, legs outstretched, "I can't believe this, so awesome…"

"That was the president of the United States!" Mattie shouted. "She talked like she was an old friend of yours, Diane. Wow! What did you do that was important enough for the president to call you personally?"

"I really can't tell you dear … wish I could, but apparently it was very important."

##

The next morning, the girls were off and running early, leaving Dennis and Ed to have lunch together.

"Mind talking shop, Dennis?"

"My favorite thing to talk about. Any particular subject?"

"Your new ship. Lord almighty, it's hard to shock me, but when I saw those beauties, they took my breath away. Sergeant Tensley showed me around, and when we got to the flight deck … whoa! You used every nook and cranny so efficiently, it is the perfect layout."

"I'm not really the one that designed it, Ed. I went to the movie set where Star Trek was filmed. When I explained how I wanted to use that configuration, the designer gave me a complete set of blueprints—and I was allowed to take all the pictures I wanted. That man had an eye to the future, for sure. It was amazing how few changes I had to make. Most of the radar and communication equipment fit perfectly."

They were almost forehead-to-forehead with Dennis drawing sketches, Ed absorbing every detail the lieutenant shared.

"Hey, guys! What are you up to?"

The three women were standing behind them, loaded down with boxes and shopping bags.

"We decided we had to look beautiful for our guys, who happen to be our dates for tonight," Diane said with a sexy smile.

"All of you are perfectly beautiful, just as you are!"

"Aww, Dennis!" squealed Mattie in delight. "You are just so sweet!"

Dennis blushed at Mattie's loud comment, and tried to change the subject fast. "You girls had lunch yet?"

"Yes, we just finished, and we have scads to do before tonight," Cathy chimed in.

Ed stood up and hugged Cathy.

"I miss these hugs. At what time shall we pick up our dates?"

"You choose the time, guys," Diane said, as she reached over and stole Dennis' water glass.

"Not on your life! You say you have 'scads' to do, so our time-table probably won't jive with yours."

"Smart man," Diane remarked, and handed Dennis his glass back, empty.

She turned back to face Cathy.

"Its 12:15, girls, think we can be ready by seven or seven thirty?"

"Eight for sure," Cathy replied.

"Why don't you just call us about fifteen minutes before you're ready?" Dennis asked.

"Smart man, again. Will do" she smiled and planted a big kiss on his cheek. Waving her hand forward, she added, "Let's go girls!"

"Bye y'all," Mattie said sweetly.

##

It was 7:25 p.m. when Dennis' phone rang.

He met Ed coming out of his room and they walked down the hall together. They both stopped dead in their tracks at the same instant.

"Dennis?" Ed asked, "are there three women there, or are my eyes playing tricks on me?"

"I was about to ask you the same question. There are supposed to be three of them. Maybe they are triplets."

"None of those can be my sisters," said Ed.

"Well Ed, whatever is going on, there are most definitely three beautiful ladies blocking the hallway."

The three could have easily passed for sisters. Their hair glistened, even in the dim hall. All three had ringlets of hair, flowing over their shoulders and framing their beautiful faces. They had strapless evening dresses, snug under the breasts, then slightly filling out to shape their bodies, and flowing to just above their knees.

"Lordy, how quickly they grow up," Ed said in a whisper.

"Right you are, Ed. What do you say we go and show them off now?"

When they walked into the restaurant, Ed with one on each arm, and Dennis with his lovely woman, many heads turned.

"Beautiful, aren't they, Dennis?" Diane whispered.

"Almost as beautiful as the lady I'm with," Dennis whispered back.

They found a lounge that wasn't crowded and danced the night away. It was an evening they would all remember for years to come.

The Facility

The limo took them to the airport Sunday afternoon. Ed and Dennis did the preflight on the general's plane, and Diane followed Cathy and Mattie around as they did theirs.

"I'm really going to miss you two," Diane said. She had come to think of them as sisters. "I had such a wonderful time with you guys."

"Thank you, Diane, for all the fun and excitement you brought into our lives. I will never forget you. We better be seeing you again!" Cathy said, as she stopped and hugged her new friend.

"Time to go girls," said Dennis.

They were cleared for takeoff and Cathy was the first to go. As her plane went for the sky, Ed was right behind. He radioed to the plane in front.

"Hey, Sis, safe journey; love ya."

"We love you too, bro," Cathy said. "Don't be so long coming to see us next time."

Cathy's plane headed east, back to Texas, and Ed banked away, his compass set north-west.

Diane had taken the second seat while Dennis sat on the buddy seat, in the middle and just behind them. They had only been in the air about an hour when Ed was cleared for landing.

Ed turned on final approach.

"Um, Ed, if this is final, where is the runway and the base? All I see is white sand."

"It's there, Diane, trust me. Have you ever heard of the Salt Flats? Perfect runway and needs very little maintenance. Each rainfall erases all the tire marks, so it's as if no one can tell we're even here."

The ship floated gracefully downward. The wheels touched, Ed dropped the nose, and there was a soft thump as the nose wheel settled into a roll.

"Well, I see no buildings. Are you two playing a trick on me?"

They were rolling straight toward a mountain when Diane noticed the sand begin to move on the huge dune, just below the mountain.

"Oh my," she whispered, "underground?"

As the ship slowly taxied into the massive cave, Diane wondered where it ended, it was huge!

"Just how big is this building, Ed?"

"It's another three miles in front of us, and a good three quarters of a mile to those offices on your left."

"Where are the barracks?

"You are in for a total surprise, Diane. All the people working here have been cleared as top secret, even the janitors. In order to work here, civilians have to sign a four-year contract, and they get a thirty-day-per-year furlough, just like the military," Dennis said, as he led them off the plane.

"Come on, I'll explain it all as we walk. The general is expecting us."

An airman was waiting for them in a vehicle that looked much like a golf cart, only it went faster.

When they arrived at their destination, Ed went one way while Dennis escorted Diane through two sliding glass doors that opened automatically.

Diane came to a stop.

"My word," she gasped. "Is this is a military installation, or are we in another Hilton? This looks more like a huge mall."

"There are restaurants, shopping, grocery stores and lots more. That's the only way to keep people here for four years. Give them what they want, and need, most of all what they are used to," Dennis said.

"We used to be able to send men to isolated stations, such as Goose Bay, Labrador, and keep them for twelve to fifteen months at a time. Since we are strictly a volunteer military now, we have to … well … baby them, or we lose well trained people."

"I understand, Dennis, but this?"

"I know, but since this had to be kept top secret, we had no alternative. Believe it or not, this installation was cheaper to build than a complete, spread out base, over hundreds or thousands of acres. We didn't have to build runways, yet we can still bring in the largest aircraft in the world, and safely land it here. The biggest expense was building the eight levels below ground. What you see here, and you will see in building number one; is that it's all one building."

"You said building number one. How many are there?"

"There are three. Number two is where we assemble our ships. After they are test flown and approved, they will be housed here, in this hangar. Number three is where the assembly sections are warehoused. This facility was built not only for our ships, but for other space flight programs to come."

They reached the elevators.

They dropped down the eight floors quickly, and exited into a hallway.

"Dennis? I've noticed that every place we have been has different colored carpets. Why is that?"

"You're very observant. The complex is so big, you could actually get lost. At each elevator and hallway is a chart of the number one facility. Each area is color coded; my apartment is in the light blue area. When Thelma sets you up in an apartment, it will be color coded too, so you can find your way around easily."

"Apartments? Don't you mean rooms? And who is Thelma?"

Laughing, Dennis said, "Apartments, Diane. You know, with bedrooms, kitchens, closets, living rooms and so on. Thelma is General Estes' wife. Come on, we have plenty of time to fill you in."

They entered the reception area of the general's office through glass doors that had lettering on them.

"Lieutenant Denehey! It's about time; good to see you!"

"Hi Anna, how do you like our new home?"

"Love it, absolutely wonderful! No traffic to dodge going to work. Shoot, I hope they let me retire here!"

Anna walked over to Diane, "Hello, Colonel, good to see you again. I've been hearing nothing but good things about you."

"Well, thank you!" Diane said, smiling.

"Just go on in, the general is expecting you."

As Dennis reached for the door knob, the door opened and a petite lady was backing out of the office.

"Estes, you old coot, behave yourself now and leave my bottom alone!"

She turned and almost ran into Dennis.

"Oops."

She noticed who it was and a huge smile came across her face. She wrapped her arms around his neck, and planted a big kiss on each cheek. Then she backed away from him, taking his hands in hers and totally inspecting him from top to bottom.

"My, honey! You finally came home, and just as handsome as ever!"

She put her finger on the second lieutenant's gold bars.

"It's a sad day when the idiots in Washington don't know right from wrong. I'm glad you didn't take the discharge, Dennis."

"Oh, it's all right, Thelma. It will turn around, some day."

Thelma looked around Dennis' shoulder and stepped to his side, beaming at Diane.

"My goodness, you have to be Colonel O'Hara!"

She turned back to Dennis

"Dennis, she's absolutely gorgeous!"

She turned back, and took Diane's hand in both of hers.

"Welcome home, dear!"

"Why, thank you so much, and you must be Thelma."

"Sorry dear, I forgot to introduce myself!"

"Not at all, Thelma. Dennis – uh, Lieutenant Denehey – told me all about you."

"I sure hope it was all good," Thelma said, winking at Dennis.

"Thelma!" a voice bellowed from the office, "quit BS'ing and send those kids in here."

"Oh hush, you old coot! Get mad at me and there will be no supper for you!" She winked at Diane. "He's going to fire me, someday!"

Diane and Dennis entered the general's office and he met them halfway across the room.

"It is so good to have you back, Dennis. And you, Colonel O'Hara, have a lot of catching up to do now. I'm very proud of the way you handled things down in Florida – good work!"

"Thank you, sir. I'm ready to start now, if it's OK.

"Well, you're a go-getter, Diane; I like that. OK then, Dennis, would you like to give her the two-bit tour and get her situated?"

As Dennis and Diane turned to leave, the phone rang.

"What is it, Anna?" He listened before shouting, "What? Who gave her this number?"

Dennis and Diane both waited to see what was wrong.

"Lieutenant Denehey? Hold on. Dennis, did you give this number to a girl named Cathy?"

"Yes, sir. Ed Mitchell's two sisters, Mattie and Cathy, were our pilots to Florida. It's a long story, sir. May I take the call and explain later?"

Telling Anna to put the call through, the general handed the phone to Dennis.

"Hello, Cathy, Lieutenant Denehey here. What's up?"

Diane saw a sad expression cross Dennis' face as he talked to Cathy.

"I'm so sorry, sweetheart. How is Mattie?"

He listened for a minute.

"Yes sweetie, we'll get Ed right away. Does he know where to call you? No, you did the right thing. I'm sure General Estes won't mind. OK, you have our heartfelt condolences from everyone here. Bye now."

Dennis handed the phone back to the general and then explained.

"Their mother passed away before they got home today. I gave them your number because they planned to enlist in the Air Force once their mother passed on. It's quite a story, but we can discuss that later. We need to let Ed know what's happened and get him on his way. Their mom is to be cremated within three days."

"Thelma, honey, could you tell Anna to get Ed and have him report here, ASAP?"

"I'll do it myself, dear."

While waiting, General Estes commented, "So, those girls want to be pilots? Do they have any qualifications?"

Dennis barely had time to give much of the girls' backgrounds before Thelma arrived with Ed.

"Ed, I hate to break the bad news to you, but your sister, Cathy, just called. She informed us that your mother has passed away. We are truly sorry for your loss, son. Thank goodness, Dennis gave them this number, so they didn't have to go through Red Cross."

"Thank you, General. We knew it was just a matter of time. The doctors had told us it wouldn't be long."

"Go pack what you need while I get your orders typed up, and we'll get you on your way. I'll get ops to get the Lear ready and have you home as soon as possible. Will two weeks be sufficient time to take care of everything?"

"Yes, sir. I'm the executor of Mom's estate, but I think that will be plenty of time, sir."

The general held out his hand.

"Ed, go pack."

Ed left after receiving condolences from the others and the general sat down and leaned back in his chair.

"Ok, Dennis, better show this girl your baby now, we'll take care of Ed."

Diane and Dennis left the general's office, heading toward the elevator. As they passed the elevators, Diane took Dennis' arm.

"Aren't those the elevators we came down on?"

"They are. Why?"

"Are we not going back up?"

"Sure, but we're going up and over, to hangar number two. It's almost four miles over there and there's a much faster way to get there, come on."

About eight yards further, Dennis stopped at what looked like a door to an elevator. It was only about five feet high and the width of an average door.

"Ah, here we are."

He pushed a button beside the door. The single door, silently, slid open.

"OK, Dennis, is this our garbage chute?"

"Get in and sit down, you'll see."

Diane gave a long sigh, but did as he asked. He followed her in, sat down next to her and then pushed another button. The door slid closed. There was a sound like rushing air, and then about fifteen seconds later, the door opened.

She looked out, into the corridor.

"What's wrong, it didn't work?"

"Sure it did, jump out."

"Dennis, no B.S. We didn't move an inch."

"Sure we did, look at the sign on the wall there."

Again, turning to look into the corridor, she saw a green sign, with white letters, signifying hangar number two.

She was still not convinced.

"Dennis, is this a joke on new people or what? You said it was almost four miles and this thing didn't move even four feet. Someone hung that sign there while the door was closed."

"Di, honey, I'm sure you've been to a bank drive through. You get a little round plastic cylinder, put your check or money inside, close it, put it back in the holder and push a button — zipppp — the cylinder is in the bank. That's how I came up with this idea. I was at the bank one day, during the time I was designing this facility and wondered if a similar system could move people. I went to the factory and visited with their engineers and got an immediate interest. Two, maybe three months later, they asked me to come back to the factory. They had built a one mile long test unit, and voila, here we are."

"You aren't kidding me, are you?" she asked, as she followed Dennis out. "How long is this one unit?"

"The whole system is a maze of tubes, and they're on every floor in this facility. It will take you almost anywhere. There's even a traffic control system, as there could be as many as fifteen to twenty cylinders going in all directions, at the same time. All are computer monitored at intersections. But now, I'll take you to see the ships."

She followed him through two double doors and into a hall-way. There they found two security guards.

"Hi, Jules, Jordan, how are you?"

"Hello Colonel," answered Jordan. "Oops, sorry, sir. We heard about what happened; sorry to hear, but it's great to have you back."

"It'll get straightened out sooner or later. And it's good to be back, thanks."

Reaching into his shirt pocket, he pulled out two security passes and handed one to Diane.

"Fellows, this is Colonel Diane O'Hara, one of our new pi-lots."

They saw her rank, snapped to attention, and saluted.

She returned the salute.

"At ease, gentlemen."

"Welcome aboard ma'am," said Jules, handing her a clip-board. "Sign in here, please."

Walking through another set of doors, and up a flight of stairs, they emerged into a room that was flooded with light.

Diane blinked her eyes several times. As her eyes adjusted, a huge, shadowy outline began to appear. When it became clearer, she was stunned.

"Oh, my God. Oh, my!"

In front of her was a massive aircraft, painted Air Force royal blue, its nose high above her head. She backed up to the wall, craning her head, trying to see the flight deck windows. Slowly, she leaned to her left, then to her right, trying to see the wings of the huge ship. Silently, as if in reverence, she walked forward, looking up and down, until she reached the huge wheels of the nose gear. She reached out and touched one of the two massive tires, as if touching a god. She slowly circled the wheels, looking up into the well of the nose gear. When she came back around the front, she was laughing.

"I pictured in my mind what she would look like, when you told us how big the ship was. I missed it by miles — she is huge, and beautiful. Does she really fly?"

"Oh yes, she does, and very fast too."

"You say you flew her by yourself. I've got to see the cockpit that allows one person to do that."

"The console in the simulator is almost identical to the one in this ship, except for a few minor modifications."

"How do we get inside? I see no ladders or steps."

Smiling, he walked to the nose gear and pushed a switch that was mounted on the upper cylinder.

Hearing a clicking sound above her head, she looked up, and saw a portion of the fuselage was separating, and starting to come downward. It was an elevator coming down, with a platform that looked big enough for three or four people.

On their way up, Dennis explained.

"It's more than an elevator. It works in three stages. In an atmosphere like on the moon, you can get into your space suit on the flight deck, and exit to the surface, without losing atmospheric pressure in the ship."

As the elevator stopped, and latched in place, Diane's mouth dropped open. Her head pivoted back and forth as she took in the sights.

"Dennis; oh, my God! This is the flight deck of the Starship Enterprise from "Star Trek." How?"

"Yep, almost to the inch. I visited the set, and not only got permission to use the design, but also got a complete set of blueprints. Whoever designed it had a whole lot of foresight. Just about all our equipment fits like a glove in each cubicle. Come on, you take the pilot's seat."

Diane pointed to the bench seat in the middle of the flight deck.

"I suppose that's Captain Kirk's seat?"

"More or less, a complete set of flight controls lowers down from overhead, that's my modification. We'll cover all of that later. For now, turn on the power, just like in the simulator."

Diane complied, and immediately heard a very light, whirring sound. She pivoted around, looking at the other consoles around the flight deck. The equipment was coming to life, as small lights started flickering on each console; some green, some red. Then, in unison, life was restored, and each console was ready to do its job.

"Press 0-2-0 on your console."

She pressed the numbers and a slight sound was heard. She looked overhead and saw two large doors slide sideways, exposing a very large viewing screen.

The large screen lit up, but there was no picture.

"On your left hand keyboard, press 26."

Diane did, and immediately saw the screen separate into 26 individual pictures.

"What you see is the entirety of the inside and outside of the ship. The outside of the ship is the top eighteen pictures. You can also remove any you want by pressing the ELM button and the corresponding numbers you want to eliminate."

Dennis smiled; he could see that Diane loved this.

"Now, if you press 19 through 26, the others will magnify. There's no blind spot, and the cameras cover inside and out, in all areas."

Diane was in awe, and sat quietly, taking it all in.

"If you want to see just what is in front of you," Dennis continued, "keep 1, 2, 3, 4, and eliminate the rest. Once you do that, you can press the MAG button, and it magnifies everything. You can see anything, clearly, up to one hundred miles in front, aft, or from the side of the ship. The communication and radar officer can do what you're doing now, from his or her console."

Diane was stunned.

"It's unbelievable what you've done here. I am so impressed! When do we fly?"

"Ouch," he replied, "be patient!"

"Me? Patient? You might want to remember who you're talking to here!"

Diane displayed her gorgeous smile

"How do I shut this down? I've got to call the girls."

"Just push the power button," he replied.

She pushed the power button and watched as each console shut down. The doors over the viewing screen and the windows closed.

As they walked down the hall to their rooms, he asked, "Want to go out to eat?"

They stopped in front of her door.

"Not really. If you want, I'll fix us some sandwiches, or whatever. We can drink some beer and shoot the breeze."

"Sounds good to me, I'll bring back the beer."

Diane took a step toward him. He knew her intent and took her hand.

"Good night, Colonel."

His eyes went quickly toward the wall and hers followed. She noticed the camera and shook his hand while whispering, "I'm beginning to hate those things already. Hell, I was planning on raping you right here."

He winked at her and walked away with a smile on his face.

Upon disarming his security system, he grabbed some beers and headed back to Diane's.

He knocked lightly on her door.

"It's open."

He walked in.

Her first words were, "Do you want something hot or cold?"

"Oh please, Diane, don't ever get cold!"

"Not me crazy! Will sandwiches do, or would you prefer a steak? And by the way, the last couple of weeks, I've been very hot, with no intentions of cooling off!"

Laughing, he replied, "Sandwiches are perfectly fine with me. Have you talked to Cathy and Mattie yet?"

"Yes, I did."

She opened the fridge, took out some lunch meat, and set it on the island that separated the kitchen from the dining area.

"They're pretty torn up, naturally, but at the same time they know she's out of her misery now, and in a better place. They said she suffered terribly the last few months. Cathy said she hoped you didn't mind them using the number you gave them, they tried to go through the Red Cross to contact Ed, but were told that it may take a couple of days."

"No, I don't mind, and I know the general didn't mind either."

Dennis sat down in a dining room chair. He leaned back against it, stretching his legs straight out in front of him.

"Their mother is going to be cremated, and that has to happen within three days of death, so they knew Ed probably wouldn't be home in time. Ed called them from the plane; he should be landing about now."

She put a plate stacked with sandwiches in front of Dennis.

Just as he picked one up, his shoulder phone buzzed and vibrated.

"Now what?" Dennis moaned, as he hit the receive button.

"Lieutenant Denehey," he said.

"General Estes, Dennis. Sorry to bother you son, but once more we have a problem. I don't know how anyone could get this information, but I just received a call from Wright Patterson."

"About what, Sir?"

"You know that our supply flights leave from different destinations to come here, and never leave at the same time, right?"

"Yes, Sir, I know about that."

"Well, a C-130 left from Dover, Delaware, this morning, coming this way. They picked up a shadow just over Ohio. The pilot made drastic course changes, three different times, just to make sure it was a shadow; it was, beyond a doubt. The pilot called it into Wright, and F-18s were scrambled. They reported it was an F-86, probably sold at auction sometime. All markings had been removed."

Dennis was pacing back and forth across Diane's living room.

She noticed the security camera kept moving, following Dennis. She knew she had turned the security system off when she came in from the hallway.

She wrote a note to Dennis: "If the security system is off, why does the camera follow your every move?"

She folded the paper, walked back to where Dennis was pacing, and handed him the paper, which Dennis took but ignored, continuing talking to the general. Totally exasperated at him for not reading the note, she stuck her foot in his way, tripping him. He fell to the floor.

Diane was apologizing as she knelt down beside him.

"I'm so sorry," she said loudly, and then angrily whispered by his ear, "Read the friggin note."

Dennis pulled the phone off his shoulder strap and stared, questioningly, into Diane's eyes. "Hold, General, I just tripped."

He got up, on his knees, and with a perplexed expression on his face, he picked up the note and read it.

"General, let me get back with you. I fell, and now I have a muscle cramp, I'll get right back with you."

Dennis disconnected the call.

He put one hand on the floor to push himself up. As he stood, he massaged the other leg with the supposed cramp in it. Diane slid her arms under his and helped him to his feet.

"Here," she said, as he hobbled toward a chair.

From the corner of his eye, he saw the camera following the two of them.

Diane led him to the chair and helped him into it. Then, on her knees, she pretended to massage the so-called cramped muscle.

"That's good," said Dennis, stretching the leg out in front of him, "would you please get my beer from the table?"

Without looking directly at the camera, Dennis saw it start to pan, following her into the dining area. Diane returned and handed him the beer.

"Why don't you put those cold sandwiches away? I need to stretch my leg, and a hot meal sounds really good now. You like Italian food?"

"Love it, but I'll have to change clothes first."

"Oh, don't bother," he said, glancing over her shoulder, "it's all casual around here."

She caught the movement of his eyes and realized that whoever was watching them might even be able to see her changing clothes.

"Ok, let me just cover the sandwiches and put them in the fridge."

"I'm going to my room to set my security system. I'll meet you in the hallway. You mind if I ask the general to join us? I think he works way too much."

"Sounds good to me, I enjoy his company."

While walking toward the elevator, Diane moved close to Dennis and whispered, "Why a restaurant?"

He put his lips close to her ear and whispered, "No cameras."

In a small room, inside the quarters of one Captain Knull, four men sat watching row after row of monitor screens.

"That Colonel O'Hara is one hot babe. I'd love to see her naked," said one of the men.

Another replied, "Oh yeah! I bet you'll get your view when she showers tonight!"

"I hope so! The lieutenant and her seem awful cozy; wonder if they've done it yet."

A third man added, "Probably so, but you know that Kutchmark babe ain't no slouch. She has a fine body."

The second man asked, "Did you see that report the general got from the Cape? What that O'Hara babe did to that prisoner?"

"Yeah, I saw it," said the fourth man, laughing. "I bet she wouldn't be so brave if she was the one hanging there!"

Dennis and Diane secluded themselves in a booth, at the restaurant. There were very few people there, so they just talked while waiting for the general.

"Cameras can't be put in public businesses, and the hotel is off limits to them also. We'll be away from roaming eyes here," Dennis explained.

General Estes and Thelma joined them.

"Dennis, my boy, I had just gotten comfortable and relaxed. Why couldn't we finish our talk on the phone, instead of here?"

"Tut-tut," Thelma responded, "I think it was a great idea, I love Italian food."

The general shot back, "You like any kind of food, as long as you don't have to cook it!"

Diane giggled at the way they bantered back and forth at each other.

In a serious tone, Dennis interrupted.

"General, I don't believe our security system is secure any longer."

The general's head pivoted to face Dennis, eyes wide, he leaned closer to him. "What do you mean by not secure?"

Dennis quickly filled him in on what Diane had picked up on, and how the events fell.

"When I went back to my apartment, to arm my security system, the camera there was also panning. My system was not on. The red light that indicates the system is activated was off. The camera should have been dead and not able to pan."

A perplexed look came across the general's face.

"How can that happen?"

"Simple," Dennis replied. "Someone has jumped the system; it would be easy to do."

"Then who, and why?" the general pondered.

"Well, this would be just a guess, but I would say that somewhere there is a dual monitoring system set up."

"Why hasn't anyone noticed it before?" Thelma asked.

"It's like hearing the ticking of a clock," Diane explained. "You get so used to it, you just ignore it. Since I'm new here, and I really don't like all those cameras, to be honest with you, it just jumped out at me."

"Can we look up what contractor designed and installed the system?" Dennis asked.

"Don't need to look," the general replied. "Capt. Knull came highly recommended from the White House. He designed the entire system, and his men helped him install it. In fact, I better call him now and get to the bottom of this."

The general reached for his shoulder phone.

"Excuse me, General," Diane interrupted, "before you call him, I have an idea, if I may."

Estes hesitated.

"Sure Diane, but he's the lead man of the whole system. If anyone can check it, and get to the bottom of this, he can."

"Maybe so, but just out of curiosity, are there any official systems we can check, besides our apartments?"

"Do you mean, like our office?" Thelma asked

"Exactly."

"Well," the general said, "if we have any muck-a-muck coming in for a conference, say, like the secretary of defense, we always shut the cameras down, particularly in the conference room. We can shut them all down throughout the entire office, but we have to notify security first."

"Why?" Diane asked. "Why notify security?"

"Well, just in case someone should get in and go through files when the office is closed. If someone shuts the system down, we get a phone call within a couple of minutes, and if no one answers, a security squad will be there on the double."

"Uh-huh," Diane said, thinking carefully. "They do call first, though?"

"Oh yes," Thelma chimed in. "I've accidentally shut it off before; the red switch is just beside the light switch, so not hard to do."

Diane was quiet for a moment.

"Why don't they call us when we shut ours off?"

"They have a video, showing us in the hallway, just before we enter our rooms," Dennis replied. "Plus, if someone doesn't have a key card and tries fooling with the locks, it sets off a silent alarm."

"Okay, so if Thelma and I went to the general's office, right now, and I, accidentally on purpose, turned off the system … a minute or two would be plenty of time to see if the cameras follow Thelma around the office, while she searches for papers, right?"

"Oh, yes, we could do that, couldn't we?" Thelma asked.

"Thelma, honey," said the general, "you sound like you're ready for an adventure!"

Everyone laughed.

Thelma replied sarcastically, "With your permission, General, may we raid your office?"

"Yes, by all means," the general replied. "But start at your desk, honey, and then go to the file cabinets. That way, if it's going to pan, it will be very noticeable to the colonel."

The two left, and the general said, "That O'Hara is one sharp woman, Dennis."

"Yes, sir, I've noticed."

"I thought you had. I've seen you smile more in the last three days, than I have in months. You know, if this turns out to be our leak area, there are going to be some heads rolling around here."

"Whose heads?"

"Knull to begin with, White House or no White House. He should have caught this. He's supposed to be the expert here."

"Who in the White House recommended him?"

"Oh goodness, let me see … who was in that meeting?"

The general sat in silence for a moment, rubbing his fore-head.

"It was me, the president, secretary of defense, a senator, the speaker of the house. The president said that the vice president was unhappy with their security system, and wanted it changed. The secretary of defense mentioned that in order to keep this place secret we would have to have the best system ever.

"The president said it was up to them, but they might want to check out this Lieutenant Knull."

"So, the president recommended him?"

"No, it was the vice president who first mentioned his name to the president, and then the secretary of defense had his people run a thorough check on him. When they found an impeccable record, they recommended him to me. Since he was military, I decided to use him instead of a civilian contractor. Saved a lot of money too."

"Do we keep records of all communications?" Dennis asked.

"Everything except mail is on the computer. Cell calls are monitored, as well as regular calls placed here, and outside the complex. As for the mail, we don't monitor it by reading it, but we do record the addresses, sender, and date from each. What's your point, Dennis?"

"Information is leaving here, and going somewhere. It has to come from here, otherwise, how would they know when to put planes in the air to shadow us? And look at all this other crap that's happened."

Thelma and Diane walked in and the men stood to let them sit on the inside.

"Well," said Diane, "it's just as I thought. The cameras still pan even though the system is off."

Shaking his head, the general said, "It's all over my head. I guess I should get Knull, the FBI, or someone in here to investigate this whole damn thing."

"Sir, who should have spotted this?" Diane asked.

"The expert who installed and designed the system, as he is supposed to inspect…"

The general stopped in mid sentence.

"Awww. jeez," he grunted. "Now I have to suspect Captain Knull. Damn, what the hell else?"

"Here's a cheerful note for you," said Dennis. "Remember telling me that we were way behind schedule on our aircraft?"

"Yes," the general replied. "I haven't had the time to fully catch back up. I'm not sure where we stand. The last I heard,

Sergeant Tensley was having problems with the wings on number two."

"Well, I feel Sergeant Tensley has a very acute sense of what's going on around him, much like our Colonel O'Hara here. I'm not sure, but I think Tensley passed out some false info so no one would know where we really stood. In the next five to six days, we will have seven more units ready to test fly."

The general sat up straight, and then leaned over to get closer to Dennis.

"Seven? Seven more units? How could that be? That puts you way ahead of your schedule!"

"Not only that," Dennis continued, "when I left the hangar a few hours ago, they were working on the tail assembly and mounting the engines in number eleven."

"Oh, my Lord, Dennis, how could they possibly be that far ahead?"

"In Sergeant Tensley's words, after all the flaws were worked out on one and two, they knew what had to be done, and the rest was easy."

Thelma spoke up and nailed the general's enthusiasm to the table.

"The way I see it, people, you could have a hundred ships. The problem is, there are no pilots."

"Well, sweetheart, for once you're right."

"Have you talked to the president about what we discussed earlier?" Dennis asked.

"You mean about young, unspoiled pilots and such? She told me, bluntly, to get whoever I could; dig them out of the garbage cans if need be, she said. Just make sure they can pass a top secret security check, and check their flight records to make sure they're clean. She's going to shake up all the military academies; she believes they're not doing their jobs. Now, in the meantime, we have to get this security issue nabbed in the butt, damn quick, before this whole mess blows up in our face and we all get canned."

"One thing," Dennis interjected, "it's too late to make a move on anything tonight. Thelma, if it's OK with the general, can you pull up all land and cell calls made from here in the last three months? That's when all our problems seem to have started."

Thelma looked at her husband and he shook his head in the affirmative.

"Sure, Dennis, no problem."

"Could you run some printouts of those too?"

"Will do."

"I also want a private suite at the hotel."

The general looked at Dennis.

"Why?"

"I'm going to put together a crew that I know I can trust, to deep scan those printouts, and I don't want anyone knowing what we're doing."

"Damn good idea," the general replied. "No cameras there!"

"Sir, it seems you're pretty tight with the president. Maybe you can get her to work the same thing from her end. She has plenty of manpower at her disposal. By the way, I have two recruits for us, if the president is indeed going to cut all the red tape for us. They are excellent young pilots."

"I'll contact the president by 0600 hours in the morning. I'm sure she'll do what she can. Just get the info on your recruits to Thelma, and she'll get the paperwork to security for a clearance check."

"Security?" Thelma asked. "Which security?"

"I believe they were already cleared, day before yesterday," Diane interrupted.

"Who are we talking about?" asked the general.

Dennis answered before Diane could.

"I believe she is referring to the Mitchell sisters, Ed Mitchell's sisters."

Diane nodded her head.

"I would take a very close look at them, General."

"I'll take your word for it, Dennis. Contact them tomorrow. Now, can we go get some sleep?"

Thelma said, "Sleep? We haven't eaten yet!"

"I'm not going to either," said the general. "I have a headache and I'm going to bed."

"Oh, pooh," Thelma said in a disappointed voice.

"Oh, pooh yourself. Order something to go."

Diane smiled as they started to leave. She absolutely adored the way they picked at each other.

"By the way, General," Dennis said, "if it were me, any further communications, of any importance might be safer in your jet — a couple of hundred miles out and on your secure line."

Dennis and Diane watched as they left.

"Was I right about the Mitchell sisters," Dennis asked.

"Right as rain, and your recommendation really helps, thanks!"

"I'm serious," he replied. "I believe they are excellent candidates for a look. They have the hours, they're very conscientious, and damn good pilots. You can contact them—still want to eat?"

"Not really. The sandwiches will do for me, and I really wanted a shower, but that's out, damn it. Do those cameras have infrared lenses?"

"Probably, and we can't do anything to make them suspicious, so just slip your nightgown over your head, before you drop your pants. I don't want whoever is watching to see your beautiful body."

Diane smiled at him. She had never had anyone that was jealous before; she thought it was cute.

"You want to go on a test flight in the morning?"

She squeezed his arm. "You better believe it!"

Diane knocked on his door at 0600 hours.

He immediately knocked back, and opened the door.

"Morning," he said, yawning. "My, you're up early!"

"I didn't sleep worth a damn in that stupid gown. I kept getting tangled up in it. Besides, I got used to having a bed partner for a while there … funny how I got used to it so quickly. Got coffee?"

"Was just going to put some on; come on in."

They went into the kitchen and Dennis pushed a button and coffee started brewing.

"I like this new-age stuff," Diane said. "I never had a coffee pot that you don't have to put in filters or water, or even the coffee. Now, how neat is that?"

"And it's fast too. That's what I like."

Diane poured them each a cup, and they sat down at the dining table.

"So, how did you get into that flight suit without exposing that pretty backside?"

"The gown helped, but I couldn't put my bra on."

"I can tell, but it doesn't look like you need one from here."

Diane looked down at her breasts, the slight imprint of her nipples were quite evident in the form-fitting flight suit.

"I'll have to put it on in ops. There is a bathroom in ops, isn't there?"

"Yes, there's a bathroom, or you can put it on in the ship."

"You would sure love that, wouldn't you?"

"Sure, I wouldn't complain, but there are bathrooms on the ship too."

Diane pointed to his coffee cup.

"Want a refill?"

"Sure, thanks. We'll have to get you fitted for a new flight suit, and we can get your new helmet in ops this morning."

"Helmets?" she asked, as she was pouring his coffee.

She came back into the dining area, set his coffee down in front of him, bent over, and looked him straight in the eyes, "But Captain Kirk's crew didn't have to wear helmets!"

Dennis shook his head and laughed.

"Only on test flights and training, Diane. You crack me up woman!"

He took a sip of his steaming, hot coffee.

"Oh, by the way, on test flights, I take the first twenty to thirty minutes alone. If everything checks out in that time, I'll come back and get you."

"And if it doesn't?"

"If it doesn't, then it gets parked until whatever kinks are found and repaired. You ready to rock and roll?"

##

They walked up to the supply counter in ops. A young, tomboyish woman came from around the shelves

"Hey, Lieutenant, I heard you were back … good to see you!"

"Same here, Shirley. This is Colonel O'Hara, a new pilot. She needs a helmet, and if the new flight suits ever arrive; one of those also."

"Nice to meet you, Colonel O'Hara; this is your lucky day. Flight suits are in and I bet there's a size that will fit you perfectly. Want to try them on?"

Diane looked at Dennis.

"Do we have time?"

"Sure, go ahead. Come into the briefing room when you're ready, OK?"

"No you don't, Denehey."

Shirley reached under the counter and pulled out two dark blue flight suits.

"I already have your name tag and everything."

Grinning, Dennis picked them up.

"You're the best Shirley."

"Only next to you," she replied as he walked away.

"Know him well?" Diane asked.

"Not as well as I'd like! He's one sweetheart of a man. I've never worked for a better person."

"Yeah," Diane replied. "I've only known him for a short time, but it's very easy to like him."

Shirley looked at Diane and smiled.

"He would be quite a catch! Oh well, this dreaming won't get your flight suit on. I'll show you where you can change, and while you do that I'll find a helmet."

"Umm, Shirley?"

"Yes, honey?"

"There aren't any cameras in there, are there?"

"There damn well better not be!" she replied. "That damned Knull is a pain in my ass as it is."

"Why's that?" Diane asked, heading for the dressing room.

"Oh, he's trying to hit on me every chance he gets. I don't like him, and, I don't trust him."

Diane slipped into her bra, and the new flight suit. She loved the color, and was happy to be away from the black suit she was used to wearing. The suit had an actual shine to the thread, and it fit like a glove. She liked the squadron name and emblem on one sleeve, and the flag on the other.

Shirley whistled at her when she stepped up to the counter.

"Damn, wish I could find something that looked that good on me, maybe I wouldn't be so shy then. It goes great with your auburn hair, too."

"Thanks, I love the stretch to it, it's really comfortable."

"Well, if that doesn't get Denehey's attention, nothing will, and I'll declare him blind! Here's your helmet, hon. Best try it on. You do have a lot of hair up there."

Diane slipped it on and shuffled it around a bit.

"Fits perfectly, Shirley. Thanks for everything."

"You bet," Shirley replied, "and good luck! Fly 'em high!"

Diane, feeling very comfortable, walked into the briefing room carrying her helmet under one arm, and her old flight suit under the other. The only two in the room were Dennis and Sergeant Tensley. When they heard her come in, they both looked up. Dennis' mouth dropped open and Sergeant Tensley was wide-eyed.

"My word," said Tensley, "are those our new flight suits?"

Dennis sat still … gawking … his mouth half open.

"Yes, Sergeant," Diane answered. "These are the new suits, so I'm told. Dennis, are you catching flies?"

Dennis clamped his mouth shut and broke into a big smile.

"Not sure what I'm catching; sure ain't flies though!"

"Well I just hope my new suit looks half as good as that one. Do you think I'll look that good, Dennis?" Sergeant Tensley asked, with a big grin.

"Hell no, Sarge, you won't come anywhere close to that. Meet Colonel O'Hara."

"Nice to meet you, I've heard all about you."

"Nice to meet you too, Sergeant. I've heard quite a bit about you also. So where is everyone? I thought we were having a briefing."

"We're going to do the test flight. We cancelled the briefing for today. Sergeant Tensley has her fueled and has pre-run the engines, so it's good to go. I've already briefed him, so let's go see how this baby flies."

"Do we come out with you?" Diane asked.

"There's an observation platform," Tensley replied. "As soon as the lieutenant is on the flight deck, and I can pull the chocks, ma'am, I'll escort you to it. If you would, just wait for me at the hangar door."

Dennis sat down in the pilot's seat, strapped in, and put on his helmet. He started pushing buttons on the console, and the whole system on the flight deck came to life. He went through his check list, one item at a time. He then pushed two switches, and the quiet hum of the number one engine sounded. Glancing at the instrument panel, he saw everything was green to go. He looked at the big view screen and saw the sergeant at the nose gear, his radio earphones plugged in to the ship's radio receptacle, so they could talk to each other.

He glanced at the instrument panel one more time.

"OK, I'll start the other two while you're escorting the colonel. Unplug and pull the chocks; she's mine now."

"Yes, sir," the sergeant said. "Good luck, sir."

From the viewing screen, Dennis saw Tensley enter the hangar. He then turned his attention to the task at hand. He pressed more buttons, and engine two came alive. A few seconds later, all three of the powerful engines were green, and purring like kittens.

Diane and Tensley were standing on the observation platform as Dennis released the brakes and the monster craft started to move. They were five stories above ground level, and could see Dennis clearly, as he came by them. He gave them the thumbs up sign as the huge ship slowly slipped by them. The sergeant picked up two sets of earphones, handing one set to Diane.

"Any vibration, sir?" asked Tensley.

"None. Smooth as glass, Sarge. I'll let you know just before takeoff, and will keep you informed as I go through maneuvers."

As the engine section passed by them, Diane asked, "Sergeant, there are three engines on that ship, the simulator only had two, what's up with that?"

"A little misinformation, Colonel, for anyone too curious. Actually, ma'am, the two engines can put him in space at any altitude, elliptical, or straight as an arrow upward. The third engine is a safety factor only."

They heard the tower give Dennis clearance for takeoff, and watched as the craft sat there, lurching, as if he were holding the reins on a wild horse that wanted to run. The craft suddenly shot down the flat runway. It had barely gone a few hundred yards, when the nose gear came off the ground, and then the whole craft was airborne. The nose was up about thirty degrees, climbing for the heavens.

"Smooth as glass, Sarge," they heard Dennis say.

The huge bird became a speck in the sky, and then quickly disappeared.

"Twenty-eight percent, Sarge … did you make some adjustments?"

"A couple, sir," Tensley replied.

"Ha! That's five percent less than number one's," Dennis said.

"I was waiting to see what effect this had before I touched number one, sir. If this holds, and it should, I'll do the same on each ship."

"Twenty-five, going to 30K, still holding twenty-eight percent at 590 knots."

Diane whispered to Tensley, "Only twenty-eight percent thrust, at that speed? That's not possible, Sergeant."

"Oh, yes, ma'am, it is, and number three is only on standby."

"Thirty K — 675 knots," Dennis said.

A short pause.

"Thirty K — 900 knots," Dennis came back again.

Diane couldn't believe what she was hearing.

"Thirty K — 1140 knots — twenty-nine percent. Beautiful, Sarge. I'm going to crank down and make a flyover."

"How far does he crank it back?"

"He'll vacuum the runway," the sergeant said, with a grin. "See him back there in the west, ma'am?"

Diane strained her eyes, looking toward the west. She saw a vapor trail dissipate as the ship came lower, and the arc of the ship dropped, as if falling from the sky. Still miles to the west, it was streaking, as if someone were drawing a line on a piece of paper. Then she heard Dennis talking.

"740K — 900 feet … 740K — 500 feet …"

"Keep your earphones on tight, Colonel, here he comes!"

"740K — 250 feet."

A swirl of dust lifted up, off the runway, behind the craft. The dust storm remained, but Dennis was gone in an instant. A sonic boom rattled the enclosure where Diane and the sergeant stood.

"Going for 50K," Dennis' voice said over their headsets. "Twenty-five — 840 knots … thirty-five — 890 … forty-five — 890 … leveling off at 50K — 900 knots."

"My God, he must have been going straight up!"

"Almost," said the sergeant, not attempting to hide a grin.

"What percent of thrust, and was the number three engine online?"

"Probably about thirty-four to thirty-five percent, and no, ma'am, number three is simply on standby."

"How long does it take number three to come up, to equal thrust with one and two?"

"No more than three seconds."

"You mean if the pilot can function that quickly?"

"Oh, no, the only time the pilot brings number three up is if he wants to; other than that, its auto. If number one or two even hiccups, three comes up; no reaction time is needed by the pilot."

"Who the hell designed those engines? They had to be a genius."

The sergeant turned to her with a big smile on his face.

"The design and function of those engines belongs to the man flying that ship. Three different companies fabricated and built his design."

"I remember them saying in the meeting that he designed them, but I guess it just didn't register that he did it all himself." Then she said, in a quiet voice, "I should have known."

"Tower? Number two," they heard Dennis say.

"Go ahead number two," the tower responded.

"Has the dust cleared?"

"10-4, number two … dust storm dissipated."

"What's the wind sock telling you, tower?"

"Nothing, number two, you tore it down again—but the little dust that's remaining tells us its calm down here."

"Sorry about your sock. Coming in from west, will turn back west for touch and go, test afterburners on one, two and three."

"10-4, see you in a minute."

##

In the main complex, a security sergeant knocked on the door of Captain Knull's office.

"Come in," Knull said. "What can I do for you, Sergeant?"

"Sir, you said to make you aware of anything unusual, and while studying the video tapes yesterday, I noticed some out-of-the-ordinary actions by Lieutenant Denehey, Colonel O'Hara, General Estes and his wife. I put Franklin on the tapes to read their lips."

The sergeant related the entire incident that had been observed in O'Hara's apartment, particularly after Denehey got the phone call from General Estes.

"In their meeting at the restaurant, Franklin couldn't get close enough to hear what they were saying, but on two or three occasions the general seemed very upset."

"Is that all, Sergeant?"

"Not quite, sir. During the early part of the meeting, Colonel O'Hara and the general's wife went to the general's reception room. Apparently, O'Hara turned off the main security camera by accident. The general's wife was searching for some papers, and when I studied the video, one of the cameras caught Colonel O'Hara watching the other camera—the one that was panning on the general's wife."

"Did they find the papers they were searching for?"

"Other than reading a couple of pages, they both left with nothing, sir."

"Hmm, could be just what they came for, to find out something. Where did they go from there?"

"Back to the restaurant. I guess the strangest part was O'Hara making up sandwiches, then not eating them, then going to the restaurant and not eating there either."

"Did the general and his wife eat?"

"No, sir, not a thing. In fact, the general acted mad most of the evening. They said that once, for just a couple of minutes, the general actually seemed pleased about something."

"A conference is what they were having. But why there?" Captain Knull asked himself, out loud.

He leaned back in his chair, letting it all sink in.

"I want all four of them watched very closely. Get Franklin to look at that video in O'Hara's apartment to see if he can make any sense of the words he can read."

"Sir, I've had him go over that already, three times. They kept their mouths well hidden, and the only words he could make out, were O'Hara's apology for tripping Denehey. After they left their apartments this morning, I went in and tried to find the note she gave him. It was nowhere to be found in either apartment, or in any trash containers on the way to the restaurant. The pad she took the paper from had no write-through imprints at all, so apparently she tore the sheet off before she wrote the note."

"Well, keep a close eye on all four of them for the next few days, and report anything that's the least little bit out of the way."

"The general left at 0530 hours this morning, no destination entered on the flight plan, no ETA or anything, just departure time."

Captain Knull sat straight up in his chair.

"Now, that's too many things happening in just a few hours."

"Another unusual thing, sir. The general's wife pulled a printout of all communications from here in the past three months, and delivered them to a hotel room."

Knull jumped to his feet, leaned over the desk, and through gritted teeth, hissed at the sergeant, "What room and who is in that room?"

"I don't know, sir. Normally, when someone is arriving here that we are aware of; we put an undercover man on the hotel. You know that we can't get in there in uniform, so we were unprepared."

"Put two damned undercover men in that damned hotel, now! I want to know who is using that room. Is that understood, Sergeant? We have to know, as we may have to accelerate our schedule soon."

"I understand, sir, but there is another problem."

Knull hit the desk with the side of his fist.

"Damn, why all at once?"

"It's our team, sir. I don't know who started the grumbling, but many are beginning to question the authenticity of the letter you showed them. Plus, they haven't seen one dime of the bonus they were told they would get."

Captain Knull sat down in his chair, elbows on the desk, fingers interlocked together, and his chin resting on them.

"Are we going to have a mutiny?" he quietly asked. "I can't ask that person to come here and talk to them. He's not to even know about this base. He accidentally uncovered this treasonous movement that we are checking into."

"What's the plan?" asked the sergeant.

"The same as I said it was when this operation began. Once we have uncovered who is head of this whole thing, at the very top of it, we call in the Marines to take over the base and secure all the aircraft. So far, the only person the general contacts is the president, and she could not finance the billions of dollars poured into this facility. It has to be a group or a foreign country."

"All incoming paychecks seem to be from the federal government," the sergeant stated.

"That's easy to forge. Get Dietz to come over here, pronto, and then return to your duties and follow the orders I gave you."

"Sir? A couple more questions about our mission?"

Knull sprang back to his feet.

"Not now, Sergeant; find Dietz and send him over here now!"

The sergeant was surprised at the vehement reaction from the Captain.

"Yes, sir, but…"

"No fucking buts Sergeant — now!"

"Yes, sir!" the sergeant saluted, did an about face and left.

Knull sat back down, thinking, *Damn, I need at least eight to ten more days. Flying that damn thing is so different, and I won't get paid if I don't deliver it. Son-of-a-bitch!*

##

Dennis stopped the craft at the end of the runway and waited for Tensley to transport Diane to the ship. When she stepped onto the flight deck, her helmet in hand, he thought, *Damn, she is gorgeous. She could have been a model.*

"Welcome aboard, Colonel."

"Thanks, where do you want me?"

Dennis covered the microphone with his hand and leaned over to whisper in her ear.

She patted him on the arm.

"We'll play later, honey, right now I want to fly."

He let out a deep sigh.

"In that case, Colonel, sit here."

Dennis moved out of the pilot's seat and motioned for her to sit there.

"You want me to fly her?"

"You beat the hell out of me on the simulator. We might as well see how you do in the real thing. Will I distract you if I sit in the second seat? I could take Captain Kirk's seat, there are identical controls there."

"Nothing distracts me when I'm flying. I prefer you take the second seat so I can keep my eye on you. Besides, if you were behind me, then I couldn't see you, and I wouldn't like that at all."

Dennis took the second seat. They both put on their helmets and plugged into the radio system.

"OK, Colonel, call the tower to clear for takeoff. I would like to see 20,000 feet, leveling out at 400 knots ... let's say in twenty-five seconds from roll time."

"Afterburners?"

"One and two engines are sufficient, number three on standby, no afterburners."

Diane pressed her microphone.

"Tower, number two ready for takeoff, climbing out to 20K in 25 seconds."

"Number two clear," the tower replied. "Roll when ready."

She held the brakes, pushed the throttles and instantly felt the ship trying to force its way down the runway. She checked her panel for oil pressure, tail temp, RPM and thrust indicator. At a given thrust, she released the brakes, and the giant leaped forward. She watched her speed rapidly gain to 150 knots, eased the nose gear off the ground, increased the engine thrust to the twenty-eight percent mark, and felt the ship leap into the air. Her speed went to 290 knots, and she hit the button to retract the landing gear. When the gear was retracted completely, and the doors that covered them closed, the resistance, or lack thereof, jumped her speed to 380 knots at 18,000 feet. She reduced the thrust to twenty-four percent and leveled off at 20,000 feet at 400 knots, heading west.

"How was that?" she asked Dennis.

"Close," he came back. "You missed it by one second."

"Are you sure Lieutenant?"

"Pretty much so. Call the tower and ask them."

She pushed her microphone button.

"Tower? Number two requesting climb verification."

"Roger," the tower came back. "From roll time to 20,000 in 24.75 seconds; good job!"

Dennis shrugged.

"Bring her around, down to 8,000 feet at 690 knots, and make a runway flyover."

Sergeant Tensley pressed the earphones tight against his ears as the huge bird came toward him. They were too high for a dust storm, but he knew the sonic boom would stir it up a little. The craft streaked by, the boom close behind.

"Very good, Colonel," Dennis remarked. "Let's do a 180, back west, 150 miles — then 180 back east at 25,000, 800 knots.

Diane reported to the tower as she made a 180, heading back west, and climbing.

"Negative, number two," the tower replied. "That is a negative. Climb to 18,000, 200 knots, and hold circle. Lear with General on board, ETA three minutes."

Diane replied, "Holding pattern at 200 knots, 18,000 feet."

She switched off her microphone.

"I wonder what news we'll have from the general."

"No telling, but I bet its more work for someone," Dennis replied.

After a few minutes, General Estes' voice sounded in their ears.

"Dennis, bring her home. I'll meet you on the ground."

Dennis looked over at Diane

"You heard the man, take her home while I grab a nap."

Sergeant Tensley, General Estes and the men in the tower were all watching as the huge ship circled, then lined up for its final approach. It came down as gracefully as any bird. She held the nose up about ten degrees to slow her down, and to let it touch down on the main landing gear first.

When the engines idled, Dennis's eyes popped open and his hands flew to the thruster's control. He started to engage the thrust and then felt the slight bump, as the nose gear touched down.

"What's wrong, Lieutenant?"

He looked at her, then back out the window, shaking his head.

"How the hell did you do that?"

"Do what?"

"Hell, you rattled me. I thought you had chopped the engines before we were down. That was the softest landing ever."

"I didn't want to wake you."

She steered the plane to the back of the hangar, where Tensley was waiting to park her. Once the ship was parked, Diane let the tail pipe temperature drop into the green on all three gauges, and then shut down the engines in sequence.

With everything shut down on the flight deck, there was an eerie silence.

"Quiet — too quiet," she said, as she removed her helmet.

They rode the elevator down and found Sarge waiting for them.

"I'm to drive you two around to the Lear. The general wants to talk to you there."

Diane hopped in the middle, and the sergeant started the guide truck.

"Well, Lieutenant, I must congratulate you," said Tensley. "You got both wheels on the ground — at the same time — best landing you ever made."

With his sheepish grin, Dennis replied, "Wasn't me Sarge, it was the colonel."

"You let her land it too? Wooohooo, I think we finally have another pilot."

Once Dennis and Diane were in the Lear, the general pulled some papers from his briefcase and spread them on the table.

"So, tell me," he asked, "how's number two doing?"

"We still have about forty-five minutes for a complete test flight," said Dennis, "and so far everything is absolutely perfect."

With a grin, the general stated, "It had to have been perfect for you to get both wheels on the ground, at the same time. That was your best touchdown ever."

"Oh, hell. Was everyone watching?" Dennis asked, and pointed to Diane. "She landed it."

"Well whoopee," the general said, laughing, and extending his hand to Diane. "By God, looks like we finally got ourselves another pilot."

"Do I hear an echo somewhere?" Dennis asked, rolling his eyes.

Diane chimed in, "General, he's a great instructor."

"Oh, B.S. Colonel, you're going to have to teach me how you did that," Dennis replied.

"Whenever you're ready," she replied, giving him a wink.

The general got down to business.

"I spoke with the president. She is, as we speak, having an Army crew see if Knull screwed up the White House security system. She's having her personal security team check all incoming calls to the White House, so, with their new computers, it will only take a couple of hours to get them. I would like for you and your crew to go to the hotel. Thelma has a large suite set up and will be there to help you, and there is a large screen the calls will be projected onto. How many people are on your team?"

"There will be five—myself, the Colonel, Sergeant Tensley, and he has two people he trusts implicitly. Thelma makes six, so that should be plenty," Dennis replied.

"In case what we suspect is true, the president has a special Marine crew standing by to fly in and secure this facility," the general said. "They'll be able to get here within an hour. We need to take over the standing guards in both hangars prior to the Marines getting here. There are sixty-five total, including Knull, but only twenty-three of them should be on duty. Since we don't know if all the security people are involved, they'll all be taken into custody until we can find out who is part of this."

"Once we get to the hotel," said Dennis, "I'll get with Sergeant Tensley and see who we can recruit to secure the guards in our main hangar. I don't think rifle bullets could hurt the ships, but if we can stop it from happening, all the better."

"OK, keep me informed. I have notified the tower of the possibility of the C-130 coming in. Whoever calls the tower to deploy the Marines is to only tell them—call C-130 Echo Charlie. The tower will then call them, and the only thing they are to say to them is 'go.' If these people have ears, they won't know what is taking place."

##

Diane, Sergeant Tensley, and Dennis were about twenty yards from the entry to the hotel when they saw Thelma. She had just come out of the hotel and was casually strolling along, as if she were out sight-seeing. As she walked by them, she didn't even look their way, but said in a low voice, "Coffee shop around the corner."

"See any security guards?" Dennis asked Tensley.

"No, I wonder what's up."

"Don't know." Dennis said. "You two go with her; I'll stick around here and see if anyone is following. I'll join you in a couple of minutes."

Diane and Tensley went to the coffee shop, and Dennis stayed behind, looking in the shop windows. He found one window that gave him a clear reflection of the hotel entrance. He pretended to be looking at some shoes on display there, and after a few minutes went by, and no one came from the hotel, he turned and lit a cigarette. There were only a few people roaming around, and Dennis's eyes scoured the plaza for any sign of a security guard or cameras. Cameras were not allowed in this area, and he wanted to make sure he didn't find any.

He finally sauntered back to the window and checked the hotel entrance one more time. He then went around the corner, and into the coffee shop. The others were in a booth at the far end of the room. He joined them and Diane pushed a cup of coffee in front of him.

"Thanks. What's up, Thelma?"

"Someone saw me go to the hotel this morning," Thelma answered. "I'm sure Knull knows about me getting the printouts off the main computer and had me followed. He has two undercover guards posted in the lobby now, and if he is what we think, he wants to know what I did with the printouts — and who is in the hotel getting them. There is a rear entrance to the lobby; let me borrow your arm phone, Dennis, please."

Puzzled, he handed her the phone. She punched in some numbers and in a moment, a grouchy voice asked, "What the hell is it?"

Thelma said sweetly, "Don't you talk to me in that tone, you old coot. This is your sweet, loving wife!"

"Oh," he said in a very soft voice. "Hello, dear."

The other three had to stifle their laughter.

Thelma quickly gave the general all of the details of the situation.

"Those men aren't supposed to be there, are they?" Thelma asked, referring to the undercover men in the hotel.

"Hell, no," the general replied.

"We want to go into the rear entrance of the lobby; can you do something to help us out here?"

"Go ahead over there, and wait outside. I'll call Knull, and then call you right back," and he clicked off.

Thelma handed Dennis the phone.

"Come on, there's coffee and other goodies in the suite."

They followed her out the rear door of the coffee shop.

Meanwhile, the general was punching in Knull's number.

"Captain Knull here," said a voice on the other end.

"General Estes here."

"Yes, sir, general, can I help you?"

"To be honest, Captain, no, but you can help yourself. I've been getting itsy bitsy complaints lately, which I normally dismiss, but this one I can't. I just got a call from the hotel manager, and apparently, you have two undercover guards lounging around the lobby. They stick out like a sore fucking thumb, been there way too long to be waiting for someone. Now, if that manager reports this to his senator or congressman, I'm in hot water. I know you are well aware of the rules for having security guards or cameras where civilians congregate or go, aren't you?"

"Yes, sir, but when my men are off duty, they have the same rights as…"

"Off duty, my ass!" the general interrupted. "Now, this is serious business; the people in those shops are well aware of who's a customer and who's not. Those folks aren't dummies, Captain. The manager called me and was going to detain them with his own security people, but, since I know you're short handed and really can't afford to lose them for seventy-two hours, I told him I would take care of it."

"Thank you, General, but..." Knull tried to say.

"No buts!" the general blurted out. "You have five minutes to get them the hell out of there. Do you understand? You tell them to clear the place and don't come back unless they're off duty, and I want their names, pronto!"

"Yes, sir!"

The general smiled, turned off his speaker phone and dialed Dennis' number.

"They'll be gone in five," he said, and hung up.

The four entered the suite and two men were already there, patiently waiting.

"This is Chuck Hennesey and this is Harold Dickerson, two of our engineers," said Tensley.

After shaking hands, Dennis, Tensley, Chuck and Harold sat down at one side of a long conference table, facing a huge screen on the other side. Diane seated herself next to Dennis, and Thelma walked around the table to face everyone.

Chuck started things off.

"While we were waiting, I saw the screen and figured out what ye might be looking for. I worked with the FBI, and we had to do this once in a while. I've already found seven numbers that came from the same number here at our facility," he said while marking them on the screen. "Five of them belong to one number in D.C., and two to a number in Virginia."

"Thanks Chuck," Thelma said. "Harold, Dennis and Chuck, could you three keep an eye out for those numbers, and the rest of us look for any others that might pop up?"

They all agreed, and began the daunting task.

Diane leaned over toward Dennis.

"Do you think you could spare me for a few minutes? I want to call the girls and see how they are handling their mother's death, and if I feel the mood is right, I will talk to them about coming out here."

"Honey, you are a colonel; I'm just a lieutenant."

She leaned closer and whispered, "Stop that shit. We're a team here and if I'm needed, then the call can wait."

Without thinking about where they were, Dennis turned his head, and his lips lightly brushed hers. He looked around and was relieved to see that everyone's attention was on the screen, everyone except for Tensley, that is. The sergeant had a big grin and was giving Dennis the thumbs-up sign.

Dennis turned back to Diane and whispered, "Sorry 'bout that."

"I'm not," she whispered back.

"Go make your call."

##

Ed answered and updated her on the funeral.

"I have another reason for calling," Diane said after hearing Ed's family news. I wanted to see if it was the proper time to ask the girls something. I would really like to have your permission before I ask them. Do you want the girls in the military, Ed?"

"Diane, you know darn well they're going to enlist anyway. Why?"

"Would you want them in the space program?"

Ed hesitated, "I know it's Mattie's dream. I don't know about Cathy. That's four years down the road anyway, finishing the academy, and then they have to get in line."

"Not really, Ed. With the experience and know-how they already have, they're way ahead of anyone coming out of the academy, except for the silly ass basic training."

Ed laughed and bluntly asked, "Why are you asking these questions? It's not as if they can just skip the academy and basics."

"They can now. If you want them in our program, I'll explain. If you don't, then there is no need."

"Hell yes," Ed said, with no hesitation this time. "I would love to have them out there with me. That way I could look after them, to a certain degree."

Diane quickly went through the president's exemption plan, and explained how the last six people had washed out on the simulator program.

"We want pilots whose brains haven't been saturated by the academies," Diane explained, "and we want to train a completely different kind of pilot, an astronaut. We have a top-of-the-line instructor in Lieutenant Denehey. We need good pilots, Ed, and you know we'll keep them as safe as possible, and your sisters are very good."

"Damn girl, you should be a recruiter."

"So, what do you think? You want to ask the girls, or wait a day or two and think it over?"

"If I didn't give them the chance to say yes or no, they would have my hide. Speaking of the devils, they just walked in. I'll put you on speaker phone."

Diane heard a click and then heard Ed saying, "Hey you two, get in here, someone special wants to talk to you."

After a little catching up, Diane said, "Girls, I have a very serious proposition for both of you, but first I want to ask, do you still intend to enlist?"

"You better believe it!" Mattie exclaimed.

"Probably," replied Cathy, "as soon as all of this is settled here."

"Alright, I want you both to listen, absorb, and think it over real good. I would appreciate an answer within a week though, but let me explain in full before you say anything at all. Are you ready?"

Affirmation was heard and Diane launched into the offer.

As she finished, it was so quiet that she finally asked, "Is anyone there?"

Ed spoke this time, "You ought to see their faces; I think they are stunned beyond belief. They both have tears streaming down their cheeks. Oh, hell, so do I."

"Well, just let them know the offer is there, but be aware a washout is always a possibility."

"I've been there before," Cathy said. "I won't wash. Oh my, thanks so much for recommending us, Diane. I love you, girl."

Diane wiped a few tears from her cheeks.

"When can we come?" Mattie asked.

"Are you sure you don't want some time to think about it, honey?"

"Think? What's to think about?" Mattie asked. "You know this has been my dream, and to have the opportunity to at least have a shot at it — not much to think about there. Just tell us when and where. Can we come with Ed?"

"I'll check with the general about that. Tell you what, Ed, I'll see if the general wants to send the Lear after you. We need to get to work as soon as possible. And Ed, remind the girls how top secret this is, and talk to no one about this."

"You got it, Diane, and thanks again!"

In the background, a voice yelled out, "Hey! What about me?"

"Who is that, Ed?" Diane asked.

"My younger bro, Captain Terry Mitchell"

"What does he do?"

"Stealth pilot, ma'am," Terry answered.

"Oh, yes, I remember the girls talking about you," Diane said, smiling as she recalled their conversation on the plane … a whole family of pilots … who would imagine?

"Hell, why not?" Diane replied.

She was just as excited as they were.

"Get all of his things in order; you know the drill, Ed. I need a copy of the girls' last flight physicals. When you get to Vegas, you know the way to get a ride. If the Lear can't be sent, I'll let you know. I'll call you sometime tomorrow and we'll set everything in motion. God speed!"

Diane felt like screaming for joy. She wasn't quite sure how she had attached herself to those two girls so quickly, and she really didn't care how. She just knew she loved them.

"Some quick call," Dennis whispered as she joined the others at the table.

"May not have been quick, but it was sure a productive one," she whispered back and then filled him in.

"How's it going here?" Diane asked.

"Look at the screen."

"Wow, are all those calls from here to D.C. and Virginia?"

"And Maryland," Dennis added, "all cell phone, and only two local numbers."

Thelma was changing the printouts and marking them. It was almost eight o'clock when they finished going over them all.

Thelma called the general, using a preplanned message in case the phones were tapped.

"Sweetheart, come and see me. Remember what tonight is?"

The general responded, "Oh yes, my sweet wife, that's why I wanted a hotel suite, so we could celebrate. I'm on my way."

"He can be the sweetest man," Thelma said, after hanging up.

Dennis took Sergeant Tensley aside.

"On what I was telling you earlier, do you think you could get some men together to subdue the guards?"

"Sure, I know just the guy to help us."

Tensley turned toward Chuck, an ex-Army man, now a civilian engineer and still someone you would not want to meet in a dark ally. Tensley motioned for Chuck to join him.

"Dennis, meet Chuck Hennesey. This is one man we can trust with our lives," Tensley said.

With a confused look, Chuck replied, "Trust with your lives for what?"

"Have a seat, Chuck, and we'll explain."

Dennis and Tensley filled him in about the upcoming plan.

"So, do you know of anyone who can help us?" asked Dennis.

"Aye, sir, I be knowing of at least thirty-two techs and assemblers, mostly ex-military, that would be very interested in helping. I would trust them all with me life."

"I think we should take both hangars, and the security room, just kill the whole network," said Tensley. "That way, if there is a monitoring room, and they are tapped into the main system, it would kill theirs also."

"I agree," Chuck said, nodding his head in agreement.

"Fine," said Dennis, "but how the hell would you get into that room?"

"All depends on when we go," replied Tensley.

The sergeant pulled a chair from the table and straddled it.

"I drink with a lot of them. I've been in there before, just shooting the breeze, and those guys get so bored. They have nothing to do but sit and watch those screens, and most of them hate Knull."

"The security room should go before the guards," said Chuck.

"I agree with you on that," Dennis replied, "but remember, we have no idea who is, and who is not, working with Knull, so be as careful as possible. We don't want any innocent people killed here. I'll take Knull myself!"

"Oh sure, leave me out of the best part! I'll try to remember that if I see him first," Tensley said.

"Tell you what, Sarge," said Dennis, "second shift is working now. Why don't you and Chuck see who you can round up for this?"

"Some, if not most, of first shift is still there, I guarantee it. They have all been staying over and working their asses off to get these ships done. They started on number 12 after lunch," Tensley said.

"Oh, by the way Sarge, the arms cabinet in number one is fully armed. Use any weapons necessary from that, if we do go. I'll catch up with you after awhile."

"Roger," replied Tensley, and they were out the door.

They hadn't been gone five minutes when the general came in and planted a big kiss on Thelma's lips.

"Great job, Mama, what do we have?"

Thelma led him over to the table where everything was laid out. She showed him the list of calls.

"Damn, why the hell is Knull calling the vice president's office so many times? That's his secure line on most, and then here are a few to his personal phone," the general noted, pointing out the numbers to everyone.

He turned to Diane.

"Colonel, a favor please."

"Yes, sir?"

"I don't recognize these two D.C. numbers. Would you call them and see who answers? Our number's blocked, so it won't show on any caller ID."

Diane wrote down the two numbers and went to the phone.

"Now, this number here," he pointed out to Thelma, "is a local number, and I don't know about it, except that it's one of the series of numbers issued to security."

He scratched his head, and then wrote down the number and handed it to Diane.

"Did you manage to get some men to help take down the security guards, Dennis?"

"About thirty or so, sir. Sergeant Tensley is lining it up right now."

Diane walked up, and pointing to the numbers said, "Chinese embassy, a Senator Tolbert, and the local number is a Sergeant Dietz."

"The vice president, Tolbert, and the Chinese embassy ... I can't believe the vice president is tied to this. Somehow, he is tied to Dietz or Knull," the general remarked.

"Excuse me, sir," Diane said. "Didn't the president say that it was the vice president who recommended Knull?"

"Yes, Colonel, you're correct, she did say that."

He picked up his shoulder phone and punched in some numbers.

"General Estes here, is the Lear ready to fly?"

He paused, listening.

"Good, pilot and copilot, 15 minutes. I'll be right there."

He turned to Dennis.

"I'm going out to call the president; keep your phone handy. If I call you, call the tower and get whatever force you have to. Do what you can to make it as easy as possible."

He scooped up the papers from the desk, kissed his wife, and left in a hurry.

Looking at Thelma and Diane, with a bleak smile, Dennis said, "I'm going to catch Sarge and get things lined up. I think you two should go to quarters."

"Quarters? Hell, I'm going for a drink. Diane, want to join me?" Thelma asked.

"I think I should help the lieutenant."

"Diane ... Colonel, please go with her."

"Yes, Dennis can handle this. He has lots of good people backing him, and he would only worry about you. I saw that little smooch earlier; he needs a clear head to do what has to be done."

Diane smiled at Thelma but spoke to Dennis.

"OK, but you get your butt back here in one piece, please."

"Will do."

Dennis winked at Diane, and then turned to leave.

"Aw, hell Dennis, go ahead and kiss her. I won't look," and Thelma turned her back to them.

"You can look, Thelma. I'm not ashamed to kiss the woman I plan to marry, in front of anyone."

There was a surprised look on Diane's face as his lips met hers, then he was gone.

Dennis caught up with Tensley at the number twelve ship.

"Twenty-three here. Chuck just called; he'll be here with the rest shortly."

"Good," Dennis replied, "we might go anytime now. The general is talking to the president and we need to be ready to go if he calls me. When Chuck gets here, take a couple of men and tool bags to number one and get weapons. Distribute them to those who know how to use them."

"I've already cautioned them about some being innocent. They're going to do their best to just subdue them; hopefully no weapons will be used."

"Who's going to take the security office?" Dennis asked.

Tensley smiled, and reached down into his side pocket on the leg of his work fatigues. He pulled out a roll of magazines.

"'Playboy' — I take them up to the guys every now and then. Between these," he held up the magazines, "two other men and myself, I think we can handle it."

Dennis smiled, "I'm sure you can!"

"I have men assigned to different guard posts. Once you give the signal, work will stop and they will split up and go to their assigned areas," said Tensley.

"I need someone to lead a group of the Marines to the security quarters, to get those who are off duty. I particularly want the one called Dietz. I'll find Knull. Do you have men already assigned to the guards in the second hangar?"

"Yup, sure do. They're to act like they're going there for parts and then they'll secure that location."

"OK, Sarge, good. I guess the one leading the Marines can open the hangar doors and lead them in. You be damned careful, Sarge, can't do without any of you men here."

"I will, sir. By the way, I'll need at least ten minutes to take the security office from the time you say go."

"You got it. Damn, you should be a general."

"A second Louie would be fine, sir."

"Pull this off and you just might get that," Dennis replied. "Here comes your day crew, Sarge. You take care; I'm going to the briefing room."

Dennis sat down. Diane was weighing heavy on his mind.

Why did I say that word — marry? We've only known each other a little while. She'll probably say no, anyway. It's clear she's a career woman, and once this mission is over, I'm going to resign, so that won't work. I've been broken down from a colonel to a second lieutenant ... I would do better as a civilian engineer, so I have to resign. I can't believe I'm even thinking this anyway.

He kept going over these things in his mind, thinking of Diane and trying to figure out a way it would work … then his phone vibrated on his shoulder.

"Denehey here."

"Dennis, Estes here … it's a go and everyone has been notified. Take care."

Dennis walked calmly to the door and opened it. He saw Tensley and put his fingers to his mouth and whistled.

Tensley and two other men walked toward him, but passed without saying a word. Dennis looked at his watch and went over to number twelve, where the men were hard at work. He watched the cameras out of the corner of his eyes, and then glanced back at his watch — six minutes had passed. At eight minutes, the camera's red lights went out, and they were dead still.

Dennis called Hennesey over.

"It's time to go."

Hennesey went back to the men, and just a minute later all noise stopped. The men went to the aisle and then separated, each going in assigned directions.

The sergeant, manning the clandestine monitoring room in Knull's apartment, stared at the blank screens in front of him.

"Captain Knull," the sergeant called out, "we have lost all our feed."

Knull appeared in the doorway, glanced in and grabbed his shoulder phone.

"Must have blown a breaker," he muttered. "Damn it, answer the phone you piss ants."

There was no answer from the security room.

Tensley just let it ring, and the guards he had captured kept asking him why he was doing this.

Knull stood there, thinking, phones aren't out … it was ringing … something is fucking wrong here.

He told the guys in the monitoring room, "Sit tight, I'll be right back."

He slipped into his security jacket, strapped on his revolver and left. When he got to the stairs that went up to the security room, two armed guards stood in the doorway.

One of the guards looked down.

"Well, well, Captain Knull, please come up."

Knull spun around, out of the guard's sight. *Son of a bitch,* he thought, *why would they take over the control room? They know, damn it! I've got to get to security quarters; they're armed. Shit, they won't obey me. This is a controlled takeover.*

He dashed for the tubes, just as one of the men guarding the security office came around the corner. Knull drew his revolver and fired. The security officer ducked back around the corner just in time.

Tensley, hearing the shot, told the other guard, "Get inside and lock the door. I'm going to check on Jack."

Gun drawn, he flew down the stairs. He ran down the hallway and found Jack, safely huddled by the corner wall.

Tensley grabbed his shoulder phone. Dennis answered.

"I guess Knull came to check on the security room and took a pot shot at one of my men."

"I checked his office and he wasn't there. He won't answer his phone either. I'm one level down. I'm coming up; maybe we can box him in. You stay put."

Dennis took the stairs, leaping up two at a time. He carefully opened the door, hit the floor and rolled, just in case Knull was there. He was just in time to see a foot disappear into the transport tube.

Damn, which way would I go? Dennis thought, trying to outguess Knull. *Up or down ... no, not up; you would lose one escape route that way. He would have to go down.*

Dennis pressed the button to bring up the next capsule. He jumped in and pressed minus 8, down to the rail line. In just a couple of seconds the door opened.

A big man from the assembly crew was running toward him.

"Lieutenant, I just saw Knull. He was headed that way," he said, pointing toward a platform.

Still sitting in the tube, Dennis said, "Slide that trash can over here."

Dennis jumped out of the tube, leaving the trash can in the doorway. The door couldn't close, which rendered the system useless.

"Don't let anyone take that can out."

The door to the next tube Dennis came to was closing. Dennis got there just in time to see that no one was in it. It was almost closed when it suddenly reopened, then closed again.

"Good, out of order," he said to no one. He stopped and held his breath. In the distance, he could hear running.

He is on the rail line, Dennis thought to himself, *heading for the end of the tunnel.*

Dennis pictured the layout of the tunnel in his mind. He didn't know if the contractors had started burrowing through to the third hangar yet. He did know there was a ladder that would take Knull to the surface.

Where does that manhole come out? Dennis thought to himself. Oh, yeah, it would bring him out in the wash and refueling area.

He jumped off the platform and slowly made his way toward the end of the tunnel. About thirty yards down, there were no more lights. With the light now filtering in from behind him, Dennis knew he would be a good target.

There was a gradual turn ahead, and he was now operating like a blind man, hugging the wall and feeling his way as he went.

He heard a loud bang, and then some cursing. It came from the area where the manhole should be. Dennis stopped dead in his tracks, listening. He heard some more cursing and then heard something hit the ground. Then there were footsteps, coming slowly, back toward him.

He couldn't get the cover off, Dennis thought to himself.

Later on, Dennis found out that number two's nose wheel was sitting right on top of it.

Dennis sat down, his back against the wall, trying to melt into it. This way, he presented a much smaller target than if he had stayed standing. He held his breath and strained his eyes, looking for any movement, even a shadow would do. He saw a slight movement against the opposite wall, and heard the light touch of boots on the concrete.

Dennis' revolver followed the shadowy figure, until it emerged into the light that had once been a disadvantage to him. Now the table was turned, and the light was in Dennis' favor. Now he could clearly see Knull, and the revolver he was carrying.

"One more step and you're a dead S.O.B. ... drop it now!" Dennis ordered.

Knull froze, his weapon still pointing in front of him.

"Drop it now, or I shoot! I won't say it again, you bastard. You deserve to die."

Knull let the nose of his weapon drop toward the floor, and then half squatting, he tossed the gun forward.

"Don't even flinch."

Dennis pushed himself to his feet.

"Put both hands on your head and start walking ahead, slowly."

They walked down the tracks until they came to a security station. Two of Dennis' people were manning it, and one came forward.

"You need some help, Lieutenant?"

"Please. Get this S.O.B. up on the platform and find something to tie his hands."

They reached down and grabbed Knull's arms, yanking him roughly onto the platform.

Above, the hangar doors opened. The big C-130 had parked, and well armed Marines poured from it. A captain was there to meet them, and take them to their destination. There was a long row of security officers standing, hands cuffed behind their backs with their own restraints. The troops and their leader trotted behind the guide, and there were looks of confusion on the security guards' faces.

"What the hell is going on here?" one of them asked.

No answer was forthcoming.

As Dennis pushed Knull ahead of him, toward the line of manacled security guards, the last of the Marines ran past him.

One of Tensley's men asked, "Want me to take him, Lieutenant?"

"Don't take him off, but guard him well."

A Marine major with another detachment of troops came through the hangar doors from the C-130. He spotted a lieutenant's bar and called out.

"Lieutenant!"

Dennis walked toward him, and they met in front of the row of prisoners.

"Who's in charge here?"

"For the time being, I am," Dennis replied.

The major looked down the row of prisoners.

"We have only an inkling of what's going on here, but we are told we're here to get your security system back in order. Can you guide us to your main security office?"

One of the prisoners yelled out.

"Major, the lieutenant and his people are committing treason."

The major walked over to the prisoner.

"Who are you shitting, Sergeant? If that's the case, then why are you in handcuffs instead of him? Traitors don't call in the Marines."

Baffled, the sergeant clamped his mouth shut.

Looking from the prisoner, to the monstrous spaceships, then back to Dennis, the major was in awe.

"Lieutenant, what the hell are those?" he asked, pointing toward the ships.

Smiling, Dennis replied, "Top secret, sir!"

Dennis saw Hennesey and called him over.

"Mr. Hennesey, please show the major and his men to the security room, and have Sergeant Tensley report back here with his men."

"Aye, sir. Follow me, Major."

When they had left, Dennis walked over and faced the sergeant who had yelled out.

"Who says I'm committing treason, Sergeant?"

"Lieutenant, I haven't a damn clue as to what's going on here. All I know is that Knull showed us a letter from the vice president, stating that we were to assist the captain in stopping you, and the general, from committing treason. He said you were planning on taking over the government by using these aircraft."

Dennis wiped his brow.

"Did you see the letter?"

"Yes, sir, I did. It was on White House stationery, with the signature and seal of the office, sir. It was very authentic looking, sir."

"Do any of you have a copy of this letter?"

One man stepped forward.

"Sir. Sergeant Dietz here. I'm second, or was second in command, under Captain Knull. Captain Knull carries the letter, or a copy of it, in an envelope in his right side, jacket pocket. I believe he uses it to recruit others."

Dennis walked down the line towards Knull and turned to face him. Reaching into Knull's jacket, he pulled out the envelope. He removed the letter, and making sure to only touch it by the corners, he carefully unfolded it. He read it and then checked the signature and the seal. He then held it up to the light, studying it.

Sergeant Tensley and General Estes came in the door. The general was all smiles as they saluted each other.

Dennis handed General Estes the letter.

"Hold it by the corners General, possible fingerprints."

As the general read the letter, he too, held it up to the light. He studied the special parchment paper that comes only from the White House.

"Damn, I didn't want to believe it. I'm going to my office and get the president on the phone. Can we check this for fingerprints or do we have to send it off?"

"We have a lab in Captain Knull's office," Sergeant Dietz offered.

"And who are you?" General Estes asked.

Dennis quickly identified the sergeant

The general stared at the sergeant.

"Were you in cahoots with the Captain?"

"Sir, I had no reason to doubt Captain Knull. I saw that same letter, knew it was authentic, and the vice president's prints were all over it. I know this, because I ran the fingerprints on it. It wasn't that I didn't trust Captain Knull; I just wanted to make sure my men, or myself, were not being duped. I am not a traitor, sir."

"Do you still have the prints and computer reports?" Dennis asked.

"In my locker, sir."

Dennis handed the letter back to the general. Then a light went off — Dietz, Tolbert and the phone calls.

"Sergeant Dietz, did you make some cell phone calls to a Senator Tolbert—and if so, was that Carey Tolbert?"

"Yes, sir, I did."

"Know who he is, General?" Dennis asked.

"Yeah, the one who cost you your rank," the general replied.

"My ex-father-in-law also."

The general's eyebrows went up at that revelation.

"Oh, I wasn't aware of that part."

"Sergeant Dietz, what was the purpose of those calls?"

"The captain told me to call him and inform him of your progress on the aircraft, sir. The second call was to tell the senator that Captain Knull was almost ready to fulfill the mission, but needed a little more time. On the last call, I was told to say the timetable had been moved up, possible suspicion."

"Suspicion of what, and what timetable?" The general growled at the sergeant.

"Sir," the sergeant replied, "Captain Knull said, when the time came, we were to arrest you, the lieutenant, and some others, then secure the aircraft and he would call in the Marines as soon as the vice president ordered it. He said there would be pilots coming in to take the flyable aircraft to an unspecified location."

Dennis and the general looked at each other.

"Was that the extent of the calls to the senator, or were other things talked about?"

"Captain Knull wrote down exactly what I was to say, and I did exactly as he instructed, sir."

General Estes and Dennis walked back down the line toward Knull.

"Knull, you can make things a lot easier for all of us," the general said, "and for yourself. If you would just open up, and give us the complete story of all the plans you have made, and who all is involved in these plans. Even though we are not in a state of declared war with the Muslim world, you could be tried by a military tribunal and face a firing squad. Let that sink in before you answer."

The general turned his back on Knull.

"Damn it, Dennis, I'm really in a quandary as to what to do with these men. It's quite apparent that they were sucked into this by the vice president's letter and Knull's recruiting efforts. They thought they were defending their nation, which is why they joined the military in the first place."

"I understand, and you're probably right, but, we don't know for sure who, or how many, really knew Knull's purpose."

"None," stated Knull. "None of them knew my intent."

"Just what was your intent, Knull?" The general asked, turning to face him once more.

"Oh, no, I'll just say that none of these men knew the real intent. When I hear the president say I won't be put to death, and put it in her handwriting, then, and only then, will I talk."

"Let's take him to my office," said General Estes. "I'm going to release all of his crew. If I hadn't seen the letter myself, I wouldn't release them, but I believe they had no idea what was taking place. There will be no arms issued until further investigation."

In the general's office, everyone listened to the president on the speaker phone.

"Captain Knull, a faxed statement is on its way, and the United States provost marshal is here to witness this statement. Along with the marshal, as witnesses, are the secretary of defense, your state senator, and head of the CIA. A courier will be there soon with the actual statement, in my own handwriting, saying you will not be put to death for your crimes against the United States of America. With this, I want your complete statement now, so we can take into custody the rest of those involved."

Knull thought it over for a moment.

"Yes, ma'am. I'm ready to give my statement.

Dennis walked into his apartment and, from habit, switched off the security system. Walking into the kitchen, he glanced at his watch and thought, damn, 2:30 in the morning. He opened the fridge, grabbed a bottle of beer and made his way back to the dining room table. He plopped down in the chair, kicking off his shoes and guzzling the beer all in the same move.

A soft voice said, "More like coffee time isn't it?"

Dennis spun around to see a very beautiful sight. There she stood, her long, flowing, deep auburn hair, falling in curls and waves around her face and over her shoulders. She was breathtaking against the light in her powder blue, very sheer, baby doll that barely hung past the top of her thighs.

"Don't you know that angels aren't allowed in single men's quarters?"

"I can leave, I guess."

"Oh, no, don't do that. I'll make an exception this time."

She walked toward Dennis, and right past him. In his eyes, she was gliding like an angel. She got two beers from the fridge and handed one to him.

"I thought you said coffee time."

"To hell with coffee, it's a little too warm for that now."

She sat down, across from Dennis.

"I do want to know what happened tonight, but I would like an answer to something else first. I believe I heard someone mention, in front of a witness, something about marriage. Was I hearing things or what?"

"Hmmm," Dennis voiced out loud. "I have never believed in love at first sight and I still don't understand how this happened, but I love you Diane. I fell head over heals for you the first time I saw you on the plane." He sat up straight, reached across the table and took her hand. "Would a beautiful colonel consider being married to a lowly lieutenant?"

Diane smiled, and with her other hand reached across and softly brushed his cheek.

"It has been very fast. It feels like a whirlwind has blown into my life…but it feels right…very right. Yes, I would consider it. You do know how independent I am and I'm afraid there will be some conditions attached that you may not find acceptable, though."

He took a long drink and stretched his legs out under the table until his feet touched hers.

"And what might those conditions be?"

She wiggled her toes under his feet and looked him in the eyes.

"The most serious condition is my work. You have to understand how much I love what I do, and I want to keep doing it for as long as I can. I want my career, and I expect no favoritism when on duty. Whatever we do or whatever the mission is, I want to do my part as an officer and a pilot. I want it to be just as if I were another pilot when on duty. Can you understand that?"

Dennis sat back up.

"I expected that, honey, and have thought about it, too. I might as well tell you up front, once this moon mission is over, I'm resigning my commission."

"I heard that, but I don't understand why. Dennis, you've designed a craft that's way before its time … those are your babies sitting in that hangar. Everyone who is anyone is aware of that, and there is so much more you can do."

"You're right, there is much more I can do, but once the mission is complete, they can't leave a lieutenant as commander, to send majors, lieutenant colonels and colonels on missions. I'm not sure I could stand being away from the woman I love, seeing her mostly on her 30-day furlough each year. It wouldn't be fair to you, or me."

"Then don't resign," she pleaded. "We will be together … here. It's for sure they aren't going to send you anywhere else. If I don't wash out, then the squadron will stay together."

"You won't wash out; you proved that yesterday morning. I'd bet that you'll end up being the squadron commander."

"Oh, be serious, Dennis. That's not going to happen. You think they would put a woman in charge of a squadron of billion dollar space ships?"

"I am serious. I do believe it will happen; and what about children? I'd like to have a couple before I'm too old."

Frowning, she said softly, "I never thought about that. Damn it, Dennis. Are you withdrawing your proposal?"

He reached across the table and took her hand.

"No, I'm not. I love you Diane, and I would marry you in a heartbeat, but you are a sensible woman and know we have to resolve these issues first."

She leaned back in her chair, pulling her hand from his. She took a long drink. She set the bottle back on the table and stood up.

"Well, let's sleep on it."

She walked to the couch, picked up Dennis' robe that was draped over the arm, and put it on. Then she left.

"Oh, damn it!" Dennis said out loud, and then thought, *why does life have to be so complicated?* He finished his beer, went to the fridge for another and flopped down on the couch, thinking and drinking.

##

Dennis awoke, startled and fuzzy headed.

What is that noise?—then he realized it was his shoulder phone—it was singing and vibrating on his shoulder. He had fallen asleep on the couch, fully dressed. He sat up and pulled the phone to his ear.

"Denehey," he said into it, still trying to focus his eyes.

"Dennis, son, were you still asleep?"

Dennis looked at his watch … ten after twelve.

"Oh Lord, General. Yes sir; I'm sorry, sir. I'll be in briefing in 20 minutes, sir."

"No, no, all operations are shut down for the next two days. After yesterday, everyone is wore the hell out. There's going to be lots of investigating going on and we need the time to clear our heads."

"I agree, sir, but what about the mission?"

"Dennis, clear that out of your mind, at least for a day or two. Since it's so late, and breakfast is past, how about meeting Thelma and me at that Italian restaurant at, say, 1330 hours? She's still giving me hell about not getting a meal the other evening."

"Sure thing, 1330 it is."

"Oh, by the way, do you have your formal A's?"

Yes, sir, in mothballs, but available. Why?"

"After all that has taken place, it's time for a damned good ball. I want to honor Sergeant Tensley and his people, you, the colonel and several others, so I feel it's appropriate."

"That's very good of you, General, but a good old beer bar would have been fine with me."

"Damn it, Dennis, I thought so too, but the boss said a ball, so a ball it will be — and you know who the real boss around here is."

Dennis laughed out loud.

"We all need a good woman to keep us in line, General. You found a great one."

"The ball is at 2100 hours, in the hotel ballroom. I'll see you at 1330."

"Yes, sir."

Quite a couple they are, he thought, as he hung up the phone. He sat for a moment, laughing at the general's honesty about Thelma.

Then, Diane popped into his mind. He put his ear against her kitchen door ... no sound at all. He headed for the bathroom, with Diane still on his mind. As he shaved, he thought, *I had to tell her my plans. It was only fair.*

He walked into the restaurant and stopped, looking around for the general. He spotted them in the back corner, in a big round booth, and there was no mistaking who the third person in the booth was. That auburn hair could only belong to Diane.

The general shook his hand.

"Good to have you here, Dennis."

"Thanks, sir. Hello, Thelma, good to see you again." He looked at Diane, "Good afternoon, Colonel."

Diane gave him a semi-cold glance.

"Good afternoon, Lieutenant."

She scooted around the half circle seat, getting as close to Thelma as possible without being in her lap. There was enough room left for three people to sit.

Maybe I should look at myself to see if I have festered whelps of some contagious disease showing, he thought as he sat in the huge gap left by Diane.

The dinner went well, all except the coolness between the two. After they ate, Diane excused herself, saying she was tired.

"Is Diane all right?" Thelma asked Dennis.

"I think she's just tired," he answered. *How can I tell Thelma any different, when I don't even know what happened?*

"Maybe she'll take a nap and feel better. I'll check on her later to make sure she's OK."

"Thanks, Thelma, you're a sweetheart."

##

Dennis stood at the door of the ballroom. He could hear soft music coming from inside and hesitated. He knew Diane would be there, and had no desire to go through the same cool attitude she had at dinner. He knew he could not get out of it though; his presence was required. He took a deep breath, and entered the ballroom.

The place was alive with people. There were some already on the dance floor, while others milled around tables that were loaded down with every kind of food and drink imaginable. The bar, at one side of the room, had several men and women around it. One stood out among the rest because of his size.

That's Hennesey, Dennis thought; *can't miss him. He looks great, very well dressed.*

"Lieutenant!"

The voice brought Dennis out of the fog he seemed to be lost in. He turned to see Tensley coming toward him, escorting a gorgeous woman with long brown hair, and a spectacular evening gown. They shook hands and Dennis thought, *I know this woman, but from where?*

"How are you, Lieutenant? You know Shirley, I believe."

Dennis took a deep breath.

"Shirley? Our supply room girl?"

"Same old me. What do you think, Lieutenant?"

She twirled around, showing off her dress.

Dennis took her hand and raised it to his lips.

"You have always sparkled Shirley, but tonight you are full blown fireworks, lady. Absolutely gorgeous. This man is lucky to be with you."

Tensley stood proud, and with a huge grin on his face, announced, "Sir, please meet the future Mrs. Tensley."

Dennis took Sergeant Tensley's hand again.

"Absolutely wonderful, Sarge! Congratulations!"

He kissed Shirley on the cheek.

"I'm so happy for you both!"

Dennis felt a tug on his sleeve.

"Excuse me, Lieutenant."

He turned and looked into the face of a very pretty young woman. Once again, he felt as if he knew this person, but couldn't figure it out.

"Excuse me, I think I'm going crazy tonight," he said with a puzzled look on his face.

"I sure hope not, Lieutenant," the young lady said.

That voice. He stepped back looking at the young woman.

"Cath? Cathy, is that you! My gosh, what's happening tonight?"

Dennis leaned over and kissed Cathy on the cheek.

"When did you get here? You look absolutely beautiful."

"Well, thank you for the compliment, and I also want to thank you for recommending us. I really appreciate it."

"You earned it, girl. You weren't supposed to be here for another day or two, what happened?"

"I'm not sure myself, but here we are! We came by invitation from General Estes, and in a very special plane, too."

"What pl-," Dennis started to ask, when Mattie came running up, throwing her arms around him and kissing him, right on the lips. When she pulled back, she looked into Dennis' shocked face.

"Thank you Lieutenant! Thank you so very much!"

"You're very welcome Mattie; it's so good to see you again!"

"How about me?" a voice said from behind him.

Dennis turned to see Ed Mitchell standing there.

"Good to see you, Lieutenant," Ed said, as he shook Dennis' hand.

"Glad to have you back, Ed, and please accept my sincere condolences to you and your family over your loss."

"Thank you Lieutenant. That is deeply appreciated by all of us."

A voice boomed over the speakers. Everyone quieted down and looked to where General Estes stood on the stage.

"Ladies and gentlemen, thank you all for showing up on such short notice. All of you ladies out there are absolutely beautiful tonight. I would say the same for the gentlemen, but my wife said I shouldn't."

There was a short burst of laughter from everyone in the ballroom.

"There are many of you here that I'm so proud to call my fellow Americans, my fellow service men and women. I'm really at a loss for words. I'm not going to give a long-winded speech, but I want to thank all of you for what you have done over the past few months, and special thanks for the successful end to what was almost a disaster yesterday."

The applause started softly and then grew in leaps and bounds.

The general raised his hand for silence.

"Ladies and gentlemen, I would ask that each of you find your assigned seats now, as we have a very special guest that would like to have a little of your time this evening."

Everyone seemed to find their seats, except Dennis. He was making his way between two rows of tables, when he noticed a movement at the other end. It was General Estes, waving his arms and motioning for Dennis to join him.

"Sorry, son, I forgot to tell you that you would be sitting with us."

The long tables were in rows, and all in the same direction, with the exception of the general's table. His was perpendicular to the others, between them and the stage.

Dennis was seated between General Estes and Diane, with Thelma on the other side of the general. Sergeant Tensley and

Shirley were seated on the other side of Thelma, while Ed Mitchell and his sisters were beside Diane.

After everyone was seated, the general returned to the stage and directed his arm toward the entry doors.

A man stepped into the aisle, and with a booming voice announced, "Ladies and gentlemen, please rise and welcome, the president of the United States, Ms. Cynthia Alexander."

A surprised gasp came from the crowd as all rose from their seats. The two white entry doors opened, while the band softly played "Hail to the Chief."

All eyes were fixed on the doors. A tall woman, wearing an elegant, one shoulder gown, entered the room. She walked down the aisle, poised and confident, with her aides beside and behind her.

A thunderous round of applause, which grew with each graceful step she took, greeted her. The military personnel that were present saluted. She walked over to General Estes and his wife, and stood between them, raising her arms to the crowd, gesturing for a moment of silence.

A gentleman handed her a microphone, and the room became quiet.

"Ladies and gentlemen," the president began, "thank you for your warm welcome to this wonderful occasion. I truly feel honored to be here, among some great American heroes. I am here tonight to honor each and every one of you, my friends and my fellow Americans. There is nothing political on this agenda; this is about you, this group of fine men and women that will go down in our history as heroes. You are writing an unprecedented page in the history of our great nation. Let me rephrase that. You're not writing a page, you're writing a book, in the history of our great nation. I know that you have faced – and conquered – some severe trials and tribulations, the most recent being one that could have had horrific consequences. We have something here that is so far ahead of its time, and I still find it almost impossible to believe. But it was all of you, each and every one that has accomplished the impossible."

She paused for a few seconds, looking over the crowd, and then continued.

"I applaud each and every one of you. I want you all to know that the American people's hearts and support, along with mine, are with you all. It's only a small gesture, but to show my appreciation, I wanted to spend some time with my heroes … all of you!"

A roar of applause rose in crescendo, and the huge crystal chandelier started singing.

Looking up, the president again raised her arms for silence.

"Whoa there, let's not bring the house down on us!"

Laughter broke out, and it too finally subsided.

"You know," she continued, "you are truly an amazing group. I want to recognize each and every one of you, individually, but as your president, I can't spend the last two years of my term to stay here and do so."

Laughter and applause followed. She waited patiently for it so subside.

"It has been my privilege, to give eight years of serving you as vice president, and now, two years as your president, and the good Lord willing, four more after this term!"

A standing ovation followed with everyone showing their support for their beloved president. After it died down, she resumed.

"Tonight, I'm going to do some unprecedented things. I feel the American people would approve. I know you all want to get to some dancing, so I am going to ask you to please hold the applause until the end of each presentation. First of all, I sincerely wish to recognize the true heroics of a team of civilians, led by Master Sergeant Albert Tensley. Your selfless acts were above and beyond the call of duty, and you are my heroes. Would Master Sergeant Tensley and his crew please stand and be recognized?"

Dennis noticed that the general had seated them all at one table.

Tensley, blushing, stood up and motioned for his men to stand with him.

Once more, the applause reverberated throughout the room as the civilian crew stood alongside their leader; their embarrassment evident in their flushed and surprised faces.

The president joined in the applause, and once again, waited patiently for it to subside.

"I personally thank you all for your contributions throughout this operation. Since you are civilians, there is only one way that America, and myself, can prove that we mean what we say. Each of you will receive the presidential Commendation of Service and Heroics for your service to your country."

Applause once more inundated the ballroom.

The noise settled and the president continued, "Over and above that, once your job is done here, I guarantee a very substantial bonus to each of you also!"

Not only applause rang throughout the ballroom, but whistles and shouts sounded as well.

"Thank you again, gentlemen."

Tensley and his crew shook hands and patted each other on the back, then returned to their seats.

"You know, I said I was going to do some unprecedented things tonight. Well, I'm just getting started. I feel, in my heart, I'm doing the right thing. I seem to have a habit of doing things that I feel are right. As far as holding your applause until the end, I see it can't be done and I understand, these people deserve every bit of it. Master Sergeant Tensley, would you please come forward?"

With a surprised expression on his face, he stood. In smart military moves, he made his way around the tables and came to within three steps of the president. He stood at attention, saluted, and waited.

"At ease, Sergeant—seeing your stiff back is making mine hurt."

A ripple of laughter and some applause came from the guests.

Tensley stood at ease, eyes upon the president.

"Just this evening, I heard you're planning on getting married, Sergeant Tensley. Is that correct?"

"Oh, yes, ma'am!"

"Is your lady present, Sergeant?"

"Yes, ma'am, she is."

He pointed toward Shirley.

"That woman sitting right there, beside my chair, ma'am."

"And what is her name, Sergeant?"

"Shirley, ma'am. Shirley Alexander, ma'am."

"Well, well, another Alexander. We may be kin Shirley."

Shirley blushed and nodded her head.

"Shirley, honey, would you please come up here and stand beside your man."

Shirley scrambled to comply, and quickly made her way to her future husband's side.

"You certainly have good taste, Sergeant!" the president remarked.

"Yes, ma'am!"

"Sergeant, I have heard nothing but outstanding reports on your performance as a leader. You are a genius in all aspects of your job, and have performed with a degree of excellence far beyond what the military demands, and expects, from its people. I want to congratulate you, on your receiving the highest presidential commendation that there is."

Sergeant Tensley swallowed hard and tried to keep his emotions in check.

"My deepest and most sincere appreciation, ma'am."

Smiling, the president picked up a card from the lectern and passed it to Shirley.

"Shirley, would you do the honors of pinning those two silver bars to your future husband's collar? As of now, he is no longer Sergeant Tensley, but 1st Lieutenant Tensley, of the United States Air Force."

Tensley's surprise could not be masked. His jaw dropped as he looked from the president to the two silver bars in Shirley's hand.

Shirley smiled, and with happy tears streaming down her face, pinned the bars in their appropriate place.

Tensley could not hold back, the tears came. Pure tears of joy. He took a deep breath. "Ms. President, ma'am, thank you. This is a dream come true."

The president, shaken by emotion herself, grasped his hand with honor.

"You earned it, Lieutenant Tensley."

She then gave Shirley a kiss on the cheek.

"Congratulations on your wedding honey."

Shirley smiled at her.

"Thank you, ma'am."

"You're dismissed, Lieutenant."

Lieutenant Tensley did an about face, as the applause roared through the room.

President Alexander took some tissues from her suit pocket, and wiped her eyes.

"General Estes, would you bring your beautiful wife and join me up here, please."

The general stood and offered his arm to Thelma. They walked up the steps and stopped in front of the president.

"Now what are you up to Ms. President?"

President Alexander laughed.

"General, you have kept me awake for so damned many nights, that I don't know what a full night's sleep is anymore! And to top that off, I heard that your wife thinks you're an old coot!"

"Oh, just now and then, Ms. President," Thelma interjected.

Laughter boiled through the ballroom.

The general, acting flustered, said, "OK, OK, now what's the point?"

The president could not contain her laughter.

"The point is Thelma might not think you're such an old coot if you had a pay raise. Thelma, would you pin this extra star on your man, please?"

Thelma took the two stars.

"Just think, my General, more shopping money!"

Laughter filled the room, and then more applause as she placed the third star on each collar.

"Thanks, Ms. President," the general said timidly.

"Oh, go sit down, you old coot! I just had to try that out — it did sound good, didn't it?

Thelma kissed her husband on the cheek.

"It works for me, Madam President."

Dennis glanced over at Diane. She seemed to be enjoying the evening, also. Their eyes met and held for a second. He wasn't sure if the smile and nod was meant for him, as her attention went back to the stage.

"Ladies and gentlemen, please don't read the shortness of my presentation to the general in the wrong way. He is so much more than a friend to me. If we had gotten into a long presentation, we would have been hugging and crying on each other's shoulders for the rest of the night. He is more than deserving of any award, or reward, that I, or America, could ever give him. If I ever needed a person to find a needle in the haystack, he would be the first one I would call, because I know he would find it." She paused. "Even if he had to sit on it!"

Another roar of laughter flooded the ballroom.

Once it abated, the president continued.

"Speaking of needles, we have had one stuck in our fannies for quite some time now. Even though we felt it, and knew it was there, we couldn't locate it. That made it really hard to remove it. There's one person in this room tonight, whose sharp eyes and sharp senses, are almost solely responsible for finding that needle, and removing it from our butt."

Applause began, but the president held her hand up, silencing the crowd.

"By now, I'm sure most of you are aware of the mess that took place at this facility yesterday. Just so you all understand how serious it was, I'd like to take a few moments to explain it to you. One military officer and two very high ranking dignitaries that represent our country committed an act of treason. This act was as bad as, if not worse than, Benedict Arnold."

She looked around the room, all eyes were on her.

"If they had succeeded, then there was a great possibility that our country would not have recovered from it. A certain captain was commissioned to steal one of the craft that you are building here. He was to fly it to China. These three traitors were to receive one billion dollars each for their treacherous act. There is so much more I could talk about right now, but to keep this as brief as possible, I'll forego the details."

The president sipped her water and continued.

"This morning, I went to the Chinese Embassy. I went to the ambassador instead of having him come to the White House. I didn't want him soiling the White House lawn, let alone the White House itself. I made him aware that we knew of their plan, and that it had failed. I also gave him six hours to gather his complete staff and be on a plane, out of this country, or else we would escort them to the Mexico border."

Every person in the ballroom rose to their feet, and applause rocked the room.

Once the room quieted again, the president continued.

"We have removed one needle, but there are many more on the way. There will be more. The last thing the ambassador said to me as I was leaving was that America will not succeed with this new craft. They know of our ship, but I don't believe they have any idea of its capabilities, or our plans for it."

She took another sip of water.

"I'm going to get back to the program now. I am going to bend and break all the rules tonight. I have personally spoken to General Estes and one other person about this, and we all agree that this reward I'm about to give, is going to a person who is most deserving of it."

Everyone's eyes were on the president and you could have heard a pin drop in the room.

"Will Lieutenant Colonel Diane O'Hara please come forward?"

Dennis saw a look of shock on her face. She looked as though someone had knocked the air out of her.

Two female voices rang out, "Our Hero!"

Cathy and Mattie clapped, and the room followed suit.

As the noise subsided, Diane stood frozen.

The president, smiling broadly, spoke again into the microphone.

"Lieutenant Denehey, as her commanding officer …" A pause and then she continued, "What the hell is taking place in the military, when a lieutenant commands a colonel? Oh, well, please escort our colonel up here; she seems a little nervous."

Laughter and applause rippled through the room again.

Dennis moved Diane's chair, stepped beside her, and offered his arm.

Diane smiled and could barely get the words out, "Thanks, I need this."

As they started toward the president, everyone in the room stood and applauded them. Dennis, in military fashion, escorted Diane to the president. He then disengaged his arm, did an about face and started back to his chair.

"Whoa there, Lieutenant, I ain't done with you yet," the president said with a drawl. "You have a job to perform here."

The people laughed at the president's humor and Dennis, once more, did an about face. He stopped about two feet behind Diane, and stood at attention.

The president shook her head and stepped around Diane. Taking his arm, the whole room heard her say, "For goodness sakes, you two, please relax!" She pulled him up beside Diane, "Now, stand there, Lieutenant; this beautiful woman isn't going to bite you. You should be so lucky!"

By now, people were using napkins to wipe away tears of laughter.

Diane and Dennis looked at each other, shrugging slightly.

"Colonel O'Hara," the president said, "I can't seem to find the appropriate words to thank you, because you deserve so much more than a simple thanks. So, as president and a fellow American,

I am going to say thank you in my own way. Lieutenant, would you please remove the colonel's rank from her collar?"

From Diane's right side, Dennis took one step forward, a left turn, one step which put him in front of her, and then a smart left turn to face her.

He smiled at her and winked.

"May I, ma'am?"

He reached for her collar.

Diane could only nod. The words wouldn't come without tears. Dennis removed each of her lieutenant colonel insignias, put them in her hand, and returned to her side.

"Normally, Lieutenant, as her commanding officer, you would do the honors, but, for my own selfish reasons, I am going to pin these on her myself," the president said, holding up two gold stars.

Dennis was shocked, but very happy for her. When he looked at Diane, he saw the tears rolling down her cheeks.

The president stepped forward and pinned a gold star on each lapel. She hugged Diane and whispered to her, "I'm proud of you, lady."

She took Diane's hand and turned to the audience.

"It is my pleasure to introduce General Diane O'Hara, of Delta Blue Squadron."

Every person in the room stood, and the applause rocked the house once again.

The president said softly to Diane, "I see you have your own fan club out there."

Cathy and Mattie were clapping, whistling, and waving, as tears ran down their cheeks.

Diane wiped tears from her eyes.

"Yes ma'am, they're two very special fans."

"So I've heard," the president remarked, squeezing Diane's hand.

President Alexander let the applause roll on, and when it went to a dull roar, she moved back to the microphone, with Diane.

"I know I'm taking up your time here, but I've never had the pleasure to honor so many in one evening. I would not be doing them justice if I did not do it properly. I will say, there had better be a cold bottle of Chablis out there with my name on it when I'm done here. And I'm not done yet."

You could tell the audience loved their president, and her sense of humor.

"I am sad to say that I neglected a portion of my duties as president last year. I was aware of a situation but neglected to investigate it completely. I have no excuse for that neglect. Tonight, I am here to right an injustice done to a great man, a genius of a man. He alone, with his insight, his inventiveness, expertise and knowledge, has jumped this country at least twenty-five years into the future. Without him, I guarantee we would not be here tonight. This facility would not yet exist, and you would not have these jobs.

I would not have the opportunity to recognize him tonight either —
Lieutenant Denehey, get the hell over here!"

Laughter and applause broke out once more, as the flustered
and embarrassed lieutenant came forward.

"Dennis, I see in my mind that you will go down, not only in
aviation history, but also in world history; as one who has contributed so much. You have contributed not only to your country but to
the world and beyond. You have contributed to the freedom of all
people, and you are certainly my hero. General O'Hara, would you
please do the honor of removing those cotton picking lieutenant
bars from his collar?"

"Yes,ma'am!"

She smiled, and smartly moved into position.

"May I, hero?" she asked, while reaching for his collar.

Dennis smiled.

"Please do."

She removed them, and then took her place beside him once
more.

"General Estes, as his commanding officer, I would gener-
ally allow you the honor, but what the hell! I've been so selfish
tonight; I think I will just continue!"

The general waved his hand.

"Please, be my guest. I'll just finish my Chablis."

The president walked around the podium, and stood in front
of Dennis.

"Sir, I am so sorry I neglected my duties. You are now reinstated to your original rank of colonel in the United States Air Force. You will receive complete back pay, plus a little promotion."

She held up two bars, with stars on each.

Dennis was choked with emotion and tried to hold back the tears.

As she pinned the bars in place, she whispered, "I know the S.O.B. deserved it, but try not to punch out any more senators."

She kissed Dennis on each cheek and whispered to him again, "I got wind of a wedding on the horizon. I better get an invite."

"You bet," he quietly answered, as she took his hand and introduced him.

The place literally went wild. They applauded, stomped their feet, and some cried for joy, including Diane.

Finally, the president had to raise both hands, asking for silence.

"Wow! Is our new General popular or what? General O'Hara, I'm going to be a tattle tale here. We usually don't tell who recommended the ones we honor, but under the circumstances tonight, I think it is appropriate. I think both men deserve a kiss from you. One is General Estes — but wait, you might want to ask Thelma first."

"Nah," Thelma shouted, "she can kiss the old coot!"

As the laughter rippled through the room, Diane went over to the general, kissed him on the cheek and whispered, "Thank you so much, sir."

The president continued, "That was number one. The other gentleman who was partly responsible, and who happens to be very handsome and unattached, is our newest two-star general, Dennis Denehey."

A deep blush came over Diane's face as she approached Dennis. She gave him a peck on the cheek and stepped back.

From somewhere in the audience, a man called out, "Come on, general, you can do better than that."

"I would hope so," the president exclaimed.

Blushing even more, Diane faced Dennis and whispered, "Do you still intend to resign, sir?"

Dennis whispered back, "Not if you consent to marry me."

Diane threw her arms around him and their lips met.

Applause and whistles resounded through the room.

The president shook their hands and reminded Dennis, "Don't forget that invite."

When the room finally calmed, the president continued.

"Tonight, we are honored with the presence of three more very special people. They are continuing in the footsteps of one of the greatest men in aviation history. This man inspired his family so much, that even the women and wives became military pilots. They will continue his legacy, and make a legacy of their own, as part of our family, and part of Delta Blue Squadron. Please welcome, three of Billy Mitchell's great-grandchildren – Ed, Cathy and Mattie Mitchell! Ed, would you please escort your sisters up here?"

She turned to the audience.

"Ladies and gentlemen, Colonel Edward Mitchell, United States Marine Corps pilot, now a member of Delta Blue Squadron."

Applause roared throughout the room once more.

"On his left is Ms. Cathy Mitchell—and on his right, Ms. Mattie Mitchell, both civilian pilots. They are going to put forward their best efforts for a spot in Delta Blue Squadron."

The room welcomed them both with applause.

"By request from General Estes, I landed in Texas to bring them here. I personally checked their records and determined they were more than qualified to be members of the United States Air Force. With the power vested in me, as President of the United States, I swore them in and waived the requirements of academy, academics, and basic training. They will receive all of their instructions here, and I'm sure everyone will help them. I feel they will succeed in their quest."

She turned to Ed. "Colonel Mitchell, here are four gold bars to show they are now commissioned officers in the United States Air Force. Since there is no place to pin them on those beautiful dresses, you may attach them to their uniforms when they are fitted. Congratulations and good luck to all of you."

The girls hugged the president and Ed shook her hand, thanking her.

The room roared with approval and the president stepped down, heading toward General Estes' table.

She picked up a glass of wine from the table, drank it quickly, and had it refilled. Everyone went back to their tables and the band began to play.

Dennis and Diane sat huddled together at their table, trying to talk privately. It wasn't meant to be. General Estes, Thelma and the president took seats opposite the two lovebirds.

"The president is staying overnight," General Estes said after the small talk played out. . "She has only seen the preliminary blueprints and wants to see the real thing."

"I don't see why not," Dennis replied. "You're the boss and the one getting the financing. When would you like to see our babies, ma'am?"

"How about when everyone recovers from tonight's party, say about ten, ten-thirty, at General Estes' office?"

People were starting to gather around their table, wanting to meet the president.

Dennis leaned over and whispered to Diane.

"Want to skedaddle, or stay around?"

"Your place or mine?"

They both eased away from the table while everyone else was busy talking with the president.

His eyes fluttered a few times, his mind kicked in gear and he looked around the bedroom. Diane's bedroom!

"Oh hell," he muttered to himself. "She did it again!"

Diane opened the door to find Dennis slipping on his pants.

"Forty-five minutes until time for your appointment with the president; coffee is ready."

Dennis opened the door for Diane, and they stepped into the reception area of General Estes' office. Two men with crew cuts in dark gray suits stopped them at the door.

"General Estes and the president are expecting Generals O'Hara and Denehey," Dennis said.

Their uniforms and general stars made no difference to these men. One of the men looked at a clipboard.

"Please pass, generals; they're waiting for you."

After they were out of hearing range, Diane said, "Those guys never smile; don't think I would want their job."

Within minutes, they had started the tour.

In the hangar, General Estes and Thelma escorted the president to the first craft in line.

"Oh, my gosh, it's unbelievable; they're huge!"

The president slowly walked around, and under the ship, inspecting every detail before returning to the group in the aisle.

"It's an engineering masterpiece — very impressive. Thelma, could I borrow your husband for a moment? I have a couple of things I need him to explain to me."

As the president and Estes walked toward the ship, Dennis noticed a movement and glanced toward the maintenance office. Lieutenant Tensley's back was toward the hangar and he was bent over a long layout table looking at blueprints.

"Thelma, would you excuse us for a minute? I want to go see what Tensley is up to."

"Sure Dennis, you two go ahead. I'll stay here and keep these two guards out of trouble."

Dennis took Diane's arm and eased her toward the office.

"Tensley, it's a day off for everyone, what the hell are you doing here?"

"I could ask the same of you two. Glad to see you though, because I didn't get the chance last night to congratulate you. When Shirley and I finally broke away, you two had disappeared."

"Congratulations to you also, Sarge. Oh that's gonna be hard to get used to, I mean Lieutenant. There goes my nickname for you, darn it.

"I won't hold it against you, General."

"So why are you working on your day off, Lieutenant?"

"I'm concerned about the micro-switch for the wings. Is it possible to replace the two micro-switches with one, so that if one did, or did not, retract or extend, they would both remain in the same position?"

"Yes, it's possible, but what I'd rather do is reinforce it, or have the factory make one of a material that won't break."

"OK, I'll get right on it."

"By the way, Lieutenant, I had no idea about you and Shirley. You two make a great couple — she's a sweetheart."

"Thanks, Diane. I'm one lucky fellow to have her. What about the president? Wow, she is sure a down-to-earth person. She is one hell of a president."

From behind them, a voice said, "Why, thank you, Lieutenant Tensley. That's quite a compliment."

All three turned to see the president, along with General Estes and Thelma, standing in the doorway, smiling.

Tensley snapped to attention, mostly out of habit.

"Stand down, Lieutenant, relax."

She walked over to Dennis.

"I would love to see the cockpit area, or I guess I should say the flight deck, as it's called now. From the drawings I saw, it reminds me of the Enterprise on 'Star Trek.'"

"Certainly, just follow me, ma'am."

Dennis sent Diane, the president, General Estes and Thelma up the elevator first.

"Step aboard," Dennis said to the president's two stone-faced guards.

"We will remain here, thank you."

"OK, let's go Tensley."

After a complete walk around, the president sat in what would be Captain Kirk's seat, if it were the Enterprise.

"I really like this. Is this magnificent flight deck as functional as it looks?"

"Yes ma'am," replied Dennis. "Functional and very efficient. The Enterprise deck was designed for this craft, no doubt in my mind."

"Wonderful. I think this is the appropriate place to ask you something, Dennis. I need your opinion on something the general and I discussed after you and Diane so quickly disappeared last night."

"Um…sorry about that ma'am," Dennis replied, blushing.

"Not to worry, hon, we could have called you but we decided to sort of hash it out first. The general and I feel that if you can get enough of these ships ready in a couple of weeks, we could eliminate the cost of the entire Shuttle and Concorde programs. We would like to hear what you three think about this."

"Well, it's a bit of a surprise," Dennis replied. "As far as having the craft ready, I feel we can have eight of them ready within a couple of weeks. What do you think, Lieutenant Tensley.

"OK, basically," Tensley began, "that means six more, which is more than possible. It's up to Dennis if they all get a test flight in that time plus training the pilots. That might make it a tight squeeze for two weeks. If they all perform as well as No. 2, with minimal write-ups, I can visualize having ten ready."

"Excuse me," Diane interrupted. "I have a couple of questions, please. I'm assuming, Madam President and General Estes, that due to the fact that our enemies are now well aware of our ships, there is no further need to masquerade launches with the

Concordes, and therefore we will use our ships to carry the Shuttle loads to the space station. Am I correct?"

"Exactly," the president replied.

"OK, now, besides practicing VTOL, how long will it take, in flight hours, for me to qualify for either flight testing, or to be a qualified instructor, Dennis?"

"If yesterday's performance is indicative of your flight abilities, I would say about five to eight more flight hours. I would like to observe you in other aspects, and other maneuvers, and there are still some systems in the craft you need to familiarize yourself with."

"You mean before I solo?"

"Yes, but let me explain this. When you solo, you will be in your ship alone, but I will be your shadow. Our brand new lieutenant here came up with a brilliant system which is being installed in each aircraft. When I am shadowing you, and if I believe you have put yourself in a compromising situation, I can take control of your ship and correct any errors, then return control to you."

"Magnificent!" The president exclaimed. "That alone would earn your bars, Lieutenant."

"Thank you ma'am," Tensley said.

"How many solo hours, Dennis? Diane asked.

"That's up to you and the individual pilot. Again, going by your performance yesterday, no more than three to four hours, and all pilots should have no less than two hours of actual space flying time."

"You mean in actual space, in orbit?" the president asked.

"Yes, ma'am," Dennis replied. "We have been restricted so far, other than the three flights I made, and space flight is considerably different from flying within the earth's gravitational pull."

"Madam President, again an assumption on my part — I have a feeling you set two weeks for a reason?"

"Yes I did, and you're a very astute person, Diane. I have a great concern for the safety of the Space Station. The Chinese and Russians have had a hell of a lot of missile and aircraft movement lately. The Russians have been moving some new missiles that we haven't seen before. They both know the importance of the Space Station to whoever controls outer space. We have been carefully maneuvering the Space Station, but no matter what we do, we can't protect it from earth. I want that shield installed quickly. If we lose the station, we lose a hell of a lot."

Everyone was very quiet, absorbing the information that the president just gave them.

"I have an idea," Tensley said, "but I need Dennis' thoughts on it. All right, our ship's cargo hold is more than large enough to store a totally fabricated, and ready to use, shielding device. Is there sufficient power in our ship to totally activate the shielding system?"

"Yes," Denis replied. "Our No. 3 could do that, even in the stand-down mode."

"I thought so," said Tensley. "I believe it would be more than feasible to assemble one of the units in our ship. We could then position the ship on the vulnerable side of the Space Station and let it act as a part of the shield, until we can install another system on the Space Station."

"Whoa, whew, hell," Dennis almost yelled. "I see where you are going with this, Sarge. Hold on and let me run a couple of calculations. Oh, wow … brilliant, Lieutenant."

Everyone was silently waiting for Dennis to finish his calculations.

"Yes, yes. We let No. 3 idle, kill Nos. 1 and 2, figuring escape velocity, fuel consumption, plus power flight to catch the Space Station, and then match up with her outer perimeter. Yeah, then open the cargo bay doors for maximum shielding exposure for our ship, and we could then shield our ship, and a third of the station."

His fingers flew across the calculator and then he finally stopped.

"We would have almost two weeks of fuel to run No. 3, more than enough time to install the control unit in the station. Yes, Lieutenant, a brilliant idea; it would work."

"How long before it can happen?" the president asked.

Dennis scratched his head, mostly out of habit.

"There's still the pilot problem. We have to get the ship to the Cape and get the shielding unit unloaded from the Shuttle. They can unload it before we go, but that's one pilot there. The techs that were going on the Shuttle can assemble it in our cargo bay, and make it function on the ground. We have to locate the other two shielding units, as we were going to send them both to the moon. We can divert one to the Space Station to be installed there by the techs. So one pilot to protect the station, one to fly in the shielding unit, the techs, and I do want another pilot to protect what we can't shield with our ship that is docking with the Space Station."

"I'll have the techs and the unit brought here from the Cape," the general stated.

"So we need three pilots, three co-pilots, an engineer, and at least one weapons person for our guard ship.

"I'll locate the other units within the next hour or so and get them on a plane ASAP," the general said.

"Let me know what you need," the president said, "and you'll have it."

"Tensley, where does No. 3 stand, as far as readiness for a test flight?" Dennis asked.

"Three and four are on the test jacks as we speak. They started wing and landing gear retractions on both yesterday, before last night's interruption. I can call two men in to complete those today. I'd like for them to run continuously for four to five hours, and if nothing fails them, they are good to go for test flight then."

"OK," Dennis answered. "Pilots and crews are our biggest obstacle right now. Ed is next in line. If he passes muster, that will make it Diane, Ed and I. I feel that Colonel Kutchmark will be OK, but that leaves us short two co-pilots. I won't go into space without that second seat."

"Since the shuttles are being done away with, maybe some of the astronauts might be interested in our program," Diane stated. "We could get enough for second seats for the mission."

"No, not really," Dennis replied. "I've been through that program and it's a whole different world. The Mitchell sisters would be a better gamble; someone totally green like that would take to our systems much quicker. Madam President, I can't tell you an exact date right now, but I'll do my best to give you something firm in the next forty-eight hours."

"I understand your predicament," she replied. "Just don't gamble with lives."

"No ma'am, I promise we won't."

"Well, General Estes, I'm out of here. I need to get back to D.C. Please escort me to my plane and I'll get out of your hair."

They watched as the president and her group left the building.

"Sarge, see if you can find two sober men to continue the retraction tests. I hate to call them in, but we need to put forth a real effort."

"Sure thing, catch you two later," Lieutenant Tensley said, and left in a hurry.

"Want to go fly, Diane?"

"Does a bear poop in the woods? I'll get my flight suit and helmet. Where are yours?"

"On my dining room table. Would you mind bringing them back with you?"

The door to the elevator opened, and Diane stood face to face with Mattie and Cathy.

"Hey there you two, come with me; I have lots to tell you!"

They all went after the flight suits while Diane explained what she and Dennis where about to do.

"Can we go along with you and see the ships? Shirley is going to fit us for our uniforms," Mattie said.

"You haven't seen the ships yet?"

"No," Cathy replied. Ed has had his nose stuck in the tech manuals every minute, getting prepared for his first flight."

"Good idea. You two may want to do the same every chance you get. I have a feeling that you're going to go sooner than anticipated."

They passed through the security station, manned by two Marines instead of the usual security guards.

Mattie was the first into the hangar. Diane smiled when she heard Mattie's screech. The two sisters stood side by side, but Mattie slowly sank, sitting down on the floor, mouth and eyes wide open, as she looked up at the huge ships.

Cathy, finally finding her voice, whispered very hoarsely, "My God, you could put a couple of 747s in that baby."

Mattie finally found the strength in her legs to get up. She ran to the front nose landing gear and shouted, "Damn it! I just can't wait!" She patted one of the huge twin tires as if it were a loving pet.

Diane turned to Cathy, "Honey, I've got to go. You will find Shirley through those double doors over there." She pointed in the general direction and took off trotting toward the big hangar doors.

##

Three hours and forty-five minutes later, Dennis asked, "Had about enough?"

Diane glanced over at him, thought for a second and then asked, "How about a couple of VTOLs before we quit?"

"A glutton for punishment, aren't you? OK, set your heading for north by northeast, our VTOL pads are about eight miles from here."

Diane turned the ship to Dennis' heading, at about 500 feet.

"Darn, some of those dunes are really high," she commented.

"Yeah, you're just coming into the canyon area now. It goes for miles and miles. When we have time, we practice speed flight in these canyons."

"Just like fighter tactical flying?"

"I guess," replied Dennis, "I never got that far. I was accepted into NASA before we got into that. There," he pointed, "off to your left … there are four pads, about two miles. Want me to do the first one?"

"Sure," Diane replied. "Let me see how it's done the first time so I'll know if it's anything like the VTOLs I flew in Texas."

"I didn't see that in your records."

"It won't be. I was just along for the ride a few times. I got the hang of it real quick and made half a dozen drops before they cancelled the tests. If they could have just synchronized those props, it would have been a great ship."

"I hear the Navy is using some of them now," Dennis answered.

"Yes, the Marines are too, but I heard they are really leery of them. They are still having mechanical problems."

"OK, here we go," Dennis said. "I'll tell you things as I do them. Start toward the pad, about 200 feet, maybe a mile out. Start changing the thruster cowls down a couple of degrees, coming in at 120 knots. As the thruster tilts downward, she will slow down. Keep dropping her down. Get down to about 100 feet, halfway to the pad, down to about 50 feet, about 80 to 100 yards from pad, creep in. Thrusters about 80 degrees down.

"As you come onto the pad, you should be almost a full 90 degrees, gently cut the power. Those candy striped posts out there are the center-of-pad markers. Whichever one is in front of you should be right in the center of the ship's nose. If you turn your head ninety degrees, one should be even with your nose, not the ship's nose. If it is, then your ship is squarely over the pad. Then you gently cut back your thrusters until you're on the ground."

Diane felt a slight bump as the huge ship settled on the pad. Dennis cut the throttles on 1 and 2 back to idle.

"Sweet," Diane said, "very sweet."

They discussed the procedure for a bit and Dennis asked, "Want to try it?"

"Naturally."

"OK, you might want to snug up your seat belt. The first time I did it, I was like a bouncing ball, bounced off one main gear to the other a few times."

Engines 1 and 2 purred to life as Diane increased the RPMs. She watched her instruments, making sure the two engines stayed balanced. Dust swirled around the giant ship as it gently rose from the ground — ten feet, twenty feet, thirty feet. Diane gently brought the nose around, into the wind and brought the throttles up. She put the thruster cowls up to eighty degrees and the monster moved forward. She put them to 50 degrees and then to 25 and the ship moved swiftly into the skies, at 280 knots and climbing for the heavens.

"Smart aleck," Dennis said, smiling at her.

"Beginner's luck," Diane came back.

Just as she leveled off at 6000 feet, a beeping sound echoed through the flight deck.

"What the hell?" Dennis yelled, as he turned to his radar screen. "Damn," he said, "someone just entered the no-fly zone. They are low, damn; they're flying the canyons and buzzing the tops of the sand dunes. Get us up to 25k quick!"

Diane was in motion as he said it.

"Tower, number 2 here, we have low-flying bogies coming fast, we are going to twenty five thousand."

"Roger, number 2. They came in under the radar. The sensors picked them up coming into the no-fly zone. Fighters are scrambling but the bogies are bouncing up and down, off the radar screen; they are so low."

"They are about fifty miles out and coming fast," Dennis replied.

"Tower to number 2, they are climbing toward you, get the hell out of there number 2."

"They just fired off a missile," Dennis said.

Diane jammed the throttles forward and the thrusters leaped to forty-five percent. The ship went to 1900 knots in a flash. Diane watched the missile on her screen and saw it wasn't gaining ground.

"What are you doing, Diane? Get us away from those missiles!"

Diane keyed her microphone, calmly saying, "May I show you, sir, a maneuver I learned as a fighter pilot?"

Dennis glanced at her; eyes squinted, not really in the mood for trying new things with the missile on their ass.

Diane was as calm as if she was sitting in a rocking chair watching the sun set.

"OK, I'm game, Diane, but we have no fire power on this bird yet."

"We do now," Diane responded.

She brought the ship around, watching the heat-seeking missile come around in an arc behind her. The bogies appeared on her screen and she came in behind them at almost 2000 miles per hour.

The two bogies were flying a wide formation, and as Diane passed under the belly of the rear bogey, Dennis saw it go wildly out of control. The sonic wind had robbed its engine of air and it had a flame-out. Dennis could see the pilot struggling to get it out of its spin. With no success, the pilot ejected.

Diane went over the top of the lead plane and it swerved sideways from the rush of wind. They both watched as the missile literally went up the tail pipe of the lead plane, and exploded.

"My, God," Dennis said. "You smoked them both."

Diane brought the ship back down to just under 200 knots. Dennis reported to the tower and gave the location on the pilot who ejected.

"Want to go back and get him?" Diane asked.

"No, let the choppers get him. Let's go home."

Diane turned the ship and brought it to 200 knots.

"May I VTOL back at the base?"

Dennis gave an unbelieving look in her direction, amazed at her calmness.

"Coming from the west, approximately half a mile, on the north side of the runway is a pad. Help yourself, General."

She smiled at him but said nothing. She saw the pad as she approached the runway and made her VTOL landing as if she was born to do it. Dennis felt a great pride in her as he thought, *at first I thought I had a tiger by the tail, now I know I have a full-blown hurricane.*

Diane taxied toward the parking spot. On the ground level, General Estes and the Marine captain in charge of security were waiting.

"In the briefing room," the general said in a quiet, somber voice.

Dennis, Diane and Tensley, sat at the long table in the briefing room. They could tell the general was not a happy camper as he picked up the phone and called the tower.

"Whoever manned the radar during that attack has ten minutes to get here. Make sure it's done."

He hung up the phone and leaned back in his chair, looking at the three sitting at the table.

"You were attacked on supposedly secure property. I want your version of what happened, Dennis. I got one screwed up version from the tower, which made no sense at all and before I call the president I want the facts. What kind of planes attacked you?"

Dennis took a deep breath.

"I have no idea, sir. If they were American, I did not recognize them."

"MiG 21s," Diane offered.

"Impossible," General Estes replied. "No MiG is allowed in this country."

"Easy enough to find out, sir," Diane calmly stated. "I had the forward cameras rolling. I was going for my first VTOL landing and, due to the dust; I turned on the cameras to help judge my position prior to accelerating out. I believe the whole confrontation will be on the film, sir."

"Lieutenant Tensley, would you please get that film and set it up. The picture will tell the story."

"Yes, sir!"

Lieutenant Tensley got up to leave. Just as he reached the door, a uniformed young woman with five stripes on her sleeves came in. She walked to the table where the three generals were seated, and saluted.

"Sergeant Kawalski, reporting as ordered, sir."

"Were you the radar operator watching the confrontation earlier?" General Estes asked.

"Yes, sir."

"Could you please give me a summary of what you saw, Sergeant?"

"We could not see them on the radar, sir. They were flying the canyons upon approaching the no-fly zone. We were not aware of them even being around until the no-fly zone sensors picked them up. Those planes had to fly over the tops of the dunes, and then drop back into the canyons. I picked them up on the screen each time they topped a dune. They had to be good; they were splitting hairs at 500 knots.

"Apparently, number 2 was lifting off and all three were showing on my screen. Number 2 reported the attack before I could notify them of the bogies. Then, everything happened so fast. There wasn't even time to speak. The lead bogey fired off a missile at number 2. One second, number 2 was there, and the next second a streak across my screen, outrunning the missile.

"Next thing I saw was number 2 streak around, behind the bogies, with the missile on her tail. Number two then went under the rear bogey and was so close that they became one blip on my screen. Then I saw number 2 go over the top of the second bogey and he disappeared completely from my screen."

General Estes shook his head.

"Is that how you remember it, Dennis?"

"Yes, sir, that pretty well describes it."

"Damn, Dennis. There are not any weapons on your ship, you take on two bogies that have missiles, and you took them both out. What made you go under one and over the other?"

Smiling, Dennis replied, "General, I was a spectator. General O'Hara was the pilot, sir."

The general's eyes went wide and his eyebrows lifted as he looked at Diane. A faint smile crossed his lips and he shook his head again.

"I should have known; Dennis has never had fighter training. So tell me, General O'Hara, why under one and over the other?"

Calmly, Diane explained, "I was flying almost three times the speed of sound and felt my turbulence would send him out of control. When I came up, in front of him, I starved his engines of air and he flamed out. At the low altitude they were at, I knew there would be no time to recover from flame-out even if he got it back under control. I went over the lead bogey to deliver the package that he had sent to me."

Tensley came in and set up the video that verified everything that had been told to the general. After it was over, everyone sat quietly for some time, thinking. The general was amazed at Diane's reaction time in the film.

"General O'Hara, you are amazing indeed. I basically knew what was going to happen after what the sergeant told me, but I could not even think that fast. Dennis, did you allow General O'Hara to do this?"

"Indeed I did, sir. I have every confidence in her. She is much faster in learning and functioning than I am. We have a first class pilot here, sir!"

"I can see that," replied the general. "You all are dismissed now. I will call the president and see what we can find out."

Back in her apartment, Diane grabbed two beers from the fridge. She tossed one to Dennis and sat down at the dining table, pulling off her boots.

"Lord, getting those heavy things off feels so good."

She rubbed her feet and looked over at Dennis, studying him.

"What?"

"Nothing, just looking at you. Did you mean what you said about me being a pilot on the squad now?"

"Sure did, you really proved yourself today."

"What about solo time?"

"If you need solo time, I need a hole in my head. Unfortunately, the training we all need is space flight time. The urgency of getting the shield on the station is going to prohibit any space time, until the day we send them all three up at once."

"Well, I ran some calculations. We already know that the higher we fly, the less thrust we need to maintain a desired speed. From studying NASA flight reports – this is just a rough calculation – but today I bounced to almost three times the speed of sound at forty-five percent. In space, I would have gone to almost 10,000 knots, or better, at thirty-eight percent. I have no idea how fast we could go at thirty-eight percent, if I brought number 3 online. The amazing thing, and something to be cautious of, is the instantaneous reaction. I no sooner thought of it, then pushed all the right controls, and was at that speed. Jeez, I was behind those monkeys way too fast."

"I know," Dennis replied, "that's why I've never pushed her much faster than fifty percent. I have no idea where I would go. I designed all the systems for instantaneous response because I have no idea what we will encounter in space. Even half a second could mean the difference between life and death."

Dennis' shoulder phone buzzed.

"Denehey," he responded.

He listened. "Damn, that's a shame; it would have been nice to have gotten him alive."

He laughed and then looked at Diane and winked at her.

"Oh, yes, sir, she would have made him open up."

A perplexed look came across his face.

"The pilot was a woman? Yes, sir, that's something we need to find out, if it's possible."

He listened again.

"I'm sure she will appreciate that, General. Yes, sir, briefing at 0800 hours, with everyone concerned."

"What's up?" Diane asked.

"Well, the pilot that ejected is dead. The canopy didn't go and she ended up ejecting through it. They inspected the seat and came to the conclusion that she was too tall for the seat safety bar to protect her head. The force of the canopy against her head shattered the helmet and collapsed her spine. Had she survived, she would be a foot shorter."

"So, the pilot was a woman? Not likely Chinese, being that tall, so either they didn't adjust her seat bar height, or she was over six feet tall."

"They confirmed she wasn't Asian; and those were MiG 21s, by the way."

"I knew that," Diane replied. "We were taught to recognize the aircraft configurations so that if we were in a dogfight, we would recognize our own and not shoot them down."

"Diane, you beautiful woman, you are a computer."

Laughing, Diane asked, "How do you like making love to a computer?"

"Well, I never thought a computer could satisfy me, but apparently I was wrong. There's one that can ... just perfectly."

He leaned over and kissed her gently. He sat back and looked into her eyes, wondering how he could be so lucky. Then he saw it.

"OK, spit it out, Diane. I know there is something else eating at you. What is it, honey?"

"I have been doing some thinking. Whoever we are dealing with had to know we were airborne. They knew we were there and came right for us. It takes a good runway to get a missile loaded MiG off the ground, and for them to know when we are up; they have to be close to the no fly zone. If there are more out there, we need to find them."

"I'll call the general. Hell, there's a lot of old abandoned air fields around that the military used that would be perfect for what they need. If they are hidden, they could be hard to find."

"Not anymore. Remember, we now have human body infrared equipment. If a human is hidden in a building of any kind, he can be found, even if in shallow underground."

"That's right," Dennis said, "I forgot about that. OK, let me call the general."

"One more thing, I wonder if they know how many ships we really have. It doesn't make sense for them to try and destroy just one. I wonder if Knull or the others passed that info on to the enemy. Dennis, the other day, when you were testing number 2, you were all but in the hangar and damned well high enough to be seen on a radar scope within, say, 250 to 300 miles. Did you test number 1 in the same area?"

"No, I didn't. I was so unsure of my ability to handle the bird, that when I was airborne, I kept her at about 100 feet until I got out to the test site, which was about 150 miles north."

"That's why they couldn't find the facility. They probably thought it was somewhere out there, who knows what the hell they think or know."

Dennis frowned.

"Damn, why didn't I think of that? I could be responsible for jeopardizing everything here."

"Not so!" Diane shot back. "Your total thought mechanism was tuned to developing, perfecting and testing our ships. Security of everything was up to others, not you."

"Now here you are, realizing all this."

"Well, hell, yes," she replied. "Who would have dreamed that the vice president of the United States, a senator and a captain, would betray their country? Especially over a weapon that they knew would destroy them and their country if it got into enemy hands? I can't even imagine MiGs close enough that would dare attack us here. So the question remains—do they have any idea how many ships we have? It just doesn't make sense for them to let us know of their presence, sacrifice two planes, and two pilots; unless they believe we only have one ship. I'll bet my stars, they think we only have that one."

"I don't get it. What difference does it make if they know we have one, or fifty-one?"

Diane got up and went to get two more beers from the fridge.

"Think about what you just said—what the repercussions would be if they thought we had fifty-one ships," she said, handing him a beer.

Once more, the light turned on in Dennis' head.

"Damn, Diane, how do you figure these things out? Hell, if they even think we have four or five, it would be all out war. It would scare the hell out of them."

"So, they have no idea. They think that number 1 is a proto-type, unproven and experimental."

"Damn, damn, damn," Dennis whispered. I wonder if those pilots could see that big no. 2 on our vertical and radioed it to whomever?"

"Not a chance. The lead bogey that fired was fifty miles away. With heat seekers he felt he had a good shot from that distance. We were just a blip on his radar, a visual was impossible. Hell, they didn't even have time for evasive moves before I smoked them."

"That's for sure," Dennis replied. "I assume you have a suggestion, Ms. Computer?"

"Um, excuse me, but I'll prefer Mrs. Denehey, when it happens, and yes, I do have a suggestion. Get all those numbers off those ships. Every test flight will be in No. 1."

"OK, I see where you are going with that. Put a number 1 on each ship. Honey, slip on some shoes. Let's go see the general."

"What? Tonight?"

"We have to, sweetheart. Everything you said makes sense and our planned strategy has to change. Even just a few hours could save our butts."

He called General Estes. Thelma answered the phone.

"I assume you wish to speak with the old coot? He's soaking in the tub. Just a minute and I'll take him the phone."

"Yes, Dennis, what is it?"

"A face-to-face, General, sorry."

"Won't it wait 'til morning?"

"It might, but I believe every hour is very important if we are to comply with the president's wishes."

"Oh, all right," the general moaned. "It better be good, I was just going to have a couple of beers before going to bed. Hell, come to our apartment, I'm still going to drink one."

Thelma answered the door and when she saw Diane, she grabbed her hand and pulled her inside, hugging her.

"Oh, honey, I am so glad you are safe. You are everyone's hero. I heard how you smashed those bogeys today, bless your heart."

Diane, blushing, asked, "What do you mean everyone's hero?"

"Just what I said, honey. You are a hero. You didn't think it would be kept a secret here, did you?"

The general yelled.

"Bring them in Thelma, quit BS'ing."

"Oh hush, you old coot, here they are. I'm having a tall Vodka Collins; what would you two like?"

"Same as you, please," Diane said.

"Just a beer for me, please, Thelma."

"Sit here, you two," the general said, as he sat down at the end of dining room table. "What's up?"

Diane quickly revealed her thoughts to the general, and he listened intently. When she finished, the general leaned back in his chair, looking up at the ceiling. He finally glanced at Diane and Dennis.

"Yes, it could mean all out war if they suddenly see three ships at the Space Station. Dennis, hand me that red phone behind you please. I can't make a decision on this without her; she is the boss."

When the sleepy voice answered, she was heard by all over the speaker phone.

"You old coot, this better be important, I was hoping for a full night's sleep for once."

The general shrugged.

"You'll have to be the judge of the importance, Cynthia. I have Dennis and Diane on the speaker phone here. Diane has presented us, with what I would call a major situation."

The pleasant voice of the president said, "Hello you two! I am so very proud of you both, for doing a superb job on those two planes this morning. Now, Diane, what's that old coot talking about?"

Diane, once again, began her story. When she got to her theory on the close-by airfields, the president interrupted.

"General Estes, do you have available equipment and manpower to check all of those possible sites?"

"No, Cynthia, I don't," he replied.

"After we hang up, I'll get the right people on it and have planes in the air by mid-morning, at the latest. Sorry to interrupt Diane, go on please."

Everyone listened as Diane completed her picture for the president.

"Madam President," Diane added, "please understand, this is just a hypothetical theory here."

"Maybe so, Diane, but I see a lot of reality in it for sure. My goodness, there has to be an end in sight somewhere. I believe you are correct about what would happen if they knew how many ships we have. Three showing up at the station would be a dead give away. Why the hell didn't my Secretary of Defense see this coming when I told him of our plans for the station?"

"I guess I had better get my ass out of bed and get some heads together," said the president. "I'll see if we can find a solution to this without starting a damn war."

"One more question before you go, Madam President?"

"Sure, Diane, go ahead."

"OK, but please don't laugh. Hear me out. During World War II, a lieutenant in the Army Air Force completely fooled the enemy by playing the numbers game with the Germans. He had so few fighters left, and Luftwaffe was creeping closer to his base every day. He knew the enemy would be coming after his base, and knew he could lose his few men and all of his planes in a single raid. He set it up so that the twenty planes he had left would stay in the air around the clock. He would send up a dozen and when they returned, the others took to the air. Out of the ones that had returned, some would be repainted quickly and the numbers on them changed. It took three and a half days. He flew his men and planes into the ground, but with the Luftwaffe being in bad shape also, it being near the end of the war, after those three and a half days, they decided to look for easier pickings. It gave the lieutenant time to rest his men and planes and then he got some new planes and pilots and did a counter-attack. So, my question is, what if we ringed the station with at least eight ships, and every few hours send two back, change the numbers from, say, six to sixteen, eight to eighteen, two to twenty and so on? I know they have to be watching the station with telescopes."

"Ah," the president replied, "I see. Eight ships deployed with more back ups available, poised to jump off to wherever ... brilliant! Girl, you should be here in D.C. with me; it's absolutely a brilliant idea. We could demonstrate our new laser cannon in the ships somehow also. Hell, I'm definitely going to consider it and talk it over with my defense people, within the hour."

"I hate to throw cold water on the fire, Madam President," Dennis interrupted, "but Diane has apparently forgotten a primary issue – pilots. At the very most, I can only have four, counting myself and Diane. Yes, I can probably have ten or eleven ships in a week, but pilots, no way."

"I'm sorry, Dennis, but I did think of that," Diane said. "You revealed something the other day, that up to then I was not aware of. You said you incorporated the ship to ship capability, where the pilot could not only fly their ship but also another one by remote. If Ed and Deana qualify, we can temporarily suspend the VTOL training and you teach us all how to control another aircraft as well as ours, which would make four pilots...eight ships."

"Is that possible?" General Estes asked.

Dennis, blushing and shaking his head, answered.

"She has done me in yet again. Hell, yes, it's more than possible. It's all computer controlled. There is a keyboard on the side of the console and all you have to do is punch in a couple of command numbers, push send, and the other ship will respond."

"I'm calling in some people now," said the president, "and I'll have that base located and taken out."

Diane once more interrupted.

"Ma'am, I have another suggestion. I would locate the base, but hold off on taking it. I would keep the fighters handy, but the base might be more beneficial to us to be left alone. When the time comes to put eight or ten in the air, they would be there to pass on info to their bosses."

"That's it," General Estes said, loudly, "I'm retiring. This damn woman thinks faster than a computer."

"Hold off on retiring, General," the president said, laughing. "We still need you. Besides, who else would let me call them an old coot? I'll talk to you in the morning, sometime. Damn it, no sleep tonight again."

Diane rolled over in her bed, reaching, trying to find Dennis. Her eyes fluttered and then opened … he wasn't there. She yawned and took in the aroma of fresh brewed coffee. Smiling to herself, she snuggled back down under the covers. It wasn't long until she heard the door open.

"Hey, sleepyhead, rise and shine."

She pushed the covers from over her head to see Dennis standing there, breakfast tray in hand.

"Mmm, coffee and doughnuts; you're spoiling me."

She sat up in the bed and noticed that Dennis was fully dressed. He sat the tray down in front of her and sat on the edge of the bed.

"How long have you been up?"

"A couple of hours; I'm going to meet Tensley in the hangar at seven."

"What time is it now?" She asked, as she picked up her coffee from the tray.

"It's 6:30. I have been working up a system to implement your plans. I'm going to ask a favor of you, sweetheart."

"Umm, I love being asked instead of ordered; what is it darling?"

"I know it's probably too soon, but I think it's worth a try. I'm going to have Tensley pull Nos. 1 and 2 out to the engine start area. I'm going to take Ed and Deana out to the flight test site in No. 1 and start checking them out. Will you take Mattie and Cathy to No. 2? That entire area is under camouflage and you can't see it from the air. Instead of reading the manual, see if they can grasp the console and pilots functions. No need to cram it; they will grasp it easier at a slower pace."

"Do you want to try engine startup?"

"You be the judge of that, honey. You will know when they are ready to move on. I'm thinking of having them in the 2nd seat, as an assistant to Ed and Deana, if they can qualify. On the trip to the station, Tensley will be your co-pilot and flight engineer. He can fly one of the ships damn good, and he knows every system as well, if not better, than I do. On the trip, there will also be a weapons person and radar operator on the manned ships. They have all been well trained and just sitting around now, waiting to fly. I also want to see just where we stand on the other ships as far as flight readiness is concerned. If No. 3 is ready, I can test fly it."

"Hey, don't push it hon. I've trained people and I know how stressful that is, and then trying to test fly too, I don't want to be a widow before I'm married."

He bent over, kissing her tenderly. He pushed a lock of hair back behind her ear.

"I'll see you in the briefing."

He smiled at her and left.

##

"Sarge," Dennis said, then quickly caught himself.

"No worries," Lieutenant Tensley interrupted. "Let's just consider it a nickname; I'm used to it, too."

"That sounds good to me. OK, here's what's going on. We had no idea we would be going this soon. You are the only trained flight engineer we have. Do you know of anyone we can recruit, who is fairly familiar with the ship's critical systems?"

"Most of the techs have been cross-trained and most would give their eye teeth to go. Hennesey would be my number one choice, Donaldson next, and Dimbrowski, all damned proficient."

"Good, if they will go," Dennis replied.

"Oh, they will. In fact, they will be thrilled to death and honored if asked. What about the unmanned ships?"

"No, no qualified pilot on board, no one will be in them."

Three days later, Nos. 4 and 5 had been test flown; No. 6 was to be later that afternoon.

In the cafeteria, Diane and Dennis discussed the mission over dinner.

"Ed and Deana are ready to go and very well qualified," Dennis said. "I filled them in on the mission and they are happy that they get to be a part of it. We really got lucky to have so many great pilots here with us."

"On that note, I have a favor to ask of you. Will you take Cathy with you on the test flight for No. 6 today?"

"I guess so, but why?"

"Let me ask this first. Where do I stand on proficiency?"

Without hesitation, he replied, "Top gun, far ahead of anyone in the squadron to date, and better than me."

"I think Cathy could quickly be as good, if not better, than I am. She is amazing, Dennis. Once she grasped the functions of the control systems and pilot's requirements, there wasn't anything she couldn't do. With every question or situation I put before her, she would go to the controls and mock maneuver the ship without incident. She is quick to realize situations and respond with calmness and no hesitation."

Frowning, Dennis studied Diane's analysis of the young woman.

"What about Mattie?"

"Oh, she will make it, a little slower to grasp but I have to admit, I got partial to Cathy and damned quick. I'm afraid I worked with Cathy considerably more than with Mattie."

Dennis again analyzed Diane's statement. *Straightforward and honest about her work with the girls, plus she has been correct about everything else. I think I can surely believe her assessment on Cathy.*

"OK."

"OK what?"

"We will give her a shot on No. 6."

Diane leaned over and kissed him.

"There is one condition though. Set a cotton-picking date for our wedding!"

Relieved, she answered, "Hell, that's easy, any time you want."

"Oh, no you don't, I set the condition; you don't get to reverse it."

She squeezed his hand and stood up.

"We can discuss it in bed tonight. I'm going to get Cathy, and a helmet."

As Dennis watched her leave, he thought to himself, *there's no way I'll ever get ahead of that woman.*

Dennis took No. 6 to the test site. It had a huge No. 1 painted on it to confuse the enemy. He put it through the rigorous testing for thirty-five minutes before radioing Diane.

"Coming to get her," was his message.

He took Cathy to the test site and showed her a couple of touch-and-go landings, and then a couple of fast climb outs. He then landed.

"Want to try the touch and go?"

"You bet," she said.

She was smiling, but Dennis thought she looked a bit apprehensive.

"OK, over here is your seat, then."

He took off his belt and climbed out of the seat.

"I can do it from here," she stated, very confidently.

"I'm sure you can, but this is the pilot's seat, and for all intents and purposes, you are now the pilot. Besides, that seat looks more comfortable and I need a little rest."

Sitting in his seat, Dennis stretched out, leaned back and watched as Cathy buckled in and prepared herself.

"What is the liftoff speed?"

"Minimum, 120 knots."

"What's the next step, before rolling?"

"Line ship upon runway, lock nose gear?"

Dennis had, on purpose, stopped crossways on the runway.

"OK, line her up, east to west."

Cathy throttled up on No. 1 engine for a right turn. The ship easily slipped into a right hand turn with Cathy steering the nose gear. She throttled No. 1 back to idle as the huge ship lined up. Cathy noted on her gauge that the gear was centered and locked it. The ship was pointing due west.

"Do your thing," Dennis said, leaning back and yawning.

Cathy locked together the throttles for Nos. 1 and 2 and advanced them evenly; watching her instrument panel and making sure everything was in the green. The ship started to surge, wanting to go, but Cathy didn't release the brakes until a given thrust percentage. When she finally released them, the ship hurtled down the twenty-mile-long runway. Intent on her instruments, Cathy waited until they were at 130 knots to lift off, the nose gear came off the runway at 10 degrees up and the large ship was off the ground. She brought the nose up to 20 degrees and the ground swiftly disappeared below them.

"Level off at 4,000 feet, drift right 3 degrees at the count of ten, start a long 180-degree turn, line her up and lets touch and go at 150 knots," Dennis said.

"Roger," Cathy replied.

An hour and a half later and still yawning, Dennis said, "Let's go home, sweetheart."

He stretched out thinking, *I don't believe this crap. I wonder how Mattie is going to embarrass me.*

When Cathy set the brakes and shut it all down, she was looking for some reaction or comment from Dennis. On departure from the ship, not one word still. Diane and Tensley were waiting.

"Well, how did she do?" Diane asked.

"Perfect landing, sir," Tensley commented.

Dennis, inwardly smiling to himself, stopped and turned to the three behind him.

"I didn't land it, Sarge; Cathy did. And you know what, Sarge? I'm getting sick of this crap."

All three were surprised at his remark.

"What crap, sir?" Tensley asked.

Dennis waved his arms in the air, at the ship.

"I design the baby, we build it, I test fly it, and what the hell happens?"

"What, sir?" Tensley asked, cautiously.

Dennis said, vehemently, "Two — not one, but two women get in that monster of mine, not the tenth time, not the twelfth time, but the first damn time, and it listens to them. They can fly it better than I can."

His voice went into a pitiful, soft tone.

"What am I doing wrong, Sarge?"

That's when the three burst out in laughter. Diane grabbed Cathy, hugging her. She turned to Dennis.

"Sweetheart, don't be upset; we still love you. Just how good did she do?"

With a big smile on his face, he hugged Cathy, too.

"Excellent Diane, she did excellent, but I need a case of beer now.

General Estes and the other pilots were in the briefing room when they came in.

"OK, what's the occasion for all the happiness? I heard you all when you came into the hangar."

Dennis put on his sad face.

"General, I'm afraid we are being quickly replaced."

The general cocked his head to the side and got a very serious look on his face.

"Dennis, have you been drinking and flying? That was the longest damn test flight yet."

"Face it, General," Dennis responded. "Women are replacing us men."

The others were trying to stifle their laughter.

"That does it, damn it, you're all drunk!"

Everyone, including Dennis, could not hold it any longer. They burst out laughing.

Diane explained it to the general and they all had a great laugh again.

"OK, so we have a new pilot…that's wonderful," General Estes said.

Dennis, finally calming down, said, "Two to four more hours of flying for her and she'll be good to go. She definitely has my vote as far as her overall skills."

"So now we have you Dennis, Diane, Mitchell and Mitchell, and Kutchmark. Five pilots, and to think we had only one a short time ago. That, for a change, is progress. Diane, the president and all of her advisors are in favor of your suggestion. They see no alternative, unless we scrap the whole program and let our enemies catch up. They're not going to even consider the latter as an option."

Diane sobered up on that announcement. She had given much thought to this program, especially after she and Dennis had discussed the fact that, with America controlling outer space, they could, with such a force as Delta Blue, actually dictate to the world if so desired. She voiced her concerns on this to General Estes.

He got up, paced back and forth. He turned to the small group after considerable thought.

"I understand your concerns. I can only ask, is there another reasonable solution? If the U.S. waits for one of the other nations to do what we are doing, then they can dictate to us. It will, in my view, be up to the people of the United States to make sure we don't have a tyrannical government. Can any of you give me any other solution? If you can, I am all ears. I will be happy to hear them. If you decide that you cannot, or don't want to participate in this action, you are free to go."

No one moved. General Estes waited, allowing all to absorb his message.

"I assume we are all in accord as far as completing our mission?"

Everyone nodded in agreement.

"All right, Dennis, this is what the president wants. A timetable for when we go, within a twenty-four hour range. On your declared schedule, our national defense will go on red alert. Around the world, where we have armament, they will be ready to take whatever measures are needed. The few actual countries that are supposedly our friends will be notified of our intentions, but only after you have solidified your positions, securing the station. Two of our most trusted friends, the U.K. and the Aussies, will be informed the day before. They are already aware, but it will be done formally. Their national defenses will also go on red alert, the same time as ours. The Secretary of Defense is drawing up a positioning chart, of places on earth, where we know strike or nuclear missiles are aimed at us. Each ship that is free of not having to protect the Space Station will be assigned areas, including the U.K. and Australia. Should any offensive missile be launched from your area, you will do your best to destroy it with your laser cannon. That aid will be of great importance, to lessen the load on our anti-missile system to destroy what you can't."

General Estes passed out papers around the table to each person.

"So, General Denehey, the Secretary of Defense would require a chart from you as to what number of ships will be available for that mission. The president wants a daily report as to each day's progress and a projected plan. I know you are personally tied up with test flights and pilot training. Assign the report project to whomever you wish, but please, make sure the reports are as accurate as possible. I am to report to the president at 1800 hours.

Sitting in his chair, the general asked, "Can you give me a partial for today's report Dennis?"

"Yes, sir," Dennis replied, "but no sense keeping everyone here. General O'Hara and Lieutenant Tensley, please stay. The rest of you are free to leave, get some rest, briefing at 0800 hours sharp."

Dennis, Estes, Diane and Tensley gathered around the planning table. None of the others left; they joined the four at the planning table. With a smile of approval, the general winked at Dennis.

"Glad you all decided to stay. Diane would you take notes, please."

Dennis dictated his report to Diane, from memory.

"First of all," Dennis began, "I have neglected to train sufficient flight engineers. For this mission, Lieutenant Tensley will assign civilian flight engineers in whom he has complete confidence. Lieutenant, please put together a list of the civilians who will be involved, along with their flight records, medical records and all other pertinent paperwork. Any who have not had a medical exam in the last sixty days will need one immediately. They are very important to us. Make sure there are standbys also. As of today, Nos. 1 through 6 craft are ready to go. Should only those six be available at launch, I will pilot No. 1 to the station, and I will go to one of the other ships to be named at a later date. No. 2 will be flown by General Diane O'Hara, No. 3 by Colonel Ed Mitchell, No. 4 by Colonel Deana Kutchmark and no. 5, I believe, by Lieutenant Cathy Mitchell."

"Believe?" asked General Estes. "Does that indicate doubt?"

"Not at all, sir," Dennis replied. "If No.7 and No. 8 are go for test flight, she will accompany me for further observation in her performance. Should she perform as well as today, then I must surely admit defeat at the hands of a young pilot."

Everyone laughed. Ed and Mattie hugged their sister.

"So," General Estes added, "if those are the only six at launch, then that leaves No. 6 to be towed.

"More or less," Denehey agreed. "As of now, General O'Hara will fly Nos. 2 and 6. Colonel Ed Mitchell will have the Space Station's new shielding device and laser cannons on board. Once he is docked, all the technicians will unload. Once he is unloaded, he will then separate and be available for the Secretary's defensive positioning. Colonel Kutchmark will take the defensive posture where the shielding can't protect the station. General O'Hara will maneuver No. 6 into position so I can tether it to the station, near No. 1, acting as a defensive ship to anyone watching."

Diane interrupted.

"Shouldn't you have a spacewalk partner, just in case? Trying to tether those ships alone is dangerous."

Knowing that Diane wanted to protect him pleased Dennis.

"Diane, when this overall mission began, we had months to prepare. Due to the urgency of what is laid out for us, it's cut to days now and everyone will take the training ASAP. Until then, I am the only one qualified, and I have spent several hours on space-walks at the station, assembling it. The only ones trained, so far, are the technicians who will assemble everything on the moon. Let's move on, but thank you for your concern, General O'Hara.

He looked at Diane's face, seeing the wrinkled brow and the worry in her eyes. He loved her so much at that very moment. He winked at her and when his crooked little grin appeared, she smiled back at him.

"If all goes as I expect, Lieutenant Mitchell will take defensive posture on the Secretary's chart. Once again, when Ed undocks, we will, as of that time, have three defensive ships. In fact, no matter how many ships are up there, that's the most we will ever have during the critical phase. If the enemy is going to attack, I expect it will happen within the first twenty-four to thirty-six hours. I don't think the techs can install the station's shielding device in that time."

"You are probably correct on that, Dennis," General Estes remarked.

"Sirs," Lieutenant Tensley interrupted. "I know I'm not considered qualified, but I've flown No. 1 under General Denehey's supervision, and I feel that I could take No. 6 up. With General O'Hara's ability to take over if I got in trouble, it should be no problem. I feel that I, along with a weapons person, would be more useful in a true defensive pattern."

General Estes looked to Dennis.

"Yes, he could, possibly. He handles the ship quite well, so he could move the ships about as needed. Thank you, Lieutenant, let's sleep on that. We may have time for a few hours if the ships are available. Where are Nos. 7 and 8 at present, Lieutenant Tensley?"

"Both are on retraction test stands now, sir. If all is well, they will be off the stands at 2300 hours. I'll come back then and put them through their paces. If all goes well with that, they will be ready for test flight in the morning."

Dennis took a deep breath.

"OK, if they are ready in the morning, those hours will be dedicated to Lieutenant Mitchell for further performance observations. That's as far as this report can go, General."

"Perfect," the general said. "The unit from the cape, with the technicians, will be here at 2000 hours tonight. They will assemble it in No. 1 tomorrow. The other new unit for Ed's ship is scheduled to land here at 0930 hours in the morning. Now, I'm hungry, tired, and thirsty."

Laughing, he added, "I'm dismissed and so are you, good evening."

Everyone laughed at the general for dismissing himself.

As they were leaving, Mattie approached Dennis and Diane.

"Excuse me, sir, ma'am, there's not a chance that I will be participating in this mission, is there?"

Dennis and Diane saw the sad expression on Mattie's face. Diane put her arm around Mattie's shoulder.

"Let's go eat and we'll discuss this."

The three walked out, arm in arm.

"Do you think Mattie was satisfied with our answers last evening?" Diane asked Dennis, as they sipped their morning coffee.

"She, like Cathy, is very confident in herself," Dennis replied. "She is a little disappointed, but I think you will find out today, while you two are training, if it has affected her in a negative way. Tensley said Nos. 7 and 8 are on the engine pad, so everything is good there."

After the briefing was over, Diane, Dennis, and Tensley were huddled together and going over a few details from the meeting.

Diane glanced into the briefing room. Ed was at the back of the room talking to Mattie and Cathy. Both of the girls were listening intently, to whatever Ed was saying. Diane nudged Dennis then nodded toward the Mitchell family. Dennis looked their way and a smile crept across his face.

He whispered to Diane, "What is it Ed says; we are a family? I think they will do just fine."

It was 0945 hours when Dennis came back from the test flight and picked up Cathy. They were done in about three hours, with Cathy shutting down No. 7. Diane, Mattie and Tensley were watching as Cathy and Dennis rode the elevator down to ground level. They seemed to be in an intense conversation.

"How goes it?" Tensley asked.

"No. 7 is ready to go," Dennis replied, cheerfully.

"How did Cath do?" Mattie asked.

Dennis laughed and rolled his eyes.

"I really don't want to talk about it. She can tell you all about it while I take No. 8 out. I'll be back in a while, Cathy."

He waved his hand behind him as he walked off.

The four moved back to the hangar door, a safe distance away, so Dennis could start the engines. Looking down on them from his pilot's seat, he saw all three were listening to Cathy's animated description of her earlier ride. He smiled, cranked the engines, and taxied out. As he glanced down, he saw the three girls waving and Tensley gave him a thumb's up sign. Dennis returned the thumb's up and took note of the time, 1310 hours. At 1340 hours, Dennis came in and picked up Cathy.

At 1730, Tensley came over Dennis' radio.

"Sir, there is a lady here who wishes to talk to you."

Diane asked, "Say, are you guys on an intended date or what?"

"Cathy, you better assure her that there is no hanky-panky going on here. She'll believe you, more than me."

"No ma'am, he is being a perfect gentleman, but if you ever decide to throw him out, let me know, OK?"

"Enough chatter," Dennis came back, "we should be in, oh … say … in an hour or so."

An hour and ten minutes later, Diane called him again.

"Dennis, what are you doing up there?"

"Diane," he replied, "I'm trying my best to confound this confounding woman. I can't seem to do it; it's embarrassing."

"Keep on trying. I'm having a world of fun," Cathy said.

At 1855 hours, Cathy set the brakes, as Tensley put chocks under the wheels. Dennis and Cathy were laughing when they stepped off the elevator. Cathy ran over to Mattie and Ed and hugged them both. Dennis walked over to the group and gave Diane a peck on the cheek and a hug.

"OK, how did it go, Cathy?" Diane asked.

"I think it went perfect," she replied.

Dennis shot back, "Ah ha! Not so perfect!"

"What did I do wrong, sir?"

"What altitude do we monitor from the hangar to the test site and back?"

Cathy replied, "one hundred and fifty feet, sir!"

"Well, you were at 149 feet all the way back. How's that, Lieutenant?"

Cathy grinned.

"Sir, if I'm not mistaken, you were fiddling with the low level altimeter. If we go check it, would it by chance be off by maybe a foot?"

"You see? You see?" Dennis yelped. "I can't get away with anything with this woman! Yep, it's off a foot."

In Russia, others were also hard at work.

The young Air Force captain was reporting to his superior.

"It's quite evident they are having considerable problems with their prototype. They test fly it almost every day and are apparently having trouble with it."

"There were no damn problems with it when it took down our two planes," the superior officer screamed at him.

"Sir," the lieutenant said, meekly, "it could not, in my judgment, have been their prototype that got our planes. Everything happened so fast, we could not follow it on the radar screen. In my humble opinion, they were shot down by missiles."

"Our satellite indicated no missile sites when we were flying over."

"Probably mobile," the lieutenant said. "When do we resume satellite coverage, sir?"

"As soon as our slow-ass scientists finish the new one that has no weapons. That bitch of an American president threatened to recover it if we did not move it. She said if it was armed, she would take the whole damn thing to the U.N. and then destroy it. Our stupid president admitted guilt when he moved it. I would have waited until their precious shuttle got there to recover it, and then I would have hit the self-destruct button to destroy them both. I would then complain to the world that the Americans were in violation of our rights to have satellites in space. But no!—we moved it!

"I agree," the lieutenant replied, "but the premier said that after losing both of our space ships, money was too tight to let the one good operating spy satellite we have left be destroyed. We have to have it. Have our ships and submarines located our two space ships yet?"

"No, I don't think those young jerks could find their own asses if they were in front of their faces. They are not training our new military properly to operate the new sophisticated and technical equipment we have. Any American could run rings around our pilots, and our nuclear subs are rotting away because we don't have trained crews. Another thing that puzzles me is why the Americans haven't tried to find our site in their desert where our planes are."

"Well, it is well hidden and camouflaged," the lieutenant stated. "There are thousands of square miles of sand out there, and that abandoned air field has been an ideal spot for us."

"Have our people reported any unusual flight activity since our stupid pilots were destroyed?"

"No more than usual. There are so many U.S. military air bases in and around White Sands that fighter squadrons are constantly in the air, day and night, practicing."

The superior slammed his fist into the desk.

"Oh, sure! While our planes and pilots sit useless because of the lack of money, and our politicians are lining their own pockets, selling our oil to the Americans, we won't even build a refinery to replace that wreck we have. It breaks down every other damn day!"

The superior picked up a piece of paper, wadded it up and shot it at the trash can in the corner, only to miss it.

"I'm stupefied as to why we revealed our presence in the U.S. by going after that one ship. We should have waited to locate their storage facility, where the prototype is hidden. They may be building others and those stupid Chinese are no damn help."

He walked over to a large map on the wall and put his finger on a spot.

"Another thing I don't understand, surely their storage area must be in the area where they are constantly testing the damn thing. It seems to just pop up from the ground, and onto our radar screen; then disappears."

"An underground facility is the most likely answer," the lieutenant remarked. "Under the sand, it would be easy to hide one."

"Had they not made the Americans aware of our intentions, had we just been patient, we could have eventually located their site and destroyed it, along with that damn prototype. Now, though, they are going to be extra vigilant, particularly in those canyons. They will set more sensors. Our four remaining aircraft will sit in the desert and rot. Those stupid Americans mark their aircraft, but now we have no idea if there are others."

"I thought we had moved some commandos into the test area to watch," the lieutenant replied.

"We did, but after those two planes were lost, the general made them get out, for fear of them being found out. Helicopters flooded the area looking for airplane parts and possible bodies. We know one of our pilots ejected, and the Americans probably have her. I'm sure they know the planes were MiG 21s, so they will be raising hell, accusing us."

"True," the lieutenant replied, "but the Americans are aware that we have supplied China and North Korea with the MiGs"

"I'm going to call the general and see if they will move the commandos back into the test area. I have a suspicion they have at least one more of those ships."

"Why would they build another when they don't know if the first one is usable?"

"Ha, those Americans waste more money in a month than our country spends in ten years on our military!"

"Sir, are we sure that the prototype we see is a spaceship? Remember how we were surprised by the stealth aircraft?"

"No, we aren't sure. Since the KGB was dismantled, we have no intelligence, in fact, we haven't got shit. It could be a fighter bomber; it's sure as hell big enough."

The next three days were hectic for the Delta Blue Squadron. Nos. 9 and 10 were test flown by Diane, with Mattie along for more training. No. 11 was on the retraction test stand, and No. 12 was just hours away from going on the other test stand. Lieutenant Tensley had also gotten in some flight test time and was approved to take No. 6 on the mission.

It was 1800 hours, on the day before the final launch. Everyone involved was in General Estes' conference room. The general set the phone to speaker as their conference began.

"Good morning everyone," the president said. "For security reasons, only the secretary of defense is here with me today. Are you ready to present us with a final launch plan?"

"Yes, Madam President, we are," the general announced. "General Denehey will present it."

"Thank you, Madam President," General Denehey began. "We have eight ships ready to launch, of which six are manned with full crews and two will be unmanned. The crew list and duties remain the same as specified in last evening's report. There will be three ships on the ground, for interchange. The returning ships will be numerically changed as planned. We plan to launch two ships at a time, five minutes apart and going vertical at 35,000 feet. The first four ships will run to the station and link up with it over Hawaii. By the time the station is over east Texas, we should all be in place, and the shield should be operational. Everything else is as presented yesterday evening. Unless you stand us down, we will launch at 1630 hours, tomorrow afternoon. We will be prepared to handle our mission, to the best of our abilities."

"I'm sure you will," the president replied. "I want to commend you all for what you have done. I never dreamed that you folks could accomplish what you have in such a short time. I want you all to know that I am proud of each and every one of you, and I wish you all the best. God speed, and please be careful. Goodnight."

General Estes looked around the table. He could feel the tenseness in the room, and he saw it on their faces.

"All right, do any of you have questions or comments?"

The clock's ticking seemed to get louder.

Finally, Dennis spoke, "OK, folks, 20 hours to liftoff. Get some rest — and I do mean rest. Personally, I don't believe they will attack us on the ground or at the station, but nonetheless, stay sharp and aware. To all of you, civilians and military alike, you are indeed the finest group of people I've had the pleasure to work with. Dismissed."

##

Diane, her head on Dennis' shoulder, quietly asked, "Do you really feel they won't attack? I would not want to see a world war."

Running his fingers through her hair, Dennis considered her question.

"I don't think Russia will, unless China starts it. They will analyze the results, and if China seems to have the advantage, then I think Russia would join them. On the other hand, I think that if China attacked us, and there was a stalemate or a decisive victory on our part, then I believe Russia would sit back and let China fend for itself. You know that neither one of them trusts the other. I also believe that whoever wins the first round, will win it all."

"There are too many ifs," Diane said.

Dennis looked into her eyes and saw the uncertainty hidden in the depths. He kissed her tenderly.

"I love you, Diane, and there are no ifs in that."

##

All were present at 1330 hours, for final briefing. Dennis stood at the lectern, with General Estes sitting to his left, and Diane next to him.

"Good afternoon," Dennis began. "We all know the plan, and three hours from now it will be executed. We all know our positions at launch, but for the sake of jogging our brains this afternoon, one more time. I will pilot ship No. 1 and Deana will pilot No. 4. Both of us will be in defensive posture to the station. Once I dock and tether, my defensive posture is null and void while tethering my ship to the station and setting up the shield. Deana will protect me until the shield is up, then she will take defensive posture over the unshielded area of the station. Are there any questions on that part?"

Everyone was quiet, so Dennis continued.

"Ed will be in No. 3, and Tensley in No. 6. Both will be in defensive posture until Diane arrives with Nos. 2 and 7. They will protect her until I can tether No. 7. Ed docks under Diane's and Tensley's protection. Once docked, Tensley will rotate to the far side of the station, in defensive posture. No. 2, Diane, stays in place in defensive posture, protecting Ed, whose ship won't be under the shield."

Dennis took a sip of water.

"All in defensive posture will be on alert to protect Cathy, as she brings No. 8 to Tensley's area, where I will tether it. She will take No. 5 around to back up Nos. 2, 3 and 4, if needed. We will have plenty of warning if missiles are fired at us, or anywhere on earth. Once I join Tensley in his ship, those in defensive posture other than Deana will be assigned by me to chase and destroy any enemy missiles. Should I not reach Tensley's ship before a situation arises, No.2, Diane, will assign those missions instead of me. Hopefully, Ed can unload in an hour or so and also be available for a defensive posture. That pretty well covers our duties. Any questions?"

He looked around the room. No one spoke.

"OK then, great. If we don't get into a dogfight with missiles, instead of going to Tensley's ship, I will man No. 7."

At that comment, Cathy's hand flew up in the air.

"Yes, Cathy?"

"Sir, in No. 7 you will have no weapons person or flight engineer."

Smiling at her concern, Dennis replied, "Correct, but I can fire from the pilot's position and my radar screen. I have to stay close to No. 1, so that when the station commander is ready to activate his shield, I can move No. 7 to No. 1, and deactivate the shield, so I can get No. 1 out of there. That's when everyone has to be on their toes to protect the station. Once I deactivate No. 1's shield system, I have to release the magnetic tether and close her cargo doors. I'm figuring that there will be no shield for three to five minutes. Thanks for your concern, Cathy. Anyone else?"

Everyone shook their heads. Dennis looked out at the people sitting before him—pilots, civilian volunteer engineers, weapons and radar personnel, and he thought, *damn, am I the only one here who feels uptight? They all seem kicked back and relaxed. Is this how a squadron leader feels before sending his people on a dangerous mission?*

Dennis continued. "I know everything is crucial, but getting from here to the space station is most crucial. Diane and Cathy will probably have the most difficult task. Even with the engineers to help them from the second seat, trying to escape into space, operating and flying two ships isn't easy. If there are any problems at all, bring the unmanned ship back. If for any reason, all three engines fail on a manned, or unmanned ship, the manned ship can dead stick land. You won't have time to worry about the other. Should it be necessary to let the unmanned ship go on, it's already programmed to go on into space and take an orbit, where we can recover it later."

God, please tell me that I'm not sending them on a suicide mission. Hours and hours spent in the classroom, explaining escape velocity, power settings, pictures, diagrams, orbits … Dennis' mind was whirling. There was no doubt in his mind that they were the finest pilots in the world, they had mastered a space ship like no other, with very few hours in training and no hours in space. Dennis' heart beat faster … *no hours in space; what are we doing?*

Dennis inhaled, taking a very deep breath.

"General, would you like to add anything, sir?"

The general solemnly approached the lectern. He looked out at his people, cleared his throat and began.

"Ladies and gentlemen, today, we are not military and civilians – we are all Americans, and I am so proud and thankful for each and every one of you. I am well aware of the lack of training you have received, yet I feel you have mastered a great feat. I have never been in space, but I have listened intently as Dennis worked with you, explaining what to expect out there, what to do, and how to react in the operation of your ships. Talk is one thing; actual experience is something all together different. I believe you have the finest vessel and equipment known to man, and I believe you have been trained well. There is only one thing I can add – a prayer. For those who wish to, please stand.

Everyone rose and bowed their heads while General Estes began his prayer.

"Heavenly Father, we ask that You be with each and every person on their missions today. Protect them, help them, be their rock and their guiding light into the deep recesses of space. We ask that You bring them back safely, and keep Your angels watching over them. Amen. God speed and God bless every one of you."

The general stepped back from the stand and everyone sat down. Dennis, again, looked out over the faces of the brave people sitting before him. He glanced at his watch.

"OK, if there are no questions or comments, everyone to their ships in one hour. First launch is in one hour and thirty-five minutes. Dismissed."

At 1600 hours, the crews were once more doing their pre-flight inspections. All ships were positioned in the order they would launch, side by side. Each would pass in front of the next ship in line, as it taxied to the runway and lined up for takeoff. At 1628 hours, Dennis and Deana were side by side.

"Ready to go, Colonel?" Dennis asked.

"Ready," Deana replied.

Dennis keyed to the tower.

"Tower, Nos. 1 and 4 are ready."

"You are clear," the tower replied.

"Release on eighteen percent, Colonel, 125 lift off."

"Roger," Deana replied.

"Let's roll!" Dennis said, and they released their brakes.

Both surged forward, together. Their nose gear left the ground and the huge ships gracefully departed the earth. Those watching followed the contrails, as each ship climbed into the colder air. When they went vertical, a burst of flames from the afterburners could be seen. In seconds, they disappeared.

Ed and Tensley, in Nos. 3 and 6, taxied into position.

General Estes was awaiting word from Dennis and Deana.

"It's a go for the chase," the general heard Dennis say.

The prearranged message meant they were safely in space and on their way to the station. There would be no further communication from the two unless they were in position, or there was an emergency.

Exactly five minutes after the first launch, Ed and Tensley rolled. They quickly passed through the contrails from Nos. 1 and 4. The general was more worried about Tensley than Ed, but in the exact amount of time as before, he heard Ed's voice.

"It's go for the chase."

The general was now worried about Diane, taking the unmanned ship.

"Lord, be with her," he muttered to himself.

He held his breath as the two monster ships barreled down the runway and smoothly lifted into the heavens. When he could no longer see them, he held his breath again, crossed his fingers, and waited. The seconds seemed like minutes.

"It's go for the chase."

"By God," he shouted, "she did it! Oh, thank you, Lord."

Everyone that knew what she had just accomplished, including the tower people, jumped for joy, clapping their hands.

"That's six," the general whispered, to himself.

Cathy rolled Nos. 5 and 8 into takeoff position.

The general's mind was at work again.

She will do it, she will. I can't imagine what is going through her mind, he thought to himself.

He heard the operator clear five and eight for takeoff, and then heard him add, "Good luck and God speed."

Everyone's eyes were glued on the two ships, in which just a wisp of a woman was in control. The general held his breath again, fingers crossed. When the two smoothly went airborne, there was a great sigh of relief. As they watched the climb and saw the explosion from the afterburners, as if in unison, everyone took another deep breath. Their eyes were glued to the only thing left they could see, the contrails. They waited, seemingly forever, before the soft, feminine voice was heard.

"It's a go for the chase."

The entire tower erupted with cheers and clapping.

General Estes took a deep breath, and said, "Thank you God."

Mattie stood beside him, holding on to his arm, tears streaming down her cheeks.

"Cathy and Ed, sister and brother, the first two Mitchells to fly in space."

General Estes put his arm around her.

"It won't be long honey; you too will visit the stars."

They weren't the only ones breathing easier. Dennis and Deana both listened for each report. Once Cathy reported, they both began to breathe again.

##

The president of Russia was packing his brief case to go home, long after the Moscow sunset, when there was a knock at his door. In an irritated voice, he shouted, "Come!"

His defense general ran into the room as if on fire, and breathlessly stated, "Sir, the Americans … the Americans just launched eight spaceships."

"What? Are you crazy, General? They don't have eight shuttles."

With a painful look on his face, the general said, "Not shuttles, sir, spaceships!"

An incredulous look appeared on the president's face and he roared.

"Impossible! Our intelligence has consistently reported there was only one prototype, and it was not working correctly. Are you sure they aren't missiles?"

"Not missiles, sir. They are ships and at least twice as large as the shuttle."

"Oh, hell, general, that's surely impossible. How could they hide eight launch towers, and do you realize what size fuel booster tanks it would take to put a ship the size you are describing into space?"

"No booster tanks, no launching towers," the general stated, with fear in his voice.

A frustrated, unbelieving president, sat down.

"General, I want you to, very slowly, tell me what was reported to you."

"Yes, sir," the general said.

You could hear the shakiness of his voice.

"Our radar operators, not far from their base in Utah, stated, that at exactly 4:31 p.m. their time, 2:31 a.m. here, two blips, flying formation, showed up on their radar screen. In less than five seconds, they were at 35,000 feet on an approximate 40- to 45-degree climb angle. At 35,000 feet, they went vertical, and he saw what appeared to be a flare from both craft. He thought, at first, they had exploded, but the flare was gone in roughly ten seconds and the two went into space, leveled off, and at impossible speeds, flew toward Hawaii."

"Is there any confirmation of that?"

"Yes, sir. Our nuclear sub stationed off the coast of San Diego confirmed the two heading for Hawaii, sir."

The president leaned back in his chair.

"Continue."

"In five-minute intervals, two more of the same craft took off, until a total of eight were in space, going in the same direction."

Shaking his head and staring harshly at the general, the president quietly, but forcefully, said, "Five minutes. I want you, the head of KGB, and the chief of intelligence here, in my fucking office; now move, damn it."

As the president sat behind his desk and waited, he wondered, *what is in Hawaii, it can't be an attack. Fuel? How can they fly at that speed and not run out of fuel after burning so much just to reach escape velocity? Where in the hell did they get an engine that*

is powerful enough to lift a ship that size into space? Surely, we are
not that far behind in technology. No booster rockets, either? Eight
at one time ... and we can't get one up, much less one into space.

The general returned.

"They are on their way, sir. Shouldn't I put our defense forces on high alert, sir?"

"No, but go yellow until our intelligence can tell me what's going on in Hawaii."

An aide appeared at the president's door. Even though it was open, he knocked.

"What do you want?" the president asked.

"Sir-si-sir," the man stuttered, "I have fu-furth-further information for the general, sir."

"Well, if it's for your fucking general, it's for me too. Come in, tell me."

The man advanced, saluting.

"Get on with it!" the president yelled.

"Our sub, off San Diego, informs us that the fir-fir-first four American ships have rendezvoused wi-with the Space Station. Two more should be at the Station when it is o-over central Arizona, if that is indeed their destination, and the other two will intercept it somewhere over Texas."

The aide ran from the room, almost colliding with the head of the KGB and the intelligence committee chief.

"Come in," the president said, glaring at them. "Sit!"

They took seats around his desk.

"General, please report to these men what you reported to me, and include what your aide told us."

With each word the general spoke, their eyes got wider and their jaws dropped. The president glared at each of them. The general finished the report and no one said a word. The silence was like a thick blanket, smothering them.

The president broke the silence with his deafening voice

"What the fuck do you have to say, you two ... two ... two asses?"

"It's not possible," the head of Military Intelligence said. "We have observed every move they made — everywhere."

"Everywhere? Everywhere, you say?"

The president laughed very loudly.

"You are so full of shit that you and your intelligence stink. The size of the facility needed to make those huge ships, has to be huge itself. It had to have been done in one of their aircraft manufacturing plants, not in the damn desert, as you thought. You are blundering, fucking idiots."

"Sir?" the head of the KGB interrupted.

"What?"

"Sir, since the KGB was ordered to work with Intelligence, we have put agents in and around every aircraft manufacturing facility in the U.S, the U.K., and Australia. They are watched twenty-four hours a day just for this reason, so this could not happen."

"Then someone has been asleep somewhere. Our satellite could find nothing before we had to remove it."

##

General Estes and Mattie left the tower, arm in arm.

"Just one, I wish I had just one."

"One what?" Mattie asked.

"Did I say that out loud? I was just thinking out loud, I guess, wishing I had just one more pilot."

"One more pilot for what, sir?"

Laughing, he answered, "I could really screw with the enemies' heads if I had one more."

"How's that?"

"We know where the base is that the MiG 21's came from. As Diane suggested, we are just keeping it under observation so they can report our launches today. If their fighters attempt to fly, then we are ready to take them out before they get off the ground. If the enemy isn't aware of our launches yet, they will be shortly."

"How would you screw with their heads, sir?"

"Well, you see, we know where all their radar sites and subs are around our country. One of our ships could easily cover the country, from border to border, in a couple of hours. We couldn't go in a straight line though, or they would know it's a single ship. If it was mapped out right, we could make them think we had an entire fleet to protect the whole damn country."

"Hmm," Mattie stopped in her tracks.

The general stopped too.

"What are you thinking about, Mattie?"

"Sir, have you ever seen the maps that airlines use to map their commercial routes?"

"Yes," he said, "looks like a maze, or even more like a spider web. Why?"

"Well, sir, given the info you mentioned, I could draw out such a route and fly it."

"Have you flown one of these birds yet?"

"Diane and I test flew Nos. 9 and 10, and she cut me loose for about six hours. Her only real complaint was my landings. She compared me to General Denehey, but told me that she knew I would improve. I had the same problem with the Lear at first, but Cathy got me straight on that."

The general laughed.

"Dennis will never get both main gears down at the same time."

"Sure he will," Mattie replied. "He does the same thing I was doing; I've watched. Coming around, before final, I was cutting it too short, so Cath got me to widen that turn into final, and get my aircraft lined up a long way before I got to the runway. Works perfect and that's what Dennis needs to do."

"Why are you having trouble with our ship then?"

"It's just the size of the ship. I'll get it. There's a lot of difference between the size of the Lear and one of our babies."

"How long will it take you to draw that map?"

"About ten minutes on a computer, sir."

"Go to the ops computer and nail it. I think you and I are going to fly."

"Really? Super great! When?"

He was hurrying off, but turned to say, "Now, if I can get the permission I need."

He stopped and let Cathy catch up.

"What would be the ideal altitude for a maximum effect on their radar sites?" he asked.

"Well, not jumping any mountains, I believe 10,000 feet would be ideal to create an umbrella effect."

"Great. Do the maps and I'll meet you in the hangar, ASAP."

##

The general took the second seat as Mattie turned engine number one over.

"What's with the black and red on this map here," the general asked, pointing to the map Mattie had produced.

"The red lines represent the large umbrella we can create, while the black lines represent the smaller one. If we want to be effective in making them believe there are several ships in the air, the red tells me we have to cruise around nine to ten thousand knots, while the black says slow down to about six thousand to sixty-five hundred knots."

"Oh, slow down to only 6000 knots? I didn't think of that. Whew, I have never flown faster than 1000. OK, what is the span of this radar?"

"Two hundred and fifty miles, Sir."

"OK, the president is having the FAA order all aircraft to not fly between 8500 and 12,000 feet. Is that enough room?"

"Oh, sure," Mattie replied, as she turned over engines two and three.

"Um, let's take the black first, Mattie."

"OK, let me feed that into the computer."

Her fingers flew across the computer keypad.

"Done," she said. "Good to go."

"What do you mean, done?"

As Mattie taxied toward the runway, she explained.

"Our takeoff is going over that hidden base of theirs. When I set my heading, and climb out to 10,000 feet, I will then flip the computers on and it will take us to the next coordinate on the map, and then turn us toward the next coordinate, until we have finished with our umbrella. So I get to just sit back and relax."

"You want me to watch the radar, just in case something gets into our fly zone?"

"No need, sir, the computers work off the main radar, a thousand-mile span. At 6800 knots, you wouldn't have time to take a breath before we hit whatever you saw on that scope. If the object is passing up or down, the computer will take us around whatever it is, at a safe distance—that way our turbulence won't wreck it. If it's between nine and twelve thousand feet, it will go over it again, at a safe distance. It will make any maneuvers it decides is best to avoid collision. There is not one pilot anywhere that could make those decisions, at that speed."

Back in Russia, the general's aide, once more, knocked on the door during the meeting.

"Now what?" the president asked.

"Sir, our radar sites in Cuba, Mexico and the U.S. have reported numerous aircraft, fitting the description of the previous ones, all over America.

The president flopped down in his chair, staring at the ceiling.

"How could this happen? Did they give any idea of the speed?"

Meekly, the aide said, "As best they can guess, four or five times the speed of sound."

"They guess? Why are they fucking guessing? Don't they know how to calculate speed and velocity?"

"Sir," the aide replied, "they all reported that in their sectors and with the widest their screen can span, that the ship appears, then is gone. It's like someone takes a pencil and drags it across their screen. It's just there, and then it's gone."

"It's quite apparent to me," the president stated, "that we don't have shit. Little or no space expertise, no Air Force, no intelligence anywhere, not a fucking thing!"

Glaring at them, he screamed, "Get out! Get out of my fucking office, you deadbeat assholes. Wait in the reception room and don't you even go to the shit house. Now — out, out, out!"

"Sir, shouldn't we go to red alert?" the general asked.

The president leaned back in his chair and stared at the general.

"How did you ever get your position, you imbecile? We have no idea what weapons those ships have. At the speed they are moving, they could come here, drop a nuclear bomb, and be back in Texas, drinking coffee, before it exploded. Stay at yellow and get the hell out!"

##

Mattie switched off the computer and called the tower for landing instructions. The nose gear softly touched down, and shortly thereafter, a maintenance man parked her and set the chocks.

The whine of the engines slowed to a silence as Mattie removed her helmet. She reached over and gently shook the general's arm.

"Sir, time to wake up."

He moaned and then came quickly awake, staring at his surroundings.

"What … what's the matter?" He looked around. "Where are we, Mattie?"

"We are home, sir."

"Home? Holy hell, Mattie, how long did I sleep?"

"You were asleep about fifteen minutes after the computer took over, sir."

"Did we finish the umbrella?"

"Yes, sir, two hours and thirty-two minutes at 6850 knots."

With a sheepish grin on his face, he asked, "How was your landing?"

"Got both down pretty smooth, sir — didn't wake you."

"Let's go to my office, Ms. Pilot; I need to call the president."

Once in his office, the general dialed the president while Mattie made herself at home, on the small couch against the far wall.

"Good evening, Cynthia."

"Well, Estes, I have to admire you. I believe your idea worked. Our communications people said that 45 minutes into your run, chatter increased everywhere, from Mexico to China, Korea and Russia. They are now decoding the tapes and I'll bet they all think we have a whole fleet out there putting an umbrella over the entire U.S. The FAA is being flooded with calls and complaints about sonic booms."

"Good, I'm glad it accomplished what we wanted it to," the general responded.

"My White House phone lines stay lit up, the different countries are calling, insisting they talk to me. I'll start returning calls in the morning. I can't tell you, Estes, how proud I am of you and your people. How did Mattie do?"

"Beautiful," the general answered. "She didn't even wake me. Uh-oh, did I say that?"

"You old coot. Are you saying you went to sleep and left that poor girl all alone?"

The general pressed a button, putting the president on the speaker.

Winking at Mattie, he said, "Just a short nap."

"Short nap my foot! I'll bet you were sleeping ten minutes from the start."

"Fifteen," said Mattie.

"Ha…is that an improvement or what? I'm going for my nap. Tomorrow's going to be a day of listening and bitching, so I need rest to put up with all that. Mattie dear, I love you and appreciate your accomplishments. Great job today."

"Thank you, ma'am, I'm glad I could contribute something."

"Something, my foot. Your action saved the U.S. millions of dollars. We won't have to rotate ships now, to try and fool them with numbers. Your contribution with one ship has probably got them thinking we have dozens of them."

"Good morning, Dennis. How is everything going?" General Estes asked.

"Not as we expected, sir. It's downright boring up here, thank God."

"I believe we all are thankful, Dennis. By the way, you don't have to worry about rotating ships now."

The general filled him in on the details.

"What is the situation with the station's shielding device?"

"About two hours ago, the tech supervisor told me they should be ready to test it in about three hours. Last night, the station crew spent about two and a half hours putting all the magnetic sensors in place on the hull. If that timetable holds, I'll have to take a walk in about fifteen minutes to No. 1 and be ready to shut down the temporary shield. I'll get No. 1 out from underneath so they can test for complete shielding of the station. Those techs worked almost all night to get this far."

"Then it's possible you could bring the squadron home in the next three hours."

"Home, sir? I thought we were to be up here a few days."

"What's the purpose? If it functions adequately, it will need no guardians. I spoke with the president last night. She has calls coming in from all over the world and she's going to start returning them this morning. We will update you about returning after the crucial calls from Russia and China are complete."

##

"Madam President, thank you for returning my call," the president of Russia said.

"My pleasure, sir. I would have called earlier, but I had very urgent things I had to attend to. What can I do for you, Mr. President?"

"Well, first of all, Madam President, I wish to congratulate you on your new fleet of spaceships. Needless to say, it came as quite a surprise to the whole world."

"Thank you, Mr. President, but let's cut the BS and get to your point."

"Very well, Madam. Since we have shared such close ties concerning the Space Station, I feel you should have, at least, told us about your intent to capture the Station."

"Mr. President, let me make this quite clear. We had no intent, and, we did not, have not, and do not intend to capture our own space station. We are merely protecting it. Those who have participated are still welcome to do so. I'm sure, sir, you have heard the rumor that there would be an attempt to damage or destroy the Station."

"Oh no, Madam, had I heard such a thing, you would have been the first to know."

"I'm sure," she replied. "Just like you would have told me that the last six MiG 21s off your assembly line would end up on American soil."

"I cannot explain that, but I'll certainly find out where they went. As you know, we have had to, for financial reasons, sell our products to many other countries, but I will…"

Cynthia interrupted

"Just stop your bullshit, Mr. President. You don't have to worry about the remaining MiGs, or the people here, as they are all in our custody. We closed down your little spy base early this morning. We may also have a couple of other little items that used to belong to you, Mr. President."

"Well, Madam, whatever you say. I will be filing a formal complaint with the U.N., against the United States, for your actions concerning the Space Station, not by my choice, but by the law in our country. I also believe you have put weapons in space, which the U.N. Charter prohibits."

"Very good, Mr. President, file away. Sir, I am very busy, so I bid you good day."

As soon as she hung up, the intercom buzzed.

"Ma'am, the Chinese ambassador called and said he wants to see you in his office as soon as possible."

"What? Why, the nerve of that little asshole, summoning me? Don't return the call and if he calls again, tell him to make a damned appointment. Tell him there won't be a time I can, or will, see him for at least ten days."

"Yes ma'am," Susan replied, laughing.

Cynthia sat back in her spacious chair, in the oval office, thinking over all that had happened. *Estes and Mattie did a master-ful job building the invisible umbrella over America. The news of the rumored fleet of ships had gotten out through the Democratic radio station, Air America, that the Republican President had not been authorized by Congress to build hundreds, if not thousands, of space ships, which is costing the taxpayers trillions of dollars. Impeachment is the only way to stop that woman...what a crock,* she thought.

"Damn," she said out loud, "our twelve ships have now turned into thousands!"

The intercom buzzed once more.

"Yes Susan?"

"Ma'am, the secretary general of the U.N. has an envoy here to present you some papers."

"Please sign for them, Susan."

"Ma'am, he was ordered to give them only to you."

"Oh, hell, I will be out in a minute."

She walked into the outer office and to the man who stood by Susan's desk.

"Can I help you, sir?"

"Madam President, yes, thank you. The secretary general wanted me to deliver these papers to you. Will you please sign here?" he asked, handing her a clipboard.

Cynthia looked at the envelope and the papers he wanted her to sign.

"Sorry, I sign nothing without reading it first."

She tossed the official looking envelope to Susan.

"Glance through those, while I read this, please."

"Madam, please, just sign and…"

Cynthia gave the man a stare that could have frozen water, and he shut up. She uncovered the sheet of paper.

The heading, in large black letters, read:

Official United Nations Summons to the President of the United States of America. You are hereby summoned to appear at 2 p.m today. This official Summons pertains to the many violations of the Outer Space Treaty that your government, the United States of America, previously signed and agreed to."

Cynthia folded the paper.

"Susan, I'm really getting pissed off at this damned, arrogant organization they call the United Nations. Give him back the papers."

Susan put the papers back in the envelope and handed them to the envoy.

"Madam, this is highly irregular. You must sign these papers."

Looking directly into his eyes, Cynthia said in a cold, harsh voice, "I don't have to sign a fucking thing. You take those papers back and tell those folks to shove them where the sun don't shine. You also tell your corrupt boss that I will be there at 2 p.m. sharp, and he damn sure isn't going to like what I have to say."

Cynthia turned around to summon security.

"Please escort this person from the White House property, all the way to the street."

"Susan, get General Estes and the attorney general on the phone, please."

"Yes, ma'am," Susan replied, with a huge smile on her face.

"Also, I want the videos of the ships and weapons that we recovered belonging to the Chinese and Russians. You can get those from the lieutenant in the photo lab. At 1:15, I want a helicopter to take me to New York. Oh, and I also need a video projector.

"Yes, ma'am."

Cynthia went back into her office and a minute later the intercom buzzed.

"I have General Estes on line one, ma'am," Susan said.

"General Estes, how do we stand on the station?"

"I was just going to call you, Madam President. I just spoke to Dennis a few minutes ago. The station's shield is in place and completely functional. Dennis tested it by firing the laser cannon at a non-critical area. The laser bounced off the shield and went out into space. Nothing is going to penetrate it. Dennis wants to know if you still want them to remain there for a few days."

"No, and here is what I would like, if possible."

##

Cynthia grabbed the pilot's arm, taking him aside as the others boarded the helicopter.

"We are going to have an escort to New York, so don't get alarmed when they arrive."

"Fighters, ma'am?"

"Well, yes, but nothing like you have ever seen before."

"Yes, ma'am, I'll be prepared then."

The chopper lifted off. Cynthia was smiling and humming to herself, but most of all watching the faces of the attorney general and the others sitting around her.

"We are going to have an escort to the U.N.," said the pilot to his co-pilot, "so keep an eye out for them."

The co-pilot quietly asked, "Do you mean those?"

A ring of ships had gathered around the helicopter.

"I thought I was going to mess my pants when I looked out and saw them," the co-pilot said. "What in God's name are they?"

The inside of the cabin suddenly went dark as the shadows of the eight Delta Blue ships blocked out the sun.

"Are we under attack?" the attorney general asked.

"Oh no, it's just our escort to the U.N.," the president replied.

"Hell," Senator Howard gasped, "they're bigger than an aircraft carrier. Are those the ones they had on the news?"

"Some of them," replied the president. "Impressive, aren't they?"

"Are they ours?"

"Oh, yes," the president said, with a smile, "one hundred percent ours."

The chopper sat down and everyone took their places. Everyone waited for the president to walk down the steps, but their eyes kept wandering to the ships, which had formed a ring around the U.N. building, and moved like a slow moving merry-go-round.

The honking of horns from the streets had stopped, as people were getting out of their cars and staring at the sight above them.

The president, her Marine guards, bodyguards and everyone else with her, marched smartly down the aisle and to the center of the counsel chamber. The secretary general stood at the lectern and nodded to the president, acknowledging her presence, but instead of taking her seat, she walked directly up to the lectern.

The Secretary General, with a stunned expression on his face, motioned with his hand and said, "Madam President, please take the seat at the table, facing the members."

"You go and sit there, I'm going to address them from right here, and I'm going to present something that many don't want to see or hear. Go sit now, or my Marines will throw your ass out of the building and out of America."

"But, Madam, I'm in charge here. You can't…"

"Either go and sit, or leave the building – your choice."

Stunned, he left the lectern, and joined the others in the room.

Cynthia walked around the lectern, placed her leather folder on it, and straightened her suit jacket. She adjusted the microphone so she would be speaking directly into it and, taking her time, gazed around the room. There were representatives from many countries, along with their assistants and interpreters. The representatives from Russia, China, Cuba, and North Korea had smug looks on their faces, as Cynthia's eyes locked on them. She pulled a sheet of paper from the folder, smoothed it out, and then once again looked at her enemies.

Her first words were firm.

"Ladies and gentlemen, to those of you who are *truly* America's friend, please, don't be offended by my presentation, as it is not meant for you."

She looked around at the faces and then continued.

"This building is in the United States of America. Americans built it, and they cover almost eighty-five percent of all expenses to operate the U.N., not just this building, but around the world, military and otherwise. Were I in your country and wished to converse with you, I would either call or write for an appointment. This morning I received a piece of paper."

She held it up, shaking it, for all to see.

"In my country, of which I am the president, I received this paper, ordering me, the president of the United States, to appear here, as if I were some lackey or servant. Well, this is what I think of this shithouse paper."

She wadded it in one hand and dropped it to the floor. There was a loud murmur throughout the council members.

A disturbance began to take place as a group came hustling through the entrance doors, into the council chambers. The people rushing in went separate ways, to different council members, whispering in their ears. As this happened, most all of the members left the chamber, and Cynthia knew they were going into the outer hallways to observe the ships.

An aide gave the president a glass of water. She stood there, sipping her water and just watched, with a smile on her face, as the members slowly began to trickle back into the chamber. She put the glass down and stepped back to the microphone.

"I do not, and would not, summon any of you. I would call and ask to meet, nothing else. America is a country blessed, and we are willing to share those blessings with those in need. During my terms as vice president, and these two years as president, I have seen a lot … and I am not happy. Most of the aid that was sent to your countries — and you know which countries you are — did not get to those for whom it was intended. That is going to stop. I am going to the Congress of the United States to make sure this practice ceases. America will never participate in, or be a part of, a one-world government. We will forever remain an independent republic. We will recognize you if you are a just country, otherwise we will be very careful about our vigilance against any aggressive moves against us, or our friends. If the corruption in this assembly does not cease, I intend to go to the Congress of the United States and ask to withdraw from the United Nations."

Cynthia saw some motion out of the corner of her eye. She glanced over and saw the Russian president whispering to his ambassador, and the first thing that popped in her mind was, *uh-oh, hear it comes.*

"Madam President, excuse me," the Russian ambassador interrupted. "What you are doing is highly irregular. The president of the U.N. Council should be addressing us, not you. You are here to answer why America has broken Article 4 of the Outer Space Treaty."

"Sir," she replied, "first of all, I saw your president telling you what to say. Secondly, I have already told you that when I finish my comments, I will answer your questions. Mr. President, if you can't speak for yourself, I would appreciate you stop using your ambassador as a lap dog. Now, if you don't want to hear my statement, there are two things we can do. You can leave, or, if the majority of the council so desires, I can take my people and go."

Cynthia spoke loudly into the microphone.

"Those who wish me to leave, please stand."

She looked around the chamber. The North Korean ambassador stood, as did the Chinese and Russian ambassadors. She noticed that the Russian and Chinese presidents did not stand.

She looked directly at them both.

"What's wrong, gentlemen? Too bashful to stand and back your ambassadors?"

There were angry looks from them, but no words were spoken. She looked around the room once more.

"You are outvoted gentlemen, now sit down or leave."

They sat down.

"The American taxpayer is sick of paying for a losing U.N. This U.N. was to bring all the hundreds of countries together, to help one another, and keep the peace. Unfortunately, none of that has happened. There are more dictators in the U.N. now, then ever before, dictators who care only about two things — building their bank accounts and leaving their people hungry and poor."

A loud chorus of dissatisfaction passed through the chamber. Someone in the crowd shouted, "What we do in our country is none of your business."

"Well, sir, depriving your people of food, medicine, and freedom becomes our business when the American taxpayer is the one paying for the food and medicine that is sent to the very people you are depriving. There is so much corruption in the U.N., it is unbelievable. The Oil for Food program was a big joke. Look at all the bribes, all the money made by U.N. members—at the expense of the people who needed your help. I know who you are, and you know who you are. Not one has been cited for their corruption, let alone prosecuted. Shame on you. Here is the bottom line people. The American taxpayer is sick and tired of paying for the world's upkeep. America pays seventy-five to eighty-five percent of the cost of this body. That is going to come to a damn halt. We can't, and won't, force you to do what's right, unless you step on our toes— and woe be to those who try.

"Now," she said, adding a long pause for emphasis, "if those responsible for the corruption in the Oil for Food program are not arrested, and prosecuted, within sixty days, the U.N. in this country will cease to exist. If need be, we will escort you out of our country. We will reorganize with our true allies and help to protect one another. Sixty days, people, that's it!"

There was shouting and cursing throughout the chamber.

"Down with America!"

Cynthia smiled and took a drink of water.

Senator Howard, who had been on the helicopter with Cynthia, stepped up to the podium and, over the shouting, said, "Madam President, you just declared something that you alone cannot enforce. The Congress and Senate will not approve the closing of this facility."

She faced him directly.

"Senator Howard, let me tell you something. When I decide to come before either chamber, I'm going to crisscross this country on radio, television and in person. I'm going to inform our people of the huge cost that the two Houses have placed on their constituents, yours, as well as every other congressman and senator. There is corruption and kickback money coming back to key people in our government and I'm sick of it. The American people are sick of it. Anyone who votes to stay with this body of dictators and thieves will personally see me go to their constituents."

"You wouldn't do that, ma'am."

"Try me and see, Senator."

Senator Howard turned and stormed from the podium, back to his seat.

Cynthia turned back to the assembly.

"I'm ready to take any questions you have."

The chamber suddenly grew very quiet.

The Russian president stood.

"Madam President, it's so nice to see you in such a jovial mood. I will speak for myself this time. A few years ago, in this very chamber, most all countries including mine and yours, signed a treaty agreeing to not put weapons in space. Why did America decide not to honor that treaty?"

Good, he stepped right into the trap, thought Cynthia.

"Mr. President, I'm afraid you're forcing me to do some-thing I detest — answer a question with a question. Mr. President, has Russia ever put or attempted to put weapons of any sort into space?"

"No, Madam President, never!"

"I see, sir. Then I declare you either have no idea what is happening in your country, or you are lying to this assembly. I prefer the latter, as I believe you know everything that goes on in your country."

"How dare you call me a liar, Madam President," he shouted.

Cynthia turned to a small group that stood behind her.

"Lieutenant, are you ready?"

"Yes, ma'am."

"Let her roll, please."

Cynthia turned and faced a large screen behind her. As three eight-foot-wide pictures popped up on the screen, Cynthia turned back to the microphone.

"Explain these three pictures, Mr. President."

Two of the pictures were of space capsules with delta wings. Beside each ship were two bodies, dressed in cosmonaut spacesuits with their helmets beside them, on the floor. The third picture was of a large satellite, sitting on the floor in a big hangar.

The Russian president stood, shouting, "See? You all see this? Nothing is sacred to the Americans. They steal our ships and satellites. Those belong to Russia and you will return them to us immediately!"

Cynthia calmly replied, "Sir, they are junk, and they were nothing more than flying coffins when you put those poor men in them. The point now is, according to international law, anything that sinks in our oceans and has done so in international waters is fair game, and whoever retrieves them first is the rightful owner. I am glad, however, that you admit they are yours. Now we will show the council what we found on those ships. Lieutenant, the next four pictures, please."

The three pictures disappeared, to be replaced by pictures showing the two different ships. The ships were standing on their tails, with something similar to bomb bay doors wide open, and a cable lifting out a skeleton container with missiles encased in it.

Cynthia spoke into the microphone.

"That container would have been hydraulically lowered below the ship, and the frame work around the missiles would have become the launching platform. Two of those four missiles had nuclear warheads. The other ship was exactly the same. Anyone in the U.N. is welcome to come to where these ships are stored and see. Bring your own scientists and engineers to check them out. Now, Mr. President, you claim the ships are yours. Are the missiles, and missile rack, yours also?"

"The satellite," he shouted, pointing at the picture, "it is ours, return it to us immediately!"

A loud murmur passed through the chamber when the next pictures appeared. The picture showed a large, open door on the satellite, and another battery of missiles were shown being removed from their launch rack.

"Mr. President, you were letting the satellite go into re-entry to destroy it. It became a salvageable object at that point. One of our brave shuttle crews risked much to salvage it. So, you never put weapons into space and never tried to put them in space with those junk ships … is that correct?"

The president, in a rage at being caught, was shouting in Russian to his people, who were stuffing papers into briefcases.

"Mr. President, we have preserved your cosmonauts' bodies and will return them to their families," Cynthia said.

The president glared at her, and not saying a word, he and his people exited the chamber.

After the commotion died down, Cynthia spoke once again.

"Ladies and gentlemen, the United States of America did not break the Outer Space Treaty. It disappeared when the Russians and Chinese put weapons into space. Yes, you in the Chinese delegation, we also recovered your attempt to put your own armed ship into space. If you want to see the pictures of it, I will oblige. We also know that your newest satellite in space is armed. Do not put it over American airspace or we will shoot it down."

The Chinese leader stood, shouting at his people, and ordering them all to leave.

"You will regret this," he said to Cynthia as he turned to leave.

"The Outer Space Treaty is dead, not broken by America, but by our two key competitors for space. They chose to break the treaty and put arms into space, so now America claims the same rights. Thank you."

She picked up her briefcase and turned to go. She saw the president of the U.N. walking away.

"Mr. President, I wish to speak with you."

He turned and waited for her to approach him.

"Sixty days, Mr. President. The French, Germans, Canadians and all others, including the United States companies, must be brought up for charges. That also includes your son. Sixty days, or America will shut down the U.N."

She turned to leave and there was considerable applause from many of the countries' representatives, including her own people. She waved to those. She saw Ed Mitchell and headed straight for him.

"How did I do?"

Ed laughed.

"Wonderful, you ate their cookies."

"Thanks, Ed, I needed to hear that."

"Remind me to not get on the wrong side of you. You would chew me up, and then spit me out."

She smiled at him. Her eyes met his, and she lingered before saying, "Come on; let's get that media conference over with."

In a large conference room at Andrews, the president stood at the lectern looking out over the packed room. Reporters and TV people waited patiently for her to speak.

"OK, folks, I am fielding no questions today. This day belongs to this wonderful group of men and women behind me. They are true patriots of this country. We are having special medals designed just for our men and women of NASA, who led the way into space for all others, and soon we will be exploring deeper into our universe, and beyond. Due to the shortness of time, I am going to introduce five of the group here, but I'm not forgetting the remainder of them who were equally responsible for the success of Delta Blue Squadron.

"There are several civilians, who unselfishly volunteered to help with this success. When the medals and plaques are ready, there will be a meeting to honor all of them. As I said, I will introduce these five, and they may field five questions each. I ask that you raise your hands, and the person fielding the question will point to whomever they wish to ask their question, and please, no shouting. First of all, I want to introduce the man that history will record as the father of these magnificent ships. With his tenacity, expertise and genius, we have built ships that have pushed America at least fifty years into the future. Without him, these ships would not exist today — General Dennis Denehey, Commander of Delta Blue Squadron."

She held her hand out to Dennis and he stepped forward, saluted, and they shook hands. She stepped to the side, allowing Dennis access to the microphone.

One man in the front row shouted.

"General, a question, please."

Dennis pointed at the man.

"Yes, sir, go ahead."

"Sir, I was at your court martial. According to the records, you were busted to a second lieutenant, and could never be promoted if you remained in the service. Can you explain what strings you pulled to now be a general?"

Blindsided by the question, Dennis glanced over at the president. She stepped up to the microphone.

"We are not here today to honor these people by degrading them with stupid questions, or to accuse them of pulling so-called strings. To satisfy your stupid and morbid question, I will answer it and erase any further doubts. There is something you people are not aware of yet, due to its secret nature, but I will say this. We have three traitors in custody who were in high positions of authority. One of these three tried to ruin this man's integrity, as well as his life. Had I done my duty, I would have caught what happened earlier and stopped it. I failed this man. I have now corrected what was an injustice. He should have been a general years ago, and this is only a small reward for what he has contributed to this nation. One more damn thing, if I hear one more question, or read any degrading comments or questions about the integrity of these people that we should be honoring, that news organization will be banned from further White House conferences while I am in office. Dennis, do you want to field your second question now?"

The rest of the conference went well, with the president introducing Diane and the Mitchell family. The president told the history of the Mitchells and all answered questions from the reporters.

When the news conference was over, the president escorted Ed and the others to their ships. She stopped with Ed, at his ship, and took his arm.

"Mr. Mitchell," she quietly said, "I will be attending a wedding soon at your base. Would you honor me and be my escort?"

Smiling down at her from his six-foot-three stance, he replied, "It would be my honor to escort you, Cynthia."

"Wonderful, expect me then."

"I can't wait," he said, saluting her and turning to step onto the elevator. He stopped abruptly and went back to her. He leaned over and whispered in her ear, "Would it be proper for a colonel to kiss the president of the United States?"

Looking into his earnest, and concerned eyes, she replied, "To hell with ranks, Ed, you can kiss me anytime, anywhere."

Ed swept her into his arms and their lips met.

There was a roar from the crowd of reporters as cameras flashed and television cameras rolled.

Everyone watched as the three craft climbed gracefully into the air and quickly disappeared into the western sky.

Senator Howard asked, "Do you think that kiss was a proper thing to do here and now?"

She turned to him, put her hands on her hips and looked him square in the eyes.

"Hell, Senator, that was for me, and if you or anyone else has a problem with it, well, you can all kiss my ass."

It was three weeks later when a commuter jet landed at a small airfield by the little village of Hohhot, in northeastern China. The plane taxied through large hangar doors which quickly closed behind it. The council leader of China deplaned. He stood there silently and looked around the large hangar where several MiG fighters, armed with missiles, were housed. Ignoring those who saluted him, he turned to the captain that was standing at attention.

"Are you in charge here?"

"Yes, honorable sir."

"How many fighters have you?"

"Twenty-eight, sir."

"Are they ready for battle?"

"Yes, sir, and excellent pilots also, sir."

"Are the others here?"

"Yes, sir, awaiting your presence in the conference room, sir."

He entered the room, and the four officers already there jumped to attention.

"Sit."

He walked to the head of the table.

"Are your missiles and the site ready?"

"Yes, sir, all is prepared. The underground missile silos are ready to fire on your signal. The final train arrived yesterday with the ground-to-air missiles to greet any intruders. The completed launch site is about 100 yards from the Mongolian border, where the train crosses over into Mongolia. It's a very deserted area for hundreds of miles, with the exception of a few small villages that are scattered about. Some of them are even deserted."

"How many missiles do you have that can reach the target?"

"Six, sir."

"What time will the target be in range?"

"Approximately 4 a.m., Sir."

"Kill the target then."

"Yes, sir."

"Have those MiGs ready to fly. How long from here to our site?"

"From the ground up, five minutes, sir."

"Good. Is the site thoroughly camouflaged?"

"Yes, sir, it cannot be spotted from the air. I went up and could only find it because I knew where it was."

"Very good. When you are ready at the site, call me a few minutes before you fire. Keep your radar on constant watch when you do fire. I'm sure the satellites will pinpoint the location, as no launch can be hidden anymore."

"I'm certain that we can fend off any intruders if they dare show up, sir."

"Good, you are prepared then?"

"Yes, sir."

"I'm leaving it to your people to succeed."

##

It was 3:50 a.m. when the Chinese leader's phone rang. He rolled over in his bed and fumbled for the phone.

"Yes," he answered.

"Sir, the target is coming in range."

"When it is in range, kill it."

"Yes, sir. We are going to fire the sixth missile five seconds after the others. We have a camera mounted in the nose of it and will have a video for you to see when the mission is completed."

"Brilliant, yes, that is good. After being so embarrassed by the American president, maybe I'll have a copy sent to her … unmarked of course."

"Sir, it's time. Do you want me to call you back?"

"No, I'll hold on the phone, do your duty."

Seconds passed as he listened to the orders being given ... then, confusion.

"What? What has happened? It can't be. Radar? Radar? Is the target gone?"

Then silence for a few seconds more.

"What? It can't be. They were direct hits. It can't happen."

Then silence once more.

Finally, back on the phone with the Chinese leader, he said, "Sir, I don't understand what happened. The first missile hit the target directly. The camera showed it before it hit. It was as if the missiles hit a shield or barrier. The target was unharmed."

The leader heard the words that the officer was telling him, but it was too unbelievable.

"Get that video to me immediately. I want to see this. Surely the Americans could not have come up with such a device without us knowing about it. Are you ready, Captain, for retaliation? I know it will be coming in the next few hours."

"Yes, sir, we are more than ready. All radar stations across the country are on high alert. We will meet any intruders and kill them, sir."

"Get that tape to me, and let me know if a strike is coming."

The leader shut the phone off and rested it back on the cradle. Then he snapped it back up and dialed a number.

"Wake up, you fool, and get my scientists to the Great Hall immediately!"

He was pacing back and forth behind his chair when the huge doors of the Great Hall opened. Several men in various stages of dress hurried into the room, bowing as they came.

"Come in, come in and sit. I am indeed sorry to pull you from your beds at this hour. I need to know something very important and perhaps one of you can help. To your knowledge, has anyone, or any country, found a way to build an electro-magnetic shielding device that would protect a small city?"

The scientists all looked at one another. Finally, one stood up.

"Sir, it has been every scientist's dream to do so. To date, no one has ever developed one to shield even a small chair. The last one I tried to design was totally impractical. The device that would generate enough power needed to shield a chair would have been the size of a four-story. To build one large enough to protect a small city would be impossible. It would have to be the size of the city, or bigger."

"Well, sir, you may be wrong, but we won't know until the video I am waiting on gets here."

It was almost 1430 hours when Dennis and the crews walked into the briefing room. Dennis' shoulder phone buzzed.

"Denehey here."

"Dennis, this is Estes. The space station has been attacked. Retaliatory strikes have been ordered by the president. Are you prepared?"

"Yes, sir. Location?"

"Northeastern China, almost, if not on, the Mongolia border. They are downloading coordinates from our satellite now. Get what you can in the air and I'll give you exact coordinates when finalized."

"Yes, sir. Out."

Everyone was getting seated for the briefing and Dennis shouted, "Hold up, everyone."

Dennis took his walkie-talkie from his belt.

"Sarge, Dennis here."

"Yes, sir?"

"Numbers 4 through 10, are they ready to go, armaments and fuel?"

"Aye, sir. Do you want them rolled out?"

"Immediately. I want seven weapons, radar and comm men, fast. Send them directly to the ships."

The old, as well as the new pilots, were listening, stone faced, and waiting for orders. Dennis did not hesitate.

"Seven ships. Qualified pilots, first seat; six new pilots, second seat. Crews are on the way and the ships are being rolled out. Delta formation on takeoff, I'll follow in seventh position in No. 4 ship. Ships are fueled and armed. When airborne, go to 38,000 feet, east-northeast. I'll give you the coordinates in the air. Let's go."

Tensley had the engines on No. 4 running when Dennis arrived.

Dennis grabbed his calculator and started punching in numbers. Approximately 8000 miles, at 18,000 knots, so less than thirty minutes to get there. *Now for the strategy.*

The six other ships rolled by. Tensley took their ship down the taxiway, behind number 10. It wasn't long before they were all climbing for the heavens and General Estes sent the coordinates to Dennis.

"Five through 10, switch to secure frequency," Dennis announced.

He pressed the appropriate button.

"Listen up, 5 through 10. I'll take the lead; form delta formation off me. Once in formation, feed these coordinates into your computer. We will go to 18,000 knots, ETA of target area approximately 22 minutes."

They each reported when they were in position, and watched their air speed indicator rapidly move up to 15,000, and then to 18,000 knots, and the computer took over.

"OK, folks, when we arrive at target area I will drop to 20,000 feet, use infrared to locate body heat or exhaust heat and pinpoint the target. I'll feed 5, 6 and 7 the coordinates. It will be daylight, and once the location is verified, I'll go north and you three join me. Spread out about 50 yards apart, weapons personnel will sweep the area. We'll be going in at 25 feet off the deck, lower than their missile launchers can get to. Numbers 8, 9 and 10, fly cover at 10,000 feet. All radar operators stay alert for any bogies. That's it, everyone; you can relax for about 10 minutes."

A Chinese radar operator picked up the seven ships as they were approaching the China border from the east. He radioed the next station in line.

"Seven craft, 38,000 feet and … I can't believe this; they are moving at almost 18,000 knots."

A voice came back.

"You are crazy, nothing travels that fast."

"They are leaving my screen and going into the next area."

"Impossible," said the other voice. "Wait, yes, I have them. All stations alert … 38,000 feet at 18,000 knots!"

At the hangar, where the MiGs were stored, an alarm went off. Pilots scrambled for their planes which had been lined up outside. Their engines came to life, and they moved quickly toward the runway.

Back at the Chinese leader's briefing, the phone on the conference table rang.

"Yes, Captain, you are on the speaker phone; what is it?"

"Sir, I don't know what is happening. Our earliest warning radar post has picked up seven large ships. Two other sites have confirmed. They are showing to be at 38,000 feet and moving faster than anything I know of — 18,000 knots, sir."

"It can't be so. It would take their best and fastest fighter pilots hours to get here from their desert base ... oh wait, they have sent their new ships! Where are our fighters?"

"They should be at the site by now, sir. I scrambled them at the first notice."

"Can you recall them?"

"I don't know, sir, but they are to protect the launch site."

"To hell with the launch site; recall them now!"

"Yes, sir, one moment."

"Radar has us," Dennis told the crew. "Slow to 1800 knots, I'm going down. When I locate the target, proceed as planned."

Dennis said to Tensley, "Sarge, infrared, please."

"Aye, sir, it's on."

"Clue me when you see anything, I'll get the coordinates."

"Aye, sir, dead ahead. I see many people running toward something."

"Weapons, can you see them on your screen? If so, sweep it."

Dennis and Tensley saw the blue beam as it flashed out in front of the ship, streaking toward its target. As fast as it came on, it was gone.

"Explosions, it's a hit, sir."

"Going north — 5, 6 and 7, come down to 1000 feet, north of my position and line up on me, going west. We will turn and I'll lead the way back."

"No. 4, No. 8 here. We have bogies spreading out from the south. Twenty-seven total … wait, there's a latecomer. There are fourteen going east to come back, and fourteen targets head on from the south, about a hundred miles."

"Can you three keep them busy? We're going around for our pass on their site."

"If they stay as they are, they will be sitting ducks. Nine and 10, take the ones from the east. Weapons, do you have the bogies from the south?"

"Yes, sir."

Nos. 4, 5, 6 and 7 were on the deck, the earth sweeping by so fast that it was only a blur.

"I have the target," weapons announced.

"All ships fire," ordered Dennis.

Four blue streaks left the cannons and explosions spread toward the heavens. Fuel tanks and missiles exploded as the train's flat rail cars sailed through the air, flying across the desert.

"Up to 800 feet," Dennis said, as the huge ships rose above the wreckage and debris.

Dennis heard the weapons man on No. 8.

"Thirteen MiGs gone; missed one, sir, but he is high-tailing it back to wherever he came from."

"Making a slow pass for inspection, and if need be, we will make one more."

Ships 4, 5, 6 and 7 throttled back to 150 knots. From 100 feet above the deck, they passed over the area. The sand below looked more like glass. The sight was something else. Rail cars were scattered across the desert, open silo doors with flames spewing from deep in the ground, and nothing was moving. The only heat signatures were from the flames.

"OK, people, No. 4 here. Let's go back up to 38,000 feet, form up, and go home."

Everyone at the Chinese leader's conference heard the captain calling on the radio. "Butterfly Squadron ... base ... reply."

He repeated it, over and over.

"Sir," he said to the Chinese leader, "no answer. Perhaps they are at battle, sir."

Then a lone voice was heard over the speaker phone.

"Base, Butterfly."

"Butterfly, where are you?"

"Cin Ho here. I had a flameout on the way but I managed an air start. I was minutes behind the squadron, when an ungodly blue streak flashed across the sky. In a minute, the squadron was gone.

Half of the squadron had gone east, and turned back in toward the enemy. I couldn't see the enemy ship, but two more blue flashes arced across the sky, and in a moment, the remaining fourteen planes were gone. Apparently, I flew into the shrapnel of our ships and my hydraulic controls are out. I'm trying to get my ship back to base."

"Twenty-seven MiGs gone; how so?"

"I don't know, sir, I don't know," the pilot answered. "I am four minutes from base, no landing gear. I'll try to set it down beside the runway."

The captain was back on the phone with the Chinese leader.

"Sir, you heard?"

"Yes, I heard; thank you, captain. Send helicopters for any survivors. I want pictures of whatever you find."

"Yes, sir. What kind of weapons do those devils have, sir?"

"Laser cannons, I fear. Get back to me."

The Chinese leader collapsed into his seat, placing his forehead in his two palms, shaking his head and muttering to himself.

Two servants came in carrying teapots, cups and rice cakes.

"Give the scientists the tea and cakes," he ordered, "and bring me a bottle of sake."

The scientists did not touch the offerings, but instead just sat there, watching the leader as he shook his head from side to side.

The servant rushed in with a bottle of sake and sat if before him, along with a glass. The leader brushed the glass aside and took the opened bottle of sake, turning it up and guzzling down half the bottle. Bringing it down from his lips, he sat it on the table and made a sour face. Finally, he looked up at the men around the table.

"China, I feel, is in big trouble. If our pilot could not see the enemy, it means that the enemy was too far away for our boys to fire their missiles. I'm afraid what was seen in space recently was their laser cannon. I am sure of it now. With a laser cannon and possible shielding devices, our weapons, and even our nuclear bombs, are useless. If they can shield the International Space Station, they will eventually be able to shield their major cities and ports. Until they get that done, their devil ships will protect America. We thought they only had one, but three went to Washington, and seven took out our missile launch site and twenty-seven MiG fighters, in less than two minutes."

##

Dennis and seven weary crews were seated around the general's conference table; some drinking beer and others mixed drinks. No celebration would be held this night, but all were ready to relax. The general was on the speaker phone talking with the president.

"Are there any further orders for now, Cynthia?"

"None, Estes. I know the people there are sad about today. No one likes to take another human life. We were forced to do what we did. Under no circumstances is this to get out to the media. If it gets out, the Chinese will have to leak it, then it's on them. We will not brag about it. A victory, yes it was, and I'm proud of our people for doing what had to be done."

How many ships can you put in the air in the next three or four days?" the president asked.

The general looked at Dennis.

"You mean another mission, ma'am?" Dennis asked.

"No, just for advertising. I'm serious about that. The Chinese, I'm sure, are now aware of the shielding device on the station. Maybe I'm jumping the gun here, but were I them, I would anticipate the U.S. would have a shielding device sooner or later to protect, at least, our major cities. Meanwhile, we have these craft that can cover great distances in a very short time, to protect the country. With an umbrella of ships over the country, all their weapons are useless. I would like to see our ships actually patrolling over our major cities, and get the word to the news people why we are there."

"I can put twelve ships up whenever you want them."

"With three at a time over the major cities, you could cover the entire country in a day."

"Yes, ma'am, easily."

"Wonderful, plus it would certainly help me get the funding for the twenty-four more I want."

"That is quite a goal, ma'am. Do you think the Democrats will go for it?"

"If they don't, after a couple of weeks of the people know-ing you are there, I'll take it to the people themselves. I bet the Democrats would change their minds then. Before I go, is Ed there?"

"Yes ma'am, I'm here," Ed replied.

"I just thought I'd let you know that you and I made front page news across the country."

"Why is that, ma'am?"

"Oh, would you stop being a stuffed shirt Ed? Among our people, I am Cynthia, not ma'am. When you wrapped me up in those big strong arms and gave me that juicy kiss; we made the headlines."

Everyone around the table tried hard to stifle their laughter and Ed's face turned a deep red.

"Uh, Cynthia, I have to go," Ed stated, rising from his seat.

"Yes, dear, bye for now," Cynthia said with a hint of a laugh.

"Hey, Ed, do we hear more wedding bells?" Diane asked.

Everyone burst out laughing and Ed sat back down in his seat, shaking his head, his face turning redder by the minute.

"OK, shut up," Ed replied, and then turned up his beer and chugged it down.

"Ed, if you don't mind, I'd like to tell you about Cynthia," General Estes said.

"No, not at all, sir."

"Well, Cynthia, Thelma and I have been friends since the tenth grade, and our friendship grows stronger each day. She never searched for fame and riches. It is her beautiful personality — not her looks, not her expertise, nothing but her being the person she is – that brought her to be the president of the greatest country in the world. She was talked into being vice president, and she was asked to run for president. She is first true to herself, then to the rest of the world. Oh, she pulls no punches either, and as far as Thelma and I both know, you are the first man she has shown any genuine interest in. I could go on and on, but I'll just say this, if you two do make it further, you will be truly blessed."

Ed looked down at his hands for a few seconds, then back to the general.

"Sir, I'll tell you a little secret. When I first heard her speak, before I knew what she even looked like, I thought, that is a special lady. When I finally saw her, and again heard her speak, I fell head over heels for her. I've followed her all the way through her vice presidency, to where she is today. I always felt she was unreachable by someone like me, so I was content with just following her progress. Why she took to me, I have no idea, but if she will have me, I will be the happiest man in the world."

Everyone at the table stared at big, soft spoken, quiet Ed. Mattie and Cathy came around to him, both hugging and kissing their big brother. Others breathed a deep sigh, while some softly clapped their hands.

"Absolutely beautiful, Ed," the general said, softly. "I'm sure she won't disappoint you, son. One hundred percent of the odds are in your favor."

The next two weeks became very hectic. The training of five new pilots was complete, along with getting the equipment from the cape and lining up engineers for the moon base installation. Six ships were patrolling the skies over major cities every day.

Diane and a new pilot, Captain Tina McBride, parked the ship. They had been patrolling the southern borders of the U.S. and Mexico and up the west coast to Seattle.

The newspapers and major news stations hailed what they defined as an "umbrella of security" for America. Many people were interviewed on the streets, as well as on radio and TV.

General Estes was watching a newscast in his office where a man and his wife were being interviewed.

"Do you agree with the Democrats, that the new ships and their patrolling our cities, is a waste of money?" The news anchor asked.

"Let me say this," the man replied. "My wife and I, along with our families, have been staunch Democrats of the old Democratic Party, since way back. Our party disappeared over forty years ago. We tried to restore and bring back our party, to no avail. The fanatics that run the party today want a welfare country, where everyone is dependent on the federal government for everything. What most people don't think about, is what the Democrats promise and give you today, they will take away from you tomorrow. Did you see that video of Diane O'Hara, in an unarmed ship? She took out two MiG fighter planes. We now know she was flying one of those new ships."

"She's a hero in our book," stated the wife.

"We, as well as our families, are no longer Democrats. Just let that Diane Workstein, Barry Landew, Amanda Closee and that drunken Fred Benaby try to stop these new ships. My family and I, as do thousands of others, feel safer and more secure, since the threat of Russia's nuclear war has ended. I will say this, Sir, I urge everyone from the old Democratic Party to switch. This president we now have is doing a superb job, and she is working for us, the American people, as it should be. I'll vote for one hundred more new ships!"

"Well there you have it folks," the newscaster was saying, as the general turned off the TV. That interview was being repeated, over and over, in other countries.

Seeing Dennis' door open, Diane walked on in.

"Hey lover, what are you doing?" she called out.

Dennis came from the kitchen and smiled at his beautiful woman. He walked over and kissed her tenderly.

"I was re-checking the inventory for the moon jump. All we are waiting on is the rest of the installation crew to get here."

Diane noticed the stack of mail on the table.

"Is that all mine?"

"I don't know, dear, I just picked it up. Check it out."

She flicked through the items, pulling out two letters with her name on them.

"Hmm," she murmured, "wonder who this is from, no return address on it."

She opened the letter, pulled out the single sheet of paper, and read it. She slammed the paper down on the table.

"What's wrong sweetheart, bad news?"

She handed him the letter and he read it out loud.

"'Suggest you check on your sister. Message will follow.' What does that mean, Diane? I didn't even know you had a sister."

"We haven't communicated in years. I've written to her several times, but never a reply. I guess I'd better call her and see what's wrong. She should be home from work by now."

She laid her address book on the table, picked up the phone and dialed her sister's number. There was no answer. She disconnected and dialed another number. On the second ring, a woman answered.

"May I help you?"

"Connect me with Tina O'Hara, please; this is her sister, Diane."

"Hmm, there is no listing of a next of kin on her application," the woman mumbled.

Getting irritated, Diane replied, "I could not care less what is on her application, just connect us please. I got a screwy letter today and it tells me to check on my sister. I want to hear her damned voice, so connect us, lady!"

"Ma'am, this is the Pentagon, not a message center. Your phone number doesn't show on our caller ID. Can you tell me where you are calling from?"

Diane, now worried, asked, "Who are you? You are certainly not a receptionist. Is my sister there or not?"

"I'm sorry, whoever you are, without positive ID I can't put you through. Have a good day."

"Wait! Don't hang up. I am General Diane O'Hara of the United States Air Force. You can check that out. My serial number is AF 7044-7924. The president will verify who I am. Has something happened to my sister?"

"Why won't you give us your location, General?"

"I am located at a top secret facility – again, the president will verify that."

"Does the president know how to contact you?"

"Hell, yes, she does, and by God if someone doesn't let me know what's going on in the next twenty minutes, I'll call her myself."

She slammed the phone into its cradle.

"What's going on, Diane?"

Dennis could see the fear in her eyes.

"Something has happened to Tina, and those assholes won't tell me anything."

Dennis wrapped his arms around her and held her tight.

"Who are they?"

"My guess is the FBI or CIA. Tina has worked for the Pentagon for quite a few years. I believe she has a fairly high position there."

The phone rang and Diane grabbed it.

"General O'Hara here."

"Diane, General Estes. The president just called. She gave me a phone number for you to call. What is going on?"

"General, I don't have time to explain right now. Maybe you would come here, sir. Can I get that phone number please?"

He gave her the number and Diane's call was answered immediately.

"Tendel here, may I help you?"

"General Diane O'Hara here; the president just gave me this number to call."

"Yes, Ms. O'Hara, I'm sorry for the inconvenience. I'm Ken Tendel, FBI. Have you heard from, or spoke to, your sister recently?"

Diane swallowed hard, try to stay calm.

"It's been over two years since we last had any communication. Why? What has happened to her?"

"Nine days ago, she did not show up for work, and did not call. Her supervisor said that was most unusual in itself. Tina has not missed one day in over three years, and even if she was going to be a little late, for whatever reason, she would call. Your sister has a very sensitive position in the Pentagon. When she did not show on the second day, her supervisor called her. There was no answer.

Worried, she went to a woman who apparently was a close friend of your sister. She asked her to take off and go to her apartment to see if your sister was all right. When she got there, she knocked on the door several times, with no response. A neighbor lady came out and told her that she had not seen or heard Tina for several days. Your sister's friend, now concerned, used the neighbor's phone and told her supervisor what she had found out. The supervisor then called us and we sent an agent right over. The agent got the super to open the door and everything was clean, and in order. The agent checked her closet. Her clothes seemed to all be there, and there were three suitcases in the closet. The agent checked for an imprint on the carpet to see if one might have been taken. There were no imprints at all. In checking the closet in the other room, some men's clothes were found. An imprint in the closet carpet in that room indicated that a suitcase or heavy container had been recently removed. Ms. O'Hara was your sister married, or did she have a live-in boyfriend?"

"Married? I don't know. The last time I saw her, yes, she did have a boyfriend who stayed with her."

"Well, Ms. O'Hara, we have checked all the states around D.C. and none have any records of her being married. Her friend told us that the last two or three times she visited your sister, there was a very rude man there who seemed to be right at home. He, in many ways, indicated to her that he resented her being there. She said she took the hint, and never went back."

"Was he a dark skinned man with a heavy accent?"

"Yes, she did mention that. Are you familiar with who he is?"

"Oh, I know the ass. In fact, he is the reason my sister and I have not communicated in the last two years."

"May I ask what happened?"

"I was on furlough for a month. I wanted to surprise Tina and visit with her for a few days. When I arrived, she seemed happy to see me and wanted me to stay. After I was there about an hour, this ass walks in, as if he owned the place. With no hint of friendliness in his voice, he asked Tina who I was. Tina got up from her chair to introduce us, telling him I was her sister. He glared at me, without saying a word, and then turned back to Tina and asked if his supper was ready. When she told him that we had been visiting, and she was sorry for being late with the meal, he slapped her so hard that she fell backwards and hit the floor. That was more than I could take. I got up and kicked his ass all over that apartment. I knocked him out cold. I kicked his Colombian ass damned good."

"You beat him up?"

"You better believe I did. No man hits my sister, ever."

"What happened then, Ms. O'Hara?"

"When I got Tina up from the floor, to my surprise, she told me I had to leave. I couldn't believe it. I left, reluctantly."

The agent laughed.

"Please excuse that, Ms. O'Hara. You are a most unusual woman."

"His name is Raul Santiago. He is from somewhere in Colombia, and was working at the bank where Tina did her banking."

"I see, we will check on him immediately. Ms. O'Hara, why did you call your sister today? Our agent said you were quite upset."

"It was because of a note I received in the mail saying I had better check on my sister."

"OK, I understand you are at a top secret installation, how could anyone get your mailing address?"

"I don't know, sir. We have our own APO address. It's on the envelope here on the table."

"Do you know who you gave out your APO number to?"

"Well, only my sister. I have written Tina many letters, trying to repair our relationship. My return address was on the envelopes, naturally."

"Anyone else?"

"No sir ... well, yes, my bank."

"The same bank as your sister used?"

"No Sir, a Texas bank."

"Very good, Ms. O'Hara. There should be some bank statements in your sister's apartment to indicate where she banked, or we can find out. We will check to see if any unusual withdrawals have taken place lately, and we will definitely be having a talk with Mr. Santiago today. That note, Ms. O'Hara, did you handle it much?"

"Well, I guess so; our post office here had to put it in our box. My fiancé, General Denehey also held the note. Why?"

"In an installation such as yours, there is a department of security. They should have the equipment to dust it for fingerprints. If you would, call them and have them do so, please. Is there a postmark on it?"

Looking down at the envelope, she replied, "There is one, but it's not readable, sir."

"Well, your security people may be able to bring it out. If a follow-up letter arrives, hold the envelope by the corners and call your security office to have them open it. I'm going to send a couple of agents to you in anticipation of such a follow-up letter."

"Will you please let me know if you find out anything?"

"Yes, I will. Is there a lot of money in your family that would benefit someone to kidnap your sister?"

"As far as I know, Tina and I are the only two remaining in our family and there is no money to speak of."

"Thanks again, Ms. O'Hara. We will be in touch."

Diane slowly hung up the phone. She turned to see General Estes quietly talking with Dennis.

"Diane, Dennis was just telling me what happened. Any news at all from the person you were talking to?"

"Nothing good, sir. He's an FBI agent. My sister, Tina, hasn't been seen in nine days."

"Dennis tells me she works at the Pentagon. Does she have access to important information there?"

"The agent just told me that she worked in a very sensitive area, so I guess so. Sir, since the big security mess, is there anyone who can dust this envelope and letter for prints?"

The general made a call.

"Any idea who might have your sister?"

"No, sir. I can't imagine her useless boyfriend doing it."

"Didn't I hear you tell the agent he was from Colombia?" Dennis asked.

"Yes, but why would he, or they, want her? From what I've heard, that country is only into drug trafficking."

"I don't know; wish I did sweetie." He hugged her tightly.

The next morning, at 0630 hours, Diane's phone rang. She rolled over in bed and had it before the second ring.

"Yes."

"This is General Estes, Diane. There is an inbound plane with an FBI agent and a CIA agent on board. They have a little more info on your sister's case. They will be brought to my office directly and you're welcome to be there if you want."

Dennis walked in with steaming cups of coffee as she rolled out of bed.

"Good morning, babe. The general called and I need to meet him in his office. There are two agents flying in now. He said they have more info on my sister."

Dennis, Diane and the general were sitting in the general's office drinking coffee when the two men, in gray suits, were ushered in by a security guard.

"Thomas Walters and Jerry Crowell, sir," the security guard stated.

"Thank you, Jim," the general said.

After the introductions, General Estes said, "I understand you gentlemen have further information on the Tina O'Hara case."

"Some," the FBI agent replied. "Whoever wrote the letter got careless. Your fingerprint man lifted a clean thumbprint from the stamp, and the letter was postmarked in Virginia, at a post office not far from D.C. The letter was written by Mr. Santiago, an alias by the way, and as far as we can find out he is a Greek citizen by the name of Anthony Savalas. At the bank, they told our agent that he had not come to work in two weeks and assumed he had quit. As is required in all FDIC banks, they had a complete file on him, fingerprints, pictures, and everything. He came on a work permit from Venezuela. How his prints got through the Bureau, we have no idea, but we put the information out over the hotline yesterday evening. Within an hour, Interpol came back to us and he is wanted in several countries for illegal sales of weapons of war. He sells everything from stolen fighter planes to missiles, weapons of all types. He is also wanted for drug trafficking. We are privy to your sister's job records, and in no way would she have any info on any weapons, of any kind. We can't figure out why he took her, unless she went willingly because they were in love."

Diane, who had been absorbing it all, leaned back in her chair, shaking her head.

"No," she finally replied. "That's not likely, but then again, why would she live with that pig the way he treated her? It's just nothing like her."

The CIA agent handed Diane some pictures.

"Is that the Santiago you know, Miss O'Hara?"

She slowly leafed through the pictures.

"This one definitely, clean-shaven, short crew cut hair. I see the resemblance, but these all have beards, mustaches, and much longer hair."

"He is known for changing his appearances. The French thought they had him boxed in about four years ago, but he got away. He high tailed it to South America, and when Interpol found his whereabouts in Venezuela, they requested extradition but were refused. Interpol was going to try and snatch him anyway, but again he disappeared, and according to his passport date, it was about that time he came to America."

Still shaking her head, Diane could not believe that Tina would go willingly, and leave all her clothes behind. "If Tina went willingly, why would Santiago, or what ever his name is, send me this note with a message to follow?"

"That's a puzzle to us also," the CIA agent responded. "If a follow up message does come, then perhaps we will find out. Do you have a daily mail plane that comes here? "

"Yes we do," General Estes replied. Looking at his watch, he told them, "It will be arriving within the hour."

"Sir, we want to separate and check the mail bags before anyone touches the letter. We will personally open and dump the bags, please."

"By all means, gentlemen, let me call the tower so they will let us know when the plane is inbound. I'll have the bags brought by security to the mail sorting room. I'll also notify the postmaster not to touch or open them."

"What if it doesn't come today?"

"Miss O'Hara, we are instructed to remain here for two weeks and go through the process. According to Interpol records, Mr. Savalas doesn't play waiting games. He's aware that he is being sought, and he doesn't stay in one area very long. It took three days from the postmark date for this letter to get to your APO post office, then one more day to get to you. Now another day and a half will have passed before you get it. Six to seven days will have passed when you open it and read it. We figure Mr. Savalas is aware of, and follows timelines pretty well. It appears he is very efficient in his operation; that's why he has survived so long. We will just have to wait and see."

The FBI agent opened his briefcase and pulled out a handful of letters. He handed them to Diane.

"Are these the letters you wrote to your sister, Miss O'Hara?"

She quickly leafed through them.

"Yes, yes they are, but none are opened."

"Yes, one is partially opened; the return address is torn off. We figure that is where he got your address from. One of our agents found it on the topmost shelf in the closet, with his clothes. It was shoved back against the wall where it could not be seen."

"Damn it, he hid the letters from her, she didn't even get them … the bastard."

"Here's one that was apparently written by her, to you. It has a postage stamp on it but was never mailed."

Diane took it. She slowly turned it over, as if afraid to open it. She carefully opened it and pulled out the pages. As she read it, tears started rolling down her cheeks. When she finished reading, she handed it to Dennis, put her head down, and openly cried.

Dennis finished the letter and laid it on the table.

Speaking solemnly, and to no one in particular, he said, "She wanted help to get away from him. He threatened to kill her many times if she ever left him, and apparently he almost choked her to death a couple of times. She feared him very much."

Diane sat up, and wiped her tears away.

"I should have killed the bastard instead of beating him up. She wouldn't be going through this now if I had."

"Perhaps," the general replied, "but you would have been in prison if you had done that. I'm glad you're here so you can help her now."

His phone rang.

"Yes. Thank you. "

He looked at the two agents.

"The mail plane is on the ground and taxiing in. Security will have the mail bags in the sorting room in about 20 minutes."

In the mail room, the postmistress came over to them.

"Gentlemen, perhaps to save you some time, you will allow me to explain something. At high security facilities, all mail is separated. Personal mail is in bag A. We record the name and address of the person who is receiving the mail, as well as the return address and the postmark. Bag B is what seems to be business mail, while junk mail and ads are in bag C."

The two agents soon had the bag marked A on a long sorting table, spreading the letters down the sorting table. Wearing latex gloves, they started on opposite ends of the table. Deftly, they spread the letters out to review them. About half an hour passed before agent Crowell picked out a letter with a pair of tweezers.

Walters handed Crowell the other envelope and they compared the writing.

"This is it," agent Walters said, as he placed the new letter in a plastic bag and then into another folder.

Back in the general's office, everyone gathered around the conference room table watching the agents do their work. They put a large brown paper on the table and put the envelope right in the middle. They dusted and brushed each side, looking for fingerprints. There were none. When the exterior was completed, agent Walters turned the envelope over, back flap up. He took a long, very thin blade, slipped its tip under the far end of the flap and slowly pulled the knife along, and under, the flap. In seconds, he pulled the flap up, opening the letter.

"Is that a hair?"

"It looks to be an eyebrow, or eyelash. Pick it off with tweezers and bag it."

They dusted the inside of the flap, finding no fingerprints. With tweezers, they reached in and brought a letter out and opened it carefully. They carried out the fingerprint dusting process on both sides of the page. There were no prints to be found. After they finished their investigation of the letter, they picked it up to read it.

"I'll read this out loud," agent Walters said. "Miss O'Hara, you are indeed much more of a woman than your useless sister. I don't know why I have always felt that Tina would bring me something worthwhile. Gut feeling I guess. She finally delivered, though. I saw your TV interview after you destroyed those MiG jets. Later you revealed that you were flying one of the new space-ships when you took those fighters out.

Miss O'Hara, you have the ability, and I'm sure the opportunity, to deliver to me a commodity that is quite priceless. I demand that you do so. After checking on this useless bitch of a sister you have, you know she is gone. I have her, and for a very short while will keep her. The first mistake you could make is going to the authorities. If you do that, it will make your job much harder to meet my demands. These are my demands and my time schedule for you to carry them out.

"You will deliver to me one of those new spaceships, completely intact. Here is when and how. This letter will be posted on the same day as the date written below. I will give it six days to be in your possession. It shouldn't take more than five days, but I'm aware of how things happen in APO centers. I'm giving you one day of grace for you to absorb this letter and start making your plans. In exactly seven more days, I demand a ship be sitting on the ground at the coordinates posted at the bottom of this letter. If it is not there by midnight on that day, your lovely sister's fate begins.

"At midnight, I will turn her over to the very hungry man who already wants her body. At 6 a.m. the next morning, a gruesome punishment begins. Miss O'Hara, I really never liked doing this, but I've found in the past that what I do always works.

"I have a very large tank of hungry piranha. The tank is more than big enough for a large human body and they can strip a body to a skeleton in two minutes flat. At 6 a.m., should you not be here, my men will push one hand into that tank until there is nothing but bone. I will seal and bind her wound for two hours. After the two hours, if you are still not here, then my piranha will feed on her arm, up to the elbow. With each two hours that you are not here, that act will be repeated.

"Believe me; I will keep her alive until midnight. After midnight, her entire body goes into the tank, very much alive. I will admit defeat and go about my business. Your choice, Miss O'Hara. That's it except for the date and coordinates he lists at the bottom of the page."

Diane's hands covered her eyes, but she could not stop the stream of tears that poured from behind them. Dennis sat beside her throughout with his arms around her.

"I cannot believe he could be so inhuman," said Dennis.

"General Estes, his past history indicates that he will carry out any act that suits his purpose. I'm afraid he's most capable of carrying out this inhuman act."

"When the hell is the date and what are those coordinates?" Dennis asked.

"Here is the letter, General Denehey. We will want a copy for our files. Meanwhile, I'll call my boss and get an agent to the post office where this was mailed from. It's a small town just south of San Diego, on the Mexican border. General, may I use your office phone? We have eight days to find them."

"These coordinates should tell us that," Dennis added.

"Perhaps," agent Crowell replied, "but Savalas knows that, too, so he won't be there early. We'll try to go in the back door, so to speak, to really find him. Most likely he will be in Mexico. These coordinates, I think, will be somewhere near the Yucatán Peninsula. Do you have a navigational map of South America, General Estes?"

The general walked around the table to a thirty-foot blackboard. Above it, end on end, were what looked like movie screens
rolled up. General Estes found the one he wanted and pulled it down
over the blackboard. The map showed Central America and Mexico

"Give me those coordinates Dennis."

Using a thumb tack, the general pinpointed the location.

"Hell, I can't pronounce it."

"There, right in the middle of those tiny islands. They're
about 90 miles off the coast. The agent was right; Savalas has
probably taken her to Mexico."

Dennis let go of Diane's hand.

"I'll be back in a minute, honey."

Dennis walked around to the large map. Diane had pulled
herself together and watched the two men. Dennis put his finger on
the map, traced around the little group of islands, and then ran his
finger over to the coast.

"Hmmm," Dennis muttered out loud. "There is tiny village,
north and south, of this larger town in the middle."

Looking at the legend in the lower right hand corner, he
studied the miles legend. With a ruler, he measured the distance
from the city to the center of the group of small islands. Still talking
out loud, but to no one in particular, he continued, "approximately

60 miles from this city to the islands. A seaplane, helicopter, or boat, could get them there in no time."

"What are you thinking, Dennis?"

"Well, General, I'm just trying to form a picture in my mind of the area, Sir. What are the chances of using one of our ships to run down there, get some pictures of the whole area, buildings, vehicles, people, and so on?"

"By golly, Dennis," General Estes said, "maybe I can do better than that. I just happen to know we have one of our newest spy satellites over Venezuela. We've been keeping a close eye on what that dictator, Chavez, is doing. You know he owns a refinery and the chain of Citgo gas stations across America. Ever since he said he would destroy the American economy, we have been watching him closely. Personally, after a statement like that, I don't understand why our government allows him to continue operating in our country. Back to the subject at hand, I'll call Cynthia and explain the situation to her. We'll see if we can't move that satellite over the area we want. I've seen some pictures taken from it, and you can count the grains of sand on the beach. If she doesn't want it moved, hell yes, we'll take a couple of our ships and do what we can."

He grabbed the letter with the coordinates and actually ran from the room, to his office. About 15 minutes later he walked back into the room, smiling.

"Done deal," he reveled, putting the letter back on the table. "They are now maneuvering the satellite up there. It will be in position in about 30 minutes and we should start receiving downloads within the hour."

Diane gave Dennis a weak smile.

"What are you thinking about, sweetheart?"

"I'm not sure yet, waiting for the pictures. I promise you this, darling; we won't allow him to do what he says. No way in hell."

The images were handed off to Dennis, Diane, and the general as fast as they came in. Dennis was placing them in order, south to north, filling up the blackboard slowly, until a complete picture began forming on the wall. Soon, the picture was complete.

"Magnificent photos," Diane stated. "Look at the detail. I can count the patterns on the thatched roofs of those huts. It's as if I am standing right there. I can even distinguish features on the people's faces."

"We have seven tiny islands between the coast and the two larger islands. I don't see any huts on any of them," said Dennis.

He pointed to the largest island on the picture.

"The largest island, this southerly one, is about 22 miles long. There's one village on the south end, another in the central part, and nothing I can see on the northern end."

"Dennis, look at the little island between the two. There is a runway, tarmac, and in damn good condition," said the general.

"Look on the road there, leading to those buildings, it's an old fire truck and what looks like an old World War II ambulance, no wheels on one side."

"What does that printing say on the left side, bottom, next to the ambulance door?" Diane asked.

Dennis looked closer.

"It's sort of faded, but I think it says property of the U. S. Army Air Corps. I wonder if it's an old American airfield."

"It probably is," General Estes replied. "I remember reading somewhere that we put alert stations all around South America and Mexico. They flew scout planes out of there. The old T-6 had good fuel range. They watched for the Japs on the Pacific side, and the Germans on the Caribbean side."

"Well, whatever it is, the runway is in excellent condition. From the tire marks I see, I would say it's been recently used. Those two long wooden structures look like old barracks. Look here, there's a Jeep by that one, with a mounted machine gun behind the two front seats and thirteen men in front, armed, but just sitting around."

General Estes pointed to an area of interest on the pictures.

"Look here, this may be the compound. There's the rusty flagpole in the center, and the larger building to the north with three jeeps in front of it. One jeep has a top and one without, and then another with a mounted machine gun. That concrete block building looks to have a steel door, and see those men standing by that old six-by?

"Yeah, I see that," Dennis replied.

"Damn, the print on those crates looks new. What does that say? It looks like United States Marine Corps, Arms Warehouse,

San Diego, California. I count eleven long crates and several other smaller ones.

Agent Walters came up to inspect the picture.

"I'll be; I better call this in."

He left the room quickly.

"There is a long wharf extended out, and a deep draft cabin cruiser with some crew members on board. General, these pictures are a gold mine."

"You bet Dennis. Are you forming a plan yet?"

"Roughly, sir. Let's get the rest of the pilots down here and put our heads together."

"Good idea, Dennis. I'll take care of it."

Soon, all the pilots were filing in, looking at the overall picture on the board and wondering what was going on. Once they were all seated, General Estes began to explain what was happening, while Thelma passed out copies of the letter that Diane had received. As all read it, their faces took on very grim expressions.

Captain McBride gasped.

"Oh my God! How could he do that to a helpless human being?"

There was no answer, but she expected none.

The general finished explaining everything, and the grim faces reflected their disgust and their determination.

Dennis took the floor and explained his intent.

"I want all of you to know, this is strictly on a volunteer basis. Anyone who wants out, at any time, can leave. We understand if you don't want to go, so don't feel bad if you decide not to. I'm also going to say this; I don't want to hear of anyone giving a hard time to any person who decides not to go. We will be on foreign soil."

Captain McBride had gone to the board and was studying the island pictures.

"Sir, excuse me, I believe I know who those islands belong to, or at least who has a lease on them. My grandfather was an Army Air Corps pilot in World War II. He had many pictures of the same islands in his album. He flew old gooney birds, the C-47s, supplying materials, mail, and equipment to a whole chain of islands down the east coast of South America. America had a 100-year lease on them, which I bet is still in effect, just like Guantánamo Bay in Cuba."

"Thank you, Captain, so we have more great background history in our group," replied General Estes. "Thelma, honey, would you run that through the computer and see if we can verify that base? It should come under Army Air Corps bases in World War II."

"All right," Dennis continued, "let's put our heads together and see if we can come up with a solid plan to use our ships to go down there, save this girl, and get rid of this Tony Savalas and his henchmen for good. We have seven days to solidify a plan and one day to implement it. According to Interpol and CIA records on his history, he himself may not come to the site where the deal is to take place, until a day or two before the supposed exchange. The CIA figures he has already taken Tina into Mexico. Noting the location he has chosen for the exchange, I would bet that the CIA is right on the money. My guess is that he will be as close as possible to the primary site, which is this small city, right here on the coast. It's approximately 50 to 60 miles from the delivery area, and there are only three ways for him to get there."

Dennis took the ruler and pointed to the picture.

"There are two seaplanes tied up to this wharf right here. There is this small airfield just west of the city, about one mile. I'll bet there is a helicopter in one of the two hangars here, and naturally, those little planes parked outside the hangars. Other than flying, he would have to go by water, which I would think would be one of these cruisers parked at the docks. I have a partial plan in mind, but I'm not going to put it out there and screw up your train of thought. The most important thing we have to take into consideration is, somewhere in all of this, Diane is likely to have a face-to-face meeting with this jerk if we are going to save Tina's life. Any questions?"

When nobody spoke, General Estes stood up.

"Just to let everyone know, the president said she has made arrangements for the satellite to make four passes a day. They will be at daylight, mid-morning, mid-afternoon, and one hour before sunset. If we need a nighttime pass for any reason, just let her know. She has the same pictures from the satellite that we are looking at. She has also put some tactical people looking into the situation to see if they can offer any helpful solutions. That's it for now."

Thelma walked back into the room and handed the general some papers.

"Captain McBride is correct, that whole chain of islands is leased to the United States, and there are 37 more years on that lease. So whoever is on those islands, we can remove for trespassing."

Everyone went to work on their own ideas. Once in awhile, someone would ask a question, or go up and study the pictures, and then return to his or her seat. Updated pictures came in once more before sunset. The only things that seemed to change were the number of people or vehicles that had moved. Nonetheless, everything was picked apart, noted, and itemized on the blackboard.

"All right my good people," Dennis said. "It's almost midnight and even my brain is getting scrambled. We still have eight full days, so let's get some rest."

Everyone stood, stretched, and started picking up the paper plates, napkins, and drinks that Thelma had brought from the mess hall. In no time, they had the room shining, and most of them departed to their quarters. Tensley, Dennis, Diane, Thelma, and the general, all sat down.

"Oh, man," Tensley said. "Those pictures have been picked apart, like picking fleas off an infested dog. Every building, hut, roof, path, road, runway, building, oh I said that already, anyway it's all there."

"Yes, it is. Tomorrow, we should sound everyone out for their ideas and then put the jigsaw puzzle together."

"Let's go get a shower and get some sleep," Diane said, yawning.

Thelma walked over to Diane and gave her a big hug.

"Don't worry, Diane, we have a wonderful team here and they will get your sister out safely."

Diane lay quietly in bed, staring into the darkness, hoping Tina was comfortable and saying a prayer for her.

"You're not asleep." Dennis' voice came out of the darkness.

"How do you know that? I'm not moving around."

"I never close my eyes until your breathing tells me you're asleep. You're worrying about Tina, but in my heart I know it will all end well."

Diane rolled over and put her arm across his chest.

"I never knew a man could be as wonderful as you. I wish I had met you years ago."

He kissed her on her forehead.

"Quit it, you're making my head swell up."

She giggled and whispered, "Oh really, should I ask which one?"

"At least you still have your sense of humor. I love you, crazy woman."

When Dennis woke up, he looked around for her, but she was not there. He smelled the coffee, rolled out of bed, and walked into the dining room. She wasn't there. She must be in the bathroom, he thought, and poured himself a cup of coffee. He walked over to the dining room table and sat down. That's when he noticed the note. Gone to the conference room, I love you. He took another drink of coffee and went to the bathroom. He rinsed his face with cold water and grabbed a fresh pair of fatigues. As he was dressing, he saw the clock … 10:45 a.m. Lord, why didn't she wake me?

When he arrived at the conference room, everyone was already there. They turned and looked at him when he entered the room.

"Sorry, everyone, I overslept. Someone I thought would call me didn't."

"Dennis, son, don't worry about it. When your body says to rest, listen to it."

"Sir, when my people are present ..."

"Enough, Dennis. Everyone here, including me, knows you have been pushing it way too hard. Your mind and body's defense mechanism kicked in and kept you resting. So don't worry about it. We have updated pictures and one thing has changed. A helicopter is parked in the field, behind the town's only hotel."

Dennis went to the board, studying the helicopter in the large picture.

"And it seems to be rather new at that. Six-seat Bell. I wonder who arrived in that."

The words were barely finished when Thelma came in, her arms loaded with a new set of downloaded pictures. She laid them on the table and gave Dennis a hug.

"Finally get a decent night's rest?"

Blushing, he replied, "Thank you, sweetheart, I did"

Dennis began leafing through the pictures. He found the one he was searching for.

"Damn, the helicopter is gone"

Diane came over and put her arm around Dennis' waist.

"Let's get the picture of the target island."

She leafed through the pictures and found it.

"There … there is the same helicopter, same numbers."

Holding it up and studying it, Diane noticed something.

"There is that jerk Santiago. You were right, Dennis."

"We'll see in the next download if he goes back to that hotel."

"OK, let's put those pictures over the others and see if anything else has changed."

Deana was at the board, putting up the pictures she had. Just as she held the new one up, to cover the old one, she stopped and stared at it. Then she lifted the one before it, and the one before that, and then she glanced back at the new one.

"Uh oh, here's something I certainly missed, and I don't see it on our board anywhere."

"What's that?" Ed asked.

"All along the northeast side of the runway, if I'm not mistaken, that is an old tank hidden in the trees. Then about 100 yards down is a Jeep with a mounted machine gun. Are the other two Jeeps still at the compound?"

Everyone began leafing through their pictures.

"Here," Mattie said. Here are these two, and another one is approaching the compound, down the road from the runway, and about 20 men behind it."

"You're right; that is not a machine gun on it. That is a handheld ground-to-air launcher, and a rack of missiles on the other side. . OK everyone, hold up. Put your pictures on the table and let's go back to the first download. Each of us start on a vertical row, and let's see if we can find out where all this equipment and men were hiding. We'll progress from this download to the next."

About 20 minutes had passed when Cathy said, "Sir, they were not hidden; they flew them in last night."

"What makes you say that?"

"Look at the far north end of the runway on the first download. Then look at last night's final download."

Dennis stared at both pictures.

"They're identical."

"Yes, sir, they are, now look at the download from early this morning."

"Oh, hell yes, great details, Cathy. There's a new set of touchdown tracks and whatever touched down was heavily loaded. You can see where he bounced and left another set of tracks here."

"I don't think so, sir. Two planes landed, one just slightly overshot, or the heavy one landed before the other. Old C-119s, sir."

"How can you determine that they were C-119s, Cathy?"

Leafing through the latest download, Cathy laid two of the large pictures on the table.

"This is the far south end of the runway, sir. Just before the end of the runway, tri-cycle landing gear tracks are going through the grass, and have crushed the shrubs on its way into that large group of trees. Now, if that's not the twin tail booms of a C-119 under the camouflage netting, I don't know my aircraft. The other 119 is in those trees on the opposite side of the runway."

"Great work Cathy. She's right, everyone, they're 119s. That means they expect Diane's compliance or at least they're hoping for it."

"Yes it does, General. Let's put this all aside for now. Apparently, we know their plans, so let's see if we can figure out a strategy to rescue Tina."

"Dennis, Diane was here before we arrived today. She has worked out a pretty good plan. In fact, everyone else has already agreed it's the best. Let's start from the beginning and pick it apart. So far, everyone has added some contributions to her plan and it seems pretty solid. OK, Diane the floor is yours."

Diane took a position in front of the satellite pictures.

"As you know, these are great pictures when the satellite is zooming in. Every detail of the islands is here. The target island lies between the two larger ones, and none of these six small islands, west and north, are occupied. The largest southern island has huts and natives that are visible. This island is approximately 25 miles long. There is a group of huts about five miles north of the other village, which leaves about 20 miles to the northern tip of the island. There are no natives seen anywhere in the second village, so I would assume that it is abandoned. The small Leeward Islands are 10 to 15 miles from the larger islands. The more northern of the two largest islands has no huts, buildings, or structures of any kind. I'm assuming that no one occupies it. There are no visible roads or paths either.

"General, if we can get some night shots, say around midnight, two in the morning, and then again at four in the morning, I believe we will find that those folks will be in bed, asleep, lights out. If I understand correctly, we can use all twelve ships. Excuse me."

Diane walked about three feet to the water cooler and filled a small paper cup with cool water. She felt warm and a little light-headed.

"Are you OK, Diane?" Dennis asked.

"Don't worry, Dennis, I'm really okay," she said, as she walked back to the board.

"Like I was saying, I believe we have permission to use all twelve ships. That will give us eleven to stand by, plus mine to go in and more or less negotiate. I propose putting one ship on each of the smaller islands. They will have to VTOL, but there are plenty of trees and shrubs to taxi into, and hide even our huge ships from aerial view. That would be six of our eleven ships. At least two ships near the northern tip of the southern large island. Two ships somewhere near the central and southern end of that island," she said, using the ruler to point out the location. "The normal southerly winds down there should sweep the sound of our ships landing away from the coast, and the target island. Maybe we'll put all five ships on the northern island. We can discuss that in a bit. I'll need two passwords set up that will fit into a conversation. One password will be a signal for all eleven ships to take to the air and circle the target island, while the other password will be to attack. Lieutenant Tensley said that he can furnish a transmitter that could be hidden, so that all ships will be able to hear my conversations. I will want one pilot with me, in my ship. I'll explain why in a minute. As mentioned yesterday, I'll have to go face-to-face with these people. I sort of know how I will, but it's something I have to work on."

"This VFR homing building is about ten yards from the runway, and at Lieutenant Tensley's suggestion, the nose of my ship will be close to the edge of the runway, pointed at that building. That way, when I step off the elevator I will go to my nose gear. That building will act as my shield if I have to take cover for any reason. I will have my new laser pistol, along with my .45 until help arrives.

"Let me back up a moment. If I give the signal to lift off and surround the target, stay under two hundred feet. Do so even when going to your set-down spots, as you can see they do have radar. The dish looks to be a fifty mile radius sweep. Those dummies put the thing almost at ground level, among that forest of sixty- to seventy-foot trees. So, at two hundred feet or lower, you will be under it. When the attack starts, whoever is the closest to this building here, takes it out first. That's where they were unloading the missiles and no telling what else. It should make one hell of a distraction when it goes. The rest of you will start from water's edge and go toward the center of the target, which will be me and my ship. Sweep with your laser cannons, level the trees and anything taller than an inch off the ground. All I ask is that you please try not to make me into toast."

Smiles and giggles went around the table, even as serious as the jest was.

"What if they refuse to negotiate?" Mattie asked.

"That is why I want a pilot in my ship. They want the ship so bad, and all Santiago sees is dollar signs. That's why I will feel comparatively safe on the ground at first. They won't damage the ship, or me, because no one there will know how to fly the ship. I'm going to pull a stunt from Captain Kirk's program.

"In one of the 'Star Trek' episodes, his people had beamed down to what they didn't know was a prison planet. They were captured, disarmed, and the bad guys ordered Captain Kirk to bring a shuttle down so they could escape the planet, their intent being to take over the starship. When Captain Kirk disembarked the shuttle, his backup pilot was hidden. Captain Kirk acted as if he ordered the computer to close the hatch and go up to a hover, where it could not be reached.

"The prisoners threatened to kill him and his crew if he didn't bring the shuttle back. As usual, Captain Kirk says, fine, go ahead, but when we die, you die. The prisoners were distracted by the threatening shuttle just long enough to give Scotty time to lock on to our heroes and beam them up. That's where my bluff will end, mainly because you guys can't beam me and Tina up."

Everyone laughed.

"OK, here's my plan from when the ship leaves me. From there, I think I can force a negotiation of some sort. If Tina isn't there, I'm going to force them to produce her, or there will be no deal, period. If they don't, it will convince me that they have already killed her. If my ship can protect me fine, if not, so be it. Turn that island into a puddle of mud and glass, and above all, don't let Santiago escape so he can harm and kill others. That, my friends, pretty well covers my plan."

She took a seat next to Dennis and he took her hand in his.

"I'll be the one in your ship, sweetheart, and I will protect you."

"What are your thoughts on this, Dennis?" the general asked.

"It pretty well covers and improves on my plan. Her having to face someone is inevitable, but it scares the hell out of me."

"Do you feel that you can pull it off, Diane?"

"Sir, it's not a matter of feeling; it has to be done to save her from those animals. I am so grateful to all of you, the president, and anyone else involved, for allowing us to use these ships to rescue my sister and rid the world of an evil man."

"America is one family, and the ships are tools of the family. Does anyone else have anything to add?"

No one said a word, but the expressions on each face around the table showed determination.

"Diane," said the general, "work on your passwords and we'll get you those overnight pictures. Let me know when you want to go. I'm going to call the president and fill her in, and I'll let her know when you have your schedule down pat."

##

Later, as Dennis and Diane reached the elevator, several people were waiting for them.

Cathy and Mattie stepped forward.

"We know it's a little early for this, but we all agreed that it would be great if you two would go with all of us to the club, and have a little bash. It's rare that we all get a chance to get together at one time, and we would deeply appreciate your companionship."

Laughing, Diane asked, "Dennis?"

Shaking his head and smiling, Dennis replied, "I think it's a great idea. Heck yeah, let's get wild. Thanks, Cathy."

"Actually it was Ed's idea, but you know how bashful he is."

He gave Ed two thumbs-up.

"Let me tell the general, he and Thelma may want to join us. Hey Sarge, go get Shirley and tell the engineers to get off their butts, drinks on me, and bring our noncoms too."

At 1 a.m., the party was in full swing, and the club was packed with Delta Blue Squadron. The jukebox played various types of music, but someone had most definitely dominated it with big-band era music and blues. Everyone was dancing, drinking, and enjoying the company.

Diane was sitting at the table watching Dennis. He was consumed in a conversation with General Estes and Chuck Hennesey, the civilian who had played such an important role in quashing Captain Knull's scheme. Mattie appeared and sat in a chair close to Diane.

"Diane, I need some advice."

She was feeling no pain, not drunk, but close.

"Sure Mattie, if I can help, I will."

"Well, there's this regulation about no fraternization, or something like that, between officers and noncoms. Is that a really serious regulation, and do they enforce it real hard?"

"Oh Mattie, I really don't know, honey. I can find out. What's up? Got a crush?"

"No Diane, not a crush, we are dead serious. I really love this man, and he loves me. I have had crushes before, but this is different."

"You aren't by any chance pregnant, are you?"

"Oh no, nothing like that, but as much as I love the service, I would resign my commission to marry him. He has never even tried anything like that, and if he had, I would have given in to him; would be my first ever."

"Well, that sounds serious. Do I know him?"

"You might. He's one of the sergeants on the security guard post at the hangar."

"Well, sweetheart, I won't tell anyone. After this mission is over, I'll make some discrete inquiries into that. I'll bet there are places where they will relax that regulation, particularly when two want to marry."

"Oh, I hope so. He has brought the marriage subject up twice, but he also mentions the regulations. He said he doesn't want to cause me any trouble, but Diane, if he asks me to marry him, I will resign if I have to."

"I'm so proud for you, and I understand your feelings, believe me. Just give me a chance to check into it, OK?"

"The main thing right now Diane, is for you to stay safe. You can bet I'll be on my toes on this mission. We will bring you and your sister home safely."

"Hey, girls, what's up?"

"Hello, Dennis. Diane and I were just having a heart to heart. You're a lucky man."

"Oh yes, I am that. We haven't had much time to really get together like this since all of you got here. Training, training, training. I do keep up with your progress though. How do you like our ships, and your job?"

"Job, what job? This is a dream come true for all of us. I could not be happier, thanks to you and Diane."

Mattie excused herself to leave Dennis and Diane alone.

"So, a heart to heart, huh?"

"She is madly in love."

"Puppy love?"

"No, Dennis, she is very seriously in love."

"That's wonderful. She may joke around a lot but she sure is serious, and damned good at her job."

"Yes, I know, and I hate to think we may lose her."

"My Lord, Diane, why? She just said she loves this job."

"Don't mention this to anyone, honey; I'm going to check into it after the mission. She is in love with a non-com, and said if there is no way around the fraternization regulation, she will resign her commission to marry him."

"We will both look into it. In my eyes, that regulation was made primarily to discourage officers from trying to take advantage of the higher position to gain favoritism. We can't afford to lose such quality people."

"I totally agree. Sweetheart, I've had enough partying. I need to work on those passwords for tomorrow. You can stay if you want, I don't mind at all. I need some food, maybe a bowl of soup or a sandwich, and then a hot tub of water, so I can think."

"I have some paperwork to do, too. I want to assign certain ships and people to certain positions on those islands. I want to assign Ed or Terry, because of their fighter experience, to take out the armory, boat docks, and the radar. That will shut off any escape routes. Then we can herd the rest of them with your plan. Your job in all of this scares the hell out of me."

"There's no way around it, but don't worry, I can handle it."

Diane and Dennis walked into the conference room early, but again, Dennis saw that everyone had beat them.

"Darn, we sure have anxious troops here. It's good to know they care so much."

"Family, Dennis, they're our family."

"Good morning Dennis, Diane," General Estes said, sounding rather perky. "You were right, Diane. Here are the satellite downloads you requested. Hell, all lights were off before midnight. Not one sign of life anywhere before sunrise. There's nothing moving on any of the occupied islands, nor the target camp."

"Good, I hope it's a cloudless night and the full moon is out. It would be much easier to land when everything is illuminated like that white sand is. No landing lights would be needed."

"OK, here's my suggestion," Dennis started. "We stagger the ship's arrival times. Let's say we send in the first six ships starting at 0230 hours, five minutes apart, and land on the farthest spots first, those six small islands. That should be complete no later than 0300 hours. Use your secure radio to let the next ship behind know you are down. Let's put three ships down on the most northerly island. At 0400 hours, when most are getting their best sleep, is when we should land the other two on the southern island. If we're lucky to have a breeze, the sound won't carry very far toward the target area. Be safe, but get down as quickly as possible and idle your engines."

Diane stood up.

"Dennis is going with me. Before any of you go in, we will be at 20,000 feet using our cameras to observe the target island. If we find it necessary to change the plan or cancel, we'll let everyone know. We're hoping that this won't alert them in any way. Once you are down and safe, Dennis and I will go to this island, about a hundred miles north of the target. We will stay there until sunrise. We want to go in at sunrise while everyone is still groggy. I'll come in from the northeast, at about 10,000 feet, so their radar will be sure to pick me up. I will VTOL at the proposed spot, with my nose gear near the concrete block building as planned. From then on, I'll have to feel my way through it.

"The passwords are Mattie, and imbecile. Mattie for you to get in the air and imbecile means attack. Shake that island like an earthquake. If things go haywire, attack is what I will say, nothing more. If that happens, I want Dennis to take out the tank and then get out of there. Don't hit his ship, as he will be in the center of it all. If I can make it, I'll be in a prone position by that VFR building. One thing though, if you toast me, I want butter and jam."

Nervous laughter passed around the room.

"You ain't gonna get toasted baby, I guarantee that," Deana chimed in.

"We're going to take good care of you Diane, no worries," Cathy said.

"I appreciate that. Dennis will assign the ships and positions."

Diane sat down beside General Estes.

"OK, folks, we have only a few second seat personnel. I don't want to take more people than necessary. There will be a radar communication person on each ship but mine. Should any of you feel uncomfortable without a second seat officer, we will scratch that ship and pair you with someone on another ship. Don't be bashful, no one needs to be embarrassed, particularly you six new folks. Trust me, we will all understand. So speak up now if you are nervous, as I want all of us back here safe, and we don't want to lose a ship."

Dennis paused, looking around the room. He was proud of each and every one of these brave people. None said a word. He walked over to the bare blackboard, beside the pictures of a strange land that they would all know too well, very soon.

He wrote the ship numbers and positions on the blackboard as he talked.

"Diane and I, ship No. 1. Deana, you will be in No. 2, island one, starting from the north. Mattie, ship No. 3, island two. Cathy, ship No. 4, island three. Terry, No. 5, island four."

Dennis turned to face Terry.

"Terry, it was you or Ed. Island four is in line with the target, and I want you on attack. I need you to take out the Armory, radar, boats, and the dock."

"Yes, sir."

He turned back to the board and began writing.

"Ed, ship No. 6, island number five."

He glanced at Ed.

"Ed, you'll take out the headquarters building, the barracks, and any vehicles there."

"Yes, sir, understood."

"Tina, ship No. 7, island six. You'll go south after liftoff, to the south end of the runway, and take out both of the C-119s."

Dennis pointed to two of the newer pilots.

"Bill Turzan, you will be in ship No. 8 and Donald Sutherland in No. 9. When you get there, go to the eastern side of the target island and separate to the north."

Dennis picked up the long ruler and pointed to the location on the pictures.

"Bill will land on this island. Donald, you go further north to this island."

"Yes, sir," they said, in unison.

"Now, Matt Ferguson, you will be in ship No. 10 and Crystal Seismore will occupy ship No. 11. You two will be on the northernmost island. It is larger, so you two get together and decide on a common spot to land. On liftoff, spread out to the east and match up with the ones coming from the southern island. Lieutenant Tensley will have ship No. 12 on the northern island. He will be my backup from the north. Lieutenant, I do want flight engineers in the second seats with McBride, Turzan, Ferguson, Seismore, and Sutherland. You five will have very knowledgeable people with you, to aid in any need you have, radar, communications, and weapons. Any questions?"

No questions were asked.

"OK, since there are none, all we have to do is figure out when we go. In the meantime, get your coordinates for where you are to land. We will leave here as a squadron, two divisions of six each. When we are within 800 miles of the target, Diane and I will go to our higher altitude, above their radar capabilities. Nos. 2 through 6 will circle in a holding pattern, while Nos. 7 through 12 will proceed to within 700 miles of the target. When you get there, you will assume a holding pattern also and notify me. From that point, I will release the ships at five minute intervals to proceed to their coordinates. As each of you land with no visible problems, contact me on the secure radio channel. When we leave for the target we will notify you; you will then go into standby for the passwords. That's it for now. Get those coordinates and if you have any questions, do not hesitate to ask."

Diane, Dennis, and the general, put their heads together.

"Diane, we will leave when you say."

"Thank you, General Estes. I want Tina out of there as soon as possible. I can't stand her being in their possession any longer than need be. Those damned animals, no telling what they have already done to her."

"I understand, and I hate to bring this up, but there is one contingency we have not discussed."

"Yes, I know. I have run the prospect of not being able to get her through my mind a thousand times. I have come to one conclusion should that happen. If I can get back on my ship, I will kill her myself. I will level that island, every building, every vehicle, any place they could hide her. An instant death for her is a billion times better than what these SOBs have planned for her. If I don't make it, I pray the rest of the squadron will finish the job."

A deep, somber look came over the general's face.

"Dennis, what say you?"

"Sir, I'm not overconfident about any of this, but I am very confident that this woman here will get the job done, and done right. On the hypothesis that we fail, we will complete the job, one way or another."

"When do you go?"

"It's almost 1100 hours. I believe tonight is as good a time is any. A good 10 hours of rest right now would easily put us on the flight line by 2300 hours. Preflight check by 2330 hours and all ships in the air by 2400 hours ... plenty of time to reach separation point, and if no problems, all should happen on schedule."

"Notify your crews and get some rest; see you in the hangar at 2300 hours.

##

By midnight, all 12 ships were in the air and headed south, as planned. At 0155 hours, the ships were given the go to get to their destinations. At 0355 hours, the last five were sent on their way, and by 0425 hours, all the ships were cleared and in place. Dennis and Diane landed on the island at 0440 hours, local time.

Diane was lying on a soft bench seat, her head in Dennis' lap. Dennis' head was resting against the headrest. Both had their eyes closed, resting, not sleeping, but their minds wandering over the events to come.

Dennis opened his eyes and looked at his watch ... 0610 hours. Looking through the flight deck window to the east, the horizon was turning a light gray. He looked down at Diane, and softly ran his hand over her thick hair. The only light on the flight deck was the soft glow of green indicator lights from the overhead breaker panel.

Diane whispered, "You okay sweetheart?"

"Yes, I'm fine. I'm going to the galley to make some coffee. Another 30 minutes and it will be time."

"I'll fix the coffee."

"No, you stay right here. I set the timer on the coffee pot before we sat down, it should be ready. You just rest."

They sat together, sipping on their coffee and watching the light as it slowly erased the darkness. The very top edge of the sun peeked over the horizon, as though it were just waking up itself to begin its daily journey across the heavens. About 50 yards in front of the ship, the white sand shone like diamonds, as the first rays of the sun danced across it. The Caribbean Ocean, meeting the sand, was a beautiful marine blue, smooth as glass, and not a ripple to be seen.

"It's so beautiful and peaceful; if only the whole world was this way."

"I know honey, if only ... you know, I was just thinking, when we get married I would like to get permission to use one of our ships to come back here for a week long honeymoon."

"Oh, yes, I would love that. You Adam, me Eve!"

"Wow, do we have to wear fig leaves?"

"Not me!"

"Wonderful ... finish your coffee."

##

Diane and Dennis were in their seats preparing for the mission.

"Check out that microphone and earpiece Sarge made for you. Call the other ships and have them check with you as to their status. Let them know we'll lift off in 10 minutes and be at the target approximately 12 minutes later. See if they read you from this distance, and if not, use the radio. We'll check your signal all the way. If it doesn't work from there, then we scratch the mission."

"Why would we scratch the mission?"

"Your communication to all the ships is vital if we are to get in and out safely with you and Tina. Without that, the odds against us are too high."

Diane contacted the ships to check their status. All were ready and awaiting orders.

"Tensley is a genius; it sounds like they are right here with us."

"Good, are you ready, sweetheart?"

"As ready as I'll ever be."

"Take her up then. I'll sit here in Captain Kirk's seat and when I see the target, I'll energize the laser and turn the cameras on. I want to see everything at ground level on the screen."

"Right, here we go."

Just minutes later, they were there.

"There's the target," Diane pointed out, "going down."

Diane started a long approach, straight in, and slowing to almost a stall. She readjusted the thrusters to VTOL at the desired spot.

"There's that tank, just inside the tree line, on your left."

"I see it, Dennis."

The huge ship moved slowly down the runway, toward the small concrete building. She turned the ship's nose at a 45-degree angle toward the building, and cut back the throttles of the engines. The ship settled softly onto the tarmac. Clouds of dust and dirt swirled up, around the ship. As the giant engines came to full idle, the clouds slowly began to settle.

"Check with the other ships, Diane, let them know you are down."

"Roger."

"There are about a dozen armed men running out of the trees, Diane."

"Uh-huh, I see them."

The men reached the runway behind the ship. Ten of them huddled around the main landing gear, their guns pointing in all directions, not knowing where the pilot would exit.

Diane released herself from the seat harness, not taking her eyes off the screen, she watched, waiting for someone to show themselves.

"I guess we're playing a waiting game, Dennis."

"Yeah, they're trying to work on your nerves."

In about four minutes, a Jeep raced out of the trees and onto the road from the compound. Two other Jeeps with mounted machine guns, and men at the ready to use them, followed the lead vehicle. About three hundred yards away, they turned up the runway, toward the ship. They stopped about twenty yards in front of the ship, and four men from each jeep jumped to the ground, kneeling, and leveling their rifles at the ship.

A tall, skinny man stepped out of the lead jeep on the passenger side.

Diane reached over and turned on the exterior phone. She heard the toy soldiers jabbering. The tall man, apparently the leader of the group, was looking toward the flight deck. He waved, and pointed to the ground.

"The ass wants me to come down; he must think I'm crazy."

Diane picked up the microphone.

"Do you speak English?"

The voice startled him, and he looked around. He quickly regained his composure and shouted, "Yes, I speak English, please to come out of your ship."

"You, sir, get those ten men from under my ship. I came here to negotiate for my sister, not to fight. Get those men away from my ship and make them all lower their weapons."

The man looked around, rattled. He was not expecting this confrontation at all, and it was apparent that he was nervous.

Finally, he shouted, "No negotiations! I am boss here, not you; come down immediately!"

"Oh, don't be ridiculous. I'm no one's fool. I will come down only when those men under my ship are gone. Send them down the runway, to that road where you came out of the trees."

The man just stood there.

"Mister, I'll only say this once more. I stole this ship from people who trusted me. My career is gone, my country is gone, and I came here to negotiate, not fight. If you want a demonstration of what I can do, I'll give you one. I'll count to five, and if those men under my ship and those men with you, including your driver, aren't running, not driving, running down the runway, then I will show you what I can do."

She took her finger off the microphone button.

"Dennis, honey, can you zero in on that tank with the rear laser?"

Dennis smiled; proud of the way his woman was handling the situation. He pulled the sighting gauge to his eyes, moving the laser cannon as he went.

"Dead center, babe."

"Good, give me one second after I say five, and take the tin can out."

She looked at the screen, the men were not moving.

She pushed the speaker button, "Sir, five seconds."

"I'm in charge here, not you; I will kill your sister."

"One ... two ... three ..."

No one was moving.

"Four ... five ..."

There was still no movement. The hot, blue-white beam sizzled from the rear laser. The trees in front of the tank disappeared. The tank flew into the air, burning and tumbling. It soared above the trees and exploded in midair, disintegrating into millions of tiny pieces of metal.

Diane observed the scene. The men under the ship lay prone on the tarmac, covering their heads. The leader and the driver were behind the Jeep, while the other toy soldiers had dropped their rifles and were running down the runway. Diane waited. She heard tapping sounds as tiny pieces of metal fell on top of the ship.

"Good job sweetheart, that's one less thing we have to worry about."

She pushed the speaker button.

"Sir, that could have been you."

He raised his head from behind the Jeep, staring up at the windows.

"Yes, I could have taken you and your men out, just as easily. You are now wasting my time. Yes, I want my sister, but not at the expense of my life and hers. You damn people put me in this position and I can never return to my country. I'll give you one minute to move all your people or I'm leaving. I'm sure other people or countries would be interested in this ship."

He stood up, yelling to his men, pointing down the runway toward the other fleeing men. She saw the men under the ship scramble to their feet. There were gone quickly, dashing down the runway.

"Your driver, also."

He signaled to the driver, who did not delay.

"Very good Sir, now remove your weapon and throw it toward the building, beside the runway. After you do that, I will come down and we will talk, face to face."

Reluctantly, he pulled the weapon from his holster and threw it. It sailed past the building, into the shrubs and weeds.

"Very good, sir, I'll be down directly."

"Dennis, would you make sure this earpiece wire is hidden?"

"Yes, it's hidden, but I'm going to let your hair down anyway."

He did so, taking out the clips and folding her long thick hair outward. She shook her head from side to side, and her hair fell over her back and shoulders.

"Perfect," he said. "He may have another weapon, so be careful."

"I will. When I get off the elevator, I'll send it up. I'll talk as if I'm addressing the computer. Take the ship up, and move all the way back to the touchdown area."

"Stay at least ten feet from him and out of my line of fire. I'll have him in my crosshairs. One wrong move and I'll fry him."

"Got to go," said Diane, "I love you."

"I love you, too. Be careful."

She kissed Dennis quickly and walked to the elevator.

When she stepped onto the tarmac, she turned back and removed from her pocket an actual TV remote. She pointed it at the ship, and then raised it to her mouth and said "Computer, raise the elevator."

The man jumped as the elevator began to rise.

She slowly moved toward the man, but angled toward the edge of the runway. He started to say something, but she interrupted.

"One moment, sir."

She spoke into the remote once more, "Computer, move to the designated area."

"What? You talk to your ship?"

Engines one and two throttled up. The ship lifted off the ground, slowly turned, and began moving off to the north.

The man tried screaming above the noise of the powerful engines. They were both forced to turn their heads because of the dirt swirling around them. The man looked horrified.

"Bring it back ... bring it back," he screamed.

Diane held her hand up, speaking into the TV remote once again. The noise subsided as the ship turned once more. With its nose pointing toward them, it gently landed on the ground.

"That is my bargaining chip. I'm here, sir, in good faith, and your boss will be fair. Anyone who threatens me will die."

Gasping and rattled, the man asked, "How?"

Diane laughed heartily.

"Did you see what happened to your tank? Imagine what would happen if that beam reached out and touched you. Just make sure you stay this distance from me. Now, let's get down to business. I'm not staying here much longer. Tell your boss I want proof my sister is still alive."

The man, still watching the huge, menacing ship, stuttered, "There is no boss. I'm the boss here, and if you want proof of your sister's well-being..."

"Oh, so you're the boss?" She pulled out a sheet of paper and unfolded it. "You must be the one who wrote this letter to me."

"What? Oh, I had one of my men write it. I don't write your language too well."

"Understand this, buster; get me the proof that my sister is alive. Until then, we have nothing more to discuss. I will be here in my ship. Until then, goodbye, Mr. Santiago."

"No, no, wait. Five minutes, I'll return with proof."

"OK, I'll wait five minutes, right here. Bring the proof that she is alive and unhurt."

He turned toward the Jeep, then back to her.

"I'm no Santiago, who is that?"

"Oh, hell, never mind ... proof, living proof, man."

He ran to his jeep and started it. He was raking gears all the way down the runway. Diane could still hear him after he turned off toward the compound. She sauntered toward the building, her back to the runway, talking into her microphone.

"Heads up, everyone, I think he has gone to get Tina."

Dennis' voice came through her earpiece.

"Don't be too sure of that Diane. You have that dummy so rattled, he doesn't know up from down. I have no idea what he went to get as proof, but I'm betting he won't come back with her live body. That guy is just a gopher."

"I know that, Dennis, he has lied all through this so far. Let's see what happens, I'll play it by ear."

"You're doing wonderful dear, I'm amazed."

"Tell that to my nervous system and my churning stomach."

"You've got company coming."

She turned to see a Jeep screaming down the runway.

"There's no one in the Jeep with him."

"I know, Dennis, damn it."

"Patience, darling, you're doing fine."

Diane walked to the tarmac and waited.

The vehicle roared up and skidded to a stop about twenty feet from Diane. He jumped out of the Jeep holding a bag and running toward her.

"Stop right there," Diane said, holding up her hand.

He skidded to a stop. He looked down the runway toward the ship, and held up his hands, as if to ward off an evil spirit.

"You're OK, but where is my sister ... a real, live breathing person, my proof."

"This is proof," he said, holding out a bag.

"Shit, man, you really don't understand English. I want real living proof."

"Your sister is not on the island, she is being held another place, and this is proof."

"What is it, throw me the bag."

He flipped it through the air, and she caught it.

"Diane, turn your back to him and listen to me."

She did as he said, fumbling to open the bag.

"If the CIA agent was right about Santiago's habits of coming to the site of the deal, I'll bet he is here. I saw that chopper in the compound when we were coming down. I'm betting he flew in here before we arrived."

She whispered back to Dennis, "Thanks sweetie, get ready to come pick me up. This time just roll, you sandblasted me a while ago."

"Sorry, waiting for your order."

She pulled the contents from the bag and held them for a moment, then turned back toward the man. She held a pair of panties and a bra in her hand. Holding them up, she screamed at the man.

"You call a bra and pair of panties living proof? I don't think so."

She stuffed the items back into the bag and threw them at the man.

"Hell, this could be off of one of your island whores."

Pointing her finger and shaking it at him, she said, "You listen to me and listen carefully, mister. I'm going to be in my ship resting for a bit. Go to your boss and tell him to either produce my sister, alive, so I can check her out, or in twenty-five minutes my ship and I will leave. I'll contact Russia, China, and North Korea. I'll start a bidding war between them. I'll get the money to go somewhere and lose myself. You bastards have forced me to give up my country, my career, and everything I valued. I'm not leaving here empty handed."

She held up the TV remote.

"Computer, come pick me up."

The man was staring past her, down the runway. Dennis had just released the brakes on the giant ship, and the thrust alone from the three idling engines, coasted it almost silently down the runway. Diane heard the soft roll of the tires, and when Dennis reset the brakes, there was a slight squeal.

"Twenty-five minutes or I'm gone."

She started to leave, and then turned back to the man.

"By the way, I'm not going to deal with go-betweens, so tell Santiago to bring her himself. I want to finalize this deal within half an hour and get this ship out of sight."

She again turned away, putting the TV remote to her mouth and saying, "Computer, lower the elevator."

"No!" The man shouted, "You cannot return to your ship, you must stay here."

She stopped in her tracks, her back to him.

Does he have a weapon? She asked herself. Should I try for my pistol?

As if reading her mind, Dennis whispered, "Have patience, he has no visible weapon. Bluff baby, bluff."

She slowly turned back to the man. Seeing he had only the bag in one hand and the other by his side, she said, "Are you going to stop me Sir? If I am hurt, not only does this ship leave and return to its base, but you will look like the dust on this runway before I hit the ground."

He looked down at the tarmac, and Diane could feel his terror. He held up his hand, palm toward the ship.

"No, no, I go, I go."

Diane stepped onto the elevator, and turned to face the man. She pushed the button and the elevator started upward. She saw the man running to his Jeep

When the elevator stopped, Dennis was there. He took her into his arms and she thought her knees were going to buckle. She clung to him, and they stayed that way for a moment.

"Thanks," she whispered.

"Come on, sit down. Sweetheart, that's the best acting I've ever seen. You are doing terrific."

"Dennis, unusual as is it may seem, I have a favor to ask. Do you have anything on this bucket of bolts stronger than water or coffee?"

He helped her down, on what they now permanently call Captain Kirk's bench.

"Knowing Sarge, I'll bet I can find anything you want."

Diane heard Tensley's voice in her earpiece.

"Budweiser, back part of the fridge crisper. Other beverages, top right hand cabinet above the fridge."

Giggling and pointing to her earpiece, she repeated what Sarge said.

"I forgot we were broadcasting. What will it be my lady?"

"The tallest glass you can find, Vodka Collins please."

It wasn't long before he returned with a tall glass in hand.

"How long has it been?"

"Approximately ten minutes."

The minutes slowly clicked by as they waited in the quiet of the flight deck.

Diane got up from the bench and moved to the pilot's seat. Twenty-four minutes passed.

"What are you going to do, dear?"

"If he's here, he's trying to play mind games with us, fray our nerves. On the mark of twenty-five minutes, I'm bringing number one and two online. At 30 seconds past, I'll lift off. If he doesn't show, I'll make one pass over the compound and then back here. I'll give him five more minutes to show, and if he doesn't, I'll have to assume it's off. I'll call the ships up and we level the island. No. 6, Ed, listen up. If that cruiser or chopper heads for the mainland, destroy them."

"Will do, No. 1."

"OK, Dennis, here we go."

On throttling up, number one and two engines surged, and all instruments started toward the green line. The ship began to bounce, wanting to be free of the earth.

" Throttle down babe, chopper coming above the trees from the southwest."

She did as Dennis told her, and the ship settled down. The chopper turned south and circled, then back north toward the runway.

"Dennis, it has missiles."

"I see that. If he powers up to fire them, he is toast. I have him in my crosshairs."

They both watched as the helicopter dropped down to about five feet off the ground, and came directly toward them.

"Dennis, if he fires, we're toast."

"He hasn't powered up, Diane."

The chopper came to a stop and hovered about 50 yards down the runway, facing them directly.

"More mind games," Diane said.

Finally, the chopper turned its nose about forty-five degrees to the west, and began inching closer toward them, sideways. Approximately twenty yards out, it softly settled onto its skids. The rotor blades slowly decreased rotation. The passenger door opened and a man stepped out.

"Santiago," Diane hissed.

"Patience, sweetheart, patience, he is ours one way or the other."

"I would prefer the other, the bastard."

Santiago confidently walked toward the ship. He stopped about ten yards away, looking toward the flight deck.

"Miss O'Hara, please come visit with me."

Gritting her teeth, Diane muttered, "I should have killed the bastard the first time."

"Please, Miss O'Hara, let's waste no more time."

Diane released her seat belt and stood up. She pressed the speaker button.

"Be right there, Mr. Santiago."

"Well, here goes, wish me luck."

"You know I do dear, where's your pistol?"

She patted her right side, ".45 in belt under jacket, laser on the other side."

The elevator came to a halt.

"Computer, retract the elevator," she said into the TV remote, as she stepped off the elevator.

She advanced at an angle toward a small building at the edge of the runway, keeping herself between the building and the man, and out of the path of the laser cannon. She stood face-to-face with the man she detested, but managed to put a slight smile on her face, for acting's sake.

"My, my, Miss O'Hara, you are much more beautiful than I remember."

"How would you know? The last time I saw you, you were out like a light. I should have killed you then. If I had, at least I would have a country to call home and a career that wasn't ruined."

"Oh, yes, Miss O'Hara. You do owe me for that you know."

"Owe you? Owe you what?"

"Perhaps sometime in the future, near future that is, a few nights in a very nice hotel."

"Don't piss me off Santiago. If you ever attempt to even touch me, you know I'm quite capable of killing you, and I will. Enough niceties; since you bastards put me in this situation, you get nothing unless I get what I want."

"Oh, I see, and just what is it that you want Miss O'Hara? I did not think you would be so hard to deal with."

"The very first thing I want is to see that my sister is alive, and check her over to see if you have damaged her."

"Ah, I can say this, she is not damaged. Now, what else do you want Miss O'Hara?"

"No more damn talk, I want to see my sister, now."

"If you insist. I did not think you cared so much."

"That, Santiago, is not the point. My sister or not, it is the right thing to do. To get anyone out of an animal's control is the right thing to do."

"Ah, morals are a downfall for idiots."

He turned toward the chopper and waved an arm. The female pilot walked around the front of the helicopter to the back passenger door, reached in, and pulled a person from inside. As disheveled as the woman was, Diane recognized Tina.

"Damn you Santiago! She looks like you have kept her in a hole. When was the last time she had a bath?"

He nonchalantly said, "Probably the day I took her."

"You fucking pig! Bring her here; I want to see what other damage you have caused."

"Now, now, Miss O'Hara ... in time, in time."

He again waved his arm. The pilot almost had to pick Tina up. She shoved her back into the chopper and slammed the door.

"That bitch of yours is now on my list, I'll kill her."

"Now, now, Miss O'Hara, be nice."

Dennis lightly whispered in Diane's ear.

"Calm down, sweetheart. It's all going our way."

Diane had to grit her teeth and swallow the words she wanted to say. She turned her back to Santiago and took a few steps away from him to regain her composure. After a minute, she turned and went back to her original place, and stood glaring at him, saying nothing. He had a smirk on his face, thinking he had Diane right where he wanted her. Diane knew that he had gotten to her, but she regained control. She calmly pulled a pack of cigarettes from her jacket pocket. She had to concentrate very hard to make sure her hand did not shake or quiver as she lit a cigarette.

Calm, calm ... she thought to herself.

Then she sat down on the tarmac, crossed her legs, and leaned back on both hands, looking up at him.

"Very, very attractive Miss O'Hara. Are you comfortable?"

She leaned forward, pointing her finger at him.

"Shut the fuck up, Santiago, just shut your mouth," she said vehemently. "You want that ship? Fine, it's yours, but this is the only way you will ever get it. I want one billion dollars ... cold hard cash."

"Are you crazy?"

"Shut up, Santiago, hear me out. I'm not crazy, just realistic. I know what it cost to build the ship and that no one else in the world even knows how to start building it. That tells me how much you can get for it. When that cash is crated in that ship, you will take me and my sister to a country I choose. Once my cash is secured, then, and only then, will you take possession of that ship. Is that clear, Santiago?"

"May I speak now?"

"Go right ahead."

"What, Miss O'Hara, makes that ship so valuable?"

Shaking her head, Diane replied, "I'm surprised you even ask that question. I guess in your case ignorance must be bliss. Just out of curiosity, how much were you going to sell that ship for?"

"I estimated that it should be worth at least ten million dollars."

Again, shaking her head and laughing, Diane leaned back on her hands.

"You, sir, would screw yourself out of billions of dollars. I'm not sure you could even buy the landing gear for that much."

He looked down at her relaxed figure, his eyes wide.

"Billions of dollars, you say?"

"One ship, billions."

His interest was reflected in his voice. He sat down, opposite of Diane, and leaned toward her.

"Explain yourself, please"

Diane sat up straight, then leaned forward and looked him directly in the eyes.

"Santiago, that is not just an airplane, it's a deep space ship. It is going to travel to the moon, Mars, Jupiter and Pluto. The special fuel and engines alone, you could not buy for a billion dollars. The laser cannon? The Russians and Chinese have been working to develop one for years, and are no closer now than when they first started. It alone is worth over a billion dollars. That ship has been filled with contingency equipment, to counter anything that scientists can think of that man might encounter in space. Every system is computerized with backup systems. It is the world's first true space ship, at least fifty years ahead of its time. We don't even know how fast it will go. The fastest we have ever pushed it is 26,000 mph in the earth's atmosphere, using less than sixty percent of its power."

He quickly rose to his feet and began pacing back and forth, muttering to himself. He came back to within five feet of her. She wanted him to start getting comfortable with her, just in case an opportunity came around that she could use to her advantage. He looked down at her, noticing how relaxed she was.

Dennis whispered in her earpiece.

"He is too close."

She could not reply.

Santiago asked anxiously, "In your opinion, how much would you sell it for?"

"If I had a buyer, like China, I don't think Russia could afford it, not a penny less than twenty billion dollars."

"Are you joking? Why would anyone pay that much?"

Diane took her time, thinking before she spoke.

"As I said before, that ship, equipped as it is now, is at least fifty years before its time. China and Russia cannot get their tiny little one-man spaceship into space. They have all crashed into the ocean, and the damned things are so small they can barely get one man in them. That ship there can easily carry three hundred people, food, and a decent payload for millions of miles into space. The Chinese and Russians know that the U.S. has at least twelve of these ships ... well, eleven now. America is going to build a military base on the moon, and China and Russia both know that if America controls space, what little power they have will be gone. Russia is bankrupt, and China has all the money they need to do what they are famous for – duplicating. Oh, yes, they will pay the twenty billion without blinking an eye."

Santiago resumed pacing back and forth, once again muttering to himself. Diane could see the dollar signs passing before his eyes.

Santiago knew that what she said about the Russians and Chinese was true. Then it crossed his mind, the Americans built twelve ships, they have the money. Maybe they will pay more than the twenty, just to keep it out of China's hands. I'll get them to bid against each other and to hell with Korea.

While Santiago was pacing back and forth, Dennis was speaking to Diane.

"You are giving him way too much info, careful."

Diane put her mouth down, close to her lapel.

"Don't worry; he is not leaving this island alive."

"Careful babe."

Santiago turned, looking at Diane.

"Did you say something?"

"No, I guess I was thinking out loud."

"About what, may I ask?"

"I'm trying to figure out which country I could go to where I'm less likely to be found."

"Yes, that could be a problem. The Americans are a tenacious lot. They have been after me for years, as has Interpol, but I have the perfect place, they will never find me."

"Oh really, maybe I can go there."

He looked down at her and licked his lips.

"Only if you go with me. I have my own private paradise, and if I get anything close to what you say, I'll never have to leave home again. Can you teach me how to fly this ship?"

Diane looked up at him, and she forced her sexiest smile.

"Maybe we can do some dickering on that."

"Dickering.? What is that?"

"Trading out, in exchange, you know."

"And what might you want in exchange?"

"Hmmm, more money would be good, but all the money in the world won't keep me safe forever. Ever since I received that last letter, it's crossed my mind just how much money I could reap from this transaction. Compared to the paltry sum I now get, and the little in retirement later on, with this transaction I could live like a queen until I die. Yet, I can't picture a country where I can have a good time and also feel safe."

She got very quiet.

"So?" he finally asked.

"I was just thinking it over. If I visited your paradise and didn't want to stay, would I be free to leave?"

A big smile played across his lips and his eyes lit up. He moved a little closer and once more looked down upon her, like a cat getting ready to pounce on a defenseless little mouse.

"How much time would it take for you to figure out if you would want to stay or not?"

"I don't know… five or six months, maybe."

"Not to be too forward, might I ask if perhaps you and I might, you know..."

"It's a possibility Raul. Just from talking to you today, I can see why Tina fell for you. There is one problem though; I will never accept treatment such as she did. I'm no man's servant."

"Yes, I know of your strengths; Tina is a weak woman. Enough talk for now. I must fly to the mainland to make some calls. Will you wait here for me to return, Diane?"

"Let's not get in a big hurry here, Raul, we're only talking. Trust is a long way off; you'll have to prove yourself over time. I still want my billion, and I want it secured. That way it's there if I need it. If you leave here with Tina, I'm on my way to talk to the Chinese. As I said, I don't trust that easily."

"I must go ashore to make arrangements; I cannot from here."

"Leave with her, and I'll leave."

A perplexed look crossed his face and he turned away from her. He put his hands on his hips and turned back to face her.

"The trust situation moves in both directions. If I leave your sister here, what would stop you from taking her and going to the Chinese anyway?"

"As I told you earlier Raul, it's a moral thing. Family. I believe in heaven and hell. If I didn't at least make an attempt to save my family, I would surely go to hell. If I fail, at least I made the effort. Hopefully that would work in my favor."

"Bah, you people and your stupid religions. My parents tried to raise me in a Catholic religion; it's all nonsense. Would you trade her for one billion American dollars?"

"She's not mine to trade, she is blood. As I said, I believe in heaven and hell."

He paced a few steps, and then turned back toward her.

"All right, I can fly the helicopter. I will leave the pilot here to guard her while I go ashore. Mind you, she will kill both of you if need be. Your sister will stay attached to one of us at all times until the payment from the Chinese is secured, as well as your money."

"That is fair enough Raul. I can live with that as long as Tina is where I can see her."

"Very well, I shall return in about an hour and a half."

"Thank you, Raul."

"I like the way you say my name Diane, you have a beautiful voice."

He was almost skipping off toward the helicopter.

"Dennis, are you there?"

"Oh, sorry, I was almost going to sleep from that boring conversation, you have such a beautiful voice ... Oh, thank you, Raul!"

"Jealous, huh? It's not like you. Ed, do not take out the chopper on the way out. I've been watching the pilot and she keeps nodding off. While he's gone, I'll find a way to take her out, I'm sure I can. No one do anything until he's on his way back. If I take her before he starts back I'll let you know. When he's on his way back, take him out Ed, dead out. At the same time, the rest of you firewall your engines, make as much noise as possible. Hopefully the noise will distract her and I'll have a chance to take her out then if I haven't already."

"... and if it doesn't distract her?" someone asked.

"Someone will pay the price. Then level this damn island. Ed, did you receive?"

"Loud and clear, he will be ashes today."

The helicopter engine was revving and the rotors spinning. It lifted off quickly, gaining altitude, and went over the top of the trees toward the mainland.

"He just passed over," Ed reported.

The helicopter pilot sat down on the hot tarmac, and immediately got up. Diane felt the heat even through her boots.

"Dennis, this tar is getting hotter by the minute. I'm going to try and get her and Tina under the ship. The nearest shade is those trees, about a hundred yards away. If she goes there, I could try to get behind the IFR building and circle around behind her and take her out."

"Diane, honey, I would have a better chance in the trees than you. I promise, she is going to be watching you wherever she goes."

"Let me see what I can do, I think under the ship gives us a better chance anyway."

"While you're doing that, there is an emergency hatch over each wheel well and I'm going to remove them now. If I have to go into the trees, you can keep her attention by walking in the opposite direction. Under the ship, you'll have to let me know which wheel well will give me the opportunity to exit from behind her."

"Good plan, go for it. Dennis, I'm going to wait another ten to fifteen minutes, let the sun do a little more work on the pilot."

"OK, but don't wait too long, it's already hot out there and that black tarmac has to be 15 to 20 degrees hotter."

"I'll watch real close. I'm even cooking right now."

Diane watched Tina particularly close, if the sweat even slows dripping from her nose, she would make her move.

About ten minutes later, Diane walked out into the sun from under the ship toward Tina and the pilot. The sweat was pouring off both. Tina was wilting fast and the pilot wasn't far behind.

"Hey," Diane called out to the pilot.

The pilot raised her pistol to Tina's ear. Diane held up both hands.

"No. Do you speak English?"

The pilot looked at her. Diane could see her hand quivering.

"Of course I speak English."

"Look, as hot as it's getting, neither of you will last another much longer. You are dehydrating fast. I'll keep my distance, but please, come, get under the ship. Come quick, I'll get you some water."

The woman licked her lips. She was wobbling on rubbery legs and tried to pull Tina up. Tina couldn't, or wouldn't, move.

"Get up. Get up," the pilot urged.

"Stop!" Diane shouted. "She's out of it, back away and let me carry her."

The pilot, realizing she wouldn't last long, responded quickly. Diane ran to Tina, and with strength she didn't know she had, picked her up and was running for the plane. The pilot was staggering after them on legs of rubber. The weapon, too heavy for her to hold, dropped to the tarmac. The pilot took a couple more steps before falling to her hands and knees. Diane looked back and saw the pilot trying to throw up. Diane sat Tina down, leaning her against the huge wheel.

"Dennis, bring water, lots of water."

She ran back for the pilot. She picked up the gun and shoved it in her leg pocket, then grabbed the pilot by both arms.

"Sorry, honey, I don't think I can carry you."

She pulled the woman under the wing of the plane and then sat down, weak, sweat pouring off of her. Dennis came off the elevator with four cases of water and came over to Diane.

"No, not me, pour water on their heads and chests and a few drops into their mouth."

He handed her a bottle and started pouring the quart bottles over their heads slowly. He turned the pilot over and poured a few drops in her mouth. Tina had slid sideways off the tire. Dennis rolled her onto her back and gave her a small amount of water to drink. Bottle after bottle was slowly dispensed over them.

"Dennis, I can't open it."

He sprung to Diane's side and twisted off the cap, giving her some to drink and pouring some around her neck and head.

"No, no, I'm just beat; give it to me."

Dennis obliged and handed her the water bottle.

"I think the pilot was on the verge of a heat stroke, trying to throw up. Is Tina moving at all?"

"She's licking her poor swollen lips. That's a good sign. Give her a little sip and the pilot a sip and keep pouring water over her head until the steam stops."

"The steam?"

"Yeah, that pilot has a crew cut, and she didn't have a hat to protect her head. At least Tina's thick hair shielded her brain from cooking. They were sitting in that damned hot helicopter the whole time asshole and I were talking. The engine was shut down, so they had no air; I imagine that's why the pilot was nodding off."

"Didn't you feel the heat out there in the open when you were talking to Raul?"

"Yes, but I was still in the shadow of that building. Raul was thinking dollars, so he wasn't worried about sweating his bum off. My bum got a little hot sitting on the tarmac, but my sweat was keeping me somewhat cool there.

"When I told him twenty billion, I had him hooked and was not about to let him off. He also seemed to enjoy my position on the tarmac."

"Oh sure, tempting him with your breasts protruding out that way."

"I guess, but it worked."

"Hey," a voice came through Diane's earpiece, "what the hell is happening there?"

"Is that you, Deana?"

"None other."

"Everything here is under control. When Ed spots Raul Santiago and goes after him, you all bring your ships in and set down here, plenty of room. Ed, you copy that?"

"That's a big 10-4, girl. What about your sister?"

"I think nothing a long hot bath won't cure. We may be in the ship when you get here. As soon as we cool off this pilot, we'll go up into the ship where we have air conditioning. It's so hot out here you can fry eggs on the runway."

"General, there are men heading for the cruiser," said Terry. "Do you want me to take them out?"

"No, I don't think so; they are just local men wanting to play soldier."

"How bout the armory and buildings?"

"Can't now, Terry. We have charge and we'd be destroying United States government property. The U.S. still owns this base for another thirty-something years, so I guess we'll be hauling the stuff from the armory out of here."

"Chopper on radar," Ed said.

"Ashes to ashes, Ed, do it. When you are done, come and join us."

"That's a big 10-4; on my way."

Diane crawled over to Tina. She lifted Tina's head and gently placed it in her lap. She lightly patted a cheek.

"Wake up baby... come on, wake up honey."

After a couple of minutes, Diane gave her a small drink of water. She coughed, but swallowed some of the water. Her eyes fluttered several times, and then opened. She looked up at Diane and moved her lips, licking them.

In a strained and hoarse voice, she croaked, "Diane? Oh, Diane, am I dreaming again?"

"No, baby, it's really me. Don't try to talk, honey; everything is going to be fine. Dennis, how's the pilot?"

"Her head is cool, breathing seems normal. I'm feeding her a few drops of water at a time, and she is taking it down all right."

Ship No. 12 touched down, reverse thrusters on full, and by the time it reached them, engines one and two were shut down. It turned in front of them, and came to a stop, nose gear in the grass. In seconds, Tensley and a couple of crew members came running up. Tensley looked the situation over and approached Diane.

"Here, honey, let me take Tina."

He carefully, and easily, lifted Tina into his arms.

"There, there, sweetie," he softly crooned, "everything will be OK. Comm Sergeant, would you help the general off the hot ground, please?"

"Thank you, Sarge, let's get her into the ship. My sis needs to stay cool. Thank you, Sergeant, I can make it. Would you stay with Dennis and help bring the pilot up as soon as possible?"

"Yes ma'am."

Just as they got on the elevator, Cathy's ship was slowing down and parking beside No. 12.

When Diane, Tina, and Tensley got to the flight deck, Diane said, "Put her on Kirk's bench, please, Sarge."

"Sure. The pretty little thing has a mighty hold around my neck."

Tina was actually smiling, and Diane was very happy to see that.

Tina tried talking, but she still sounded like a bullfrog.

"Pretty? You say I'm pretty? I am filthy and I stink. I would like to sit, not lie down, please."

"Sure thing. Under that wee bit of dirt, there is much beauty."

He sat her down on the soft cushion of Kirk's bench.

"Thank you sir, very much."

Her voice was considerably stronger.

"It was my pleasure, Tina."

"Are you sure you feel strong enough to sit up, sweetheart?"

"Oh yes, sis, it will be a while before I'll want to lie down. I felt I was melting into the pavement out there. Oh how I wanted to get up, but couldn't."

Deana and Cathy entered the flight deck, with Dennis, the sergeant, and the pilot of the helicopter, close behind. Dennis was clutching the pilot's right arm, while the sergeant had her other. Her eyes were open, but she was still having a problem standing.

"Would you put her into the crew's quarters, please? Lay her down easy and put pillows under her head. Try to get her to drink some water, but only small amounts at a time."

"Diane?" Tina said with an even stronger voice. "Is there a place in here where I could possibly wash my hands and face?"

Diane burst out laughing.

"Thank the Lord!"

"What's up?" Cathy asked.

"Oh Cathy," Diane said, still laughing. "My wonderful little sis. Just minutes ago she was on the verge of dying, and now she's worried that she is too dirty to be around all of us."

"Tina, if you will allow us, Mattie and I will help you get to the shower," Cathy said. "I'm sure we can dig up something to resemble clean clothes."

Diane heard a noise and looked around to see Ed stepping off the elevator.

"How did it go?"

"He is sure enough gone, but not the way we thought he would go."

"What do you mean?"

"He must have seen me coming and he went down on the deck. He was cruising at a pretty good clip when I pulled up beside the helicopter. I was on the passenger side, and he must have known what was coming when I pointed the ship's nose directly at him. He opened the door and out he went."

"What? He jumped out of a moving helicopter?"

"Oh yeah, right into a mess of sharks. He kept trying to climb out of the water, even though they were tearing him apart."

"Oh, Lord, what a horrible way to go," Captain McBride remarked.

"I guess it was his retribution time," Diane replied. "He wanted to feed my sister to the piranhas, but instead, he was eaten by the sharks. The CIA said he has done that before, and you know what they say, paybacks can be hell."

A voice called out, "Listen up folks."

Everyone focused on Dennis, who was at the communications station.

"I just reported to base. General Estes told me to tell all of you, that once more, he couldn't be more proud of anyone, than he is of this entire squadron. I scribbled some notes here, so maybe I can quote what he said. He said that no group in military history has been thrown together in such a helter-skelter way, with so little training, and in such a short time, and then became a team of perfection. He is definitely proud of the men, but he is in total awe of the bravery and expertise of our women in uniform."

Everyone on the flight deck applauded.

"Another item," Dennis continued. "The general said these comments are for us all – officers, as well as noncoms and our civilian employees. Quote, we are standing at the door of history, but we will not open it. We are going to kick it down, reach out into the universe, and be welcomed there, end quote."

The applauding resonated on the flight deck.

"Great job everyone. Now, we have two ladies here that need attention, and we need to get them back to the base hospital. They have suffered through a terrible ordeal, especially Tina, my soon to be sister-in-law."

A squeaky voice interrupted him and everyone turned to see Tina standing on the raised station platform, on the aft flight deck.

"I'm fine, and I don't need a hospital, just a lot of your wonderful company and lots of food; I'm starving."

She was wearing a pair of shorts and a lightweight, sleeveless sweater. She was badly sunburned on her legs, arms, and face, but there was a shine to her skin from scrubbing off the days of dirt and grime. Her hair was still wet, but brushed neatly, with bangs falling over her forehead. Her white smile was brilliant and genuine, and even from a distance her sky blue eyes sparkled.

Everyone applauded the beautiful young woman and Sarge stepped out of the crowd, toward her.

"Ah, you see? She is indeed a beautiful woman that no grime could cover. It will take no time for us to get you home, but in the meantime, with the permission of our kind commander, I may be able to persuade my personal friend, and the best chef in the world, to serve you up some appetizers."

A deep, baritone voice sounded over the flight deck intercom.

"Aye, you be too late me kind friend, and I thank you for the compliment, I do. I already be in the galley, preparing me fine cuisine for the young lassie."

Sarge laughed and shrugged his shoulders.

"Well it looks like Mr. Hennesey is on the ball and has everything under control, so I will leave it with him."

"A couple more things," Dennis interjected. "I will join Ed, on his ship. We're going to have to load up everything from the armory, and I'm going to need some volunteers."

Everyone's hands flew up at once.

"Oh Lord, I should have known better than to ask that. Tina, we'll use your ship. Everyone else that is not a pilot will go on Tina's or Ed's ship. There is going to be a lot of stuff to load and it's very hot out there. I don't want anyone having a heat stroke, so drink plenty of water. If any one of you feels the slightest bit unusual, stop what you're doing and get in the shade. Please, and I know you will, look after each other. While everyone is loading, Tina and I will go through the headquarters building for any paperwork. Let's see if Mr. Raul left any behind that could implicate other people, or countries. I have a feeling this is his main headquarters, and I hope I am right. Everyone else can load up and head home. We'll see you back at base."

##

The sun was ready to set across the salt flats back at the base as Ed and Tina sat their ships down and coasted to a stop, ready to taxi in. Dennis heard Tina's voice on the ship-to-ship intercom.

"Have you ever seen such beauty? The salt sparkles like diamonds, and those soft, pink clouds above us are gorgeous. I never knew the desert could be so beautiful."

Ed's soft voice came back, "There is real beauty everywhere you look. It's a shame that most will never recognize or see it."

Tina's ship, holding all the ammo and things they collected from the armory, taxied into hangar number one. The forklift workers immediately began unloading it and taking it to the base armory for safe keeping.

The general met Ed and Dennis at hangar number two's door, as the very tired crew members entered.

"What took the two ships so long to get back?"

"To begin with, we found a literal gold mine in armament. Didn't we, Ed?"

"Oh yeah, a gold mine, a diamond mine, and more."

"Are the FBI and CIA agents still here?"

"They left right after you did. Why?"

"I was right earlier when I thought that base we just closed was Santiago's main headquarters. We have tons of paperwork for them to sift through. Above all that, we found in the safe, lists of contacts – those who sold him armament, planes and everything else he had. Unfortunately it names some people that are pretty high up in our government and military."

"Oh, Lord, it's going to hit the fan then. I'd better let the president know so she can be prepared."

"He kept great books, that's for sure."

"Right, Ed, but we have all discovered a great deal more about Mr. Santiago, or Mr. Savalas, I should say, after the others got back."

"Oh really, what's that General?"

"The chopper pilot that Diane brought in with her gave us a wealth of information on him. Savalas hired her about two months ago as his personal pilot, after she got out of the Air Force."

"She was in the Air Force, sir?" Ed asked.

"In a way. She was a commercial airline pilot, a captain. She volunteered for the Academy, but supposedly a slight twitch in her left eye failed her medical. Hell, I didn't notice it until she told us about it. Anyway, when she woke up, she was surprised to find herself in a military hospital. In fact, it took a bit of convincing before she would believe me. She was convinced that Savalas was a legitimate businessman, and was flying him all over the United States and Canada in his Lear jet. She gave us a list of his warehouses. He has them in Seattle, San Diego, El Paso, and outside of Phoenix. They extend all along the southern coast and as far up the East Coast as New Hampshire. Hell, he was openly staying at the largest hotels in the country and gambling in Vegas, right under our noses. His jet is stored in a private hangar outside San Diego, and she said there's a safe, and a large six-drawer filing cabinet with combination locks on each drawer."

"Well, sir, if she is so straight, how the hell did she end up with him, and why was she holding Tina as hostage?"

"That's a story by itself. In fact, the president contacted the Attorney General and the FBI immediately. So far, her record is as clean as a newborn baby. Her high school record is exemplary, as well as her records from the airlines she worked for. They said that they hated to lose her because she was so dependable and very qualified in her job. Two of her fellow pilots told the agent that her dream was to become a fighter pilot. She acquired a legal visa into Mexico, and a permit to fly in Mexico. Everything legal and above-board so far—but now for the real kicker, she said that Savalas had convinced her that his company had developed this new aircraft, and that a group of thieves, supposedly us, had stolen it. He told her that Tina was the sister of the ringleader who stole his plane, and that he was using her as a hostage to recover it."

Dennis was shaking his head.

"That's just plain crazy."

"An unbelievable story, but yet it has a hell of a ring of truth to it. They're still investigating and they can only hold her for 72 hours without charging her. If nothing shows up, we'll have to release her. She also told the agents that Savalas offered to pay her under the table, but she insisted on a paycheck. Everything checked out at her bank, she even deposited her bonus checks. With all this information, we now know at least one of the bank's Savalas deals with."

"How much did Savalas pay her?"

"A little above average for a personal pilot and some hand-some bonuses. I'll bet she was worth it though, from her record as a pilot, and she did report all of it. Oh yeah, another little tidbit—she told us that Savalas approached her several times, wanting her to spend the night with him and she refused. She told him she was engaged and would not cheat. She told us that she was not engaged, she just did not want to be with him."

"General, you know what's strange?"

"What Ed?"

"From the time I started reading, I have always loved good spy and espionage stories, secret agents and the like. Take James Bond. Now, he was the man. I often thought I wanted to be an FBI or CIA agent, until I found that flying was my true love. Since I've been with this organization, and it's only been a short time, I feel sorry for James Bond."

"Sorry? Why in the world do you feel sorry for him?"

"Well here we are, real life people, no fiction, and I've had more exciting adventures than James Bond ever thought about having."

The three of them laughed heartily.

"Ed, maybe you should write your own book."

"I just might do that Dennis, but let's make some more history first. There's no telling what else is out there that I'll be able to write about when I have to retire."

"I can just see you Ed, sitting on your porch in a squeaky rocking chair, recounting some of your stories to your grandchildren."

"I'll be able to tell some whoppers, that's for sure. Well, I think it's time for a bath. Anything further, sirs?"

"Everything is off for the next three days Ed. Do what you want and have fun. Come back fresh, the moon jump is on the agenda."

"No patrols? No flying?"

"You can if you want Ed, any ship, any time."

"I might make a patrol sir, over D.C."

Laughing, the general said, "Call first, Ed. I bet she would change her agenda real quick."

"Thank you, sir."

General Estes and Dennis watched the big Marine as he headed for the elevators.

"For some unknown reason, General, I see another wedding on the horizon."

"I wouldn't be the least bit surprised Dennis."

In another place around the world, the dictator of North Korea was pacing the floor. His air force general, the defense general and the leader of the North Korean Secret Service watched the very nervous dictator.

"Where is he? Where is Santiago with my ship? We have paid him millions in advance, and the one billion American dollars is packaged as he requested. Now where is my ship?"

"Sir, he has always made delivery before. Sometimes late, due to unforeseen circumstances, but he's always delivered."

The dictator glared at his Secret Service leader.

"I know. That's why, on your word, we advanced him millions of dollars."

The dictator began pacing the floor again.

"Two days ... that's all. Two days, and I'll have the agents find him, kill him, and get my ship. And you ...," he hissed, as he turned and pointed to the Secret Service man, "Oh, never mind, we will see."

The dictator walked toward the door.

"I want my ship," he repeated, as he left the room.

Dennis walked into his apartment and heard female voices coming from Diane's room. He glanced over and saw her door was wide open. He went to the door and peeked around the corner to see Cathy, Tina, and Diane bent over, heads in the refrigerator.

"What's the matter Diane, air conditioner quit?"

Diane jumped, grazing her head on the freezer door above. With a welcoming smile on her face, but rubbing the side of her head, she walked over and hugged Dennis.

"Glad you're back sweetie. What took so long?"

He whispered in her ear as she hugged him.

"I would have made it back sooner if I had known I was going to see a pretty butt in short shorts sticking out of the refrigerator."

Diane laughed and planted a big kiss on his lips.

"Oh you, is that all you ever see, my butt?"

"Oh no sweetheart, I observe and appreciate all the scenery."

She kissed him again.

"Me too, handsome. Come on, come on in."

"Let me get a cold one and I'll be right back."

"I stole yours. I was just putting them in our refrigerator and there's more on the way, I just ordered it. I'll get you one."

She pulled him into the room. Mattie and Cathy surrounded him.

"Hey, General, is a general allowed a kiss from a lowly lieutenant?"

"This one is."

He laughed and bent over slightly. As usual, and as he expected, Mattie planted one on his lips, while Cathy, being a little bashful, kissed him on his cheek. With his arms around both of their shoulders, they went over to Tina.

"Hey girl, good to see you here. How do you feel?"

"I'm fine Dennis, thank you."

Tina glanced over at Diane.

"I certainly approve of my future brother-in-law, sis. You always said that you would eventually find the right man," she glanced over at Dennis, "but I was always afraid she would grow old and be a prune faced old maid."

Everyone laughed at that.

Dennis whistled.

"Girl, you are still so sunburned, are you sure you're OK?"

"Yes, I'll be fine. Thanks for your concern. Now, may I give the general and future family member, a kiss?"

"Well you sure can."

Dennis leaned over and they both kissed each other on the cheek.

Diane handed him a beer, and slipped her arm into his, snuggling closely with him as they settled on the couch.

"So, why did it take so long for you fellows to get back?"

Just as Dennis began telling her what he had told General Estes, the phone rang.

"Cathy, would you please get that? You'll have to use the speakerphone; the battery is dead in the handset."

"Sure thing."

Cathy walked over to the table and pushed the button for the speakerphone.

"Hello."

"Hello, is that you Cathy? I thought I had Diane's number, this is Cynthia."

"Cynthia? Oh my gosh! Madam President please forgive me, how are you?"

"I'm fine dear, thank you. How are you and Mattie doing?"

"We're just fine, Madam President, thank you for asking."

"When are you girls going to learn? On personal time, I'm Cynthia to all my friends, so please drop the Madam President thing. I think you all know you're my friends."

"Yes, Cynthia. This is Diane's phone. We all got together at her apartment."

"Wonderful, everyone should get together and party. If anyone deserves it, your squadron does. I'm sorry to bother you all, but could I speak to Diane, if she isn't tied up?"

"Hello, Cynthia, and how are you?"

"Ha, totally swollen up with good old American pride."

"That's wonderful. It's nice to have that feeling."

"Well, Diane, you should be feeling that right now. I just finished listening to the tape from your mission, and honey, it was better than any movie I have ever seen. Darling, you should have been an actress. You pulled it off so sweet, it was unbelievable."

"Oh no, ma'am, I had no idea it was being taped. My language, I know it was bad."

"I don't even want to hear an apology from your lips young lady. You are a true American, an American hero. When you deal with pigs, you usually have to wallow in the mud and dirt with them. Getting your sister out of his filthy hands was the most important thing. You and your squadron did the whole world a great favor. All of you brought home much more than anyone realizes. I'm thinking of replacing the CIA and FBI with your squadron. Sorry about preaching on this call, but there are times I just have to express my real beliefs. The real purpose of this call was to inquire about your sister. How's Tina doing?"

"Well Cynthia, first of all, we thank you for your wonderful compliments to me, and the squadron. Right now, Tina's worst problem is bad sunburn, thank God. In fact, she's sitting here right now, listening."

"That's absolutely wonderful. Hello, Tina."

"Who, me?" Tina asked, pointing at herself. "Oh, my gosh, my president is talking to me. Thank you for caring."

"Sweetheart, not only is it my job to protect you and all American citizens, it's my duty. I'm really glad you're all right and will fully recover."

"Madam President, I am so proud that you do care about the little people under your watch. I'm very proud of you."

"That, Tina, is the finest compliment I could ever receive. To me, there are no little people in this country ... you people are America. Well, I hate to, guys, but I have to go. Cathy, Mattie, Tina, and my sweet Diane, God bless. Don't forget my invite, Diane, and take care of that handsome hero."

"Thank you, Cynthia," Dennis spoke up, "she is taking very good care of me."

"Oh, damn, Dennis, didn't know you were there. You're still my hero, you know. Hugs everyone, and goodbye for now."

It was 0500 hours and all the crew members were present in the briefing room. Dennis looked out over the group, and realized they were as anxious as he ... the big day had arrived.

"Good morning, everyone. Our big day has come, and for the life of me, I could not fairly choose who would go, and who would not. Each and every one of you deserves to make the journey. You have all worked hard and excelled above all expectations. In order to be fair, I have decided to have a drawing."

Dennis picked up a box and held it in the air.

"In this box are folded slips of paper. There are ten numbers, with one through six being first and second seats on the three mission ships. Rank, or time in grade, will be first seat. Seven through ten will be first and second seat on two ships that will stand by at the space station. One for standby rescue at the station until we return. That ship will be relieved every two days. The second ship will be for refueling; in case we need to once we're in orbit. The three ships making the journey will be with a full load, so we don't know how much fuel we'll need to get into orbit. Should any one of us use more than eighteen percent, we will all refuel and leave together. That is a huge safety factor, so better safe than sorry. Once we're on our way, the refueling ship will return to base. Once the rescue and refueling ships are in place, a simple four and five ready, will be our signal to jump off for orbit. Once we are in orbit, again, a simple 1, 2, 3, go, will be sufficient to bypass the station. If there are any nays, we all stop. Any questions so far?"

Dennis looked around the room.

"OK, let's continue. I know you're tired of hearing what I'm going to say next. I also know that you're fully knowledgeable about it, but I want it fresh in your mind today. Computer analysis shows we can actually save one percent of our fuel if we go to a steeper climb-out altitude to achieve orbit. We will find out today for sure. Once we achieve over 10,000 knots, at a 40-degree up attitude, we will go for a one minute altitude change to a 60-degree climb-out attitude. My order will be, at 10,050 knots, go 60 degrees now. When we break into orbit, we should be at 26,000 knots. Use forward air thruster, reverse engines one and two, idle number three, and slow to 18,000 knots. If fuel is go, we'll set our computer headings according to our navigator and astrophysicist, Captain Pat Conklin. She will be on my ship. Captain Conklin, tell us please, about how long it will take to set our course?"

She stood beside her seat.

"I have already given you two rough estimates. They are listed in your packet. If your calculations for liftoff and orbit entry stay the same, then we will only have to make minor navigational corrections as we go. If your calculations are off by five minutes, then I will have to make major corrections. Now, if you stop to refuel, I'll need from you an estimated time of departure, then I'll recalculate according to where we are over the earth at that time. Once the jump has started, I'll take some new shots and give you a more accurate heading with any corrections, if needed, along the way. Simple."

"Ha, for you maybe," Dennis said, laughing. "But most of us are used to setting headings by a compass."

Chuckles went throughout the room.

"Thank you, Captain, and welcome aboard. We know, in astronomical miles, it is very close to 239,000 miles to the moon. I want to set our speed at 17,500 knots, so it will take about 14 hours to get to the moon. Yes, we could get their much faster, but I feel that this first experience, if nothing else, will be mentally tiring. I want everyone rested when we do arrive there, and totally alert. Everyone will get relief from their positions for at least a six-hour break. All of the radar operators are going to have to be on their toes, as there are a lot of meteors and space junk out there. I have contingency plans and instructions that will be given out before we get to the moon. I'm not going to scramble your brains with that right now. Another very important thing that I insist on... every crewmember will have his or her space helmet hanging at his or her station, with the small emergency oxygen bottle attached to it. The installation crews are more familiar with their suits than we are, as they have been training in them for months. I want that helmet with you wherever you go, period. We will have ample warning of any small pressure leak, get your helmet on, turn on the emergency bottle, secure that helmet, get your backpack on and hooked up. Everyone help each other. OK, let's pull the names."

Dennis slipped his hand into the box and pulled out the first slip of paper.

"Terry Mitchell, you will be with me in ship No. 1."

He then pulled out a slip of paper from the flight engineer's box.

"Skip Tracy, you will be our flight engineer."

He repeated this for each ship.

"Ed Mitchell, you will be on ship No. 2. Diane O'Hara, you will accompany Ed Mitchell. Flight engineer will be Mr. Hennesey. Cathy and ... imagine that ... Mattie, you two will be on ship No. 3. Tensley will be your engineer. Ship No. 4 will have Deana Kutchmark and Bill Turzan. Engineer will be Mr. Donaldson. No. 4 is our fueling ship. Crystal Seismore and Tina McBride will be in ship No. 5 and Mr. Dowden will be the engineer. No. 5 will be our emergency rescue ship. Don Sutherland and Matt Ferguson will be in ship No. 6 and Pete Dominic will be the flight engineer. If any ship cannot make the jump, or has to return, 6 will replace it. All other ships will be standby defense. OK, folks, we have one hour before ships 4 and 5 are to take off. Let's get to our ships."

Ships 4 and 5 flashed down the long runway. Everyone watched as the huge ships lifted gracefully. With their noses turned up, they climbed into the light gray, dawn sky, which was patiently waiting for the sun to push the darkness into the west. They quickly became mere spots, with their contrails tracing their progress high above the earth.

Ships 1, 2, and 3 moved off the taxiway and positioned themselves in a Delta formation. Everyone waited for the tower to say when the two ships were in orbit. It wasn't long.

"Ships No. 4 and 5 in orbit, turned back west to intercept Space Station."

"Nos. 2 and 3, let's review our checklist while waiting."

The minutes slowly ticked by.

As Captain Conklin had predicted, to the minute, the message finally came.

"No. 4 ready."

"No. 5 ready," was heard, a few seconds later.

"Nos. 2 and 3, lock nose gear and start roll on my three count. Lift off at 160 knots, retract, forty-degree attitude at two hundred feet. One, two, three, roll."

The nine mighty engines roared to life, starting slowly, and then quickly gaining momentum. They streaked down the glistening salt flats as the rising sun reflected from it. The three ships' nose gears lifted from the runway at the same time. Everyone watched as the landing gear of each ship retracted at the very same moment. They turned their noses to a 40-degree angle, climbing toward the huge, blazing fireball that had decided to grace the day with its brightness. They quickly became specks, following the fading contrails that 4 and 5 had left behind.

Dennis watched the airspeed indicator, as it was rising very fast. He calmly spoke into his microphone.

"We're coming up on 9000 knots ... check, 9000 — 9200 — 9400 — 9600 — 9800 — 10,000, up 60, one minute, now, after-burners."

If anyone could have seen them, the giant masses of metal would have looked like a bullet leaving a gun barrel as they streaked upward, leaving the new daylight of earth behind and entering the darkness of space.

Again, Dennis was watching his airspeed as it crept toward 24,000 knots.

"24,000 check ... at 24,500, after burners off ... 24,400 — 24,500 off."

Dennis glanced out of the flight deck windows and into the dark vacuum of space.

"Tower," he announced, "ships 1, 2, and 3 achieved orbit, now turning."

Dennis keyed back up.

"Ship No. 1, go, fuel usage at seventeen percent."

"Ship No. 2, go, at seventeen percent."

"Ship No. 3, go, at seventeen-point-five percent."

Dennis checked his readings.

"Very good 2 and 3, reduce airspeed to 17,000, set computers at 17,000 on predetermined heading. Brake on now."

The forward air thrusters ejected a spray of air from the nose of each ship. Numbers one and two engines went into reverse thrust. Any indication of slowing could not be felt inside the ships. Again,

Dennis was very carefully monitoring airspeed. His calm voice, once more, went out over the radio.

"18,000 knots, pause, check, at 17,500, cut engines one and two, idle number three. Cut air thruster at 17,200, check, 17,500 — one and two, 17,400 — 17,300 — 17,200 — cut thrusters."

He waited a few seconds.

"Hold 17,000, holding, holding ... on the money. Ships 2 and 3 report."

"No. 2 on the money, sir."

"No. 3 perfect, sir."

"Captain Conklin, when you are ready."

"Two minutes, sir."

"Hey there," a voice came over the radio, "Commander Simon, Space Station."

"Hello, Commander, how are you?"

"Fine, General. You folks wouldn't happen to be in a hurry would you?"

"You might say so. We didn't disturb you, did we?"

"Nah, you went by so fast, I think you almost sucked us into your air stream. I just called to wish you a safe journey. Your refueling ship is on its way home, and the other is docked under our shield."

"Thank you, Commander, see you on the way back, safe journey yourself."

"Thank you, Space Station out."

Captain Conklin read off their new headings, and everyone fed the updated information into the computer. Each computer adjusted the heading using only the ship's air thrusters.

Dennis readjusted his seat.

"Well, Terry, what do you think?"

Terry's eyes were locked on the forward flight deck windows. He sighed and looked upward.

"Well, sir, I believe it might take hours to tell you how wonderful I feel at this very moment. I'm just finding it hard to believe that I'm really here, on my way to the moon. I have always been a huge fan of the "Star Trek" series, and I don't know how many times I watched the cameras zoom in on the stars, and then I felt sad that it was just a sci-fi show. Now, here I am, seeing a repeat of those scenes, except, now I'm actually here. It is really beautiful out there."

"Yes, it is, much more clarity out here. Do you need a break, Terry?"

"No, sir, I'm fine."

"Hold down the fort, I'm going to see how everything is."

"Hey, Skip, how are the passengers doing?"

"They went to their quarters, sir, but they're fine."

"Good, everything else?"

"Great, all crew members good and I checked the cargo hold – all secure."

"Would you make sure relief schedules are followed? When you are ready for your relief period, I'll stand watch."

"Have you seen Captain Conklin?"

"I believe she is in the navigator's quarters."

He walked around to the far side of the flight deck. The navigator's quarters were her private quarters, but were also set up with a hydraulic chair that would raise the navigator up into a special section of the fuselage which contained a large, extra thick, bulletproof glass dome. The navigator could take their shots and read the stars, which would tell her exactly where she was in the universe.

Dennis knocked on the door.

A muffled voice said, "Come in."

Dennis walked in and glanced around. He saw her legs, a few feet in the air, her head and shoulders in the dome.

"Is everything all right, Pat?"

"Be down in a second."

The hydraulic chair started down. Her head and shoulders came into view.

"Is everything all right, Dennis?"

"Oh yes, just checking in on everyone. Taking more shots up there?"

"Oh no, just watching a dream come true."

"May I ask what that dream might be?"

"To be right here at this very moment. It being a historical moment is icing on the cake. My love for the universe was much more than a fascination. Ever since memory has served me, I have been drawn to the stars like a magnet to steel. Now, here I am, one of the first women to travel to the moon, and hopefully beyond, before I get too old."

"That's a very beautiful way of putting it, Pat. I believe your wish to go beyond the moon could very well come true, very soon in fact."

"Oh, really? Now you have really piqued my interest. Can you elaborate on that statement?"

"Yes, I think now it would be permissible. These ships have been more successful than even I dreamed possible. I anticipated many major problems, but they have performed so perfectly that I can see us on Mars in less than a year."

"Do you have the fuel capacity to go there?"

"Well, Pat, as of now, even with the heavy payload we have, I believe we could go to Mars twice and still make it home."

"We have already gone to the moon, so why not set up a base on Mars instead of the moon?"

"For several tactical reasons, not to mention the practical ones. First of all, we take small steps into the future, not leaps. I don't know if you are aware of the problems we've faced from other countries trying to stop our progress. The Space Station should have been finished over five years ago. We still believe that the two shuttles were sabotaged, just to stop the completion of the Space Station. They have already tried to destroy it twice, once very recently.

"The Space Station is a stepping stone to the moon, and the moon a stepping stone to beyond. We have found that we're going to have to protect each step from our enemies, from the ones we wanted to take with us on the journey to the stars. We know now, that we will have to go it alone with only England and Australia. We have fully protected the Space Station, and once this mission is over, we will swarm it and finish it in a couple of months. We will get it rotating to provide it with normal gravity. The moon base is another step, and it will protect itself, our continent, and our allies."

"May I ask how you are going to do that, Dennis?"

"Sure, the enemy is already aware of the new weapon on our ships, the laser cannon. We have already mounted one on the Space Station and there are two new ones in our cargo hold. The laser on the station is quite capable of taking out any missile that is fired on earth. Our ability to detect an armed missile has improved so much, that once it starts liftoff, we will know if it is armed, and we can destroy it before it reaches its peak from the launch pad."

"Whew, that is really something. If it's nuclear, a lot of people beneath that missile are going to die when it explodes."

"Well, if that were the case, I would say better them than us. Fortunately, that's not the case. When the laser hits it, it's dust, immediately. There will be no nuclear blast, period. The laser on the moon will have the same capability. The domes that will be erected this trip will be protected by the same shield as on the station. Should they fire missiles at the base, our lasers can pick them off faster than they can be launched. We'll have to finish our talk later Pat, I want to finish my rounds and I need to get some rest."

##

Dimitri Kozolov, the president of Russia, was in a cabinet meeting. He was talking to several members when he noticed a young man, just inside the chamber, with an arm raised. Dimitri motioned for him to come forward.

"What is it, Lieutenant?

"Sir, I was told to inform you that the Americans have put five of their new ships into space."

"So what? They have been putting multiple ships up for some time now."

"Yes, sir, but not quite the same. Three of them went on into deep space, sir."

"You mean directly into deep space, or a higher orbit?"

"They're almost two hours into space now. An approximate trajectory has them intercepting the moon within another twelve to fourteen hours."

"What?" Dimitri shouted. "That's insanely impossible!"

The young man stepped back from the infuriated leader.

"Sir, that's what I was told to report to you. I don't know anything else, sir."

Dimitri turned away, walking toward a large window, his mind was racing. He jerked back around, facing the young man.

"Lieutenant, are you from the defense minister?"

"Yes, sir."

"You get to him immediately. In no more than 20 minutes, I want every damnable scientist involved in our space program in my office. Those who are in Kazakhstan, I want them on a conference phone when I arrive. Go."

The young lieutenant looked like a track star as he left. Dimitri turned back to face the others. With much anger he shouted.

"This country is standing on the very edge of a cliff, ready to topple off. A huge part of the problem is your responsibility. While lining your own damned pockets, at the expense of our military and space programs, you have pushed this country to the edge. Starting right now, the money you have stolen will be returned directly to the defense minister's office. I'll warn all of you now, do not try to leave this city, or this country. Should you try, you will be shot on the spot. Within two days, I expect billions to be pouring in, and for those of you who do not return the money, your families will be arrested, and you will watch them be shot, before you are shot."

He stomped from the room, leaving a deep silence behind him. When he entered his office, his defense minister was waiting.

"The available scientists are on their way, sir. My secretary is on the phone gathering the ones in Kazakhstan to a conference room. She will ring on your phone the minute they are gathered."

"Very good, here is a direct order that I want you to carry out immediately, from that phone over there. I want a set of secret servicemen on every cabinet member now. I want others at their families' locations. If any of them try to leave, mothers, fathers, wives, children, any of their family, if they try to leave this city or country, I want them shot right then and there. No questions asked.

"If money, in the multimillions, has not started flowing into your office by noon tomorrow, I want the cabinet ministers and both sides of their families rounded up and arrested immediately. The money that should start coming in is strictly for our military and the space program. I will personally dispense those monies, where I deem necessary; no one else is to touch it. I also want you and my treasury secretary in my office at 1 p.m. tomorrow. I want a full account of every cent that comes in and who it comes from. Is that all clear?"

"Yes, sir, I'll get on it right now."

Dimitri walked over to the conference table.

"Please sit gentlemen."

All of the scientists found a seat around the table. The tension could not only be felt, it could be seen on each of their faces. Dimitri pulled the conference phone closer to him, and then stood up, looking at each of the men around the table. He pushed a button on the phone.

"Kazakhstan; is everyone present and can you hear me all right?"

"Yes sir, all are present and the connection is excellent."

"Then I say this to all of you. The time for arguing, squabbling, and shouting, is over. Concerning the new American spaceships, I believe some of you have fed me very bad theoretical information. As of this moment, three of those ships are now on a trajectory to arrive at the moon within the next ten to eleven hours. I will concede to the possibility that one of them could be a refueling ship, but my gut tells me that two are loaded with enough equipment to set up a moon base. We cannot allow them sole possession of the moon. We must, at the very least, establish a claim to some portion of the moon. You there, in Kazakhstan, what is the status of the ship on the launch pad?"

"Critical, sir, there is still the problem in the computer."

"Can we launch successfully without the computer?"

"The chances of success, I would say, is no more than fifty-fifty without the computer. The cosmonaut is a very bright young man, and he trains hard every day. In my eyes, sir, he has had a minimal amount of training."

"Have we no more experienced men?"

"The best ones we had died in the last two attempts, sir."

"Has the problem with the booster rockets been fixed? There's no sense trying a launch if we're going to dump the ship into the ocean again."

"We're very confident, sir, that problem has been resolved."

"Where do we stand on the new ship in production?"

"It is almost complete, but we can't get the engines and computers from the French."

"And why the hell not?"

"Money, sir. We still owe them for the last two ships, and they insist we pay them before they will give us the ones for this ship."

"Damn them, after all the business we do with them? The Americans won't even deal with them anymore. Oh well, in a couple of days we will solve that problem, but in the meantime I want you to search out other sources. If we have a successful launch and get into orbit, what are the chances we can get to the moon, land, plant our flag, and establish a base site?"

"That could be accomplished. But, with absolutely no backup systems, if they have any problems at all, the ship may go to the moon all right, but more than likely it would bypass it and drift on into space."

"All right, damn it; suppose there were no failures ... could what I outlined be accomplished?"

"Yes, sir, we could establish a base site. Remember, this ship was not designed with the fuel capacity to land and return. It was meant to circle the moon, and use the moon as a slingshot to return the ship to earth. After that, there would be fuel enough for the retro rockets to fire and then slow him enough for reentry. He might have enough to get back into orbit; other than that there's no telling."

"I see. Well, gentlemen, we are truly in a desperate situation. If we are to maintain some semblance as a world power, I think we're going to have to gamble. So here are my orders. Prepare the ship for launch. I expect to have it launched within the next thirty-six hours."

"Sir, that is not..."

"Enough! Now do as I say, or I will replace you with someone who will follow my orders. Is that clear enough?"

"Yes, sir, quite clear," came the grim reply.

##

"Sir, it's time."

"Thanks, Skip, I'll be right out."

Dennis rolled out of his bunk and went into the bathroom. This ship's commander's quarters were small, but efficient. He splashed some water on his face and headed for the flight deck.

"OK, Terry, I understand we are in the moon's gravitational pull. How much so?"

"Our speed has increased from 17,000 to 17,100 knots."

"Let's see how well our reverse thrusters are working, again."

Communicating with the other ships, Dennis guided them through a meticulous braking process down to 4000 knots.

Terry reported, "4000 knots, sir, and holding ... holding ... holding, positive."

"Ships 2 and 3, report."

"Ship No. 2 positive, 4000, sir."

"No. 3 positive, 4000 knots."

Dennis was ecstatic.

"Wonderful, no fuel usage at all. In exactly 19 minutes, we'll drop to 2500 knots. The moon's gravitational pull will again try to increase our speed. Use your forward reverse air thrusters, as needed, to maintain 2500 knots. Now, for added stability of our ships, wings are to be extended completely, report when complete. Terry, extend our wings."

Once more, Dennis waited patiently, watching on the TV monitors, the slow movement of each wing.

"Extension complete and locked, sir."

Nos. 2 and 3 likewise reported completion.

"We are now adding an unknown factor," Dennis continued. "This is where we all become real pilots... no computers. Due to the size and shape of our ships, we are nothing similar to the original moon Landers. I want Nos. 2 and 3 to maintain orbital speed of 2400 knots, using your engines one and two evenly. I will make the first drop to approximately 1000 feet altitude. If I do it correctly, the computer will receive every function. When I'm on the surface, on the earth side of the moon, I will contact you on ship-to-ship communications. Should it not work the first time, I'll come back around and repeat, letting the computer read out my errors on the first pass. You must keep on ship-to-ship communications, because that is the only way we can talk to each other from one side of the moon to the other.

"Once on the surface, I will have 2 and 3 come around, to the earth side, and you will download information from my computer. When that is complete, your receiving light will go to green. Nos. 2 and 3 will return to the original starting position, turn on all cameras for mapping of the back side of the moon, and let the computer take over. It will bring you around and set you down. No. 3, wait until No. 2 is on the surface and then repeat. Any questions?"

"None, sir, but Mattie reminds you to get all three landing gears on the surface at once. Good luck."

Dennis heard a giggle and immediately knew it came from Mattie. Even that little bit of humor seemed to ease the tension.

"Yes Mattie, I'll give it my best shot. One more word of caution: If for any reason you have to throttle up and climb out, do so, then let us know. Let's relax for a few minutes, stand, stretch, whatever. This first time around could be a little tense."

A few minutes of silence passed.

"No. 2 to No. 1."

"Go No. 2."

"Dennis, if we were married, this would be a honeymoon to beat any other. Look at that beautiful moon, and then the earth behind us. It's a gorgeous setting."

Dennis glanced up at the screen. The rear camera showed a breathtaking image of earth.

"Beautiful indeed," he replied, "but what about that Caribbean island? You Eve, me Adam."

"Oh, hell, Dennis, don't tell everyone."

"Sorry dear, I guess I already have."

"Hey, come on, when is the wedding? Mattie and I may want to do some peeping Tom stuff on that island."

"It's a secret," Diane responded.

"Better turn off your GPS then, Mattie is very good at sniffing out things."

"Thanks, Cathy, I'll have to remember that."

"Darn Dennis, I shouldn't have mentioned it."

The joking helped everyone loosen up.

The three almost ghostlike ships floated through space. Eyes seemed glued to the ship's viewing screen, as the small specks approached the shining moon.

Diane whispered into the microphone.

"There's Mars and Saturn. Lord, it looks like I could almost reach out and touch that huge planet."

They slowly drifted up to the moon. Once more, Dennis' calm, clear voice was heard over the intercoms.

"OK, folks, it's my show. I will communicate no more until I am on the surface, as Terry and I will be busy for quite some time. He and I will communicate on an open line; you will hear it all. No. 2 and No. 3 can go down to 5000 feet above the surface, but maintain your airspeed at 2400 knots.

The three ships slowly turned into the darkness behind the moon, dropping down toward the surface. They looked like feathers drifting on a still air. Mars, Jupiter, and Saturn, shone brightly.

Captain Conklin was at her observation station, snapping pictures of the three planets and in total awe of the beautiful sight.

"My Lord," she whispered to herself, "what a beautiful universe you are allowing us to see."

Time seemed to stand still, as everyone in the three ships watched the huge screen. They were mesmerized by the beauty and greatness of it all.

A deep silence permeated the ships. The only thing heard were the calm, clear voices of Dennis and Terry as they were taking their ship down. The tension was great on the crews of 2 and 3 as they listened to their friends doing what had to be done.

Then, everyone heard Dennis give a long sigh.

"OK, Terry, we're going around, into the light."

He moved the ship forward, and saw the light he was about to enter. The ship gracefully came from behind the moon, and earth reappeared on his screen.

"Radar, stay sharp, going down."

"Clear, sir, looks to be one hundred fifty miles to desired location, closing fast. One hundred miles, seventy-five, fifty, twenty-five. Suggest VTOL function. Five miles now."

Dennis throttled one and two up a bit, kicking down the directional thrusters. The ship slowed to about 40 feet from the surface, and clouds of black dust swirled behind the huge ship as it settled closer and closer.

"There, sir," Terry said, pointing at the screen, "a ship's length ahead, perfect spot for all three ships. Total VTOL."

The huge ship hovered, engines slowly throttled back, and a slight, but noticeable jolt, as the landing gear settled into the thin coating of dirt. The swirling of dust surrounded the massive ship as it settled down. Number one and two engines were shut down, then off. Only number three was still idling. Dennis reached out and pushed two buttons on his console.

"Both generators are in the green; shut down number three."

Silence followed as everyone breathed a sigh of relief.

"I can't believe it," said Terry. "We just landed on the moon."

"Yes, it's hard for me to believe that we are really here. Communications, bring Nos. 2 and 3 around."

In short order, 2 and 3 arrived overhead. Their computers received the information from No. 1's computer. Nos. 2 and 3 returned to the starting point and it was not long before 2 was on the ground, and 3 was en route. When No. 3 finally settled on the surface, Dennis' calm voice once more came across the intercoms.

"Great job, people, and welcome to the moon. Communications, please get base on the air."

In seconds, General Estes was on.

"Dennis," the anxious voice said, "Estes here."

"Sir, the eaglets have landed."

The cheering in the background was so loud at the operations office that it echoed through the speakers of each ship.

"Thank God," said General Estes, over the cheers. "We're so proud of all of you. What a tremendous job you have done. America is back on the moon, and your tribute to the first men there is most appropriate."

"Thank you sir, every person up here has, and will, continue to earn that praise. From the time the wheels left Earth until they touched down on the moon, was 13 hours and 58 minutes. Everyone performed to perfection. Next on the agenda is to let everyone relax for a few. We'll start unloading in about an hour."

"You relax. I have to call the president and let her know you're all safe."

"No. 1 to ship No. 2, what's going on over there? It's awfully quiet."

"Stand by, sir, the first and second seat are in the conference room. I'll patch you through."

"No, that's all right, just tell the general to call me when finished."

"Will do."

"Hey, Skip, why are you dressing out? Are you planning a little moon walking?"

"The good captain of engineers asked if we could start unloading. His people are quite anxious to get started."

"Do you feel relaxed enough to go out?"

"Yes, sir, almost too relaxed. I can actually relax more by doing something."

"Who is going with you?"

"Six well trained engineers."

"Just be careful and don't go floating away."

"I didn't come all this way to float off into nowhere, sir."

"Have fun then."

"Dennis, do you want cargo hold cameras on?"

"Good idea, Skip. Keep an eye on those folks."

"No. 2 to No. 1," said Diane on the ship-to-ship intercom.

"Hey sweetheart, what's with a conference this time of night?"

"No conference, a review board. Dennis, you are not going to believe this until you see it. Apparently, we're not the first to set up a base here."

"Oh, come on, are you seeing pyramids, or faces on the moon?"

"Not quite. When I was circling, waiting to be brought around, I thought I was hallucinating. I saw something on the screen. Then I got the call to come around and land. Ed and I were just reviewing the video, and Dennis, there are at least five white domes that we can see, maybe one more."

"Diane, honey, lean back in your chair and relax."

"Dennis, don't be silly. Ed sees exactly what I saw."

"It has to be a faulty video, hon."

"All right, don't believe me. Ed is preparing images that we'll send you in a bit, out."

"Ouch, Terry, I think I upset her."

"Is it possible, sir?"

Rubbing the back of his neck, he thought about Terry's question.

"To be honest, I'm not sure of anything. This eerie landscape, as with the Mars probe, can form some pictures in your mind. That face, in the picture from Mars, looked exactly like the head of some very old statues found on the earth. Thirty-eight megaliths are in Castle Rock, England, and legends are that they are men, petrified by the gods."

"I heard that, sir. There are many such oddities around the world."

"True, and that's probably what they see. Communications, is there a transmission from No. 2 yet?"

"Yes, sir, there's one coming through now."

Dennis and Terry walked over to communications and waited for a printout. Terry and Dennis both stared at it, and Terry gave a low whistle.

"That, Dennis, is no hallucination."

"No. No, it isn't. I just find it hard to believe. Here are the five domes she was talking about and it looks like the edge of another."

Dennis walked back to Kirk's bench and sat down, confused.

"No. 1 to No. 2; you there Diane?"

"Yes, I'm here."

"Now you can say I told you so. Terry and I are studying it. Are there any other pertinent pictures, to sort of follow up on this?"

"Yes, a few. I wanted you to see that one so you would not think I was seeing things."

"I'm sorry I doubted you, honey. Can you give me some oversight as to what details you saw?"

"Yes, I could see the buildings on the right side of this one picture in the center, and about 50 to 75 yards from the buildings is a long, wide runway. It looks smooth, but way too short for a large aircraft to land. Maybe a Learjet could land, but it looks more like a perfect VTOL pad."

"Can you send those shots over, please?"

"On their way, it's a shame the night vision lens was on the camera instead of infrared. We could check for heat signatures."

"Good idea. There are four fuselage belly cameras and I believe the one behind the nose gear will show infrared. The other three will show night vision if it's dark."

"I'll check it out, call you in a few."

Terry retrieved the new pictures.

"Someone had to do this, sir. It does look like a short landing strip."

Dennis spread the pictures out on the bench and studied them.

"Damn, Terry, now this is a big puzzle. Why would anyone come here and build all of that? I mean, of all places, on the backside of the moon?"

"The only thing I can think of sir, is they want to hide it from Earth."

"I can honestly say this, if it were the Russians or the Chinese, the whole world would know about it."

"Well, think of it this way, this base may be the reason they tried to stop us from coming here, so we wouldn't find out about it. The new Hubble telescope can all but count small pebbles, so they kept it from view."

"I guess that's a possibility, Terry. Let's see what our infrared will show us, hopefully something more."

"No. 2 to No. 1."

"What did you find, Diane?"

"No heat signature, sir. No sign of life at all. It did show something we couldn't see on the other picture. On the landing pad, there are still some imprints, like some kind of tire tracks. It could be something similar to tri-cycle tracks, like we have on our ships. We didn't see anything else."

"Were there any signs of a flag that could represent some country or nationality?"

"There are no markings that I could see either, Dennis."

"I'm going to call base and inform them. Are you unloading your ship?"

"Ha, the minute I shut down the engines, the fellows on board were raring to go. Mr. Hennesey is operating the boom and cargo elevator. Have you looked out at the site lately?"

"No, is it slow going?"

"Just the opposite. Those engineers are like swarming ants. The flooring is down and anchored on two of the domes, and four men are already on the third. Those huge domes, man are they big. At the rate they are going, we can leave for home tomorrow."

"I'll take a look and then call the base. Out for now."

Dennis turned around, to the console, and pushed another button.

"Communications, get the base please. Terry, give us the building site on the big screen."

The pictures flashed onto the screen. Terry cut off all cameras except the cargo hold and the site.

"My word, Terry, Diane was right. Look there, they have them all three inflated."

"What are those platforms on each end of the site for?"

"According to the layout, those are for the laser cannons. See those two big crates over there? The laser cannons are in those."

"Are they drilling holes now, sir?"

"Yes they are. Once they hit rock or something solid, they will shoot anchor rods into it. Everything is bolted together and anchored solid. They had to do the same for the metal flooring. Once everything is installed in the buildings, they will be able to work without spacesuits. When the generators and compressors are running and the air locks are inside the doorways, then they can create an atmosphere. The buildings also have their own heating systems – just like being at home."

"Sir, base is on."

Dennis sat down in his seat and pushed radio on for the deck speakers.

"Base, this is Eaglet One."

"Yes, sir, General, what can we do for you?"

"Is General Estes available?"

"I'll have to call him, Sir."

Dennis looked at his watch.

"Ouch, I didn't realize it was 2:30 in the morning down there. What I have to tell him is very important, so please wake him."

"I'll get him on, and then patch him through."

Dennis watched the engineers, almost floating in slow motion as they moved around tirelessly. They were unpacking the laser cannons like mice tearing the wrapping off a candy bar.

"Dennis, nothing wrong I hope?" General Estes asked, in a sleepy voice.

"No sir. Sorry to wake you, but I believe this is important enough that you should know about it. Sir, what would you think if I told you that we're not the first to set up a base on the moon?"

"Dennis, that's too incredible. My God, who could they belong to?"

"That's a good question, General."

"You said there were no flags, or insignias?"

"None that can be seen, sir. I suggest we go back around, set down, and inspect the site."

"Send me those images and I'll forward them to the president. She is going to love me for waking her so early, again. As soon as she and I talk, I'll get back with you. I have no idea what the protocol is for other's properties on the moon. Out for now."

Dennis went to the communications station and had him send the pictures to Estes.

Terry was watching the site engineers at work.

"My word, apparently those weapons are done. They're already running out the cables. Five men lifted that huge laser and set it in place. That sucker looks like it weighs at least a thousand pounds, if not more."

"Remember, Terry, only one-sixth the gravity here, so that which weighs a thousand pounds on Earth only weighs about 160 pounds here."

"Yes, sir, and it sure makes them look like Superman."

Dennis laughed.

"Sure does, how about some coffee?"

Dennis made them both a fresh cup of coffee. They sat on Kirk's bench relaxing and watching the engineers work.

"Diane was right," said Terry, "at the rate they're going, they will be done in no time. Even the old crates are back in the cargo hold."

Skip entered the flight deck, carrying his helmet. He helped himself to a cup of coffee and joined Dennis and Terry.

"Tired Skip?"

"Not one bit, Sir. I thought it would be tiring working in this environment, but it's not. All the trash is on board, tied down and the cargo doors and elevator are locked and sealed, sir."

Dennis handed him the stack of pictures.

"What are these, sir?"

"They are the backside of the moon. Diane caught them on the cameras as she was circling to be brought around."

"Sir, I can't believe this," he said as he leafed through the pictures. "How?"

"You got me, Skip."

Communications interrupted.

"Sir, base is online."

Dennis pushed the radio button.

"Eaglet One here."

"Needless to say," General Estes began, "we are all flabber-gasted here. The president said there are no treaties or agreements anywhere concerning moon property. Unless you find something that shows it belongs to another country, then go there and investigate, see what you can find, ASAP. We have to know what's going on before we can make any further decisions. How is the progress there?"

"According to the captain of the engineers, another six to eight hours and we can head home."

"My goodness, Dennis, I thought it would take at least three or four days."

"So did I, Sir, but the way everything was preassembled on Earth and crated, it has taken them no time to put it together ... plus those engineers are work horses."

"Wonderful. Do you feel up to going to this site to investigate, or are you going to get a night's rest first?"

"General, I won't be able to rest until I do a thorough investigation."

"Let us know when you can. Out."

Dennis stared at the darkness outside the flight deck windows.

"Terry, will you contact the captain of engineers to make sure everything out there is secure?"

"Will do."

Dennis switched his radio over for ship-to-ship intercom.

"Ed, are you there close?"

"Yes, sir."

"Good, I would like for you and Hennesey to get suited up and come to my ship. We're going to do some exploring."

"Yes, sir, will be there as soon as possible."

"No. 2, are you on?"

"Yes Dennis, I heard. Are you forming teams to explore what I saw?"

"Yes, that's what I am doing now."

"May I be a part of the team, sir?"

"Diane, please, I..."

"Dennis, remember our discussion a few days ago? No favoritism. Besides, if you don't foresee any danger, then what's the problem? I'm the one who discovered that, I think I have some right to help explore it."

He thought about what she said and knew she was right.

"Suit up and bring Cathy with you. Out."

Dennis turned, looking for Terry.

"Did you talk to the captain?"

"Yes, sir, all secure."

"Thank you. When we lift off, we will back off from this spot before getting airborne."

A few minutes later, they were ready to go.

"Terry, bring number one and two online; let's go take a look see."

In just a few, short minutes, they found the base.

"There's the pad Terry, set us down there, please."

The huge ship hovered over the designated site, and then slowly felt its way to the moon's surface. It landed at the far end of the short runway.

"Out of pure curiosity, sir, why did we set down here?"

"Simple, Terry. Remember the landing gear tracks on the in-frared? I didn't want to blow them away or cover them up. I want to see if that's what they really are. Mr. Hennesey, do we have a measuring tape on board?"

"Aye, sir, that we do."

"Terry, turn on all the forward floodlights. They should light up the whole place like a football stadium."

As the lights came on, they lit up the entire area, like day-light.

"My word, Sir, those things are huge. They look to be at least 50 yards in diameter and they look brand new."

"You're right about that Mr. Hennesey. We could probably put two or three of ours inside one of those."

"Aye, it's as dark as can be inside them too."

"It could be an inner lining to give that appearance."

"Aye, could be."

"Alright, secure your helmets and let's get our backpacks on. Mr. Hennesey, bring your measuring tape. You and I will check out those tracks. Ed, take Cathy with you and start at the third inflat-able, working your way down to the left. Check for footprints that may be near the entrance. See if you can find any insignias, print-ing, signs, anything that might tell us who owns these. I'm not sure, but I'll bet those are airlocks at the entrances. Let's not attempt to force our way in. Terry, you and Diane check out the ones to the right. Check your oxygen and let's take a walk."

They all went their separate ways.

"Oh yeah, I would surely be a graceful dancer in the ball-room at home," said Terry.

Diane laughed.

"It is a bit cumbersome. I think more weights on our boots would help."

"Yes, in the beginning one has a tendency to force himself and tire easily, I've found out. We haven't had a chance to train like those engineers. They've worked for hours today and they're probably ready for a lot more. Once we're used to it, they say it's almost impossible to get tired."

"Terry, I think we're close to where those tracks were. They were almost directly across from the very first inflatable. Lord, Terry, I didn't realize we had come this far from the ship ... looks to be about one hundred and fifty yards."

"Probably so, Diane, one short step up here, is like three or four on earth. Did you bring that ultraviolet flashlight?"

"In my hand. Let me see what I can find."

Diane carefully searched the area with the light. She advanced slowly, and after about twenty feet, she stopped. She stooped down and studied the ground.

"It's gear tracks, double tires. Big ... very big. Assuming it was parked facing the buildings, this would be the nose gear, so any prints of the main gear should be to my right and left at about a forty-five degree angle."

It wasn't long before she found both main gear tracks. She measured from the nose gear to one main gear, then across. Diane whistled.

"Well, should gear designs hold close, I would say this ship was just a wee bit larger than ours."

"True, but I've never seen a tire with the patterns shown in these prints."

"Could be that those squiggles, or what some would call worm patterns, could have been caused by the disturbance when it lifted off."

"That's possible I guess, but where they seem undisturbed, they sure look evenly spaced. Okay, let's go join the others."

It literally felt like a hop, skip, and a jump over to the others.

"Anything, Ed?"

"Only these two posts. They are in the same spot, to which I assume is the entry on these three. This left hand post has something similar to a keypad. It probably uses a combination of numbers to open the portable door to the air..."

He did not get to finish, as a loud yell echoed in their helmets. They looked around to see Mr. Hennesey come flying above their heads, almost horizontally, through the air. He landed on his back and a plume of dust rose up around him as he hit the ground. Dennis yelled.

"Check his suit and make sure his oxygen is on."

Dennis went over to him.

"Lie still, Hennesey."

"Sir," he gurgled, "I'm OK, I'm fine."

"Just stay put while we check your suit."

"This side looks good Dennis."

"This side looks good also. Hennesey, we're going to roll you over to inspect the back of your suit, just relax and let us do the work."

"I have an emergency patch ready, Dennis."

"Good girl, be ready to slap it on any tear you see. Ed, let's roll him."

They rolled him onto his side.

"Legs look good, Dennis."

"Waist up is good also, Ed. Let's put him on his back. Mr. Hennesey, how do you feel?"

"Fine Sir, but a wee bit ridiculous lying here."

"Do you feel strong enough to get up?"

"Aye, sir. I had some air knocked out of me when I landed on me back pack, but I'm fine now."

"Ed, take that arm, let's get him up. His air supply and suit pressure are constant, so that tells us his suit is fine."

They pulled him to his feet and everyone scanned his suit again.

"Can you tell us what happened, Hennesey?"

"Aye, sir, that I can. I was trying to look through the glass in their airlock. When I was about three feet in front of the building, an invisible huge fist hit me, and here I be, flat on me back."

Dennis turned toward the building and cautiously stepped to the posts, a few feet from the entrance. He bent down, picking up a handful of tiny pebbles. He threw them at the entryway and there was a quiet hissing sound. Small sparks flew, as each pebble bounced from an invisible force field.

"A shield," he said, into his microphone. "They are covered by a force field."

"Well, so much for exploring."

"I don't know, Diane. Ed, let's take a look at that post with the buttons on it. If we can figure out what these symbols mean, maybe the computer can help us out. It has to be a combination of them, somehow."

"Does anyone here have a pad and pen?"

"Right here."

"Thanks Diane. Let's place a sheet of paper over the keypad. I think the indentations are deep enough that we can trace an exact copy of the key symbols. It seems that each one has a peculiar beginning and end. See how the forward line, prior to the symbol; has a curl to it, and the end sort of squares off? They all seem to be a little different."

"I see what you mean, Dennis. Ed, will you hold this sheet of paper over the keypad?"

In the process of tracing the symbol, Diane pushed too hard on a key and it lit up.

"Oops, I hit a key Dennis, and the light under it is on."

"Which one?"

Dennis leaned over, checking it out.

Ed picked up a pebble and tossed it at the building. Again, it repelled the stone.

"Well, apparently no help there. Go ahead and finish Diane."

Diane meticulously traced each design.

"Here they are," she said, handing the paper to Dennis.

"Okay, great. There's no sense in standing around out here. Let's go back to the ship and see what we get when we feed these into the computer."

They sat down at the conference table and Diane began drawing larger pictures of the keypad.

"Oh, so my lady is an artist too? What else don't I know about you?"

"A lot sweetheart, a whole lot."

She looked up at him and smiled, and then held up her drawing of three of the keys.

"What do you think?"

He looked at the three pictures carefully.

"Perfect. Can someone feed these into the computer to see if it can interpret them? I have some other things I need to be working on."

"I'll do it, sir."

"Thanks Mr. Hennesey."

"I want to stretch my legs and get another cup of coffee. Diane, why don't you get up and stretch? You've been at that tedious job for over an hour already."

"I'm on my last one now. Go ahead and get your coffee, I'll be done here in five minutes."

A voice came over the conference room intercom.

"Communications here. We have incoming company, sir."

Everyone stopped what they were doing and looked at the speaker.

"One of ours?"

"Negative, sir, from outer space. Two bogeys, sir."

"Damn, wait a minute. We don't see anything coming from earth. Which way are they coming from?"

"Sir, you won't believe this, but when they blipped onto my screen, they were coming almost directly from Mars."

"From Mars? Sergeant, are you sure they aren't meteors?"

"Positive, sir. Their signatures are those of two darn fast moving ships."

"I'll be right there."

Dennis looked at the surprised faces around the room, and knew they were seeing the same look on his face.

"Come on everyone; let's get a look at that screen."

They left the conference room and went onto the flight deck. They gathered around the large, pale green, radar screen.

"My God, they are ships," Dennis said. "Look at the way they are moving across the screen, hell, we can't even fly that fast. ETA Sergeant?"

The operator looked closely at the numbers around the screen.

"ETA 35 minutes, sir."

Dennis' mind was racing. He stood there for a moment, rubbing his chin and thinking.

"Communications, get 2 and 3 on ship-to-ship. Tell them to get everyone on board – emergency procedure. Get off the surface as soon as possible and get to 30,000 feet, defensive posture. I want to know the minute they are up."

"Yes, sir."

"Terry, I'm first seat, you're second. Everyone strap in and don't forget your helmets. Weapons, as soon as engines one and two are up, charge up."

"Do you think they are unfriendly, sir?"

"I don't know, Ed, but we can't take a chance staying on the surface. We would be sitting ducks, or whatever would be the appropriate analogy where they come from. Terry, bring up one and two."

"Yes, sir."

The soft, purring sound was music to Dennis' ears as it gained RPMs.

"Number one coming up, sir, almost in the green."

Dennis picked up his helmet and glanced again at the radar screen.

"Lord, they're coming fast. There's no way we could outrun them. Face-to-face, that's it."

"Number one in the green and number two coming online, sir."

Dennis bolted for his console. He strapped in and waited for number two to reach green.

"Sir, incoming communication ... from one of the incoming craft."

Dennis, surprised, turned and looked back at the communications sergeant.

"Are you sure?"

"Yes, sir, they are hailing us."

"Patch it through on the open speakers."

"Done, sir, you can talk."

"This is the squadron leader of Delta Blue, from Earth. You wish to talk?"

A calm, smooth voice came through the speakers.

"Yes, Lieutenant ... oh, sorry, I forgot you were promoted to a General. Yes, General Denehey, we wish to speak to you and hopefully meet your beautiful bride-to-be, again."

Totally confused, Dennis replied, "Sir, may I ask how you know my name and our relationship?"

"In due time, General. I see you are prepared to lift off and have powered up your weapons system. Please do not fire on us. If we were hostile, I could have destroyed your ship 15 minutes ago. We are friendly, sir. I see your other two ships have also come up. Please tell them not to fire on us."

"One moment, I'll be right back with you."

Dennis muted himself and turned, looking back at communications and radar stations.

"Communications, radar, are their weapons powered up?"

"No sir, there is no indication of that."

"Terry, idle back one and two. Weapons, kill the weapons system."

Everyone gave him a questioning look, but didn't say a word.

"Sir, you're putting my crew at risk," Dennis said to the incoming vehicles, "but for some reason I trust you. My other ships will stand ready."

"Good enough, General. We will be setting down in approximately seven of your minutes. Out."

Dennis unstrapped.

"Terry, cameras on, let's see what we're facing."

Dennis looked around at everyone.

"I don't know why I trust their words, but I do. Any comments?"

"Sir, I do too. Don't ask me why, but just the calm manner and his familiarity of you and Diane puts me at ease."

"Communications, inform 2 and 3 of developments and have them stand ready."

Everyone on the flight deck had their eyes glued to the huge viewing screen.

"Sir, they're coming down."

Two large ships appeared on the viewing screen. They looked like huge mosquitoes, with long pointed snouts and long wings with drooping ends. They were about two miles off to their left.

"Oh my, it's the Klingons!"

Everyone sort of melted at Hennesey's comment, and laughed.

The two large ships were parallel and never turned a nose to them. Instead, they started coasting sideways, toward the landing pad. Approximately a hundred yards from Dennis' ship, they settled down as soft as a feather. When the dust settled, the calm voice was once again heard over the speakers.

"General, permission for three to come aboard."

"Permission granted, Sir. When you get to my nose gear, I'll send down the air lock and elevator."

"Thank you, sir, be there directly."

Once more, everyone on the flight deck went to the viewing screen and watched as three figures, in silvery spacesuits, literally floated to the surface.

"By gory, sir, did ya see that? No elevator and one of them is but a midget."

"Yes, Mr. Hennesey, I think we all saw it … antigravity."

"Aye, sir, and look at them. They're not walking. They be floating to us."

"Jet packs, I guess. Let the air lock down, Terry, let's greet our visitors."

Everyone drifted slowly to the elevator. The hiss of the released air, from the air lock, was heard. Three figures slowly emerged, removing their helmets. A tall, young woman shook out her hair.

Mr. Hennesey blurted out, "Oh, be gory sir, they do not look like Klingons, they look like us, and my goodness, the wee one is no midget at all, just a wee lassie."

"Very observant, Mr. Hennesey."

The young man and woman were all smiles as they exited the elevator. Behind the woman was a young girl, with wavy blond hair that folded down over the sides of her face and over her shoulders. There was a beautiful, white smile, on the child's face. The young man took the woman's hand and stepped toward Dennis. He extended his free hand.

"General Denehey, I am Jules Verne the sixth. Thank you for having us. Please meet my wife. Therina, meet General Denehey."

The beautiful young woman stepped up and offered her hand.

"My pleasure, sir ... I've heard much about you."

Dennis and the rest were amazed, to say the least.

"My pleasure, Ms. Verne."

Looking down at the pretty little girl, Dennis asked, "And who, may I ask, is this?"

"Our daughter, Alania."

Dennis stooped, offering his hand.

"Welcome, Alania."

"Oh, thank you, sir. I'm thirsty."

"Well, young lady, I'm sure we can help take care of that thirst."

Dennis stood up and looked at Jules.

"Jules, I know you. I can't think from where, but I do know you."

Therina walked over to Diane and extended her hand.

"You would be Diane. I have also heard much about you."

Smiling, but baffled by the familiarity, Diane took her hand.

"You've heard of me? May I ask how?"

"Jules has described every detail of each of you, along with the friendliness which all of you extend to others. There is one minor fault in his description of you."

"Oh, and what would that be?"

"You are much more beautiful than his description."

Diane burst out laughing, and actually hugged Therina.

Therina's blue eyes sparkled. She noticed the large man as he walked up beside Diane.

"Well, hello Mr. Hennesey," she said, as she extended her hand. "I am Therina. It is nice to make your acquaintance."

"Aye, lass, I am Mr. Hennesey, indeed I am, but how did ye know?"

"If you'll forgive me, I was told that you are like a big teddy bear, and I see that in you."

Mr. Hennesey blushed.

"A big teddy bear? I like that description. I'm sorry to interrupt you lassies, but I heard the wee one say she was thirsty. May I have the privilege of taking her to get a drink?"

"The wee one?"

"Aye, the wee lassie, Alania."

"What a beautiful dialect, Mr. Hennesey. It's the first time I've heard the Scottish accent. Yes, Mr. Hennesey, I'm sure my wee lassie would enjoy your company, and thank you."

Therina stooped down, brushing a lock of hair behind Alania's ear.

"Alania, Mr. Hennesey wants to take you to get something to drink. Would you like to go with him?"

Alania looked up at him, and with a beautiful smile on her face, she held both arms up to him.

"By gory, I think she may like me."

He leaned over and picked her up gently, into his huge arms.

"Ms. Therina, would you care for something yourself? We have several beverages including cool water and coffee."

"Yes, please. Would you, by any chance, have Coke?"

"Indeed we do, and for the wee Lassie?"

"If you do have Coke, she will be your lifelong friend, I assure you."

"Then Coke it shall be. And for your husband?"

"Definitely the same, if you have plenty."

"Aye, there be more than enough. Let us go get a Coke, young lassie."

Alania wrapped her arms around his neck, hugging him.

Everyone was soon introduced, and the tension seemed to disappear. All of Delta Squadron were surprised, and relieved, by the warm greetings from their visitors. It seemed that all of their other encounters had been hostile, and this was a welcome change.

"Let's all go to the conference room and sit."

"General, would you mind if I call you Dennis? I so enjoy the atmosphere of your unit, so much like family."

"Not at all, Jules, and thanks for reminding me. We're like a big family, but we know at certain times we have to revert back to military protocol."

Mr. Hennesey entered the conference room, Alania in one arm, and a case of beverages in the other.

He put the case of Cokes on a long table. With Alania still in one arm, he handed a Coke to Therina and Jules, and then passed them around the table.

"Oh my, this is such a delicacy," Therina stated.

"A delicacy, why is that?"

"We don't have these beverages at home, so when Jules and Jordan would come back from a visit, they usually brought some. It's gone quickly, as we share it with family and friends."

"Jules, excuse me everyone, but my curiosity is killing me. I know you from somewhere, but where? With you coming to us in that ship, I can't quite place you."

Jules smiled and his eyes twinkled.

"Yes, in fact, we have met on quite a few occasions. My brother and I greeted most of you at the security post in hangar two."

"Oh yes, that's right. Then you are on our security force. Wait a minute, this makes no sense. Are you now listed as AWOL?"

"Not at all, Dennis. We are just *sort of* on that job. Jordan and I merely tapped into the computer system, putting our names on the duty roster. No one there even knows we exist. You see, we have been keeping an eye on your progress. Once I saw your fuel formula, I reported that you were very close to coming into space. Then, when I saw the development of those magnificent engines, we knew you had it."

"You saw my fuel formula? How could you have possibly seen it?"

"We have our ways. In some future time, I will tell you about it."

"Why are you keeping a close eye on us?"

"Many reasons. The council watches all warlike peoples. From before the days of the Romans, to the present time, someone or some country, has wanted to conquer the earth and dictate to them. As long as it stays on your planet, we do not interfere. Now that there are those of you who are ready to move into space, we are very watchful. You see, sir, we will not permit any wars to develop in space. When the Chinese fired those missiles at your Space Station, the council was in the process of punishing them, but you reacted quickly and firmly. The council was very impressed with the humanity you showed, and the just punishment you dealt out. They were quite happy that you didn't go further, as you could have done so with ease."

"Jules, this council you speak of, is that your government?"

"They are a legally elected body of all the populated planets that are known to us."

"Are you saying, Jules, that there are more populated planets out there in space?"

"Oh yes, Dennis, many more."

Shaking his head, Dennis got up from his chair, rubbing the back of his neck. He turned around and looked at Jules and Therina, then over at Alania who was snuggled up in Mr. Hennesey's lap.

"Jules, if I wake up and find that all of this is just a sci-fi dream, I'm going to be very sad."

Everyone laughed.

"Communications, I almost forgot about 2 and 3. Please have them stand down and land here. Jules, there are so many things

I want to ask, but I'll stick to the pertinent questions for now. The first thing I would like to know, had your council decided to punish the Chinese, in what way would they do so?"

"Just guessing, Dennis, had they just fired a regular explosive missile, probably not much more than you did. Since one was nuclear, the council would have destroyed the entire government and their military, had it exploded successfully. As a warning to all countries on your planet, the entire population of China would literally disappear."

"We didn't know that one was nuclear. Why didn't it explode?"

"It did not reach its target, Sir. When it was detected, Jordan destroyed it."

"Who, may I ask, is this Jordan?"

"My younger brother, he's in the other ship. In fact, he has just told me that the Russians have launched a small ship of their own, and it is now in orbit around the earth. They're probably going to try to use the earth as, what you call a slingshot, to come this way."

"Just told you? How?"

"This lapel insignia is a sending and receiving device. He has been listening in, but my earpiece is how he informed me."

"In that case, we are in his debt for taking out that nuclear missile, thanks Jordan."

Jules raised a finger to his ear.

"He says you are welcome, glad he could help."

"You say the council has the power to destroy all the population of China. How?"

"Sir, without going into a lot of history right now, let me say this. When all of the planets came together, a hundred centuries ago, all the weapons of destruction were given up to the council. A lot of them were destroyed, but then they realized that one day we might have to defend our right to exist. We do not hesitate to use them, when threatened. If the entire council deems an action defensive, they have the ability to do away with all human life on a planet. They would do this with no harm to plants, animals, or buildings."

Dennis sat straight up, his eyes wide.

"Are you serious, Jules?"

"Very serious, Sir. Had we thought for one second that your base here was offensive, you would not have been allowed any weapons in space. We are well aware of America's intentions. I have to admit, in no way whatsoever, did we trust your last president. Ms. Cynthia Alexander is just the opposite. She has fought the fight, from the vice presidency to present, a very honorable woman. The only warning I am permitted to give you, is this... your Democratic Party of years past were honorable people. I hope the people today will see that this party is trying to guide America into socialism, then communism, which has forever failed. Dennis, I'm sorry, I'm afraid we cannot stay as long as we would like, but we'll get back together soon."

"Excuse me, sir, may I ask ye a question?"

"Certainly, Mr. Hennesey, what is it?"

"You introduced yourself as Jules Verne, the sixth. Is that correct, sir?"

"You are correct, Mr. Hennesey. "

"Would happenstance have it that you are kin to the great French novelist, Jules Verne, who wrote those magnificent books about his journeys into the earth, under the seas, and the like?"

"Yes, that would be my forefather, Mr. Hennesey."

"Ah, me thought so, sir, I did. I remember reading his stories, but the mystery of what actually happened to him, well, has it ever been resolved?"

"Mr. Hennesey, let me straighten out a couple of things about my grandfather. He was no more French than you are. He was born and reared in Scotland, and then a small community called Kilmarnock. Yes, he wrote many of his novels in France, and as they often do, the French took credit where credit is not due. He only wrote books to finance his inventions and travels. There is more truth than fiction in most of his novels, but he had to make them sound fictional, as no one would have believed him then. Indeed, only a handful today would believe him.

"According to his journals, he loved the earth, but was worn out and disgusted with the wars, murders, and butchering of humankind. Believe it or not, my grandfather was equal to your Einstein. He found the secret of controlling atomic energy. Somewhere around 1860, he became determined to find a more peaceful planet to live on. He had met an Austrian astronomer, who swore he had seen a planet that resembled earth remarkably. He said it was between Jupiter and Uranus, somewhat sandwiched between Saturn. He said that he had seen it three different times in 10 years, and that he had seen continents, and at times clouds.

"Grandfather and the astronomer found enough people to finance building a space ship that used atomic power, as he had used in his submarine. No, Grandfather did not die in 1905. He, and the astronomer, along with some of the families who financed building the ship, left the earth. As they approached the moon, something went wrong. They didn't lose all power, but could not escape the pull of the moon. Finally, Grandfather knew he would either have to land on the moon, or eventually crash on it. He hoped he could repair whatever had created the problem. They were forced to land on the site of the last inflatable.

"He managed to do enough repairs to keep their air supply, and knowing that it would be a long journey to the other planet; they had brought more than ample food supplies. They rationed out the food, but after awhile it began to dwindle. A young man, who had joined them on the journey, was a telegrapher, and had brought his equipment. For weeks, he had spent hours each day sending out SOS signals. Everyone told him that he was wasting his time, but when he asked what else is there to do, they finally left him alone. He saved all of them. One day, weeks after they had landed, a huge ship came to investigate the strange signals, and found them. They transported them to their planet, and here I am today."

Everyone in the room was mesmerized by the story. When Jules became quiet, Dennis stood up, again rubbing his neck and pacing the floor. He finally stopped his pacing, turned, and looked directly at Jules.

"Jules, I see you, I hear you, I see your beautiful wife and child, and I know that those ships are real. All of you are real. If this isn't a dream, I'm in deep trouble. Have you any idea what would happen to me, if I go back home and report what I have been told here to the general and the president? Anyone who even attempted to back me up would be put in straitjackets and tucked away in a mental hospital and never heard from again."

Jules stood, smiling, and patted Dennis on the back.

"Dennis, I understand your quandary; let's go back to your flight deck and I'll show you something."

Everyone filed out of the conference room and onto the flight deck.

"Can you turn on your viewing screen and illuminate the inflatables?"

In a few seconds, the large white buildings were staring back at them.

"That furthest one to the right, Dennis, is our family Museum. All of my grandfather's original journals are preserved in there. They can easily be read, page by page. The original formula for controlling atomic energy is there, as well as the log of the space flight and the journals of his trips on the earth and on his submarine. There are thousands of pages, all hand written. Even those of the astronomer are preserved there. Many of his artifacts are in there, and best of all, the spaceship. It still sets on the same spot where he landed here. The only thing missing is the submarine. We know exactly where it is, and one day we will retrieve it and bring it here.

"The next inflatable covers the graves of my grandfather, grandmother, father and mother, and a few of our family members who have died since. The astronomer is also buried there. The third one contains what you and your country will get from our council, if your government stays on the track of freedom. Should your country give in to the socialist movement, then what's in there will never come to your country. There are many items in there that will jumpstart your country into the future for hundreds of years. The next two, are the equipment that keeps the temperature in the buildings just right, like the generators for the lights and the shields over the inflatables. The last two there, you will find many things that may help you and your country in many ways. I'm going to give you the combinations to all of the buildings, except the one. Unfortunately, we cannot stay this time and give you a personal tour, and there is one condition. There are to be no pictures taken of what's in any of the buildings."

"You have my word, Jules, none will be taken. I can still feel that straitjacket, somehow."

Jules laughed.

"Therina please let me have your communication unit and earpiece."

She handed it to her husband, who in turn, handed it to Dennis.

"Dennis, if your president remains in a state of disbelief, you can use this to call me at any time. In fact, here's what I'll do. You call me and set a time. I'll come and pick up anyone in your squadron, the president, and General Estes and his wife, bring them back here and give them a personal tour. Perhaps I can even get a council member to attend. Whatever, I'll do my best to convince your people that it's not a dream. Exactly north, northwest of hangar number two, 2.3 miles, are two very large sand dunes. Should your president wish to make a quick journey back here, drive between the two dunes and wait for me. I'll pick up those who wish to go."

"I can't ask for more than that, Jules. Thank you."

"No problem. What? All right Jordan, I will. Excuse me, Dennis, is there a young lady, Mattie Mitchell, on this mission."

"Yes, she's on the other ship. Why?"

"Well excuse me everyone, I'm afraid that Jordan and Mattie have an attachment. Jordan is a lovesick puppy. Oh, hush up Jordan, yes, she is here but on another ship, and yes, you are a lovesick puppy."

Everyone was laughing.

"Jules," Therina scolded, "be kind to Jordan. If I remember correctly, his older brother courted me in much the same fashion, probably worse."

Again, laughter spread around the deck.

"Jules, Jordan is welcome to call her ship-to-ship, if he would like."

"Oh, that would make him very happy. Jordan, you can call her ship-to-ship. Oh, settle down boy. She's on ship No. 3."

Diane thought about Jules' question.

"Oh my," she said out loud. "Jordan must be the security guard that Mattie is in love with. Well, I guess that solves our having to seek relief of that regulation."

"Will someone please tell me what's going on with my sister?"

"I'm sorry, Ed, Jordan wants to know if you will mind if he comes to visit Mattie, on earth?"

"Jules, I know you aren't kidding, but I have no idea how far you live from here. Anyway, no matter how you look at it, I would consider that a long, long, long distance courtship. If he is willing, I won't stand in his way. In fact, I wish him all the luck in the world with that little heifer."

The laughter rolled on the flight deck. No one could remember Ed saying that many words at one time.

Alania, still in Hennesey's arms, said, "Mr. Hennesey, here please, it sure is empty."

He took the empty container, and looking into her pleading eyes, got the message.

"How about Uncle Henny fetching some to take with ye?"

Her eyes lit up.

"Oh, could you, sir?"

"Yes, I could, but I should ask your mother and father."

"We would be most grateful for the gracious gift, sir," answered Therina.

"Let me help you, Mr. Hennesey," said Dennis.

Shortly, they returned, carrying four cases each. They set them by the elevator.

"Thank you, but that is way too much."

"Please accept them as a small token of our appreciation for your friendly visit."

"Thank you, Dennis. I assure you that it will be deeply appreciated."

"If you can wait but just a wee moment, I'll get me helmet and carry them to your ship."

"Thank you, Mr. Hennesey, but I can handle them just fine," Therina said.

She pulled a chrome rod from a small slit in the leg of her suit. She pointed it at four of the cases and they literally floated off the floor. As she moved the rod, the cases followed. She stacked the four cases on top of the others and then moved them all to the elevator. Everyone stared in amazement.

The visitors started to put on their helmets when Alania said, "Wait Mommy."

She ran off the elevator and to Mr. Hennesey, holding up her arms so he could lift her.

"I'll surely miss you, wee one."

She gave him a quick kiss; right on the lips, hugged him, and then leaned back.

"I love you, Uncle Henny, but I have to go."

He put her down and she ran to her parents. Jules put her helmet on and they waved at the crew as the elevator went into the air lock.

Diane looked at the big teddy bear.

"Why, Mr. Hennesey, if I didn't know better, I would say those are tears I see."

"Shush, woman, do nay tell everyone."

She walked over and laid her hand on his arm.

"That was very touching. You have to be a little soft-hearted or you become a bitter person."

"Aye, 'tis true love, 'tis true indeed."

They all watched as the three figures disappeared into their ship. In only a few seconds, the two ships, in tandem, rose from the surface like feathers. They retracted their landing gear and then leaned slightly, nose down. At first they moved slowly, until they were above the inflatables, and in an instant, they were gone, into the heavens.

"I'd meant to ask how fast they could fly."

"Very, very, fast, Dennis."

Dennis turned to his console.

"Communications, put on ship-to-ship, please."

"Done, sir."

"Nos. 2 and 3, report."

"No. 2 here, sir, can you please help us? What is going on? We are about to die of curiosity here. Who were those people and why are they gone?"

"I'm very sorry that you did not get to meet them. Diane and Ed will fill you in later, and Mattie, if you would kindly clear the air, you may be getting a call shortly."

"Oh, from who?"

"Just be patient and you will find out. Meanwhile, where is the captain of engineers?"

"Yes, general, I'm here."

"How much time will it take to complete the site?"

"We have everything complete except the quarters for those three who are staying. That will take about thirty minutes. Everything else – weapons, radar, radio, site shield, generators, atmosphere, heat, A/C and basic plumbing – finished and tested. All primary systems are functional, with back up systems."

"So you're saying that within the next couple of hours we can all leave for home?"

"Yes, sir, once back on site, an hour to an hour and a half, we can be in our seats."

"Captain, you and your men are indeed a great team."

"Thank you, sir."

"Ed, Diane, get your people back on your ships and..."

"Sir, communications here, incoming message from Mr. Verne."

"Patch him through on speakers, please."

"Done, sir."

"Jules, may I help you?"

"We have a problem, Dennis. The Russian ship is in trouble. Apparently, he lost power and control, and is tumbling. He is off course and will probably miss the gravitational pull of the moon, and drift out into space. He is about seven hours from you. We can easily get to him, but if we do, we can't return him to earth. On the assumption he has family there, it would be best if you could get to him."

"We will contact him and see how much air he has left. If sufficient, we'll go get him."

"We will stay on this frequency. If you can't get to him, we will. Out."

"Diane, Ed, return to your ships, please. Diane, try to pick up the emergency frequency and find out from the Russian what his problem is, and most of all how much air he has. Darn, I wanted to at least examine the museum."

Dennis looked back to where Ed and Diane were, only to find they were already on the elevator, helmets on, and going into the air lock.

"Terry, get the cameras on and let me know when they're up. If that Russian has enough oxygen, I'm going to at least have a peek into that museum. I've got to convince myself before I face the general and the president."

Dennis went to the flight deck windows and looked out at the inflatables. He thought to himself, I should not doubt Jules, but Lord, I just have to see this first.

He walked back to Terry as they patiently waited to hear from Diane. Minutes ticked by, and then Diane's voice came over the speakers.

"Dennis, the Russian, a Lieutenant Kozinski, told me he was adjusting his course when he hit the thrusters and everything went dead. He can't find the problem, and his ship is in a one minute, forty-five second, wing over wing roll."

"You mean he can't bring up his backup systems?"

"Would you believe they launched that ship without a computer, or one single backup system?"

"Damn, no wonder those Russians lose good men left and right."

"He told me that he can nurse his oxygen supply for maybe another eight hours, maximum. He is rationing his emergency power."

"Is he, or does he, sound panicky?"

"Not in the least. He makes it sound as professional as can be."

"Where are you?"

"Ed's on the deck, I can be there in three minutes."

"Get the engineers busy. I'll go after the Russian. If he has that much oxygen, I can get to him in plenty of time. Diane, I have to at least peek in that museum."

"I understand, Dennis, I would too. Radio me when you're up, I'll have radar keep an eye on the Russian and give you his exact position."

"Tell him I'll be on my way to him shortly, out. Communications, get Jules on his frequency and tell him we will get the cosmonaut, and please thank him very much."

"Will do, sir."

"Terry, I'm going to the museum. When you see me at the building, bring on one and two. I'll only be a few minutes."

Dennis slipped his helmet on as he headed for the elevator. He found his training as an astronaut helpful, as he seemed to bounce quickly to the museum. Once at the posts, he pulled the small pad from his thigh and looked at the combination for that building. He carefully pushed the buttons in the order Jules had written on the pad. When he looked up, the interior of the building was illuminated brightly. He very cautiously inched his way to the air lock entry, with his hand stretched out in front of him. He did not realize that he had been holding his breath, expecting to be hit by the shield, until he reached the door. Then he exhaled, and started breathing again.

The door was similar to a revolving door. When he pushed through a couple of steps, the door seemed to lock and would not move. He saw the red light above the door. It was steady, then flickered a few times, then went to green. He pushed on the door again and it moved, letting him enter the building. Directly ahead of him, at the end of a long aisle, was the spaceship. It was so much bigger than what he had imagined. Standing upright, he had to almost lean back to see the top.

"Unbelievable," he muttered to himself.

He slowly advanced down the aisle, seeing only the ship. About halfway to it, he realized he didn't have time to wander and discover. He saw the big open door, into the ship, and the ramp leading up almost inviting him to explore. Once more, he tore his eyes from the ship and looked at his watch.

"I've got to go," he said out loud.

He turned, seeing a myriad of glass cases with books, journals and sky maps on display. He went quickly to the airlock, where he turned once more, his eyes locked on the ship. He forced himself to turn and push through the airlock. Once more he had to wait, and when the light turned green, he pushed through into the darkness. On the post, opposite the one with the pad, a red light flashed. 40, 39. He realized he had to get out before the system reset itself. He passed the post and then turned and watched. In a few seconds, the lights went out. He picked up some pebbles, tossed them at the door, and saw the sparks. Satisfied, he quickly turned and bounded across the distance. When he stepped off the elevator, he went quickly to his seat and strapped in.

"Take her up, Terry."

The engines powered up, and in seconds they were lifting off.

"Pass over the base, Terry. Radar, No. 2 will give us the position on the Russian ship. Terry, set the heading, boost us to 10,000 knots and then we'll figure the ETA."

In a few seconds, Terry was locked on, and the ship quickly jumped from 5000 knots and steadily climbed.

"No. 2, are you there?"

"10-4, No. 1, I'm here."

"What is departure status?"

"The engineers are coming aboard. We're splitting your passengers between us. Lift-off, oh, approximately 15 minutes. Will call when both are up and on the way."

"Don't hurry, be safe. It shouldn't take us long to get the cosmonaut on board. Once on correct heading for home, set speed at 15,000 knots; I'll catch up and we'll go home together."

"Sounds good to me. I'm looking forward to a good night's sleep in a bed, out."

"Captain Conklin, report."

"I have the coordinates on the Russian ship, sir. Once there, I'll plot our heading to intercept the other ships. We will only be slightly off when we get to him."

"Radar, when you can get the fix, an ETA please."

"What did you see in the museum?"

"Terry, I only spent a little time; the ship is there. Lord, how I wanted to go aboard and inspect it. My honest opinion, I do believe it was functional. It is huge, and when we come back, I will check out that engine. So far, we have nuclear powered ships and submarines, but we haven't figured out how to use it for airplanes or even space ships. Verne has, in that ship, the answer to the problem. If we could harness atomic power, whoa ... and I wouldn't guess how many journals, books, and notes are there. I saw them, and I'm convinced that Jules was telling the truth. Now, all I have to do is convince the general and the president."

"Do you really have to even mention Jules?"

"Could you hold back that kind of information from your commanding officer, Terry? Especially if it could directly affect the outcome of what could be a perfect relationship with a truthful ally?"

"Not under those circumstances, sir."

"Sir, radar, at 10,000 knots, one hour and twenty minutes ETA. At 11,500, sixty-eight minutes."

"Thank you, we will bump it up to 12,000, plenty of time to complete this mission and get with our teammates. Twelve thousand, please, Terry."

"Going to 12,000, General."

Dennis looked around the flight deck.

"Mr. Hennesey, are you available?" Dennis asked, speaking into the ship's intercom.

"Aye, sir, I be in the cargo hold."

"May I ask just what you're doing in the cargo hold, Mr. Hennesey?"

"Certainly, sir, I'm installing the satellite recovery boom on the cargo crane. When I'm through, I'll attach the satellite recovery hook. If that wee bit of a roll is constant on the Russian ship, I can stop the roll with this boom. Then, depending on how he can exit the ship, pick him off with the satellite saddle and tuck him in the cargo hold, sir."

"Mr. Hennesey, we could not do without you. You're always ahead of problems."

"I try, sir."

"Communications, please get me base. Radar, and ETA?"

"Forty minutes, sir."

"We have plenty of time, as long as he accurately assessed his oxygen supply. At thirty minutes before ETA, hail the Russian cosmonaut; I need to discuss the situation with him."

"Sir, base is online."

"Base, this is Eaglet One."

"Estes here. Update please."

"Eaglet Two and Three on their way home; Eaglet One on a short rescue mission."

"Oh Dennis, not again. What the hell are you rescuing, a can of Budweiser?"

"Sir, don't make me laugh. I'm too tired."

Dennis quickly told General Estes of the situation with the Russian cosmonaut. He thought it best not to bring up Jules just yet.

"All right, son, do you see any problems in getting him?"

"Not at the present, sir. Once on site, I can better see what has to be done."

"Can you tell me what you found at the other base site?"

"There is so much detail in what I have to explain that I would prefer to do it when we get home."

"So, you really learned a lot then?"

"You better believe it, sir. Some of it, at first, was so far-fetched that I was almost ready to denounce it. But now, I'm totally convinced that what we found is actually a fact, no fiction to it."

"Now my curiosity is really stirring, Dennis."

"And sir, I do believe it is imperative that the president be there also. What I have to say will affect our entire nation."

"OK, Dennis, now you really have me going. What the hell am I going to say to the president that will induce her into flying here?"

"Just exactly what I said, General Estes. Sir, I have to leave you with that. Rescue at hand, see you soon, out."

"Quick thinking; it was getting a little touchy, wasn't it?"

"Sir, communications, 29 minutes to ETA, Lieutenant Kozinski on hold."

"Does he speak English? What a hell of a time to think of that."

"Yes, sir, very good English."

"Patch him through. ... Lieutenant Kozinski, General Denehey here, commander of Delta Squadron."

"Hello, General, a very welcome sight you are."

"We're just minutes away from you. How is your oxygen supply holding out?"

"Very well, sir, enough for a couple more hours."

"Very good, and how is the roll of your ship now?"

"It has slowed somewhat, a rollover about every minute."

"Excellent. How do you exit from your ship – top, side or where?"

"I can eject my canopy. My cockpit is much like that of a fighter plane."

"What? Are you serious? Is it that small?"

"Somewhat cramped, sir."

"Stand by, Lieutenant, I'll be right back."

Dennis muted his microphone.

"Terry, break her down quick, or we'll overshoot. Hell, where is my mind. See if you can get her down to under 300 knots."

"I'll have to use one and two, sir, and forward thrusters."

"Do it now, or we might blow him away. Move right, immediately. Radar, keep us updated."

They could feel the braking power of the reverse thrusters on both huge engines.

"Two thousand and slowing. Fifteen hundred. One thousand. Six hundred. Four hundred. Two hundred."

"Radar, where is he?" Dennis asked.

"One thousand yards and closing."

"Brake to eighty and then shut down the engines. Brake her down to zero with reverse thrusters."

"Seventy-eight knots, sir. There he is, to our left, on the screen."

"Stop her. ... Use engine one to bring us within two hundred yards. ... Kill number one. ... Use thrusters to bring us up close. Mr. Hennesey, report."

"Aye, sir."

"Open cargo doors. The lieutenant will eject his canopy when you stop his roll. Let me give him instructions, stand by."

Dennis took his microphone off of mute.

"Lieutenant Kozinski, sorry, I almost overshot you."

"My God, to have a ship that big, oh my."

Dennis told him of Mr. Hennesey's plan.

"Once you are stable, eject your canopy. He will extend the boom over your cockpit with a large, leather-like object, suspended between two large support arms. You will have to climb into it. Wrap your arms around whatever you can and hold on. He will slowly retract the boom and lower you into the cargo hold. He will get a tether line to you in the hold. Do you understand?"

"Yes, sir, I understand. I do not worry, sir."

"OK, Terry, get us up beside him. Lieutenant Kozinski, in case you lose your grip and lose the saddle, don't worry, we will come and get you."

"Yes, sir, I trust."

"Mr. Hennesey, the show is yours."

"Aye, Sir."

Even the communications, radar and weapons men were intensely watching the viewing screen. Captain Conklin was also on the deck, watching history's very first, deep space rescue mission.

Mr. Hennesey maneuvered the booms into place. He snagged the first upright wing that came up to his boom. He stopped its movement. Everyone let out a long sigh as he lifted the boom away, an inch or so, just to see if it would start to roll again. The ship was stable.

"You would think he had done that a thousand times," said Pat.

Mr. Hennesey's voice came over the speaker.

"Sir, I will keep my boom where it is. When he ejects that canopy, the propulsion may want to make it a roll again. If it does so, I will stop it. Please tell the good Lieutenant that there are two tight tethers attached to the saddle. When I lower it to him, I'll lay the saddle right across the forward part of his cockpit. I can nay believe they would put a man into space in such a ship."

"Understood, Mr. Hennesey, I'll relay it to him."

They all watched as the canopy came off the ship, went up several feet, and continued floating into space. They could plainly see the wing come up, meet the boom, and stabilize. They watched the lieutenant as he crawled out, onto the saddle, and grabbed the tethers.

In a few short minutes, Mr. Hennesey announced, "All secure, closing cargo doors."

Cheers erupted on the flight deck. Pat grabbed Dennis' arm and he saw tears in her eyes.

It wasn't long before Mr. Hennesey and the Russian cosmonaut came through the air lock, and onto the flight deck. The

Russian's hand was resting on Mr. Hennesey's shoulder, and both were talking like old friends. Once more, the applause broke out and the Russian cosmonaut grinned from ear to ear. He was not a big man, only five feet, eight inches tall and weighed about one hundred and sixty pounds.

His voice was clear, but there was a slight, emotional shakiness, as he said, "May God bless, and I thank all of you, my friends."

Hands clapped and the young man looked down at the floor to hide his tears, as the stress of the ordeal finally caught up with him.

Mr. Hennesey laid his hand on Kozinski's arm.

"Come, my friend, a cup of coffee will serve us both. He led the young man toward the galley.

Dennis cleared his throat.

"Terry, back us away from that piece of junk, at least a mile or two. Weapons, power up the laser, I'll want that piece of space junk in ashes."

"Yes, sir, gladly."

In seconds, Terry said, "Weapons, it's all yours, fire at will."

They all watched on the viewing screen, as the streak of blue flame flashed toward the tiny ship. When it hit, there was merely a puff of smoke.

"Nothing but molecules and ashes left."

"Very good. Captain Conklin, report."

"Sir, I've just given Terry the new coordinates."

"Thank you, Pat. Put those in the computer, Terry, 17,000 knots, let's catch our crews and go home."

They caught up with ships 2 and 3 and told them the good news of the successful rescue. They pushed the ships to 20,000 knots and let the computers take over.

"Terry, why don't you take first break?" Dennis asked.

"Sir, if you don't mind, I'm wound too tight. Would you mind taking first break?"

"Not at all. Communications, radar, weapons, flip a coin. Two of you get some rest, four hours, then the other one relieve. Captain Conklin, get some rest, we will soon be home."

Dennis went to the galley, and when he entered, Mr. Hennesey and Lieutenant Kozinski were drinking coffee and talking. When Kozinski spotted him, he jumped to his feet and saluted him.

"My General, I am so sorry I have not come sooner. I had to get myself under control. I did not want to appear, before such a great man, as a weakling."

"Whoa, Lieutenant, don't worry, sometimes even I weep and am nervous. There is no shame in that at all. We're just glad that we could come to your aid. You have been through a horrible ordeal and you did damned well, very well. Now sit, relax, and enjoy. Mr. Hennesey, I'm going to grab 40 winks. Terry is at the helm and there is one man on communications, radar, and weapons. You did one hell of a fine job back there. You're one cool cat. You two get some rest when you're ready, I'll only call you in an emergency. Good night, good morning, what the hell ever it is."

"It sounds like you may need a wee nap. Have a good rest, sir."

In his quarters, Dennis punched in ship-to-ship.

"Ship No. 2, report."

"No. 2 here, sir, one moment, I'll patch you through."

He started to stop her, but it was already too late. Diane's voice came through the intercom.

"Hello lover!"

"How did you know it was me?"

"I told Tina not to even put the president through if she called, only you. Otherwise, I would throw her overboard."

Dennis laughed. She seemed to always be able to put a smile on his face.

"I understand. I'm going to grab 40, just wanted you to know that I love and miss you, sweetheart, very much."

"Awww, I love you too. Tonight, we sleep in our own bed. Pleasant dreams and goodnight darling."

"You too, love you. Out."

Dennis' eyes fluttered open and then closed again. Somewhere, a buzzing sound was irritating him, interrupting his sleep. After a minute, he realized it was the intercom. His eyes opened wide and he rolled over and hit the button.

"Dennis here."

"Good evening, Sir."

"Hello, Mr. Hennesey, everything OK?"

"Everything 'tis lovely, sir. I just wanted you to know we are a wee bit under an hour out from the Space Station. Any orders, sir?"

It took a few moments for Mr. Hennesey's comments to register.

Dennis almost shouted, "What? Mr. Hennesey, how long have I slept?"

"That I do not know, sir. I went to sleep after you left the galley. I relieved the good Lieutenant Mitchell about five hours ago."

"Oh my God, Mr. Hennesey. I've slept the whole trip. I told Terry four hours."

"Sir, I asked him about that, and he repeated the orders you gave to the noncoms only."

"Oh, hell, he's right. I didn't tell him to wake me in four hours. Are we still at 20K?"

"Aye, sir, that we are."

"OK, coordinate with Nos. 2 and 3, bring her down so we match the station when we arrive. Hail the station and tell No. 4 to undock; we'll all go home together. I'm going to take a quick shower and shave. I'll be out soon. Oh, Mr. Hennesey, get an ETA to base and contact them."

"Aye, sir, consider it done."

The four ships came in a line, from the west. Passing the hangars, and in a long arc they circled back to the west, each dropping down into final approach. Ship No. 1 touched down on its main gear, nose in the air, slowing it. The nose gear gradually dropped, touching the earth. Dennis rolled past the large crowd that had come to welcome them back from a very historical mission. The other ships followed seconds behind, like graceful birds, each touching down softly, and once more caressing Mother Earth. Dennis waited for the others on the taxiway. When they were all in line, they slowly taxied back, toward their nest.

"Quite a welcoming committee," Dennis said, on the ship-to-ship intercom. "It looks like the whole facility is here."

As they left their ships, the huge crowd was clapping, whistling, and cheering. Dennis saw General Estes heading quickly toward him, with several other people in tow. He saw NASA patches on the arms of a couple of four-star generals. He didn't recognize anyone, and wondered what NASA reps were doing there.

General Estes, with a huge smile on his face, saluted Dennis' crew and then came directly over to Dennis. He grasped Dennis' hand in both of his.

"You folks have done it again, son, congratulations."

"Thank you, sir, we're glad to be home."

General Estes introduced the NASA people and two U.S. senators. They all had high praises for each and every crew member, as they progressed down the line. Dennis introduced them to each, including all of the engineers and the Russian cosmonaut. When they had finished, General Estes pulled Dennis aside.

"Son, would you please address the crowd from that platform over there, just a minute or two? They are proud of all of you, and you just completed your mission way too fast. We intended to throw a proper fanfare, but this is all they could throw together with such short notice. The president wanted to be here when you got back, also. She's on her way now and should arrive in a little more than an hour. She is quite anxious to hear what you have to say."

"I certainly hope so, sir."

Seeing the look on Dennis' face, the general asked, "Is there some reason she may doubt you, son?"

"Sir, what I have to disclose is monumental. In the beginning, I had some serious doubts about it myself. It's still like a dream, in a way, but I can prove everything that I will be telling you."

"Hmm. Well, Dennis, as always, we can go for broke. Now go and address your family."

Dennis stood silent for a moment, looking out over the throng of people. He took a deep breath and spoke into the microphone, his voice clear and calm.

"OK, folks, I was asked to do this, even though I am lousy at public speaking."

The crowd was silent, and he continued.

"I have made a fool of myself before, so what's a couple of more minutes?"

A ripple of laughter passed through the crowd.

"I will say this, to all who hear me. It is all of you, and my crew members, that should be up here talking. Without each and every one of you, none of this would be possible. Our mission would never have taken place. To me, your contribution to our success is just as important as anything I did. We are a family. A family that has come together, walked together, and accomplished this historical mission ... together. This mission, now and in the future, will benefit you, me, our children, and all of mankind. Thank you and God bless you, and God bless America."

He walked slowly from the stage.

The applause trickled through the crowd and then quickly grew to a thunderous ovation. The general shook his hand.

"Wonderful son, just wonderful."

Dennis looked around for Diane.

"Sir, while we are waiting, I'm going to do something that I've already been accused of. I'm going to chase that Budweiser."

"Where to, son?"

"The officers' club, sir, and my crews are going with me, all of them."

"Well, the president is coming in, let's say, under the radar. Thelma and I would join you, but we will be meeting her. I will send for you as soon as she is ready. We'll meet in the conference room in my office."

"There are a few of my people that I'll want to accompany me, Sir."

"Anyone you wish, Dennis, there is more than enough room."

Dennis rounded up the crews and they all went for a well deserved break.

About an hour later, Dennis' shoulder phone vibrated.

"Denehey here."

"Estes here, she'll arrive in fifteen."

"We'll be right there."

Everyone gathered in the general's office.

"Well, Dennis, did you chase down that Budweiser?"

"Yes Sir, I enjoyed two nice cold ones. Diane would not drink anything because of this meeting. I just wanted them to kick back and relax. This first mission, even though everything went off so well, was nerve racking for all of us. Eventually, it will become so routine that it will merely be an afterthought."

"I can only imagine, Dennis. The president is already on the ground and should be here in a minute."

"Shouldn't we have at least been there when she landed, sir?"

"No, Diane, for whatever reason, she wanted to meet here."

"Hmm, then I wonder who met her?"

"Now, now, Diane."

"Oh, come on Dennis, ten-to-one she comes in with Ed Mitchell."

"Wasn't he at the officers' club?"

"Oh Lord, you two sound like an old married couple. I can see you now, sitting in your rocking chairs on your front porch, watching the cute young'un and wondering who her next boyfriend will be."

"That bad, General?"

The door opened. Cynthia and Ed entered the room, together. They all came to their feet.

"Okay, stop, sit, relax, no mushy protocol," Cynthia said, as she walked over to Diane and hugged her. "You know, it would have been a first in the honeymoon department, if you two would have just gotten married before you left."

Diane smiled at the thought.

"It seems I sort of mentioned something to that effect as we were making our turn to go behind the moon. Cynthia, it was a gorgeous setting. As we made the turn, there was a bright, circular beam, around the very edge of the moon, dividing the front and back side of it. Then just off to our right were Mars, Jupiter, and Saturn. Oh, they were so big and beautiful; I could find no words to describe it. You would just have to see it for yourself."

"Well darling, maybe one day I'll get to see all of that beauty. In the meantime, Dennis, I am at a loss of words for you. No one in the history of this world has made so much progress, in so little time. You and your crews have benefited all of mankind, in more ways than I can say. Since the ships are now publicly known, there are scientists, and every pharmaceutical company you can think of, from around the world beating down our doors, wanting to set up labs in them. "

"I understand there are certain experiments that perform better in an atmosphere of weightlessness, but I had no idea the demand was that great."

"Only hours ago we leaked to the press the story of your moon mission. My reason for doing so was twofold. The Democrats are fighting tooth and nail against more funding for the ships. I have my public relations staff working on a program for me to take to the public and show the value of the squadron and how these ships are defending this country. I'm also going to show them your encounters with the Chinese, using the video from the ships, along with the treasonous acts of the vice president, the whole smear. When I go public about wanting more ships, and how the Democrats are holding up progress, ten-to-one there will be enough minds changed to get any damned funding needed.

"Now, one even better than that and then I'll shut up. On my way here, I got word from the White House that since the story came out this afternoon; major companies are calling and offering to pay to build the new ships. Those ships will belong to America. We get them to the moon and set up plants and labs, and they will foot the whole bill. Tourist companies and even Vegas are calling. If we accept just the offer from the major companies right now, we can build three new ships. That will be a decision that you folks here will have to make, not the politicians in D.C.

"One more thing, General Estes, in no way can we allow one of these ships to get out of our hands. I don't care what the cost is, they must be secured."

"I will personally handle that, Cynthia."

"Excuse me, sir," said Diane. "It will be very easy to secure each ship on the ground. When the new shields are installed, we will only need to be able to energize that shield from the outside, just like the inflatables on the moon."

"Great idea. OK, Dennis, I've hogged the floor long enough. Since General Estes has informed me of the deep importance of your message, I brought two key individuals from Congress; I need to bring them in."

"Madam President, I must ask you not to. This information is for yours and General Estes' ears only. I had no right to, but I gave my solemn word that it would go no further. Only those who were present at the meeting are to know of this, at least for the time being. All three crews have sworn not to let it out."

Cynthia sat down between General Estes and Ed, a puzzled look on her face. She looked over at the general.

"Were you aware of this?"

"Cynthia, I quoted you almost verbatim what was said. He all but refused to discuss it on the radio."

"Ed? Your opinion?"

"Cynthia, I was there. I saw, heard, and witnessed it all. I have no doubts in my mind about any of it, and that is why I gave my word to not divulge it. To be quite honest, I don't think even you will want it out in the public forum."

"I have no doubt that you are all in concurrence. But, if it is as important as you say, and will affect this entire nation, do I have the right to withhold it from Congress and the people of this country?"

"To be quite honest, Cynthia, I see no difference in this situation and the one you had when building these ships. There is a time to hold things back, and there is a time to expose them."

Cynthia leaned back in her chair and laughed.

"OK, you got me there, Dennis. You have my word; it will go no further than this room."

"General, sir?"

"Yes Dennis, no further. Spit it out son."

Dennis sat down across from the president and began his story

The Presidential Denial

Dennis began his story with the discovery of the base by Diane. When he got to the part where the ships were seen and then landed, the president's eyes got wide and she looked at Ed for confirmation. He merely nodded his head, not wanting to interrupt the story. During the part where Dennis was telling of Jules Vernes' spaceship, and their leaving the earth, Cynthia could no longer contain her disbelief. She pushed her chair back and quickly got to her feet, looking at everyone around the table. She was mouthing words, but uttering not a sound. She stepped away from the table and walked a few steps with her back toward them. Finally, she turned back to them, shaking her head.

"You ... you expect me to believe, for one second, that first of all, two UFOs came from the direction of Mars, landed, and had a meeting with you. Second, that in the late 1800s, the days of horse and buggies, that a French novelist, of all people, invented and fabricated an atomic-powered spaceship. Then, in the early 1900s he left the earth for a new paradise. I'm sorry, I cannot believe it. What the hell were you drinking, or smoking? My Lord, I'm so glad I didn't bring those congressmen in here."

Everyone in the room had their heads bowed, looking at the top of the table ... everyone except General Estes. He was astounded, and also in doubt about what had been said, but what surprised him more was Cynthia's outburst.

She glared at everyone, and almost gasping for air, she continued.

"How could you possibly expect me to believe such nonsense? My God, if this is some kind of joke, it is certainly not funny. Ed, I find it hard to believe you are a party to this."

With that, Ed looked up at her and rose.

"Excuse me, Madam President," he said, in a firm, but calm voice. "First of all, you question the integrity of all of us who have served this country, and you, so honorably. I was there, ma'am, and I too questioned what I saw and heard, as most of us did. We haven't asked you to believe, just to listen to the truth as we know it. I ... oh, never mind. I would like to be excused."

He moved around the table, toward the door.

"Just a minute Ed, I ..."

"Sir ... Dennis, unless you order me to stay, I'm leaving this room."

"No, Ed, I won't order you to stay; you are excused."

He quickly turned and walked out of the room, his back straight and proud.

Everyone looked at Cynthia. Her face was drawn and her lips pressed together, as she watched the door close.

General Estes felt bad for her.

"Cynthia, please come and sit, catch your breath."

Her gaze went to the general; her mouth opened as if to say something, but then closed, her lips drawn tight and thin. Suppressing whatever it was she intended to say, or a sound that may have given away her emotions, she sat down next to General Estes. Everyone averted their eyes from her to allow her time to regain her composure. The entire room was in silence for some time. Finally, the general broke the silence.

"Cynthia, honey, for too long now, Dennis and all of his people have busted their tails for this country. Dennis took that ridiculous court-martial and stayed, when he could have walked away and became a very rich man in no time. I have never – not once – had reason to doubt one word the man has ever spoken. Not in all the years I have known him. Now, as preposterous as all this sounds to you and me, there has to be something to it. What, I have no idea, but I'm convinced there is absolutely no reason for him to make this up. Personally, I want to hear the rest of it."

Cynthia looked at General Estes, not saying a word, but nodding her head. With a slight smile on his face, he turned to the small group around the table.

"Dennis, in what you have told us so far, do you have any proof, any at all?"

Dennis opened his briefcase and removed several printouts.

"Sir, these are some images taken from my video recording of Jules' and Jordan's ships coming in to land. We have the entire video, showing the original approach, landing, deplaning of Jules and his family, and their crossing over to our ship. He asked that no photos be taken of them on board the ship; none were."

He handed the photos to the general, who spread them out so he and the president could study them.

"Good Lord," he muttered, "those ships look like something from a science fiction movie."

After a few minutes, Cynthia looked at Dennis.

"You say you have the video from your ship? May I see it, please?"

"Yes, ma'am."

Again, reaching into his briefcase, he pulled out the packet and handed it to the president. She looked at the cassette and turned it over, back and forth, side to side, examining it.

With a little impatience in his voice, Dennis said, "Ma'am, it has not been tampered with."

The general held up his hand to Dennis.

"Dennis, please, get the video player and monitor."

##

"I don't see anything," said the president, "except for that big yellow ball."

"That ball, Cynthia, with the various rings around it, is the planet Saturn," explained the general, who pointed at the monitor.

"There … those two tiny sparks of light. They are moving and moving fast. They're getting larger."

They both moved their heads closer to the monitor.

"They are taking shape, Cynthia, see the wings?"

"My God, General, they are ships … ugly ships!"

They were holding their breath as they watched the two ships land. The general and the president did not seem to be breathing. Then, just aft of the nose, a figure emerged and two others, all dropping softly to the surface.

"Wait, stop it there, General. Can you back that up to where they are coming out of the ship?"

"Sure, hold on Cynthia, I saw it too. There, there it is."

"There is no elevator. They are coming down like feathers. And they aren't walking, they're just floating across."

Then they were gone from view and only the two ships stood there, like golden insects in the darkness.

The general turned off the video and let out a big breath. He leaned back in his chair and inhaled deeply.

Cynthia just sat, staring at the blank screen. She came out of the trance and leaned forward, elbows on the table and her forehead in the palms of her hands, her fingers massaging her scalp.

"Lord," she said, in a very low voice, "Spielberg would pay millions for that video."

With those words, everyone began to breathe again.

"OK, where the hell do we go from here?"

Dennis stood.

"Madam President…"

"Stop there Dennis. First, I know words are small, but for now that is the best I can offer. From the bottom of my heart, I sincerely apologize for my very harsh words. Let's start over again, please, just plain Cynthia."

She had such a sad look on her face that everyone smiled to try and make her feel better.

"Well, Cynthia, Jules made a proposal," and Dennis explained about the trip.

"Not only a trip though, he would also like, very much, to meet with you and discuss everything, much of which I didn't have an opportunity to tell you about at this setting."

"Would you care to finish now, Dennis?"

"If you don't mind, ma'am, right now, I think Jules could do a better job. Would you care to talk to him?"

Looking around, she asked, "How?"

He handed her the small button and the ear piece, explaining how it operates.

She looked at it, lying in her hand.

"This is a phone ... to him?"

"In a way, yes, and it works very well."

"Here," she said. "You call him and put it on speaker, please."

Dennis took it back and firmly pressed the pendant. In a few seconds, it buzzed. Dennis then pushed it twice, and a female voice was heard.

"Dennis, what a pleasure, we have been expecting your call. How are you and Diane?"

"We are fine. How are you and Alania?"

"I'm fine, and she is holding tightly to a Coke. I take it you want to talk to Jules?"

"Yes, Therina, please."

They heard her call out.

Cynthia murmured, "Will wonders never cease?"

"A moment, Dennis. Alania wants to know if Uncle Henny is there; she loves that man!"

"No Therina, he's not, but I will be sure to tell him that she inquired."

"Thank you, Dennis, here is Jules."

"Dennis, how are you?"

"Fine. Jules, the president wishes to talk to you."

"Are you serious, Dennis? That lady would talk with me?"

"Certainly, Jules, is that all right with you?"

"All right? Most certainly, it will be an honor."

Cynthia gently took the pendant.

"Mr. Verne, Cynthia Alexander here; thank you for talking to me."

"Ms. Alexander, it is indeed my pleasure, and an honor to speak to the president of the United States of America. How can I be of service?"

"Well, sir, to be quite honest, I find myself in a very awkward and unbelievable time."

"Ms. Alexander, I do understand, and I will do all I can to help you through this. We too, were taken aback, when we found your people had advanced so rapidly in your technology. We had thought that you would not truly advance into space for at least another thirty or forty years. Yet, here you are, and thank God you have excellent people in your command. I assume Dennis has offered you what I have proposed?"

"Yes, he has, Mr. Verne, and a very gracious proposal it is."

"Not at all, Ms. Alexander, as it stands, you are welcome to come into the Space Alliance."

"Alliance? I'm sorry, what alliance?"

"Oh, I'm so sorry. I see that Dennis has not gotten that far yet. It will merely be a discussion, if we meet. It is not mandatory, and it will be your decision if you join or not. There is no force, nor requirements in any way. I think it advisable if we discuss it face to face, rather than on a radio signal. Let Dennis explain it more thoroughly, and then if you desire to meet with me, just call."

"Mr. Verne, please, I will have Dennis tell me all about it. Regardless of that, I wish to meet with you. One question though, please."

"Most certainly, I will answer what I can."

"Ahem, silly question, perhaps, but do you reside on Earth?"

"Oh, no, we do not."

"May I ask where, sir?"

"My regrets, Ms. Alexander, but that, at present time, I am not permitted to say. Perhaps, in the near future, you can be told all the particulars."

"I understand, sir. When do you propose we meet?"

"I will leave that to you. Anytime, at your convenience is fine with me. I do recommend, Ms. Alexander, that you accept my suggestion of a trip to our museum. It will help to alleviate any further doubts on your part."

"Well, sir, I will admit, a trip into space has never appealed to me. As long as I can see land, I am content. May I ask how long the trip from here to the moon would be, in your ship?"

"I can tell you this. We can set down at the site in one hour and twenty minutes, after liftoff. For those of you who have not had the pleasure of space travel, if you like, I will give you the scenic tour, which would take 2 hours and 45 minutes. You will be able to see much more of the stars and planets, and so much more clearly than you can see them from Earth. Once we are around the moon, I will give you time to take a very good look at Jupiter, Mars, and Saturn, as they actually are."

"I accept, sir. When?"

"I can pick you up as soon as the day after tomorrow, at 3 p.m. Eastern Time or 1 p.m. at your present location."

"You know where I am?"

"Your signal, at present, tells me exactly where you are on earth. Is that where you want me to pick you up?"

"Yes, please."

"Is Dennis still there, please?"

"I'm here, Jules."

"Then you heard our arrangement?"

"I did."

"Do you remember where I told you I would land?"

"I do. In fact, I more or less spotted it when I came in on final approach."

"Wonderful, now I must ask a great favor of you."

"Certainly, I will do my best to accommodate."

"It's Mattie. You could stop Jordan from his constant harassment of me if you could bring her with you. He is about to drive all of us crazy."

Everyone was laughing, except for the president and General Estes, who had puzzled looks on their faces.

"Darn Jules, is that all? I'm sure I can honor that request."

"I will certainly find a just reward for that favor, Dennis. Peace will be restored to our household."

"No reward necessary, Jules. I assure you."

"We shall see, my friend. You know the agreement we have, about who is to know of us. My ship can comfortably accommodate fifty people, with private quarters for the president. Communications are provided so she can stay in touch with her people at the White House."

"That is very gracious, Mr. Verne. I will stay with my people, private quarters are not necessary, but thank you."

"Very well, Ms. Alexander, one more thing. Would you mind if I bring my wife and daughter? They are very anxious to meet the famous President of the United States."

"Not at all, Jules, and I am looking forward to meeting all of your people...and Jules...when we meet, please, just call me Cynthia. We can revert to protocol if necessary."

"Very well, Cynthia, a lovely name. Dennis, I'm sorry, I have another pest hanging all over me. Alania has to know if Uncle Henny is coming."

Again, laughter spread throughout the conference room.

"Jules, you tell that lovely child that he will be there if I have to hog tie him."

"You should see her smile, Dennis, she is quite happy now, thank you. It's 1 p.m., day after tomorrow at your site. Any problems, let me know, and oh, my ship will be cloaked until I land."

"Will do, Jules, until then, take care," said Dennis.

Dennis turned and looked at the president.

"Well, 1 p.m., day after tomorrow."

"Dennis, I know I am still being skeptical, but, if he does show up, and can do all he says, then I will be a one thousand percent believer. Now, what does he mean, his ship will be cloaked?"

"I can only guess. Have you noticed that at every turn we make, more and more frequently, so many things that were shown on "Star Trek" are actually happening? The cloaking device…the Romulans had that. It made their ships invisible to the eye and to radar detection. I guess that's what Jules means."

"Oh, Lord, what a weapon that would be if it were to get into the wrong hands. Say, what's this thing with Mattie Mitchell and who is Uncle Henny?"

"Jordan Verne is Jules' younger brother, who met Mattie when he and Jules were here, posing as security guards. That's another part I did not get to. Anyway, apparently, Mattie and Jordan have intentions of getting married."

The president snickered.

"Does she even know that he is not from here?"

"She does now. He called her ship-to-ship while we were on the moon."

"Uncle Henny is Mr. Hennesey, right over there," said Diane, pointing to the big guy who had recently entered the room, "the engineer that was on Dennis' ship. Alania, Jules' daughter, fell in love with him. He gave her a Coke. She is about three years old, I think; anyway, they consider Coke a delicacy, as they don't have any where they are."

"Oh, that is funny, Diane….great PR for America. After all of this, I think I need a drink. Dennis, we'll get back together and you can educate me on everything before Jules arrives. Uncle Henny is trying to get your attention there, Dennis."

"Yes, Mr. Hennesey, what's up?"

"Lieutenant Kozinski, Sir, I have nary an idea how it was found out so fast."

"What?"

"That he was even here, sir. A message came to ops from, I guess, the FBI or Immigration, wanting to know if he was here. Naturally ops told them the truth. Whoever it was, said that the Russian Embassy called and wanted him back. They want him back in Russia."

"General Estes," Cynthia inquired, "were there any of the reporters here that I was going to send for PR?"

"Yes, there were three pool reporters: newsprint, radio and TV."

"So, that's how it got out so fast."

"Well, Mr. Hennesey, it's not unusual for a country to want their citizens back, particularly a trained cosmonaut. Is there a problem with that?"

"Ma'am, he doesn't want to return to Russia. He says they will make him go on another suicide mission. He wishes for asylum, ma'am."

"Suicide mission...what do you mean?"

"Cynthia, allow me. Do you remember those two ships we recovered? The ones you referred to as flying coffins?"

"Those I showed at the UN."

"His ship was one of those. I would not use the pieces of junk for lawn decorations. The one we pulled Lieutenant Kozinski from, did not even have a working computer. Not even for launch. He is a master pilot just for being able to get it into orbit. I'll never understand how he, so accurately, got that ship into a position to slingshot it into its correct trajectory to the moon. There were absolutely no backup systems for the man, and how he functioned at all, in that tiny, cramped cockpit, which Ed could not even fit in, is a miracle. It was indeed a suicide mission, bound to fail."

"Aye Sir, and one of the pilots from the two ships we recovered earlier, was the lieutenant's younger brother, the last of his family."

"Dennis, what do you recommend?"

"Ha, an insane asylum if he even wants to go back. I would not hesitate to give him asylum, Cynthia."

"Where is this Lieutenant Kozinski, Mr. Hennesey?"

"In the hallway ma'am and he be a wee bit worried, I must say."

"Please, bring him in."

"Aye, you bet, Madam President."

Mr. Hennesey walked to the door, opened it, and motioned for Kozinski.

"Lieutenant Kozinski, please meet our president, the president of America."

Like a tree, the man snapped to attention, saluting her.

"An honor, a true honor to meet such a great lady."

"At ease, Lieutenant."

Cynthia extended her hand.

A confused look came across his face, almost stuttering, he asked, "What, you would shake my hand?"

Cynthia laughed.

"I certainly would, Lieutenant. It's an honor for me to shake the hand of a very brave man."

He reached out, gingerly, and took her hand in his. A huge smile came across his face.

"What a wonderful country, when its president will shake the hand of a common man."

"Sir, no one in America is a common man; all are equal…you, me, and everyone. You don't have to worry Lieutenant; you will never have to return to Russia, unless you want to."

"Do you say I can be an American? I have studied hard, hoping someday to come. I studied your Constitution, a beautiful thing; I can recite it for you word for word. I know your Pledge of Allegiance under God, and I know the history of your great country."

Everyone was smiling at the man's sincerity.

"You probably know more than I do, Lieutenant. I would say you are on the fast track to becoming an American citizen. I also think that General Denehey may have just the right job for you."

Leaning in closer to Dennis, Kozinski whispered, "You would give me work? Ho, I will sweep your floors, sir, anything. You and your Mr. Hennesey, a very brave man, I owe my life to both of you."

Dennis was tickled with this fine young gentleman, and he took his hand.

"No my friend, there will be no sweeping of any floors with these hands. If all goes well, your abilities and knowledge will be put to better use, if, and mind you it's a big if, you wish to train to be one of our astronauts. You don't have to. Understand?"

A very shocked look crossed his whole countenance, as his eyes searched each solemn face in the room.

"Is no joke, Madam President? I can be American... a wonderful American astronaut in one of those magnificent ships? It is too much, a shock, please pardon my weakness, my tears."

He lowered his face, wiping tears away.

"It is no joke, Lieutenant. You have lost enough, and now it's time to gain."

She reached across and lifted his face, looking into his eyes.

"You are far from being a weak man, Lieutenant Kozinski. There is no shame in tears. It only shows the world that you are a loving human being. Now, what do you say, let's get this show on the road?"

You could see the sparkle in Lieutenant Kozinski's eyes, as he said, with a salute, "Yes ma'am."

"General Estes, do you think we can get this man on the fast track to citizenship?"

"Consider it done, Cynthia. We will take it from here."

"And I will let you take it; I have to find Ed and eat crow."

Once again, Cynthia extended her hand to the Russian.

"Welcome to America, Mr. Kozinski. You are no longer in the Russian military, and when the time comes, I'm quite sure, General Denehey will assign the proper rank."

The Russian shook her hand, vigorously.

"I will make you proud, Madam President."

"You already have, sir. I'll see you soon, I'm sure."

As the general escorted the president out, Dennis went to the little group sitting by the window.

"Mr. Hennesey, will you take care of our Mr. Kozinski's quarters, and the like? We will get all the details ironed out when we return."

"Are we, or you, going somewhere, sir?"

"Yes, Mr. Kozinski. If you would have a seat, Mr. Hennesey and I will be right back. Sarge, would you come with us? Diane, honey, would you introduce the others to Mr. Kozinski, please?"

"It would be my pleasure, Dennis."

"Let's go, you two."

In the hallway, Dennis filled them in on the trip with Jules.

"You don't have to go, but a certain young lady is going to be awfully disappointed if you are not there."

Mr. Hennesey's eyes lit up.

"Awww, me little Alania, I will be happy to go, sir."

"Good. Sarge, can you join us too?"

"Well, sir, my Shirley is so patient, but I have promised her that day."

"I have an idea, Sarge. Shirley will have to start ordering supplies for the new moon base, soon. She is probably already aware of that, as everyone else is. As the only qualified person, she will have to set up a supply on the moon. Ask her if she would like to go on a pre-honeymoon trip. There will be plenty of room for her."

"You are serious, sir?"

"Dead serious; do it."

Dennis stepped back into the conference room and found Diane.

"I'm sorry to be using all our time here, Diane."

"Don't worry, sweetheart, but I do have a suggestion."

"Your wish is my command, me Lady," he said, bowing.

"Oh yeah, we shall see about that. Look, Cynthia has gone to find Ed. General Estes said he was in the officer's lounge, drowning his sorrows. I'll bet Mattie and Cathy are there with him. We need to tell Mattie that she is going with us, so, lets grab a couple of cold ones, unwind a little, and then fall into our long lost bed that has been waiting for us."

"The bed has been waiting? Waiting for what?" Dennis said, with a devilish grin.

"That, my love, will be your decision."

"Oh, yeah? You say that every time and you end up making the best decisions."

##

They stood just inside the entrance of the officer's club until Diane spotted Mattie and Cathy.

"I'll get us a drink and be right over."

She gave him a peck on the cheek and practically ran over to the girls.

"Hey, girls, how are you?"

"I'm fine," replied Cathy, "but I can't get Mattie to quit moping."

"Why? What's wrong?"

"Well, it seems that she is still in shock. She keeps moaning, wondering how it is going to work when they are literally from two different planets."

"Why couldn't he trust me enough to tell me, before I fell in love with him?" Mattie cried.

"Whoa, girl. Now tell me, if he had come to you and said, Mattie, I don't live on planet Earth. I am from another planet. Would you have believed him?"

Mattie cocked her head, looking at Diane, with a slight grin on her face.

"Well, I don't think so … No, I would not have believed him. More than likely, I would have thought he was either crazy or trying to get away from me."

"Here's the deal. The day after tomorrow, at noon sharp, be in hangar two, where our ships are. Dress out for a regular space flight, helmet, backpacks and the works. We are all going on a ride, to the moon. No questions now. If you want to go, be there, and Mattie, you will see Jordan … day after tomorrow."

Mattie sat up, smiling from ear to ear.

"Here's your drink, Diane, and look what the dogs drug up," said Dennis.

"Hey Sarge, Shirley … good to see you!"

Diane gave Shirley a big bear hug.

"Have you seen Ed or Cynthia?" Dennis asked.

"Oh boy, have we ever. Look way back there," Cathy replied, pointing to a dark, back corner of the room. "I don't think we had better bother them right now."

"I think you're right," Diane replied.

At a small table, Ed and Cynthia were sitting opposite each other.

"Ed, I am so sorry that I did not believe you. I don't know what came over me."

"No, Cynthia, I've been sitting here thinking, and if I had been in your shoes, I would have probably done the same thing. I don't know what I was thinking. I mean, it was hard for me to believe when it was right there in my face. How could I expect you to believe such a story, especially the way it was sprung on you? So I was wrong to walk out before we had the chance to finish."

"So you forgive me?" she asked, with a pout on her face.

Ed laughed and took her hands in his, across the table.

"Only if you forgive me first."

"Well, I'm going to do more than forgive you Ed; I'm going to ask you to marry me."

"What? Me? You would marry me?"

"You silly fool, you better believe it. I would be proud and honored to be your wife. But if you don't want to marry me, I'll understand."

"What? Lady, you have had my heart for a very long time. I have wanted to ask you to marry me since the first time I saw you. I just figured I really didn't have a chance in the world. As a matter of fact, I think this should be done properly. There is something I have had for a very long time that needs a home."

"Oh, and what might that be?"

Well, I expected to do this in a more romantic place, if I ever got the courage to do it," he said, as he pulled a velvety, black box, from his pocket, "but anywhere you are is romantic, so," he opened the box and got down in front of her, on one knee, "Will you marry me, Cynthia?"

Across the room, Mattie gasped, "What are they doing over there? Is he proposing to her?"

Everyone looked at Cynthia and Ed.

"Will I marry you? Oh, Ed, you better believe it!"

He slipped the ring on her finger and she stood up, hugging him.

Everyone watching started whistling and clapping. They all ran over to Ed and Cynthia, hugging them and congratulating them on their engagement.

"Oh, this is too much! I am so happy for you guys," Diane said. "So when you set a date ..."

"As a matter of fact, we already have," said Cynthia.

"Oh my God, really...when?"

"Tomorrow!"

"You're joking — right?

"Nope, not at all. Hey, I have a great idea. Why don't we have a triple wedding? I told you all that I wanted to be at your weddings; well, this way I would be, for sure!"

Diane covered her mouth, her eyes wide.

"Oh my God," she mumbled through her hand and turned to Dennis.

"What's wrong, Diane," Dennis asked. "You don't like that idea?"

She took her hand away from her mouth and said, "Don't like it? I love it! But, what do you think?"

"I think it's about time and, with our trip to the moon coming up, who could ask for a better honeymoon spot?"

Diane jumped up, grabbing Dennis around his neck and hugging him. Mattie was beside herself, jumping up and down and clapping her hands.

"Sarge, Shirley, what do you think?" Cynthia asked.

"Well," replied Tensley, "I think that if this wonderful woman is still planning on marrying me, it's a wonderful idea … Shirley?"

Shirley, being the timid one, tried to talk, but only squeaking would escape her lips. Finally, she just nodded her head vigorously, up and down. She had tears rolling down her cheeks.

"Are you OK, honey," asked Tensley, pulling a chair over for her to sit down.

She sat down and held up her hand for him to give her a minute.

"OK? Oh yes, I am. I'm just so surprised that it took my breath away. I'm the happiest woman in the world."

"Well," said Diane, "you have some competition for that title, I'm afraid."

"I think this calls for a celebration," exclaimed Mattie. "Drinks are on Dennis!"

"Ha-ha, funny lady," said Dennis. "But she's right, for once, drinks are on me."

They found a long table toward the middle of the room that was empty. They sat down and Dennis took their orders for drinks. While Dennis was at the bar, the wedding conversation began.

"Personally," said Diane, "I have no desire for a big formal wedding, but I will go along with whatever you two decide."

"What do you suggest, Diane, you know how I hate all this formal stuff already."

"I was hoping you folks would suggest something like that," Shirley interjected.

"I love you both for going along with the idea. Cynthia, Shirley, my idea is that the three of us go out and buy a dress, that you prefer, for an informal wedding, or you can wear anything you may already have, in fact. I'm thinking I'll buy something like an off-white evening dress, knee length, shoes and other items to match. It won't bother me a bit if you get something identical. My man is the all important one that I want to please."

"Can't the three of us go together," Shirley asked, "I want to, at least, be similar. I don't want to stand out."

"It will be a pleasure to have you, dear. Cynthia?"

"Great idea Shirley, I definitely agree."

"All of us have to admit we have too many friends to exclude anyone from the wedding. We have plenty of time today to get everything in order, and to notify the squadron and facility of the upcoming marriages. I'll have posters made up and sent out within the next two hours to be posted on every bulletin board throughout the facility. I look for a flood of people to show up, so I suggest we get someone to volunteer to go to the hotel and make arrangements for both adjoining ballrooms. Who do you think we can get to volunteer?"

Dennis returned.

"Our drinks will be delivered as soon as they're ready. What's going on here?"

"We have decided what we're going to do for dresses. The three of us are going shopping and I'm going to have posters made and put around the facility."

Diane looked around the table.

"You fellows are good candidates to volunteer to help us, don't you agree?"

"Tell us what to do, and we'll get right on it," said Tensley.

"First of all, make sure we have the two adjoining ballrooms. Then, find out from the hotel what kind of arrangements they can make for us for drinks and hors d`oeuvres. There will be a flood of people, so there should be orders enough for at least 5,000 people."

"My God," Ed said. "If the hotel does that, it's going to keep the staff working all night long."

"So be it," Cynthia replied, "its party time!"

"What about music, after the wedding?"

"Good question Dennis," replied Diane. "Cynthia, what do you think?"

"Can't have a wedding without music, we have to have that first waltz, together. Shirley, is there anything you prefer? Speak up girl; this is your wedding too."

"I have one request," Shirley replied. "I don't know if it would be proper, but I would sort of like to have a father figure to give us away."

"Who do you suggest, Shirley?" Diane asked.

"I think General Estes would be the ideal person to give us all three away, and Thelma to be our maid of honor."

"Excellent idea," Cynthia replied. "Excellent!"

Tensley spoke up, "You've mentioned everyone except one crucial person."

"Who have we forgotten?"

"Someone official has to perform the wedding," Tensley replied.

"Oh Lord, you're right Sarge, we did forget that, didn't we?"

Everyone cracked up laughing.

"Well, I think the general and Thelma are going to be surprised since they were volunteered."

"They'll love it," Cynthia replied.

"The question is," Tensley interjected, "which chaplain are we going to use, since we have three denominations on site. We have Jewish, Catholic and Protestant; what's your choice?"

Cynthia spoke up, "I don't care who it is, as long as he can perform the marriage ceremony legally."

It was finally suggested that the Protestant chaplain be requested to perform the ceremonies with the other two chaplains assisting. Everyone was happy with that.

"Does anyone else have any other suggestions before we go about our duties?" Diane asked.

Everyone shook their heads.

"All right, the drinks are here. I'm going to finish my drink, comfortably and slowly, no rush, then we can leave and get to work on the weddings," Diane said.

About an hour later, Diane's cell phone rang. The three women were in a dress shop in the middle of trying on dresses. She saw that it was Dennis' number.

"Yes sweetie, what is it?"

"The hotel is all set. They have volunteered both adjoining ballrooms and all the refreshments will be ready. We need to know what time you want to perform the ceremonies, as we are in the chaplain's office now."

Diane went inside the hall of the dressing room.

"Hey, you two, Dennis needs to know what time you want to have the ceremonies. He is at the minister's office right now."

Diane soon stepped out of the dressing rooms and called Dennis.

"Its set, 11 a.m., honey."

"OK, sounds good. Now we're off to General Estes' apartment to let them know they have been volunteered to be a part of our weddings. Then, the three of us are going to our quarters. Do you prefer we wear civilian suits or our uniforms?"

"That is up to you guys, but you should all wear the same thing, the uniform of your respective services, or all wear suits."

"That is a big 10-4, sweetheart," Dennis replied. "Oh, and then we're going to have a great big party. It's not every day that three great guys get three beautiful women to marry them."

"OK, after we're finished shopping, we may just beat you to the party. We are going to have to start early in the morning with getting our hair fixed and so on."

##

The brides met around 7a.m, joined by Thelma, in Cynthia's suite in the hotel.

"I have four beauticians ready to take care of our hair as soon as you girls are ready. After that, they will also do our makeup, or you can do your own if you prefer."

"Oh, my Gosh, this is a treat. I want the whole shebang."

"Me too!" Thelma exclaimed.

The gals enjoyed their pampering, while the guys laid out their clothes, alongside their bundles of nerves.

Dennis called Ed.

"Ed, I'm all ready to go except for changing clothes, and I'm not going to change just yet. I'm going to call the other two and suggest we meet downstairs and get some breakfast. What do you think?"

"I've got to do something, that's for sure. I'm going crazy just sitting here thinking about what's taking place. To think, yesterday I was a slap-happy free Marine, and by the end of today, I'm going to be married to the most important woman in the world. Now, can you outdo that?"

All four women – Thelma, Diane, Cynthia and Shirley – gathered in the dressing room, just off the main ballroom. They were sitting at their dressing tables, primping.

"Shirley, I'd like to ask you a question," Thelma inquired, "but before I ask, I understand that you requested the general and I be involved in the wedding."

"Oh, yes ma'am, I certainly did, and I'm so proud to have you here."

"I understand you wanted my Hubby as a father-figure. I thought I read in your files that you had a father, in the military, is that correct?"

"Yes ma'am, it certainly is. My father is a major in the United States Army, in Germany. He knows I am going to be married; we stay in close contact, particularly since mother died."

"So, you and your father are on good terms?"

"Oh, yes ma'am, very much so, I love my Daddy very much."

"Would you mind if we used him as a substitute, instead of my Hubby?"

Shirley's eyes opened wide.

"I would be proud for my Daddy to be here, but since this came up so suddenly, there was no way to let him know in time. He's in Germany and there is no way he could get his furlough in time to get here now."

"Well, it just so happens, Shirley, that Cynthia found that your father was processing through McGuire Air Force Base in New Jersey."

Shirley's lips were trembling, as she asked, "New Jersey?"

"Before I say anything else, if you ladies don't mind, I would like to bring a gentleman in here."

Thelma opened the door and a tall, gray-haired man, wearing the uniform of the United States Army, entered.

Shirley went berserk.

"Daddy? How …"

"Come here, honey. You can thank your president for this."

Shirley jumped all over him, hugging and kissing his cheeks, as the other three watched with tears in their eyes. After a bit, Shirley turned to the president.

"I don't know how, but I'll forever be in your debt."

In the front of the ballroom, Dennis, Tensley and Ed were seated, nervously awaiting the proceedings.

Ed looked at his watch.

"Ten minutes."

The three chaplains entered together, through a huge archway, and approached the podium. The archway had been installed by the hotel for the occasion, and was covered with red, white and yellow roses. Flowers were everywhere. The chaplains conversed for a few minutes and then motioned for the grooms to come forward. As the three men stood at the podium, the Protestant minister introduced the rabbi and the priest, and they all shook hands. The minister looked out over the faces that filled the ballroom, from wall to wall.

"If you three gentlemen are ready, we will start the ceremony."

Dennis, Ed, and Tensley, all nodded their heads, confirming they were ready.

"One thing, gentlemen, do you all have your rings?"

All three quickly fumbled through their pockets and brought forward their little black velvet covered boxes.

Getting the signal that the brides were ready, the chaplain took a deep breath and pointed to the organ player, and the wedding march began. Everyone's attention went to the back of the room.

Diane and Cynthia appeared, looking toward the podium. General Estes moved in between the two ladies. He presented both arms. The ladies tucked an arm into his and they took several steps forward, and then stopped. Shirley came into view behind them. Her father stepped from the side of the aisle and presented his arm. There were already tears streaming down Shirley's face as she smiled at her father. Thelma came out and stood beside Shirley. As they proceeded down the aisle, there was a soft murmur in the crowd. The women had chosen identical dresses, fairly plain, but form fitting. Their hair was covered with sequined embedded netting that glimmered as they walked beneath the chandeliers. There was nothing plain about the three brides-to-be, as they were all radiant in the beauty of the moment.

General Estes, Cynthia, and Diane, passed through the archway and took a small step onto the red, velvety carpet, of the podium. Shirley, her father and Thelma, waited, as the general presented Cynthia to Ed, and Diane to Dennis. Shirley's father, never having met Tensley, shook his hand, and then presented his daughter to him. He then joined General Estes and Thelma. The Baptist minister was standing behind the microphone, with the rabbi and priest slightly behind him. He whispered to the six to turn toward him, side by side.

The chaplain again looked out, over the crowd, and switched on the microphone. "This is the most unusual, unprecedented wedding that I have ever performed, and with the largest crowd ever. I am as nervous, if not more so, than the six young people in front of me, so I have backup behind me, just in case."

A small titter of laughter passed through the crowd.

He proceeded with the vows and presentation of the rings.

"Now ladies and gentlemen, please embrace, and kiss for the first time as husband and wife."

As the minister watched, he wiped the sweat from his brow with a crisp, new handkerchief. He then shook the hands of each of them, as the crowd roared its approval.

General Estes, Thelma and Robert, Shirley's father, came to the newlyweds and shook hands all around. The men received their kisses from the brides.

"If you folks will follow me," the general announced, "we'll go into the other ballroom while the hotel staff dismantles this from the dance floor. The hotel has a very nice surprise for all of you. They walked to the end of the podium, stepping down, and the crowd separated to give them an aisle to proceed to the other ballroom. The wedding parties walked into the other ballroom and looked across it to see a large table with three, three-tiered wedding cakes, standing slightly apart.

Diane whispered to all of them, "I knew I forgot something!"

Balloons and flowers adorned the room.

General Estes and Thelma led them across the room and around to the large table, as the rest of the guests filtered in. They all stood, looking back and forth at each other, grinning like chimpanzees, and watched as the people came in and crowded around.

Diane whispered to Dennis, "Look at this crystal. How did they have the time to do all of this? It is beautiful.

"Mrs. Denehey, are you going to slam that cake into my mouth?"

"If you didn't have that beautiful uniform on, I probably would, but I'll be nice, for once."

The three couples watched as everyone settled down.

"All right kids, cut the damn cake and let's party!" said General Estes.

They all went through the process of cutting the cake, and helping each other with their first taste, as tradition provided.

"What is that set up across the room? That's not hors d`oeuvres."

"Compliments of the hotel, Diane. There is plenty for everyone and more waiting."

The general then pointed to the other end of the room, where there were three large tables.

"I know you said no gifts, but you will have to talk to these people. The one on the left is for Dennis and Diane, the one in the center is for Cynthia and Ed, and the one on the right is for Tensley and Shirley." There wasn't a word said as the surprised looks on their faces told it all. They were astonished. The gifts were stacked almost to the ceiling on each one.

"The stores are saying that almost everything they had on the shelves had been bought out today," said General Estes.

Dennis leaned over and whispered to Diane, "I wonder how many new coffee pots we got."

Diane playfully slapped him on the arm, "Don't complain, it's the thought that counts."

All the normal proceedings went forward. Soon, they heard the band strike up in the next room.

The first music was "Hail to the Chief," and the crowd roared with approval.

Cynthia said, "Hey, lets go and get through that waltz, I need a damned drink, I am thirsty as all get out."

They all filtered back into the other ballroom and danced, drank, and had a wonderful party. It wasn't long before the newly-weds excused themselves and snuck from the ballroom. It was pre-honeymoon time.

##

The bus idled, air conditioning on high to keep the twenty-seven people comfortable.

"Well, Dennis, it's ten to one."

"Cynthia, you have to realize, we don't have a clue as to how far they have to travel just to get here. I'm sure they will be here in a few minutes."

"I know, Dennis. I'm just jittery, and still so darned skeptical about all this."

"I was also, so I understand."

"To be truthful, you don't know just how much I want this to be true."

"I'm glad it is, Cynthia, because without help, the Russians and Chinese will take war into space."

"Sir, a dust storm is beginning to develop," said Cathy, pointing in front of them.

"Dennis and Cynthia looked to where Cathy was pointing.

"No, Cathy, that's our tour bus."

"It's only wind and sand, Dennis."

"Watch and learn, dear."

"It looks like a dust devil from out in the desert," said Cynthia.

"It's 12:58, Cynthia!"

They all stared at the spot as the sand blew violently, in a circular motion, around an invisible force. All of a sudden, the sand began to settle back to earth. It looked as though someone was opening a stage curtain as the landing gear on Jules' ship appeared. The curtain slowly rising, to expose part of a golden fuselage, and then for the finale, the entire ship sat in front of them.

"My word," said Tensley, "they have actually developed a cloaking device."

"Oh my, I do see it, but my mind can't absorb this, Dennis."

"Believe it, Cynthia, it is real."

Dennis pressed the center of the radio that Jules had left him.

"Good afternoon, Jules, a fascinating show, my friend."

"Thank you, Dennis. Would you folks care to come aboard? Drive your bus to the left side of our ship, there will be steps there."

"Sarge, you heard the man."

They slowly moved around the long, drooping wing, to the side of the ship where the part of the fuselage began unfolding. The top of it slowly folded outward, then horizontal, and then slowly lowered itself to the ground.

"Dennis, please tell your driver to come aboard with the rest. I'll move the vehicle to a safe distance before we start."

"How will he do that?"

"Don't even ask, Cynthia, if he says he can do it … he can."

"Please, everyone, come aboard."

Cynthia led the way with Dennis following. The rest were behind them.

Cynthia stopped at the steps.

"Good Lord, it's an escalator, what next?"

"It's quite a ways up, Cynthia," Jules informed her.

She stepped onto the slow moving steps, and one by one, everyone followed. At the top, stood three figures in shiny silver, form-fitting suits. A tall young man with light brown hair, slender, and displaying a wonderful smile stood beside a woman with long brown to auburn hair, who was holding the hand of a little blonde-haired girl. The little girl was nervously waiting to move, but her mother held her in place.

The little girl could hold it no longer when she saw Mr. Hennesey.

"Mommy, Mommy, I see my Uncle Henny. See? See?"

Her smile turned into laughter.

"Yes, Alania, I see him, patience dear."

Cynthia topped the stairs and Jules reached out a hand as she was stepping off. She accepted his hand and smiled at him.

"Thank you."

"Madam President, such a wonderful honor. Thank you so much. Please, step over there until everyone is aboard and I'll make the introductions. There is a rack over there, that all can hang suits and helmets on. You will have no need for them until we arrive at our destination."

Tensley and Shirley were the last ones up, and Alania could contain herself no longer. She pulled her hand from her mother's and leaped across the floor. Had he not been there, ready, she would have bowled him over. He gathered her up, in his big arms.

Her hands behind his neck, she leaned back and said so seriously, "Oh, Uncle Henny, I missed you."

"Well now, my wee lassie, even though 'tis only been a couple of days, I still missed ye too. Oh, and I nay forget your present. Mr. Jules, before I forget, in the back of the bus, sir, several cases of your favorite beverage."

"Why, that is most generous, Mr. Hennesey; it was not necessary though."

"Sir, it is from everyone, including our president, and you know I must take care of this wee lassie here."

"Most generous, I assure you. I shall have a couple of crew members retrieve it and take them to the cargo hold. Meanwhile, I welcome all of you aboard. Once we are up, I will come back with my wife and meet everyone. If you will go through that door, there are many comfortable seats. You may strap in if you wish, though it isn't necessary."

When they walked through the door, what they saw was amazing. Instead of a cabin with rows of seats, as in a passenger plane, it looked like a huge, very comfortable, living room. Couches and easy chairs placed randomly and carpet so deep and plush, it was like walking on air.

"Everyone, please take a seat. We have not been introduced yet. I am Jules. This is my lovely wife, Therina, and I suppose most of you now know Alania, our daughter. While they are retrieving your most generous gift and moving your vehicle, please make yourselves comfortable. Mr. Hennesey, it's apparent that Alania would like to stay with you. Will she be a bother?"

"A bother, oh, by no means."

Therina walked over to Mattie.

"You are Mattie Mitchell, is that correct?"

"Yes ma'am, how did you know?"

"Oh Mattie, I have had your picture, through Jordan's words, imprinted in my mind. There is one who wishes for you to come forward with me, I hope you will. I can't stand much more of his worries."

Blushing prettily she asked, "Jordan?"

"No other, would you like to come and gag him?"

Mattie glanced around.

"Yes, yes I would."

"We will be taking off shortly. Be comfortable, we will join you soon," Therina said to her guests.

She took Mattie's hand.

"Come on dear."

##

As the ghostlike ship silently started its slow turn, high above the moon, the passengers stared at the huge TV screen in front of the cabin. The huge planet, Saturn, its magnificent rings, its yellow to orange glow, simply mesmerized the entire group. The cabin area was pure silence.

Cynthia squeezed Ed's arm as Mars slipped into view, and a small portion of Jupiter was sliding onto the screen.

"Ed, I just can't believe I am here."

Ed leaned over and whispered in her ear

"Well, Mrs. Mitchell, you are here. Soon, you'll be the very first president of the United States, or any other person of high position from Earth, to walk on the moon."

"It's an honor for me Ed. It feels like we are going down."

"Yes, we are dear. They are making a long, gradual decent, to let everyone see all the surrounding planets and star systems from a different view."

The huge ship softly settled on the surface.

Dennis thought it was funny, once the ship settled down; it was like turning on a light. Everyone began talking, whereas before, it was dead silent.

"Well Cynthia, so far, what do you think?"

"To be as honest as I can Dennis, I am simply overwhelmed. I really…"

The president was interrupted as Jules' voice came across the cabin radio.

"Madam President, Ed, Dennis, and Diane, please meet me at the front of the cabin."

Puzzled, the four left their seats and went to meet Jules, who was just leaving the flight deck.

"Madam President, my apologies. I did wish to give all of you the tour. I have been ordered by the Council to stand by my communications system to attend an emergency cabinet meeting. So, Dennis, if you don't mind, I will send a couple of crew members to help you. Would you please take your delegation through the museum first? I'm not sure, but that may be all I will have time for. We may have to cut this tour short. I suggest you start immediately and I will call you if, and when, all of you should return to the ship."

"Is it serious, Jules?"

"Madam President, all I know and call tell you at this moment, is that it's been over five of your centuries since our Council of Planets has called an emergency meeting. I will tell you what I can, after the meeting is done."

The museum was such a fascinating place, and the visitors were so caught up in some of the history of their actual past, that they lost track of time.

A loud speaker broke the silence.

"Dennis, please bring your delegation back on board, as I must cut this tour short. Please accept my deepest apologies to all of the delegation. My crew members will close up for you once you are on board. Thank you."

Once everyone was back on board, Jules appeared from the flight deck, with a very grim look on his face.

"I'm sorry, once again, to cut this tour short, but I must get you home and return to mine. Madam President, I am going to tell you what I am permitted to. We are preparing to move all of our people from our planet, and preparing also, for war. Whatever it is that is a threat to our planet, is apparently so horrific, that the Council will not talk of it on radio communications. Now, the Council has instructed me to tell you, that possibly, what is threatening our planet may possibly be a threat to yours also. We won't know for sure for at least two of your Earth weeks. If it should be a threat to you, we will definitely make you fully aware. Otherwise, at the present time, we do not wish to alarm you."

"May I ask why you are preparing for war?"

"We colonized two livable planets several years ago, just outside of our solar system. We have always tried to plan ahead for any eventual planetary disaster or problem, but nothing on this scale. Those two planets are now being claimed by another race. They have sent a message to us to move from those planets, or face the consequences.

"Now I must take you home … immediately."

To be continued....Look for the second volume to be coming out soon!

About the Authors

David M. Spriggs and Debbie E. Barnum are a father-daughter team embarking on a journey into the adventures of the mind and of the imagination, while, simultaneously casting light on, and educating their readers of important, and often even dangerous issues in America of government and military corruption, critical security flaws and concerns, and many other pressing topics that are, at times, given very little attention by current media. Both Spriggs and Barnum take a no-holds-barred approach in their writings of such issues, in an effort to accurately and vividly bring to the forefront the true dangers facing America if no initiative is taken to stop these dangerous problems of corruption within our own government, as well as the frontal attack by other nations on the wonderful country we call "home".... the United States of America.

David Spriggs, born in Scioto County, Ohio, in 1934 and raised in Pittsburg, Pennsylvania, currently spends his time as a freelance writer and poet. Since childhood, David's love and curiosity for airplanes, space, and the undiscovered led him to join the Air Force in 1951 at the mere age of seventeen. These ten years of military service afforded him the opportunity to travel to twenty-seven countries, while specializing in maintenance of various types of aircraft.

David is seventy-three years old and over his lifetime has seen many changes around the world. He is concerned with the falling economy, government corruption, the Iraq war, and the problem with other nations who will do whatever it takes to stop America's forward progress into space.

He presently lives in Texas and enjoys studying World History, ancient history of our land and anything space related. He is heavily into politics and loves writing. His one wish is for American's to open their eyes and see what is going on in the world around them. He believes all American's should get involved so there will still be a "land of the free" for their children and grandchildren.

Debbie Barnum, born in Sherman, Texas, and raised in Savoy, Texas, currently spends her time helping her father put his words in print, as she believes the stories he has to share are very important and should be shared with the world.

Debbie drove a truck for 11 years and has been afforded the opportunity to travel in all the lower 48 states of our great country. She believes that the problem with our government today is the lack of the American people's involvement. "Our country is on a down hill slide and unless the American people wake up and get involved in what is going on around them, they can kiss the United States of America goodbye. We must take back our government before it is too late."

She is married to Barry Barnum and presently resides in Odessa, Texas. She enjoys writing, reading, bingo, scrapbooking, and most of all, just being a housewife for her husband that she describes as the "most wonderful man in the entire world."